FOLLOWING THE DRUM
WITH CORPORAL JOHN

MALCOLM ARCHIBALD

Copyright © 2024 by Malcolm Archibald

Layout design and Copyright © 2024 by Next Chapter

Published 2024 by Next Chapter

Cover art by Lordan June Pinote

This book is a work of fiction. Names, characters, places, and incidents are the product of the author's imagination or are used fictitiously. Any resemblance to actual events, locales, or persons, living or dead, is purely coincidental.

All rights reserved. No part of this book may be reproduced or transmitted in any form or by any means, electronic or mechanical, including photocopying, recording, or by any information storage and retrieval system, without the author's permission.

For my son,
Alexander Thomas Archibald

"The Royal Scots have stamped their name on almost every battlefield in which our army has been engaged. They have been commanded and trusted by such consummate commanders as Turenne, Marlborough, and Wellington. It has indeed been their habit to fight all over the world: there is scarcely a region where they have not left their mark. That is the way with all our regiments, but the Royal Scots have been longer at it."
Lord Rosebery, 1915

"My lads, ye see thae loons on yon hill there? If ye dinna kill them, they'll kill you!"
Sir Flockhart Agnew of Lochnaw, Battle of Dettingen, 1743

FOREWORD

In the period in which this story is set, King William and then Queen Anne ruled the three separate kingdoms of Scotland, Ireland, and England, as well as Wales, which was then normally included, politically at least, with England. Although the story begins in 1701, six years before the Union between the Scots and English parliaments and thus the creation of Great Britain, I have used the term British to describe the various regiments that fought beside Davie Flockhart.

Contemporary writers, and even some more of more recent vintage, may have used the term English Army and even English battalions. Given that many were Scottish, Welsh, and Irish, that term is plainly incorrect.

CHAPTER 1

EDINBURGHSHIRE, SCOTLAND, OCTOBER 1701

F lockhart stumbled and fell, with the earth frosty and cold beneath him. He lay for a moment and looked up to the dark sky. Bright stars glittered like a million eyes watching him, with a scimitar moon glowing above the ridge of the Pentland Hills. An owl called somewhere, with its mate quickly replying, the sound eerie.

"Davie!"

Flockhart ignored the voice. He lay still, savouring the peace and the feeling of fresh air across his battered body. He stretched out, saying nothing.

"Davie! Come on, man!"

Flockhart lifted his head, looked around, and slumped down. His fingers curled around a patch of crisp grass.

The voice sounded again.

"Hell mend you, then, David Flockhart! Stay where you are and freeze, damn you."

Flockhart peered through the strands of lank grass, watching the men slump away. Round-shouldered, exhausted, with ragged, filthy clothes covering battered, dirty bodies, they looked less than human. They were two-legged animals suited only for labouring until they died of fatigue, accident, or disease. They knew nothing better than work and suffering.

Don't go back.

The thought eased into Flockhart's mind.

Don't go back again.

As it gleamed within his brain, the idea betrayed everything and everybody he had ever known. It was an intrusive nugget that he savoured, holding it to him as a secret he could never share.

I failed the last time I tried. Where would I go?

Anywhere is better than here. Anything is better than this.

Flockhart saw his colleagues slump into the collection of hovels they called home, the damp-infested huts that clung like ugly parasites to the rich Lowland soil. He heard the voices raised in discordant clamour, heard a woman's eldritch laughter and the roar of a man, and then a door opened, allowing fire-gleam to escape. Flockhart saw the interior of the hut, the bundle of rags for a bed, the tousle-haired, filthy infants fresh from their stint down the pit, and then the woman kicked the door shut. Darkness again, with the discordant yelling of marital disharmony.

Don't go back.

Run away.

A dog barked, joined by others in a snarling, howling cacophony that ended in high screams when a man began swearing, accompanied by the thumps of savage kicks. A woman laughed, a door opened, and a dog fled outside howling. Somebody threw a bottle after it and slammed shut the door.

Don't go back.

Flockhart lay still with the idea fluttering within his head. Until the previous month, he had never contemplated anything other than his present life. He knew nothing else and nobody else except the men and women with whom he worked. He only knew the limited orbit of his existence, a score of names, and the never-ending toil under the earth's crust.

Run.
Run.
Run.

Flockhart crawled backwards along the rutted track with no idea except to escape without anybody seeing him. When he judged himself safe from casual observation, he rose, turned, and ran. Flockhart moved clumsily, sliding over the slippery ground, running without direction or thought. He wanted only to put distance between him and the pit.

Run, Davie, run!

When his legs were weak, and the breath rasped in his throat, Flockhart stopped. He slumped to the ground, looking around. He did not know where he was, except he had never been so far from the pit. The landscape was unfamiliar under the wan moonlight, large fields enclosed by frost-rimmed drystone dykes, with a line of neat, stone-built cottages near a larger farmhouse. Flockhart saw a glow in the sky to the north and guessed it emanated from the lights of a town. He had heard of a city called Edinburgh, although he had never visited or imagined he ever would.

The weariness of a long day's work, followed by the stress of flight, overcame Flockhart. He rolled into the lee of a wall, found a patch of soft grass, and closed his eyes. He knew he would wake well before dawn, as he had done all his life. The cold was irrelevant; he had never known anything except hardship.

Flockhart woke hungry, as always. He looked around, momentarily unsure of his surroundings. He heard the clucking of hens, guessed they were in a nearby barn, and moved towards the stone-walled building. The door was closed but not locked. Flockhart pushed it open, ignored the clamour of disturbed hens, grabbed a couple of eggs from the ground, and fled before the farmer appeared.

A dog barked, awakened by the sound of disturbed fowls. Flockhart ducked his head and ran, stumbling over the rough ground. When he thought himself sufficiently far away, he sat in the shelter of a wall. Glancing around, Flockhart ate the eggs raw, washed them down with water from a fast-flowing river, and continued, head down and legs already aching. He headed for Edinburgh, unsure what he would do when he arrived and already regretting his decision. Flockhart hesitated, wondering if he should return; although the consequences would be unpleasant, it was a life he understood, the only life he knew.

"Hey! You!" A harsh voice broke the morning's bird chorus. "Thief!"

Flockhart saw three men, presumably from the farm, with two carrying heavy sticks. He ran without thought, blundering across fields, stumbling over drystone dykes and staggering over newly ploughed land. A herd of dun-coloured cattle scattered before him, their hooves thundering hollowly on the ground. The shouting grew fainter, and Flockhart glanced over his shoulder to see the men standing at the edge of the field, watching. One shook an impotent fist, mouthing meaningless threats.

Flockhart hurried on, passing through a small village where thatched cottages huddled beside a simple kirk, and men watched him suspiciously. He pulled up his shirt to hide his neck, ducked his head, and hurried on. A group of women around a well stopped gossiping as he passed, and a cart creaked from a side street, drawn by a bare-ribbed horse. Flockhart hunched his shoulders and shuffled onwards, aware the good neighbours despised his type.

I should have remained at the pit. I don't belong in this outside world.

Flockhart did not know how long he had walked. Inured to hardship, he ignored the ache in his legs and kept moving. Flockhart grabbed a towel from a clothesline to wrap around his neck and stopped in mid-afternoon when Edinburgh unrolled before him. He had seen the castle from a distance, but now the size of the city daunted him.

I didn't know there were so many people in the world.

The great bulk of Arthur's Seat rose over eight hundred feet to a bruised grey sky, with Edinburgh's streets and tall tenements emerging through the smoke reek of a thousand chimneys. The city stretched from the castle on its volcanic plug to Holyrood Palace a mile down the people-congested ridge. Flockhart viewed the tall, dark tenements rising unbelievably high and wondered what sort of place it was, so much larger than the tiny pit settlements he knew.

Wrapping the towel tightly around his neck, Flockhart moved on, disregarding the curious glances of the increasing number of people he passed as he neared the city. The houses grew more numerous as he approached, the traffic busier, with carts, horses, and the occasional carriage. Flockhart bowed his head when he saw the latter in case his owner was searching for him. He kept in the shadows, ill-at-ease, suspicious of every casual glance and unsure what to do next.

Flockhart entered Edinburgh from the south, staring openmouthed at the number and scale of the tenements and the crowds in the streets. People of all descriptions and classes mingled with a babble of noise and smells that assailed Flockhart's senses. He heard the rattle of drums and watched men in colourful clothes encouraging passers-by to join them in the alehouses and taverns, but he decided they could not mean him and moved on. Flockhart passed a life-size model of a red-coated man outside a roaring tavern, saw a well-dressed man looking at him, and moved hurriedly on. He pulled the towel tighter around his throat, stepped into the street to escape the crowds and flinched when a cart nearly ran him down.

"Get out of the way, you country Jock!" the driver snarled, glaring at him.

"That was close!" A slender man in a brilliant red coat guided Flockhart onto safer ground. "Are you all right, my friend?"

"I'm all right," Flockhart said, freeing his arm from the slender man's grip.

"You look like you need a drink," the man said, smiling broadly.

Flockhart felt instant suspicion. Strangers did not buy him a drink. Instead, they avoided men like him. "I'm all right," he repeated, ensuring the towel covered his throat.

"I'm paying," the man was around thirty-five, Flockhart estimated, with a nut-brown face and bright, hard eyes. "Josiah Nisbet."

"David Flockhart," Flockhart replied cautiously.

The tavern was busy with men crowded around tables as busy barmaids carried tankards of thick beer and glasses of spirits. Nisbet guided Flockhart to a corner table and ordered two tankards of ale and two glasses of rum.

"Relax, David," Nisbet said. "Have a drink." He drank deeply from his battered pewter tankard.

Flockhart glanced around the room. He was not used to being surrounded by strangers. He watched the door, fearful that Lord Eskbank might enter.

"You're not an Edinburgh man, are you?" Nisbet said.

"No," Flockhart agreed. He measured the distance to the exit, ready to run if challenged.

"You're a countryman." Nisbet pulled at his tankard, eyeing Flockhart. "Drink, man; it's free!"

Flockhart lifted his tankard. The ale was thick and cool, welcome after his recent exertions. He drank slowly, keeping his eyes mobile.

"That's the way." Nisbet grinned at him. "A countryman, but not a farmer. A carter, perhaps?"

"No," Flockhart said, disliking the direction the conversation was taking. He adjusted the towel around his neck and placed his tankard on the much-scarred table. A group of men watched him, openly grinning.

Nisbet looked up as another man pushed through the crowd to join them. "Here's Corporal Junar."

Corporal Junar was a stocky, broad-faced man wearing the

same type of scarlet jacket as Nisbet. He dragged over a stool and sat beside Flockhart. "Good day, young fellow."

"Good day," Flockhart replied. *Corporal Junar? Is he a soldier?*

"Corporal Junar, meet my new friend, David Flockhart, who was nearly killed by a cart a short time ago."

"Dangerous things, carts," Junar said, smiling. "You look like you've been on the wrong end of a hard time, David."

Flockhart realised his clothes were more ragged and his appearance more poverty-stricken than his companions or anybody else in the inn. He swallowed more of his ale, saying nothing.

"You need a change of fortune, my friend," Nisbet said. "You need a life with regular food and pay, good friends, travel and the chance to make bounty money."

"And women," Junar added. "Women who flock to you because of who you are." He laughed good-humouredly. "Flocking to David Flockhart, eh? I had not intended to say that."

"And clothes," Nisbet looked pointedly at Flockhart's filthy rags. "Two new sets of clothes every year. How would you like that, Davie?"

Flockhart smiled. "I'd like that fine," he said. "Are you soldiers?"

"We are," Junar admitted freely. "I am a corporal, as Josiah told you, and he is a private. Sergeant Dunn is around somewhere."

Flockhart tested his rum. "I've heard about soldiers," he said, trying to sound knowledgeable. *The men in the pit said they were dangerous, but these two are friendly.*

"Have you never met a soldier before, Davie?" Junar sounded genuinely surprised.

"No," Flockhart finished the ale in his tankard and lifted the rum.

"What do you do?" Junar asked.

Flockhart touched the towel, glancing at the door.

"Dear God in heaven," Nisbet said with a sudden realisation. "A countryman with a pale, dirty face who has never met a soldier! You're a collier, aren't you?"

Flockhart felt the atmosphere alter as both men stared at him. "Yes," he nodded, unable to hide his shame. Colliers were the lowest level on the social scale, the outcasts of society, unwanted, unloved, despised, and scorned.

Nisbet and Junar glanced at each other. "What do you think, Corporal?" Nisbet asked.

"I think we could be making trouble for ourselves," Junar replied quietly. Leaning forward, he flicked the towel from around Flockhart's neck. "That sort of trouble."

Flockhart did not hesitate. Pushing back his chair, he leapt up and dived for the door, only for a third man to wrap a pair of brawny arms around him.

"Not so fast, my lad."

Flockhart struggled, but the man pinioned his arms with some skill.

"What's the trouble?" The newcomer was older than Junar and Nisbet, with deep grooves around his mouth and nose in a weather-darkened face. As he tried to break free, Flockhart noticed the man had leaned a halberd, a long pole arm with an axe-like head, against the whitewashed wall of the room.

"We thought this man was a potential recruit, Sergeant," Junar said. "But he's a collier. It looks like he's run from his owner."

"Let's see that collar." The sergeant had a voice like gravel. He released Flockhart, pulled him closer, and thrust a powerful finger under the tight brass collar that encircled his neck.

"I didn't know colliers had a slave collar," Nisbet said.

"Only those that cause trouble," Sergeant Dunn told him. "This lad must be a troublemaker."

"He doesn't look it," Nisbet defended his choice of a potential recruit.

"Let's have a look. There's writing on the collar." Dunn

pulled Flockhart closer and squinted at the engraved copperplate writing. "It says: 'David Flockhart found guilty of theft in trying to escape his lawful owner. He is the property of Lord Eskbank of Eskhall.'" He pushed Flockhart back onto his chair. "Sit there, son, until I decide what best to do with you."

Nisbet stood between Flockhart and the door, no longer the jovial friend. He put a hand on the hilt of the long bayonet that hung at his waist.

"We can't recruit a collier slave," Junar said. "Lord Eskbank will demand him back, and we'll get into trouble with the officers."

The sergeant grunted, reread the inscription, and rapped a hard knuckle off the brass collar. "We're a bit short-handed, lads, and need every man we can find. Down in England, they're taking convicted thieves, footpads, and even highwaymen. If Flockhart here is a collier, he's used to long hours of hard work, which should make him an ideal soldier."

"Lord Eskbank will demand his return, Sergeant," Junar insisted. "The law says that slave owners can regain their property in any circumstance."

"You're well-versed in the law, Corporal Junar," Dunn said.

Junar closed his mouth and looked away.

"Well, now, Davie Flockhart," Dunn said. "You're a problem, aren't you? Corporal Junar and Private Nisbet have gone to great expense and trouble in catching you, yet you might not be suitable for a soldier of the king."

Flockhart said nothing. He was not sure he wanted to be a soldier. He eyed the door as an official-looking civilian entered, but the man ignored him and sat in the opposite corner.

"You have a choice," Sergeant Dunn continued. "You can join us and have a glorious career wearing the king's scarlet, or we can return you back to your owner. Lord Eskbank will doubtless have you flogged or however he tortures his runaways and keep you confined in his deepest and dampest pit for eternity."

Flockhart tensed himself to run for the door.

"The choice is yours," the sergeant said. "Join Orkney's Regiment and a glorious future or return as Lord Eskbank's property."

"I'd rather be a soldier," Flockhart chose what he hoped was the lesser of the two evils.

He knew he had made a momentous decision. The way ahead seemed clearer, without the dark spectre of the pit with all its memories.

CHAPTER 2

EDINBURGH, SCOTLAND, OCTOBER 1701

When Sergeant Dunn nodded, Flockhart saw the scar on his forehead. "Then a soldier you shall be," Dunn said. "You hear that, lads? We have a new volunteer in Orkney's Royal Regiment of Foot. Let's get that slave's collar off you, my friend."

"It's riveted in place," Flockhart said. "Lord Eskbank's blacksmith put it on."

"Did he, by God," Dunn said. "Well, what one blacksmith can put on, another can remove. Come on, Davie boy; you're with me, and we'll leave these two to gather more happy recruits for our regiment."

"Where are we going?" Flockhart automatically covered his brass collar.

"To find a blacksmith," Dunn told him, lifting his halberd from its resting place against the wall. Already obsolete, the pole weapon had an axe blade on one side, a hook on the other, and a spike on top.

Flockhart wrapped the towel around his neck as Dunn led him from the tavern to a blacksmith's forge in one of the wynds that stretched steeply from the High Street to the Cowgate.

"We need your help, Smith," Sergeant Dunn said, spinning a

shilling in the air. He flicked off Flockhart's concealing towel. "We want that collar removed."

The blacksmith looked doubtfully at Flockhart's collar. "Taking a slave from his owner is theft," he said. "Taking off a slave collar is probably against the law as well."

"I am the thief, not you," Flockhart told him. "By running away, I have stolen myself from His Lordship."

Sergeant Dunn slammed the shilling on the anvil and covered it with his hand. "Nobody will know except you and us," he promised. "And you can keep the collar; a nice piece of brass could be useful."

"It could," the blacksmith agreed. He nodded. "Let's see your collar, then." He examined the brass. "It's well made. I'll have to cut it off. This will hurt."

Flockhart nodded. "Cut away, Smith."

"Sit on the anvil and brace yourself," the blacksmith said, taking a pair of pincers and a short saw from the wall.

Fifteen minutes later, the blacksmith removed the brass collar, leaving two red ridges and a strip of puckered white flesh on Flockhart's neck and throat. Flockhart rubbed the place, feeling the skin tender beneath. He breathed deeply. "Thank you, blacksmith," he said.

"Your skin will harden in time, Davie," Dunn told him as the blacksmith placed the collar carefully in a tub with other scraps of metal. Dunn slid the silver shilling across the anvil to the blacksmith. "You've done your bit for king and country, Smith," he said.

They stepped into the street, where a rising wind dragged clouds above the high tenements, and rainwater wept from the slated roofs.

"Welcome to Edinburgh," Sergeant Dunn said. "Welcome to freedom from servitude and an honourable career."

"What happens now, Sergeant?" Flockhart asked.

"You stay in the castle for a few days and then take ship for the Low Countries." Dunn grinned. "Have you ever been in a castle before?"

Flockhart shook his head. "No, Sergeant."

"Have you ever been on a ship before?"

"No, Sergeant." Flockhart had never dreamt that his life could contain such variety. Even walking through Edinburgh's broad High Street and staring at the cliff-like buildings was novel.

"You have an entirely new world opening up before you," Dunn said. "A world of travel and adventure, a world where you will find new friends and a new respect for yourself. If you obey the rules and do as the NCOs and officers tell you, Private Flockhart, you will get along fine."

"Private Flockhart?"

"Here!" Sergeant extracted a silver shilling from his pocket and casually flicked it across to Flockhart, who caught it in mid-air. "That's the King's Shilling."

"The King's Shilling?" Flockhart repeated. "What does that mean?"

"It means you have accepted my offer to join the army, my lad. Once you get to the castle, you'll be attested, swear an oath of loyalty, and get a full guinea as a bounty. We'll get that coal dust and muck washed off you and find a shiny new uniform. How's that?"

"Why would the king give me a shilling?" Flockhart kept pace with Dunn up the slope of the High Street towards the castle. A few uniformed soldiers watched them, some smiling knowingly.

"King William is a generous man," Dunn said solemnly.

"I didn't know we had a King William," Flockhart replied.

Dunn glanced at him. "Have you heard about the Protestant succession?"

"No," Flockhart admitted.

Sergeant Dunn raised his eyebrows. "We have a Protestant

king," he said. "William is King of Scotland, Ireland and England and rules Holland as well."

Flockhart nodded, staring at the castle that towered ahead of them.

Sergeant Dunn realised that Flockhart had little interest in things royal. "Come on, Davie. The castle is only a short step away."

Flockhart hesitated when they walked up the final few steps of Castle Hill to the ancient grey castle. A sentry stood on either side of the drawbridge, each resplendent in a long scarlet coat with a black tricorn hat square on his head. They acknowledged Sergeant Dunn's arrival by jumping to attention, much to Flockhart's surprise.

Flockhart looked around, feeling out of place among the ancient grey buildings. Soldiers marched all around, with men polishing long cannons that pointed over the city of Edinburgh and the Nor' Loch to the fertile countryside that stretched to the blue smear of the Firth of Forth beyond. Many carried a long musket, and a few held a halberd.

"Sergeants carry halberds," Dunn explained, noting the direction of Flockhart's gaze. "You'll soon learn the ranks."

Flockhart thought the soldiers looked unbelievably smart as they marched straight-backed around the castle while a solitary man in an ornate wig rode past on horseback.

"That's Captain Brisbane," Dunn explained. "He's our company commander. If you are fortunate enough to speak to him, you'll address him as Sir, as you will call all officers."

Flockhart nodded, watching as Captain Brisbane dismounted, handed the reins to a hurrying man, and walked into one of the buildings.

"In here, Davie," Dunn said quietly, guiding him into a dark building that towered three stories towards the weeping sky. Tall windows frowned onto a central courtyard while another sentry slammed to attention, holding a long musket at his side.

A dozen ragged civilians looked up as Flockhart stepped

inside the building and entered a stone-vaulted chamber with a bright fire at the far end. A pair of sentries stood inside the door, watching the civilians.

"Another to join the happy gang," Dunn announced loudly. "That's thirteen now."

"Thirteen for Orkney's Royals," a stocky, mournful-faced civilian replied from the gloomy rear of the room. He scratched his head beneath a shabby wig. "Are any more expected, Sergeant?"

"No, sir," Dunn replied.

"All right." The mournful man walked to the head of the room. "Shut the door, Sergeant."

The door shut with a bang that echoed through the room, sending something of a chill down Flockhart. Some of the potential recruits started at the sound.

"Silence!" Sergeant Dunn roared, the sheer volume of sound shocking the civilians. The recruits were silent, staring at each other, and some began to doubt their impulse to follow the drum. Flockhart joined the crowd, automatically putting a hand to his throat.

"Raise your right hand!" Sergeant Dunn shouted as the mournful man lifted a small book and opened it at a well-thumbed page. "Raise them!"

The men obeyed, wondering. One tall man winked at Flockhart and stood erect.

The mournful man gabbled words Flockhart did not clearly hear, although he understood they referred to His Majesty, King William of Scotland, England and Ireland.

"Now say, I do so swear," Sergeant Dunn ordered.

Flockhart mumbled the words without understanding the meaning. "I do so swear."

"Now you have sworn allegiance to the King and his successors," Dunn told them.

The mournful man lifted a document and rattled off a list of rules and regulations. "I have now read you the Articles of War.

Congratulations. You are now soldiers in Orkney's Regiment, the Royal Scots, the Royal Regiment of Foot."

With his duty done, the mournful man left the room. Flockhart did not know who he was and never saw him again.

"Right, men," Sergeant Dunn said, no longer smiling. "Follow me, and don't straggle." He led them across a rain-battered courtyard and down a slippery slope to a low, dark building which smelled of dust. Passing soldiers watched them with a mixture of disdain, indifference, and amusement.

"This is the clothing store," Dunn informed the recruits. "Every man will receive a three-cornered cocked hat, well-laced, a coat with long skirts, two shirts, a waistcoat, a pair of grey kersey breeches, a pair of yarn hose, a sash, two neckcloths, a pair of strong shoes, and a sword and sword belt."

Flockhart stared at this magnificence, for he had never owned more than a shirt and one pair of breeches. In his experience, shoes, a hat and a coat were only worn by Lord Eskbank and Graham Cummings, his grieve. Other recruits looked equally impressed, with only the tall man accepting the clothes as if he deserved them.

"Don't celebrate yet," the tall man said. "The Regiment will take the cost of the uniform from your wages."

"You will keep your uniform neat and clean at all times," Sergeant Dunn told them. "When you march or in action, you will button back the corners of the skirts to give greater freedom to your legs." He demonstrated with his coat. "All right, quartermaster, they're all yours."

The quartermaster was an old soldier, overweight, with pouchy eyes and two fingers missing from his left hand.

"Get them lined up," he growled. "Send them through one at a time."

The red coat was heavier than Flockhart had expected, lined with white and with a white sash with a bright white fringe. He looked at the light grey breeches and wondered at the two pairs of grey stockings, items that Flockhart had never worn before.

The shoes were heavy and clumsy, with no distinction between the left and right foot, while the sword scabbard smelled of leather.

"These objects will need to be washed before they wear a uniform," the quartermaster growled, eyeing the recruits. "I've never seen a more filthy bunch of recruits." He pointed to Flockhart. "Especially that one. Did you rake it from a midden?"

"That procedure is next," Sergeant Dunn promised. When the quartermaster had issued clothes to all the men, he led them to another small courtyard where a pump sat on a cobbled surface.

Flockhart followed the rest as he examined the sword. It was plain and robust, with its blade, grip, and guard inside its black leather scabbard with brass mountings. On an impulse, he withdrew the weapon from its scabbard, feeling it comfortable in his hand. The blade was thirty inches of glittering steel and sharp enough to shave a man.

"Strip!" Sergeant Dunn ordered as Corporal Junar and another lean corporal entered the courtyard, both carrying short canes.

The recruits glanced at each other in confusion until the corporals encouraged them with loud shouts and smarting cuts with their canes. Flockhart pulled off his clothes and stood still, waiting for orders. He kept one hand over his throat and noticed that some of the men covered their nakedness.

"Wash! You and you!" Dunn pointed to two men. "Work the pump. The rest of you, wash!"

A small crowd of soldiers gathered to watch the fun, with half a dozen women among the audience. One man threw a cake of soap to Flockhart, who caught it with both hands.

"Who did that?" Corporal Junar tapped his cane on the scars on Flockhart's back. "Somebody's flogged you. Are you a deserter?"

Flockhart felt momentary panic until the sergeant stepped forward. "He's no deserter, Junar," Dunn said. "I'll vouch for that." He spun Flockhart around. "You're covered in scars, Flockhart, not just the marks of the whip." Dunn saw the blue scars across Flockhart's upper body.

"Every collier is covered in scars," Flockhart defended himself.

Dunn stepped back, examining Flockhart as a possible soldier. His upper body was impressive, with well-developed muscles, but his legs were weak. "We'll have to build you up for marching, Flockhart," Dunn said.

"Yes, Sergeant," Flockhart agreed. *It's Flockhart now, no longer Davie.*

The lean corporal fetched a long-handled, stiff-bristled brush and scrubbed vigorously at the recruits, which brought howls of laughter and crude advice from the females in the audience.

Flockhart endured the process without protest.

After the recruits were stripped and washed, the regimental barber shaved them, removing all the hair from their heads and bodies to ensure no lice or other vermin entered the regiment. Flockhart found the process less humiliating than most, for nudity was nothing new, as men often worked naked in the pits. He sat or stood in stoic silence, obeying each instruction until the barber dismissed him and called in his next subject.

"Line up!" Dunn barked. "Watch and learn!" He showed the men how to wear their uniforms, supervised their first clumsy attempts to dress and then herded them into a long chamber beneath the castle to be fed.

"You'll sleep in the castle tonight," Corporal Junar told them. "And tomorrow, you'll march to Leith." He glowered at them, a picture of scarlet-and-white splendour. "Cheer up, my lads. You have joined My Lord Orkney's Regiment, the Royal Regiment of Foot, and you are bound for glory and honour. God save the King!"

"God save the King!" Flockhart repeated, and half the recruits joined in. The tall man bellowed the words as one pale-faced and slender recruit began to cry.

CHAPTER 3

ESKHALL, EDINBURGHSHIRE, JANUARY 1702

John Arthur Mayfield, third Lord Eskbank, stood with his back to the fire and a glass of claret in his hand as Graham Cummings, his grieve, related the news from his pits.

"How many tons of coal did we produce this week?" Lord Eskbank asked and frowned at the answer. "Not good enough," he said. "I want more than that."

"Yes, my Lord," Cummings said, bobbing in a bow. "We had flooding in number three shaft, sir."

"Well, pump the water out!" Lord Eskbank said.

"I have the pumps working twenty hours a day, my Lord," Cummings said.

"Work them twenty-four hours a day, damn it!" Lord Eskbank snapped. "Drive them to it."

"Yes, my Lord." Cummings hesitated. "There is something else, my Lord."

"What?" Lord Eskbank snapped. He tossed back the last of his claret and signalled to a servant to refill his glass.

"A collier absconded, my Lord," Cummings nearly whispered. He saw Lady Joanna stir on her chair at the opposite side of the room. She bent over her lap dog.

"Oh, the naughty boy, Charles. Isn't the runaway a naughty boy?"

Lord Eskbank glanced at his wife before he replied. "Find him! I need all my property working to raise the total output." He held out his glass as the servant poured his claret.

"Yes, my Lord. I have searched the neighbourhood," Cummings said.

"Search again. If one man succeeds in absconding, others may follow his lead," Lord Eskbank said. "Find him."

"Yes, my Lord," Cummings agreed.

"Who was it?" Lord Eskbank asked.

"David Flockhart, my Lord. He's caused trouble before." Cummings stepped back as Lord Eskbank glared at him in sudden anger.

"Flockhart? The one I had whipped and put in a brass collar?"

"Yes, my Lord," Cummings said.

Lord Eskbank's face darkened. "Find him," he ordered. "I don't care how long it takes or where you have to go. Find Flockhart and bring him back. I will make an example of him that will strike fear into all my property."

"Yes, my Lord," Cummings said.

Lady Joanna stood up, dropping the dog from her lap. "Yes, find him, Cummings." She smiled, showing small white teeth. "Find Flockhart and bring him to me."

"Yes, my Lady," Cummings said.

"I don't care what it costs," Lady Joanna said. "I want him back."

Something in Lady Joanna's smile made Cummings shiver. "Yes, my Lady."

❉

Sergeant Dunn, Corporal Junar and four armed guards escorted the recruits down Leith Walk to the port of Leith as passers-by watched them with a mixture of sympathy and trepidation. Women whisked their skirts aside to avoid contamination from the soldiers, men stepped away, and some stared as the small column shambled towards their ship.

"Going for a soldier makes us the lowest level of society," Flockhart's neighbour murmured. "Only a small step above Egyptians or colliers."

"Any step is better than no step," Flockhart recognised the tall man from the chamber. "I was a collier."

The tall man looked surprised. "Did your owner free you?"

"No, I ran away." Flockhart held the man's steady grey eyes.

"He can drag you back."

"He'll have to find me first," Flockhart said, striding down the broad street. A cart rumbled past, with the driver pointedly looking away from the soldiers. Flockhart tried to look small, wishing he was on board the ship, safely away from prying eyes.

The tall man inched closer. "Your old master can drag you back from the army as easily as anywhere else. I hope you didn't give Sergeant Dunn your real name."

"I did," Flockhart told him.

"You are David Flockhart, then," the tall man said. "I am Adam Leishman."

They nodded at each other in tentative friendship, neither yet ready to trust the other. Half a dozen mariners watched as they boarded the two-masted snow, *Martha's Pride*, with Sergeant Dunn nodding familiarly to a bald, stocky man who Flockhart took to be an officer. He looked about him, fascinated by the smell of tar and the sight of tall masts, ropes, and canvas.

"Get them down below," the stocky man ordered. "We leave on the next tide."

The words meant nothing to Flockhart. The NCOs pushed them down a short ladder to a long, gloomy compartment with little headroom and less air. Three hanging lanterns provided minimal light.

"Settle down, lads," Corporal Junar shouted. "We're going overseas. Just find a space and keep the noise down."

"Have you been on a ship before?" Leishman asked.

Flockhart shook his head. "I've never even seen one before."

"It's going to get noisy and uncomfortable," Leishman told him. "Try to wedge yourself against the bulkhead – that's what we call walls inside a ship – or the sea will throw you around. It will get boisterous crossing to the continent."

"Is that where we are going?" Flockhart asked.

"The regiment's based in Holland," Leishman said. "They only used Edinburgh Castle to gather recruits. We'll be joining the rest of the Royals."

"How do you know so much?"

"I was a soldier during the last war," Leishman told him. "The regiment I was with was broken – disbanded, and I don't like civilian life."

"Why is that?" Flockhart asked.

"Once you're a soldier," Leishman said, "you're not much use for anything else except labouring or begging. I prefer life in uniform to either."

Flockhart nodded. "It will be better than working down the pit."

As the recruits looked around them, wondering about the close confinement and unpleasant aromas, a couple of seamen poked their heads through the door.

"Have a good voyage, lads!" one man said, laughing as he pushed the door shut. Flockhart heard wood grind on wood and guessed the seaman had barred the door.

"Hey!" one of the recruits shouted. "What are you doing?" He strode to the door and tried to haul it open, swearing when it did not budge.

"He's making sure we don't leave," Leishman said. "The sailors don't want men like us running loose when they're trying to sail the ship. We'd either fall overboard or get in the way."

"How do you know?" An anonymous voice asked from the dark.

"I've been on a troopship before," Leishman replied.

"You were on a ship, and now you're a soldier," the voice sneered.

"And now I am a soldier," Leishman agreed.

Martha's Pride began to rock, gently at first and then more violently, shifting from side to side and then forward and aft, tossing the recruits around. Simultaneously, the noise of groaning and creaking timber increased exponentially.

"What's happening?" Flockhart asked.

"Nothing to worry about," Leishman reassured him. "We're leaving the harbour and heading into the Firth of Forth. The ship will get livelier when we hit the German Ocean, so expect to be thrown around a lot."

Flockhart did not reveal his ignorance by asking what the German Ocean was. He kept quiet, listening to the constant creaking of the timbers and the crash and splash of the sea against the hull. He closed his eyes, fingering his neck and throat as the dark and ominous noises brought back memories.

The roof above them creaked. Flockhart looked up as his father hacked at the coal with his pick, gasping with effort. His father lay on his side to enable him to reach the seam. "Is the roof going to cave in, Father?"

"Maybe. If it does, Davie, you run. Don't wait for me."

A trickle of dust escaped from above, landing on the rough floor at Flockhart's side. His father was naked as a baby, filthy with coal dust and grime, panting as he swung his pick at the eighteen-inch-high coal seam. He shifted slightly and pushed a load towards his son.

"Get the coal, Davie!"

Flockhart obeyed, dragging the coal from beside his father and piling it into the truck behind him as fast as his seven-year-old hands would let him. One sharp edge opened a cut. Flockhart ignored the blood, aware that coal dust would soon seal the wound.

The creaking increased, and a small stone fell from the roof to bounce beside Flockhart. He looked up fearfully as his father released another half hundredweight of coal and shoved it back to him.

"Clear the coal!" his father snarled, "or I'll take my belt to you!"

Flockhart dragged at the coal, ignoring his broken nails and torn fingers. "The roof, father!"

His father coughed, spat black liquid onto the ground and wriggled backwards to ease away from the coal face. "Best get away," he said. "Mr Cummings won't be pleased if we leave the seam, but there's no help for it."

"Yes, Father," Flockhart agreed. He put his shoulder behind the truck and pushed, with the small wheels grating over the uneven surface.

"Push the bloody thing!"

The tunnel only allowed room for one person at a time, and Flockhart struggled to propel the heavy truck. He strained, hearing the patter of falling rocks behind him as his father rammed the top of his pick against his backside and shoved.

"Get a bloody move on, Davie!"

The roof collapsed before they cleared the face, with one chunk of ragged rock creasing Flockhart's father's head. He grunted, shook away the blood and pointed to the truck.

"Get that bloody truck out of the way. We don't want to lose the coal!"

"Don't look so worried," Leishman said. "Ship's timbers are meant to sound like that. It means they are breathing with the fabric of the ship."

Flockhart remained near the entrance of the dark space, fighting his apprehension. The memories of the mine were too vivid to forget.

"A ship's a living thing," Leishman continued. "It moves with the sea. I'll let you know if it gets dangerous."

Flockhart nodded. He felt the ship lurch to one side and held onto the bulkhead. "What's happening?"

"We're in the Firth now," Leishman said. "Short, choppy seas. Depending on the wind, we could be in the sea in half an hour, and then we'll really kick around." He grinned. "Relax and move with the ship. *Martha's Pride* is sound enough; she won't sink under us."

Flockhart felt the nausea rise in his throat, hot and acidic. He swallowed hard and vomited noisily on the deck.

Leishman laughed. "Welcome to a sailor's life," he said.

Flockhart looked up miserably to see half the recruits also vomiting on the deck, with the men more used to travelling by ship watching with unsympathetic amusement. As *Martha's Pride* reached the open sea, her movement became ever more violent, and Flockhart held on to the bulkhead, vomiting and groaning by turns. He did not remember much about the passage to the Low Countries, except it was a nightmare of suffering. After a terrible night, the crew allowed the recruits on deck to find the ship heaving and tossing and the masts gyrating against a grey-white sky.

"Up you get, lubber!" A grinning seaman greeted him. "Don't fall overboard, now."

Sergeant Dunn appeared, immaculate in his scarlet coat and with his tricorn hat miraculously in place despite the blustery wind.

"We need men who can keep moving and fighting through discomfort," Dunn stood before them, balancing easily on the moving deck. "Form up!"

The recruits formed an uneven line, with Corporal Junar pushing them into place.

"Use Private Nisbet as a marker!" Dunn ordered. "When I give an order, he will obey, and you will follow his actions."

For the next two hours, Sergeant Dunn taught the recruits basic commands, using Nisbet as an example. Flockhart listened and copied Nisbet's movements, allowing the fresh air to clear his aching head. Nothing seemed real, not the cracking and billowing of the sails, the whine of the wind or the constant slapping of the sea, yet he knew that he had to learn.

"That will do for now," Dunn said eventually. "Dismissed."

He pointed his halberd at Flockhart. "Except you! I want a word with you!"

Flockhart waited until the other recruits vanished below.

"What do you know about the Earl of Orkney's Regiment, the Royal Regiment of Foot?" Dunn asked.

Flockhart shook his head. "I know they are a regiment of the line," he said, standing at attention beside the main mast and trying to keep his balance. He was surprised that the worst of his seasickness had passed.

"They are more than that," Dunn told him. "The Royal Regiment, the Royal Scots, is the oldest line regiment in the British Army, with an ancestry that dates back centuries."

Flockhart remained at attention, trying to ignore the shaking of his limbs, the spindrift that spattered the deck and the moaning of the wind in the rigging. "Yes, Sergeant," he said.

"The Royal Regiment, your regiment, can trace its ancestry to 1421 when Scottish soldiers became a permanent part of the French army. At that time, Scotland and France were Allies. However, that part of our history is obscure. We do know that in 1625, a soldier named John Hepburn raised a Scottish regiment to fight for Gustavus Adolphus of Sweden, a Protestant king."

"Yes, Sergeant," Flockhart wondered why Dunn had singled him out.

"European politics are always complex, and Hepburn's regiment joined the French service and amalgamated with the Scots already there to form *Le Regiment d'Hebron*, or Hepburn's regiment. In 1632, King Charles the First of Scotland and England agreed to allow Hepburn to recruit in Scotland, with Charles' royal warrant and the Privy Council of Scotland's consent."

Flockhart tried to remember the details.

"You'll know that regiments are identified by their colonel's name, and we were known as Douglas's, then Dumbarton's, and now we are Orkney's, named after Sir George Hamilton, the Earl of Orkney."

Sergeant Dunn did not move as a wave broke against the

hull, sending ankle-deep cold water sluicing over the deck. Flockhart followed his example, for he was accustomed to cold and wet.

"You'll be wondering why I am telling you this and why I am happy to release you from slavery," Dunn said. "Well, I'll tell you. I was a slave for five years. I was a seaman, you see, bound from Leith to Lisbon, and a Barbary corsair captured our ship."

Flockhart had never heard of a Barbary corsair and did not know where Lisbon was.

"Barbary Corsairs are slavers and pirates," Dunn noticed Flockhart's incomprehension. "They sail from North African ports and attack Christian ships and sometimes small towns, rob them and take captives as slaves."

Flockhart nodded. "Yes, Sergeant." *I thought only colliers and salters were slaves. I did not know there were others.*

Dunn waited for a moment as the shipmaster bellowed orders that saw a rush of seamen alter the set of the sails. *Martha's Pride* moved more easily on the waves.

"The Moors held me as a slave for five years and treated me worse than any Christian would treat a dog. I was only freed when the Royals came to Tangiers, so I joined the regiment and have been here ever since. It's my home."

Flockhart nodded. "Yes, Sergeant."
Maybe the Royals will be my home as well. I certainly can't return.

Sergeant Dunn held Flockhart's gaze for a long moment. "That's all, Flockhart. Dismissed."

Flockhart stumbled back to the stinks and stuffiness below decks, determined to be the best soldier possible.

CHAPTER 4
EDINBURGH, SCOTLAND, FEBRUARY 1702

Cummings hesitated before lifting the iron ring and tirling it up and down the risp at the door, creating a loud rattle that echoed inside the house. The tirling ring resembled a lion's mouth, gaping open to show a row of sharp teeth. Cummings thought it looked menacing as he waited for a response.

He stood at the door, looking around at the steep descent of the West Bow, which coiled down to the Grassmarket. The tall tenements rose opposite him, with people passing on the busy street and a water carrier slogging up the slope with his heavy burden.

The door opened a moment later, and a medium-sized man lifted his eyebrows.

"Yes?" The man looked ordinary, with a face that would be lost in a crowd and clothes that were slightly rumpled, good quality but worn from use. Yet Cummings sensed the latent power as the man waited for Cummings to explain himself.

"My name is Graham Cummings. I am the grieve and mine manager for Lord Eskbank. Do I have the honour of addressing Mr Mungo Redpath?"

"That's my name," Redpath confirmed.

Cummings bobbed in a bow. "I believe you specialise in solving problems and locating absconded servants."

Redpath nodded. "That is something I do."

Cummings stepped back slightly. "I have a problem I need you to solve, Mr Redpath. I have a man who has absconded."

"Have you considered using a Sheriff Officer or a Messenger-at-Arms?"

"My master prefers that this problem is solved privately, Mr Redpath, without bringing it to the courts or alerting the public." Cummings knew Sheriff Officers had local responsibility to pursue a sheriff's warrant, while Messengers-at-Arms could enforce court orders and pursue criminals nationwide and even overseas if necessary.

Redpath's expression did not alter. "Do you have the necessary funds to pay for my services?"

"I do," Cummings said.

Redpath opened the door wider and stepped back. "Come in and give me the details, Mr Cummings."

The door led to a short corridor panelled in dark wood. Redpath ushered Cummings through the central door of three and into a square room. The walls were plastered and painted green, with three square pictures of intricate designs on the left-hand wall and a square rug on the polished wooden floorboards.

Three chairs stood beside the single square table, flanked by a long, double-fronted display cabinet on the right-hand wall. Faint sunlight reflected on a display of glasses on one side and three curved knives on the other.

Redpath took a sheet of paper, quill and ink, sat on one of the chairs and invited Cummings to sit opposite. "Now, Mr Cummings, what do you want of me?"

"I want you to find a man named David Flockhart, the property of Lord Eskbank."

Redpath dipped his quill in the ink and carefully wrote the name. "Property? Is David Flockhart a collier or a salter?"

"He is a collier," Cummings said. "He worked in the pits at Stobhill, south of Dalkeith."

"It's illegal for a collier to abscond," Redpath confirmed. "Has Lord Eskbank notified the relevant authorities about his desertion?"

"He has not," Cummings said. "I have already explained that His Lordship does not want this affair to become public."

"You did," Redpath agreed. "Why is that?"

"His Lordship does not want any possible scandal to attach to his family," Cummings replied. "He is endeavouring to find a suitable match for his daughter."

Redpath added to his notes. "As you wish. Give me a description of the runaway."

"Flockhart is five foot five, with dark brown hair and brown eyes." Cummings was ready for the question.

"Does he have any distinguishing marks?"

Cummings nodded. "He has the collier's usual quota of scars, plus we had the public hangman whip him for previously absconding, and he wears a brass collar."

Redpath paused for a moment. "What sort of brass collar?"

"A brass collar two inches wide with his name and Lord Eskbank's name on it."

Redpath's quill was busy on the foolscap paper. "Flockhart will try to get rid of that as soon as possible," he said. "I'll try all the blacksmiths. Which direction did he run?"

"I don't know," Cummings said.

"I'll find out," Redpath told him. "For how long has he been missing?"

"Two weeks now," Cummings replied. "I tried to find him myself before I contacted you."

"The longer Flockhart's been missing, the harder it will be to find him," Redpath warned. "I'll need to be paid in advance."

Cummings had anticipated the demand. "How much?"

"Three guineas down payment, two guineas a week and expenses. I'll keep detailed accounts, Mr Cummings."

The advance fee was more than Cummings had expected. He fished in his pocket and handed over the money, hoping Lord Eskbank would reimburse him. If not, he knew a protracted search would send him into bankruptcy.

"I hope you are as good as your reputation suggests, Mr Redpath," Cummings looked around as the door behind him opened and two people walked in.

"Meet my partners," Redpath said. "Duncan Grant and Ruth Gordon."

Duncan Grant was the largest man Cummings had ever seen, well over six feet tall and broad in comparison. He nodded without speaking. Ruth Gordon looked tiny in comparison, yet Cummings could see she was taller than most women. When she curtsied and smiled, Cummings saw she would capture the heart of most men. He smiled as he felt a surge of optimism; Redpath alone seemed a pretty formidable figure, but with his two partners inspired great confidence.

"Find my escapee," Cummings said, "and bring him back."

"We will," Redpath promised as Gordon patted his arm with a small hand.

※

Flockhart did not know the name of the town where Orkney's regiment was quartered, only that he was somewhere in the Low Countries, and it was neat and clean. He stood beside Leishman and another recruit named Young, feeling far from home.

"Attention!" Sergeant Dunn called the recruits to him. "Listen! This town is divided into areas, with one company billeted in each area. Major Hamilton has allocated this street to our platoon, and you will stay where I tell you until I order you elsewhere. Are there any questions?"

"No, Sergeant," Flockhart replied.

Dunn gave detailed instructions, telling each man where he would live until the next campaigning season started. He finished with a short reminder. "All right. You will listen for the drum and repair instantly to your quarters when ordered. You will not linger in the taverns when told to leave; you will not molest any civilian nor brawl with the other regiments. Do you understand?"

"Yes, Sergeant," the recruits shouted.

Flockhart shared a small tavern with the elderly owners and five other Royals, including Leishman, Young, and two quiet recruits. The final Royal was William Darvel, a middle-aged veteran with a lugubrious face and the broken blood vessels that suggested heavy drinking.

"You recruits do what I tell you," Darvel growled, "and we'll get along fine."

Leishman stamped his shoes on the floor and moved closer to the iron stove in the centre of the room. "We're the same rank," he said. "You've no more authority over us than we have over you."

Darvel looked Leishman up and down, took a bottle from the floor at his side and slumped onto a chair. Quiet when sober, he soon became loquacious when he drank, roaring out old marching songs with obscene choruses and speaking of past battles in distant wars. Flockhart did not know how Darvel obtained the beer and spirits he hid when Lieutenant Murray performed his weekly check.

Murray was one of the better officers who gave warning before he arrived for an inspection, allowing the men time to squirrel away any bottles or stray women who accidentally found their way into their quarters. Flockhart soon learned to avoid the officers with their better-quality clothing and shoulder-length wigs. He became as adept as the others in the essential military skills of avoiding trouble and seeking alcohol.

"You recruities," Darvel said as he cradled a bottle to his chest. "You don't know what soldiering is. Wait until you've smelled powder smoke and seen the French advancing against you with their drums beating and the sun gleaming on their bayonets. That'll learn you."

"Have you seen much fighting?" Peter Young asked.

"More than you'll ever know," Darvel replied, putting the bottle to his lips. "I was at Sedgemoor against Monmouth's rebels, Tangier against the Moors, the great mutiny of 1690 and through King William's War against the French."

Flockhart listened without comment. He had never heard of any of these events. The colliers in his pit lived a narrow life where the outside world did not matter and could not intrude. He knew about bad air and rock falls, weights of coal and the black spit, deep shafts, and flooding. Until he absconded from the pit, he had no interest in anything else. Life was about toil, suffering, survival, and finding a woman to share his burden. Nothing else mattered. Nothing else could matter.

"All this, and we get paid as well," Flockhart marvelled. The parades and drills did not concern him. He was out in the open air, with regular food and work that was far easier than toiling down the pit.

"We get paid eightpence a day," Leishman said, "but the army claws back most of that to pay for our food and uniform. Money is different here in Holland, so you won't see any money you recognise. You'll be using Dutch guilders and stivers, with a stiver worth about an English penny. If we march into the Spanish Netherlands, you might see a pistole or a French louis d'or, both of which are worth a guinea."

Flockhart nodded. He had never had much money, so the details did not interest him.

"We'll be at war soon, Davie," Leishman said. "And then the king will need all the soldiers he can get."

"What's this war all about anyway?" Young asked. "I know we are fighting France, but why?"

"The French want to put their candidate on the Spanish throne, and we want to put ours. If the French win, they'll control Spain and the entire Spanish Empire in the Americas and Asia, making them the strongest power in Europe and maybe the world."

Flockhart listened to the answer, hungry for knowledge that his previous occupation had denied him.

"If we're going to fight France about Spain," Flockhart asked. "Why are we in Holland?"

Leishman settled back in his chair, allowing the heat from the stove to seep over him. "You see, fellow soldiers and bottle companions, Spain controls the Spanish Netherlands," he jerked a thumb to the southeast. "Over there, and Spain also holds much of Italy and the New World, the Americas. Holland, where we are, shares a border with the Spanish Netherlands, and the French have already marched their troops in."

"What has that got to do with us?" Flockhart asked.

"Bugger all," Leishman said. "Except that our King William is Dutch and wants to curtail the French. He doesn't want them as neighbours and is their most stalwart enemy and the protector of the Protestant religion." Leishman shrugged, opened the stove door and added a log from the pile at his side. "The Frenchies are an aggressive breed, always wanting to attack somebody."

"Does that mean that the Dutch are on our side?" Flockhart tried to make sense of the tangled skein of European politics.

"We're on theirs, rather," Leishman tried to explain. "King William was the Prince of Orange and head of the Dutch Republic long before he became King of Scotland and England. We wanted a Protestant king, and he wanted our manpower for his wars."

Flockhart pulled his empty pipe from his pocket and thrust it in his mouth. "Did we not have a couple of wars with the Dutch once?"

"We did," Leishman agreed. "In European wars," he said. "Allies can alter yearly, but you can be assured that King William will be on the opposite side to the French, whatever happens. This season, our Allies are the Dutch, the Austrian Empire, Hesse and Hanover. The French and the Spanish who support the Bourbons, the French royal house, are our enemies. Bavaria might join the French, and Prussia and Denmark could be on our side. Add Portugal and Savoy to the mix, stir, and you get an unholy mess."

"I've never heard of most of these places," Flockhart admitted.

Leishman smiled. "It doesn't matter a twopenny damn. You're a soldier, Flockhart. Your job is to obey orders and fight the king's enemies, whoever they are. We don't have to understand the whys and wherefores. We leave that to our leaders, whoever they may be."

Flockhart nodded. "War is more complicated than I knew."

"This next war will be complicated," Leishman agreed. "At present, France has all the advantages. They have a central position with interior lines and have occupied a small nation called the Electorate of Cologne, making it difficult for the Dutch Republic to communicate with Vienna, the capital of the Austrian Empire."

"Is that bad?" Flockhart asked, sucking on his empty pipe.

Leishman nodded. "Yes, Allies must coordinate their plans. If we can't communicate, we might fight separate wars, and the French will defeat us individually."

"You mentioned an Electorate," Flockhart said. "What does that mean?"

"Some rulers of the German states are called electors," Leishman said. "They have the great privilege of electing the emperor of Austria, who theoretically rules them all."

Flockhart struggled with the unfamiliar names and concepts. "How about the Navy?" Flockhart asked. "Can't we use the Navy?"

"Only at sea. Not for wars fought on land," Leishman said

with a smile. "But that's not our worry. We obey orders and fight whoever fate puts in front of us."

Flockhart accepted Leishman's military wisdom. His new life was more interesting than his old, provided Lord Eskbank did not find him.

CHAPTER 5

THE DUTCH REPUBLIC, SPRING 1702

Sergeant Dunn eyed the recruits, tapping his halberd on the frost-hard ground. "I will teach you to become soldiers," he said quietly. "Not just any soldiers, but soldiers in Orkney's Foot, the best regiment in the army."

Flockhart looked up, resolved to become a good soldier. He listened to Sergeant Dunn's instructions and followed them carefully, learning how to march, what each drum beat meant and how to dress according to regimental requirements. When unsure, he asked Leishman's help, ignored Darvel's sarcasm, and slowly progressed.

Dunn drilled the men, bellowing at them if they moved a second too soon or too late.

"Move together!" Dunn snarled for the tenth time that morning. "Move together, or the French will ensure you don't move at all." He walked the length of his men, staring into every face. "The French are good soldiers, and we must be better to defeat them. Learn or die!"

The recruits struggled with the complexities of drill, sweating despite the chill as they concentrated on Dunn's commands and the tapping of the drum.

"You can't see the point in all this drill," Dunn told them. "I assure you there is a reason for everything I make you do. You must learn to move as a body, on the word of command, and without hesitation. The General will give orders when we face the French, and we carry them out. If we do it well, we will be victorious. If we don't, we'll be left as dung on some foreign field."

Dunn paused for a moment. "You'll recognise the General; he's the man who rides in a coach and four when ordinary mortals like you and me march. When he's near a battle, he'll mount his horse, which will have leopard skins over the saddle to keep it clean."

The recruits listened. Flockhart saw the mixture of faces, from the scarcely intelligent to men broken by life's experiences and men desperate to become soldiers. He saw the cunning and the brutal, the hopeless and the keen. All had one thing in common: they were all confused by the new skills they had to learn.

Flockhart soon learned that the drums controlled his life. The rattle of the drum regulated every important section of his day, with different beats giving different orders. The first drumbeat was at daybreak when the Reveille ordered men to rise from their beds and the sentinels to stop challenging strangers. Used to early hours, Flockhart rose immediately.

For the first few days, strident-voiced corporals helped the recruits rise by bellowing in their ears, tearing off their thin blankets and kicking feet, backs, ribs, or any other prominent part of their anatomy.

The recruits washed and shaved in a tub of cold water, ate a coarse and scanty breakfast, and ran when the drums beat the Troop. Assembling in the parade ground, they answered their name at roll call and faced another day of drill, drill, and more drill. Flockhart's head swam with the incessant orders as he learned how to march in step with scores of other men, lifting and placing his feet in time with his neighbours.

The drums dictated how to move with his company. It told

him when to eat and when to parade. The drums beat Retreat at sunset for the men to gather for roll call and the beat to order the men to listen to the orders of the day. At nine in the winter's evening, the drum called Tattoo and men returned wearily to their quarters for another roll call and bed.

The rattle of the drum echoed through Flockhart's head that first winter and spring he spent with the Royals, but the drum calls were only one part of his military education. He also had to learn how to fight.

Sergeant Dunn stood before the recruits with a pale sun clearing the pearly morning mist away.

"Each of you now has one of these." He held up the musket in both hands. "This little beauty is your best friend, companion, wife, and saviour. You will love and hate her by turns, but most of all, you will look after her." Dunn grinned. "In short, exactly like a real wife."

The recruits listened in silence, some surprised at the weight of their musket. Flockhart held his weapon without difficulty as years of working at the coal face had developed his upper body and arms into herculean stature.

"This is your musket, your flintlock musket, which is a major improvement on the old matchlock," Sergeant Dunn paced as he spoke, walking back and forth across the group of recruits.

"With a matchlock, you needed to have a slow match coiled around your wrist to fire your weapon. With a flintlock, you do not. It is a far superior musket, and you are all privileged."

Flockhart glanced at his musket, noting the firing mechanism, which looked beautifully designed and absurdly simple as a method of killing a fellow man.

Sergeant Dunn continued his teaching.

"With the old matchlocks, we had to form in six ranks because the weapons took so long to reload. The front rank fired and filed to the rear to reload, and then the second rank did the same, and so on. It took the firing of five ranks before the front rank was loaded and ready to fire again. This much-improved flintlock has cut the loading time in half and reduced misfires, so we need only three ranks, with the front rank kneeling."

Flockhart glanced along the ranks, where the recruits listened. The less intelligent already looked confused.

"Where once we had powder horns and bandoliers of shot, now we carry greased paper cartridges," Dunn held up a cartridge as an example. "Our rate of fire has doubled. A good soldier can fire a shot every minute. A very good soldier may fire twice that." He paused. "I will make you all very good soldiers or break you into dust."

The mixture of promise and threat, carrot and stick, was typical of Sergeant Dunn's style, Flockhart learned. The sergeant lowered his voice, walked around the men and stopped directly before Flockhart, who noticed Captain Brisbane watching from a distance.

Dunn ignored the officer. "You will learn twenty-six evolutions with your musket and a further seven with the bayonet."

That's even more to remember, Flockhart thought. *There's a lot more to being a soldier than I imagined.*

"Your musket has a forty-six-inch-long iron barrel and a wooden butt," Dunn hammered the recruits with information. "Iron rusts in damp weather." He stepped close to Leishman, the tallest recruit. "If I find one speck of rust on your flintlock, I will have you at the triangle."

Flockhart knew that meant a flogging with the cat of nine tails. He resolved to keep his musket rust-free. Lord Eskbank had ordered him whipped once, and he did not want to repeat the humiliation and pain.

"We fire volleys by platoons," Dunn said. "You will only fire when an officer or a Non-Commissioned Officer gives the order."

The Non-Commissioned Officers, sergeants, and corporals had authority over the men; they were the first line of command and often the only source of authority who spoke to the rankers. The officers were distant figures who spoke to the NCOs, seldom to the veterans and never deigned to recognise the recruits. Flockhart saw them as God-like beings who lived in a different world from the men.

To rise to the exalted ranks of corporal, a soldier had to acquire the near necromancy of reading, writing and arithmetic, arts to which Flockhart had never been exposed. He obeyed orders as best he could, basked in the open air, and tried to avoid punishments.

"You will need to keep your nerve," Dunn said. "If you are ever involved in a battle, you will face the French at sixty paces distant and exchange volleys until their nerve breaks and they run. We are the Royals. We will never run. That is when discipline is important."

Discipline in the Royals was strict, if not as cruel, as some other regiments. Defaulters could be sentenced to twenty-four hours on bread and water, or ordered to wear their coats inside out, showing their shame to the regiment, or subjected to a simple, cutting, reprimand. Only the most serious cases would stand before a regimental court martial, where the colonel would invariably order the guilty to be flogged.

Captain Brisbane drifted closer, sitting astride the horse that seemed part of him. He listened to Dunn's instructions, flicked back his flowing wig, and nodded approvingly.

Sergeant Dunn walked along the line, stopping before selected men to ensure everybody paid attention. He halted three inches in front of Flockhart and lowered his voice to a bellow.

"As well as your musket, you will have a seventeen-inch triangular bayonet. You will use this bayonet to gut your opponent. You will not use it to cut up food; you will ensure it is always clean and rust free."

The recruits nodded, eager to show their desire to keep their musket and bayonet clean.

"This little bump here," the sergeant touched the top of the muzzle. "Is your foresight. It is also where you lock on your bayonet. The wooden stick beneath the barrel is your ramrod or scouring stick, used for ramming down the powder, wad and ball."

The recruits listened as the sergeant showed them how to hold their muskets when marching and firing. They copied his movements, but they were clumsy, uncoordinated, and hesitant.

"The flintlock mechanism is simple and effective," the sergeant said. "You see the hammer or the cock? That cock looks like jaws, and within the jaws is a piece of flint." He demonstrated.

"When you press the trigger, the hammer drops, and the flint strikes a metal plate called the anvil. The contact pushes the anvil backwards and creates sparks which land in the pan underneath." The sergeant looked up to ensure his audience was paying attention.

"The pan holds a small amount of gunpowder, which you will put there. When the sparks ignite the powder, it explodes the main powder charge in the barrel, propelling the ball at great speed toward the enemy."

Flockhart held his musket thoughtfully, wondering if he could fire it with the intention of killing a man. He thought of Lord Eskbank and the conditions in the pit.

Yes. I could fire at a man. I will picture every Frenchman I see as Lord Eskbank or Cummings the grieve. They are my enemies, not some anonymous Frenchman who has never harmed me.

Dunn stepped back. "A bullet from this musket can penetrate one inch of wood at three hundred yards range. You can imagine the damage it will do to a Frenchman at sixty yards."

When Flockhart aimed his musket for the first time, he did not imagine an anonymous Frenchman in his sights. His target was Graham Cummings, the Grieve, or Lord Eskbank himself. He squeezed the trigger gently, savouring the thought of his one-ounce lead ball smashing into His Lordship's guts.

❋

"We'll have to find a suitable husband for Moira," Lady Joanna said. "She is ready for marriage now, and I don't want an old maid cluttering up my house."

"Time enough for that," Lord Eskbank said. "I have better things to do than run around begging people to take Moira off our hands. There's that blasted absconded Flockhart, for instance."

"Is this runaway so important?" Lady Joanna asked, stretching lazily on the bed. "He's only a serf."

"Yes," Lord Eskbank replied. He stood naked at the window, watching the gardeners working. He ran his gaze over the walled garden where the gardeners grew the fruit and vegetables for the house and the grand sweep of the lawn towards the North Esk River that lent its name to his home of Eskhall.

"Why is Flockhart important?" Lady Joanna asked, moving her head so the morning sun did not dazzle her.

"If one man successfully escapes, others may follow his lead. I need more workers, not less." Eskbank turned from the window to admire his reflection in the pier-glass beside the bed. "I want to expand my pits, Joanna. Although the late bad weather flooded many of my mines, I already supply much of the domestic coal to Edinburgh, and with this talk of Union, I might also move into the London trade." He paused. "I am not sure how yet. I'll need to find somebody who can help."

"Trade is so dreadfully boring," Lady Joanna did not hide her yawn. "Do we have to involve ourselves in such matters?"

Lord Eskbank smiled. "We can live off our rents," he said, "but I want more than that. We lost money with King William's Ill years and more in that Darien nonsense. I mean to recoup everything I lost and more." He stepped across the room, aware Lady Joanna was watching every movement. Looking sideways, he could see himself in the pier-glass, tall, athletic, and handsome in the morning sunlight.

Lady Joanna nodded. "I know, John. I understand all about our financial affairs. I am not some noodle-headed simperer. The

Company of Scotland was an excellent idea, poorly executed and sabotaged by the Dishonourable East India Company. Planting a settlement in the Spanish-owned swamp of Darien was a disaster."

Lord Eskbank stared at her. "How the devil do you know all that?"

Lady Joanna yawned. "Oh, don't be boring, John. Come to bed and prove yourself rather than parading like a rampant youth." She pushed back the bedcovers. "If you must talk about business, John, discuss it with Jamie Douglas. Queensberry will help." She watched Lord Eskbank approach through hooded eyes. "And consider Sir Hugh Crichton for Moira. He's well connected and personable."

Lord Eskbank hardly heard his wife's advice as he slid into bed and closed the bed curtains. But was she sufficiently friendly with the Duke of Queensberry to call him Jamie?

CHAPTER 6

DUTCH REPUBLIC, SPRING 1702

"We are infantry," Sergeant Dunn said. "Infantry is the backbone of every army. You will also meet cavalry, which is more mobile than us because horses have four feet, and we only have two." He waited for the laugh and snarled at them to keep quiet.

"Enemy cavalry is dangerous," Dunn said. "They can break through a weak line and will slaughter a disorganised battalion. Whatever happens, keep in formation, for cavalry cannot break a hedge of bayonets. The French cavalry comes close, fires fusils – large pistols – and wheels away while ours charge with the sabre."

Dunn tapped the musket he carried and lowered his voice as if imparting a confidence. "Your musket has a longer range than a French pistol. Trust your officers, obey their orders, and you can overcome enemy cavalry."

Flockhart learned basic foot drill and musket drill, the manual and platoon exercises, and words of command; he learned how to march, countermarch, form up in ranks, obey orders at the "tap of drum," company drill, and "handling of arms."

The routine altered as the recruits became more indoctrinated into army life, with less drill and more responsibilities. Every day, a subaltern, known as the Officer of the Guard, was on duty in the guardroom, where the patrol sergeant reported to him that all was in order or otherwise.

Whenever an officer came close, an NCO hurried Flockhart out of view in case such a disreputable specimen should offend an officer's susceptibilities. Flockhart considered it an important day when Sergeant Dunn allowed him to remain as young Ensign Forbes made his rounds.

"You're nearly fit to be seen, Flockhart," Dunn told him. "It's time you learned more of a soldier's duty."

"Yes, Sergeant," Flockhart agreed.

"I'm putting you on guard duty," Dunn told him. "I'm assigning you to the quarter guard with me, Corporal Junar, and another eleven privates, including Young. You follow orders, and you'll learn what to do." He smiled. "You'll soon feel like a real soldier."

In the evening, the drums tapped out the "setting of the watch," and the guard increased to eighteen men. Dunn gathered the quarter guard. "Our duty is to patrol the town, keep down undesirables, watch for sneak thieves, and arrest any stray drunks."

Flockhart nodded, glad to be doing something useful rather than endless drilling and training. Dunn waited until the drums beat Tattoo, then called on his patrol. "We're touring the taverns and inns," he said, "and removing any stray Royals. We don't want any brawls."

"Yes, Sergeant," Flockhart said.

"Don't interfere with the civilians," Dunn ordered, "unless the civilian authorities request our assistance. We are not here to molest them or take over their town."

"How about women, Sergeant?" Peter Young asked.

"We have camp followers," Dunn replied. "Some are genuine wives; others are women looking for a husband, either temporary for a night or two or more long-lasting."

"I mean local women, Sergeant Dunn," Young said.

"Leave them well alone," Dunn hardened his tone. "We don't want trouble with the townsfolk."

Young grinned. "The women won't complain about me," he said, looking around the Guard. "Once they've had me, they'll follow the drum and beg for more."

Flockhart joined in the general laugh.

Sergeant Dunn led them around the town, advising stray Royals to return to their quarters. The first two taverns were quiet, but in the third, a couple of veterans sat with women perched on their knees and the smell of drink on their breath.

"Right, lads," Dunn said. "The drums have sounded Tattoo. It's time you were gone."

The first veteran, a wiry man in his late thirties, shook his head. "We're not moving," he claimed.

Flockhart took a deep breath, unsure what to do. Sergeant Dunn did not hesitate. He stepped forward, hauled the woman from the veteran's knee, and threw her on the floor. As she sprawled there, protesting, the veteran rose to his feet. Dunn slammed him back on the wooden bench with a punch to the chest.

"Get out!" he snarled.

The second man, younger and heavier, swore and tried to disentangle himself from his woman. Dunn jerked a thumb to the door, pushed the woman aside, and dragged the man off the bench.

"Get back to your quarters!" Dunn ordered.

Flockhart watched as both men staggered down the street.

"That's how we treat insubordination in Orkney's," Dunn said. "We deal with it immediately, without court-martials or the wooden horse."

Flockhart had heard horror stories of the wooden horse, where errant soldiers sat astride a narrow plank for hours with bundles of muskets tied to their ankles.

Once the recruits mastered the basics of army life, the NCOs introduced them into the battalion's structure.

"You are all Royals," Sergeant Dunn said. With the sun gleaming on his uniform, he looked a splendid sight as he paced before the recruits. "But you will also be a member of a platoon, with an ensign in command, and a member of a company, with a captain in command. When a battalion is at full strength, without battle casualties or sickness, it will consist of eighteen platoons."

Flockhart listened, trying to absorb all the information he could about his new life, so different from hacking coal in the stinking, poisonous dark.

"Sixteen platoons are from the battalion companies and two from the grenadier companies," Sergeant Dunn continued.

Flockhart had seen the grenadiers, the tallest and strongest men in the regiment, made even taller by their mitre caps. As he was slightly under average height, Flockhart knew he could never aspire to be a grenadier.

"The grenadiers are all trained in throwing grenades, which are fist-sized, round weapons filled with powder, with a fuse projecting from a small neck. The grenadiers carry a pouch holding three grenades and light the fuse from a slow match they have wound around their left wrist. Some grenadiers also carry a hatchet for chopping down enemy palisades. They are the shock troops who march at the head of the regiment."

Flockhart glanced at Leishman, who was sufficiently tall to be a grenadier. Leishman shook his head, denying the possibility.

Dunn stopped to shout at a man who had lost concentration, then called the platoon to attention. Captain Brisbane passed, riding a pale horse and appearing other-worldly in his splendour. He paused to listen for a moment and moved on, slim, elegant, and unapproachable.

Sergeant Dunn relaxed and continued. "In battle, the battalion is organised into three firings of six platoons along the front, with every third platoon firing together. We call these platoons firings. While one firing is shooting at the enemy, the other two reload, which means we deliver each volley from all along the front of the battalion."

Flockhart wrestled with this new concept.

"You will always fire in volleys, and only when an NCO or an officer commands you to," Dunn repeated what he had already said several times.

Flockhart nodded. He could see no reason to fire unless ordered.

They drilled hour after hour, day after day, now learning the complicated manoeuvres and commands that would eventually see the commanding officers move their regiments and brigades around the battlefield like chessmen. They learned how to open and close ranks and to move automatically on the word of command. They learned to load and fire automatically until even the slowest man could fire two rounds a minute.

Flockhart learned the official words of command.

"Handle cartridge!"

"Prime!"

"Load!"

"Draw ramrods!"

"Ram down cartridges!"

"Return ramrods!"

"Make ready!"

"Present!"

"Give fire!"

"Why do we say give fire?" Sergeant Dunn asked and immediately answered himself. "In the old days, before we started pampering you with flintlocks, we applied the slow match to the touchhole, thus giving fire."

After weeks of training, Flockhart began to feel like a soldier, one of a unit rather than an individual, yet he always retained something of himself. The essence of his character that had compelled him to leave the pits remained intact. He may have been evolving into Private Flockhart, but he was also Davie Flockhart, with memories and a soul of his own.

※

"You lads get on guard," Sergeant Dunn ordered. "I'll be with you later. I'll check the candles and fires to ensure they are all extinguished and report them to the Officer of the Guard." He gave a twisted smile. "If any of you ever make sergeant, you'll know that our work is never done."

Flockhart did not smile. The possibility of him ever reaching the terrifying heights of a Non-Commissioned Officer was so remote he would not consider it. His sole ambition was to be accepted as a soldier, spend as much time outside as possible, and never return to the pits.

Garrisoning a quiet town in a Dutch spring may have bored some Royals, but Flockhart found satisfaction in patrolling the dark streets. He never complained about being on duty or tired of glancing at the night-time sky, breathing the chill air, or viewing the moonlit countryside.

"You're a strange man, Davie," Leishman told him as they stood at the edge of the town, watching an empty road. A solitary tree stood at a bend, spreading bare branches to the sky like a man supplicating a heartless god. "Most men would do anything to avoid guard duty at night."

Flockhart nodded. "Most men haven't spent most of their lives underground, Adam," he said. "Walking upright and breathing fresh air is one of the best feelings imaginable."

Leishman nodded. "I can only imagine," he said. "You might make a decent soldier, Davie. You take the world as it comes without expecting too much."

"There's a lot to learn," Flockhart said. "I hope I remember all the moves when we are facing the French."

"You will," Leishman told him. "All you need to do is follow the rest. Listen!" He lifted his head. "Can you hear that? Hoofbeats!"

"I hear them," Flockhart said.

"It might be a French patrol," Leishman cocked his musket and checked the priming. "The campaigning season will start any week now, and the Frenchies will want to know what we're doing."

Flockhart felt a prickle of excitement. "Should we call the sergeant?"

"Not yet," Leishman said. "Wait until we see what's happening."

The hoofbeats increased in volume until Flockhart could distinguish three horses and cocked his musket. "They'll be here in a minute."

The riders appeared around the side of the tree, with one slightly in front.

"Halt! Stand and identify yourselves!" Leishman repeated the words in Dutch. "*Halt. Ga staan en identificeer uzelf!*"

The leading rider pulled on his reins and replied in English. "Who the devil are you?"

"Identify yourself!" Leishman ordered.

Flockhart aimed his musket directly at the speaker. "Who are you?" He put first pressure on the trigger, ready to fire.

"We are English gentlemen, and we don't have to answer to the likes of you!" the man replied.

"What's your business here?" Flockhart asked, hearing Lord Eskbank's arrogant voice. "Speak before I blow a hole right through you!"

"What's happening here?" Sergeant Dunn sounded calm as he approached the sentries.

"These rogues are threatening us," the leading horseman said.

"These soldiers are doing their duty," Dunn told him. "Who are you, sir?"

"I am Sir Charles Braithwaite, and these gentlemen are my

travelling companions, come to meet Captain Brisbane of Orkney's Regiment."

"I'll take you to him, Sir Charles," Dunn said. He faced Flockhart. "Uncock your muskets, men, and resume your guard."

Leishman waited until Dunn had taken the three horsemen away before he spoke. "You sounded keen to fire, Davie. Do you hate the French so much?"

"I don't hate the French at all," Flockhart replied.

"Then why?" Leishman asked.

"I thought they were Sheriff Officers or Messengers-at-Arms Lord Eskbank had sent to bring me back," Flockhart explained.

"Would you have shot them?" Leishman asked.

"Yes," Flockhart replied at once.

"You'd swing for it."

"Better that than returning to the pit," Flockhart told him.

Leishman saw the iron in Flockhart's eyes and shivered. "Maybe so," he said. "Maybe so."

❇

Mungo Redpath stood outside Stobhill Pit, allowing the atmosphere to seep into him. He ignored the evening birdsong and the scent of grass and wildflowers that perfumed the air and stared at the pithead settlement two hundred yards away. The houses were less than huts, merely temporary shelters of boulders and mud with rough roofs of branches and heather thatch. They stood amidst a morass of churned-up dirt, with a beaten mud track from their doors to the pit entrance.

Redpath heard the growl of voices as the colliers, male and female, emerged from the depths. All ages from three to forty-five, they were filthy, with weary, glaring eyes and round shoulders, dressed in rags that barely covered their nakedness. They slumped from the pithead in a ragged mob, with two children dropping to all fours with weariness.

"You lot!" Redpath shouted. "Wait there!"

Some of the colliers shuffled to a halt. Others ignored Redpath, and a few faced him, hefting their shovels and picks in truculent defiance.

"I want to talk to you," Redpath stepped closer, throwing back his coat to reveal the pistols thrust through his belt. "I am looking for David Flockhart," he said.

The colliers glared at him, wordless. One man lifted his eyes towards the large figure who stood five yards behind Redpath with a blunderbuss held in both hands. They ignored the woman with the pack pony.

"He's not here," a woman said. She brushed back her matted hair with a filthy hand, glowering at Redpath.

"Where is he?" Redpath addressed the woman. "Come now, you must know something."

"He's gone," the woman said. A man stepped to her side, clenching massive fists. The others shuffled closer to Redpath, staring at this stranger through red-rimmed eyes.

"Where?" Redpath asked.

"Dinnae ken," the woman said, turning away. Her companion remained where he was, fists ready.

Redpath moved to intercept the woman. "Did Flockhart mention anything before he left?"

"No," the woman said. Two more colliers stepped forward, both carrying picks. They glowered at Redpath while others shifted towards Duncan Grant, ignoring his blunderbuss. Three children lifted stones from the ground and held them menacingly.

"I'll make it worth your while," Redpath said, placing a hand on each of his pistols.

"How?" the woman asked.

"Show them," Redpath ordered, and Ruth Gordon led the pack pony forward. She stopped and opened one of the saddlebags to reveal half a dozen bottles of spirits.

The woman eyed the bottles. "Aye. Davie Flockhart wanted to leave the pit," she said. "Ever since the rock fell on his wife."

Redpath handed the woman a single bottle, which she held to her half-covered breast. "What else did he say?"

"Mary was carrying his child," the woman said, cradling the bottle to her, eyeing Redpath suspiciously in case he demanded it back. "When the rocks fell on her, it done something to Davie."

"Where did the rocks fall?"

The woman jerked her head towards the pit. "Doon there. She was at the lowest level, picking up her load to carry it to the surface when the roof caved in and trapped her. She was crushed and squealing. Davie tried to get her oot but he couldnae."

"She died?" Redpath asked.

"Aye." The woman put out a hand for another bottle.

"Did Davie say where he was going?" Redpath nodded to Gordon, who pulled out a second bottle of spirits.

"No." The woman shook her head.

Satisfied he would get nothing else useful from the colliers, Redpath nodded to Gordon, who replaced the second bottle in the packsaddle and walked the horse away. Redpath followed, leaving Grant and his blunderbuss to watch the colliers return to their homes.

"If you were an escaped collier here," Redpath said, "where would you go?"

Grant joined them, and they looked around, with the Pentland ridge to the west, the Moorfoot Hills to the south and the rising grassy ridge of Camp Hill to the east. To the north, across the fertile plain, they could see Arthur's Seat and Edinburgh Castle on its volcanic plug.

"I'd go that way," Gordon said. "City air is free air."

"As would I. That's where we're headed," Redpath agreed.

CHAPTER 7

THE DUTCH REPUBLIC, SPRING 1702

"Captain Hume is bound to sea,
    Hey, boys, ho boys,
    Captain Hume is bound to sea,
Ho!
Captain Hume is bound to sea,
And his brave company;
Hey, the brave Grenadiers,
Ho!"

The sound of somebody singing woke Flockhart. He lay for a moment, unsure where he was. The darkness carried a familiar dread, but the smells were different. He tried to move and groaned as the pains in his legs increased. His head swam with all his recent new experiences chasing each other around his mind, and all the orders and movements he had to learn, the different beats of the drum, and the instructions for drill and musketry. The song continued, penetrating his consciousness.

"We'll drink no more Irish beer,
Hey boys, ho boys,
We'll drink no more Irish beer,
For we're all bound to Tangier,
Hey, the brave Grenadiers,

Ho!"

Flockhart pushed himself up, ignoring his aching legs, for pain had always been part of his life. He heard his companions' snoring, stepped over their recumbent bodies, and headed for the door. Although the voice was familiar, he did not recognise the song.

"Now we drink the Spanish wine,

And kiss their ladies fine,

Hey, the brave Scottish boys,

Ho!"

When Flockhart opened the door, he saw Sergeant Dunn standing in the street, naked as a baby with a bottle of wine in one hand and a sword in the other, roaring out his song.

"Sergeant!" Flockhart stepped closer. "You'll wake the regiment!"

Dunn swayed, drank from the bottle, and glared at Flockhart. "Who are you?"

"Private Flockhart, Sergeant," Flockhart reminded him.

"You're a Moor!" Dunn said. "Get away from me, you murdering Moorish devil!" He swung his sword, missing Flockhart by a yard and nearly overbalancing.

"I'm not a Moor," Flockhart stepped backwards. "You'll get into trouble, Sergeant!" He looked around, but nobody else had appeared. A sliver of the moon shone between silver-fringed clouds, with myriad stars ghostly in the night sky.

"You look like a Moor," Dunn peered closer and took another swig from his bottle. "You're not taking me back, you poltroon! I'm not being your slave again, you murdering, blaspheming Moorish bastard!" He swung his sword again, with the blade hissing through the air without endangering Flockhart.

"It's me, Sergeant," Flockhart said. "I'm not a Moor!"

Dunn swore and began to sing again, roaring out the words between swigs of his bottle.

"When we come to Tangier shore,

Hey boys, ho boys,

When we come to Tangier shore,
Ho!
When we come to Tangier shore,
We'll make our granadoes roar,
Hey, the brave Grenadiers,
Ho!"

"Come on, Sergeant," Flockhart held Dunn's sword arm. "Let's get you to bed before we alert the night patrol and you get into trouble."

"I'll kill the bastards," Sergeant Dunn shouted. "I'll kill every murdering Moorish bastard here." He swung his bottle like a weapon, glowered at Flockhart, and swore. "Do you know what the Moors do to their prisoners, Flockhart?"

"No, Sergeant," Flockhart said, twisting Dunn's hand backwards so he released the sword, which clattered onto the ground.

"They like young European men," Dunn drank from his bottle again. "I was a young seaman, a ship's boy when the corsair captured us. Do you know what the Moors do to ship's boys?"

"No, Sergeant," Flockhart held the sword and put an arm around Dunn's shoulder. "Come on, Sergeant. We'll get you to your quarters."

Flockhart saw two men of the Quarter Guard walking towards them, muskets in hand and feet crunching on the ground.

"You don't know?" Dunn shouted. "Then I'll tell you!"

"Not tonight, Sergeant," Flockhart began to drag Dunn towards his quarters, keeping his head down to avoid being recognised. Dunn dropped the bottle, which rolled noisily across the ground, spilling the last of its contents.

"What's all the noise?" Corporal Junar thrust his head from an open door.

"Sergeant Dunn needs some help, Corporal," Flockhart said.

"Bring him in," Junar ordered, understanding the situation. He helped drag Dunn inside the house, took the sword from

Flockhart and laid the sergeant on his empty cot. "Now you get back to bed."

"Yes, Corporal," Flockhart left hurriedly. The two men of the Quarter Guard had passed without comment, and clouds obscured the moon. Flockhart stepped carefully over his sleeping fellows and lay down, unsure if he had done the right thing.

I'll find out in the morning, Flockhart told himself, as the words of the *Grenadier's Rant* joined the confusion of orders in his head.

The following morning, Sergeant Dunn took the parade looking as fresh as if he had enjoyed a full night's sleep and as immaculate as ever. He never mentioned the incident to Flockhart again.

❋

"The campaigning season will start soon," Dunn told his platoon. "You might wonder why we have been concentrating on drill and close order movement all winter."

Flockhart had learned that Sergeant Dunn's questions were rhetorical and did not require an answer. He kept his head still and his face immobile.

"Warfare is about marching and manoeuvre," Dunn explained. "Success and victory depend on the senior officers' ability to form and position battalions and brigades to the correct place at the correct time. For that reason, close order drill is vital. You may hate it, but you will learn it. Drill accustoms you to immediate obedience and teaches the officer how to handle his men."

Flockhart stared ahead, his face expressionless as he watched a flight of birds rise above the rooftops. *I have had enough theory now. When will we fight the French?*

"In battle, a man's instinct is to shrink away from the enemy's fire," Dunn said. "Constant drill will ensure you will obey orders rather than follow your instinct." He looked over his men. "Are there any questions?"

There were none. The men had learned never to disobey an order or rise to a question. They had learned the first lesson of becoming a soldier: obedience.

❄

The farmer grunted and leaned across the gate as Redpath questioned him. "Aye," he said. "We sometimes get pestered with sorners [1] and the like. We've had fewer recently, but just the other month, we had a wandering man."

"What was he like?" Redpath asked.

The farmer ran a calloused hand down his face. "He was a rough-looking fellow. An Egyptian,[2] maybe, or something of that sort. He opened my barn door anyway and let the hens out. It was no thanks to the sorner that I didn't lose them all to Tod."

"Tod?" Duncan Grant asked.

"Aye," the farmer said. "Foxes are bad round here. His precious Lordship doesn't let us kill them so he and his friends can have their sport."

"I see," Redpath nodded. "Describe this sorner." He held a silver shilling between his finger and thumb.

The farmer considered for a minute. "He was a rough-looking fellow, as I said. He was dirty, filthy dirty."

"Could he have been a collier? A coal miner?"

"Aye," the farmer said after a moment's reflection. "He could have, at that. A dirty, ragged, round-shouldered man."

"Was he a tall fellow?"

"No, just ordinary height, man, unsteady on his pegs, as if he didnae walk much."

---
1. Sorner: a wandering beggar or vagabond. They could combine into a gang that often terrorised isolated farms or small settlements.
2. Egyptian: a Gypsy; when Romanies first arrived in Scotland, people believed they came from Egypt.

"Did you see in which direction he walked?" Redpath asked, spinning the shilling with finger and thumb.

"He didnae walk," the farmer said. "He ran rather, that way," he pointed with a stubby finger. "Towards the toon."

Redpath nodded, spun the shilling again and replaced it in his pocket. "We're on the right track," he said and mounted his horse, ignoring the farmer's protests about the shilling.

❋

"Right, young Flockhart," Sergeant said as they sat in a tavern with a smoking lantern swinging above their heads. "Do you know why we are here?"

"For a drink," Flockhart said, peering into his tankard.

"Why are the Royal Regiment, the Royal Scots, based in the Dutch Republic rather than in a cosy tavern in Edinburgh near our loved ones." He held up a hand. "I know you're reluctant to return to Scotland in case Lord Eskbank drags you back to the mines. Why do you think the regiment and King William's army are here."

"We're here to fight the French," Flockhart said. He had never given much thought to the politics of the situation.

"Why are we fighting the French?" Dunn asked. "What have the French ever done to harm you or me?"

Flockhart shook his head. "Because it's our duty," he said, pleased with his answer. "We are King William's soldiers and fight for him."

"Do you know anything about France?" Sergeant Dunn asked.

"No," Flockhart admitted, rubbing his throat.

"I thought not," Dunn said. "The King of France, Louis XIV, has joined with Spain. Together, France and Spain are the most powerful force in Europe. Bavaria has allied with them, and because Spain owns half the Netherlands—the Spanish Netherlands—they threaten Holland, our major Protestant ally."

Flockhart nodded. "I see," he said.

"King William, as King of England, has joined a Grand Alliance of England, Holland, and the Austrian Empire, with Denmark and Prussia maybe also on our side against France, Bavaria, and Spain." Sergeant Dunn stopped. "Have I lost you?"

"We are Scottish," Flockhart said. "Why are we fighting in an English army?"

Dunn grinned. "It's confusing, isn't it? We share the same monarch, you see. King William is King of Scotland as well as of England, so Scottish regiments fight for him. You'll find the Cameronians and the Scottish Fusiliers in the infantry and the Scots Dragoons on their grey horses. There are also Irishmen and Welshmen, all because we share the monarch."

Flockhart nodded.

"France has the largest and most successful army in Europe, far bigger than King William's forces. France also marched into the Spanish Netherlands before this war began, so they occupy a very strategic area."

"Can we push them out?" Flockhart wrestled with these new facts.

"Maybe," the sergeant said. "The French also grabbed what are known as the Barrier Fortresses, which control the Upper and Middle Meuse River, except Maastricht."

As Flockhart had no idea about geography, the names meant little to him.

"River transport is vital for Europe," Dunn explained. "Now, the Treaty of Ryswick, which ended the last war with France, gave the Barrier Fortresses to the Dutch Republic, so the French have no right there. The French also marched into the Electorate of Cologne, which means they could easily close any communication between our two allies, the Dutch and Vienna, the capital of the Austrian Empire."

"The French are winning the war without actually fighting," Flockhart said.

"Wars are about fortifications, sieges, and strategic marches,"

Dunn said. "The first thing the French did after they occupied Flanders was build a line of fortifications from Namur to Antwerp—the Lines of Brabant, they call it."

Flockhart nodded. "When do we stop doing drill and start to fight them?"

"When the campaigning season starts again," Dunn said. He signalled to the barmaid to refill their tankards. "Things are even more complicated, Flockhart, because the Austrian Emperor has internal troubles due to a major revolt in Hungary. He'll have to use a large part of his army to put down the rebellion and still maintain a watch on the Ottoman Turks on his eastern frontier."

"Is King Louis XIV as powerful as he sounds?" Flockhart asked.

"He is," Dunn replied. "The Catholic King, or the Sun King, as he is known, seems to have had divine favour for the past few years. He rules from his palace at Versailles, which is the next best place to heaven if you ignore the court intrigue. He has the most successful army in Europe. In the last war of the League of Augsburg, he gave us a right bloody nose at Steenkirk."

"What's he like, this Sun King?" Flockhart asked.

"We've never met," Dunn said, smiling, "but I hear he likes his splendour, with a fancy periwig on his head, high heels on his feet, and silks and frills in between." He produced a long pipe and cleaned the bowl with a knife before filling it with tobacco. "Louis will have a harem of sycophantic courtiers, of course, bowing and fawning to him, doting on every word and agreeing to every whim of His Catholic Majesty."

"He doesn't sound like much of a soldier," Flockhart said.

"I doubt he's fired a musket in his life," Dunn said. "However, his marshals have. They've defeated us, the Dutch, and the Empire's generals time and again."

Flockhart frowned. "Is the Empire powerful?"

"It used to be known as the Holy Roman Empire," Dunn said. "Now it's the Austrian Empire. It was once one of the most important powers in Europe, a collection of states that dominated central Europe and stopped the Turkish Ottoman Empire from conquering us and making all Europe Muslim."

The sergeant was quiet for a minute as he lit his pipe. "I've met the Moors, and God forbid they ever have power in Europe."

Flockhart remembered Dunn's drunken admission and wisely kept quiet.

"God did forbid," Dunn told him. "The Austrians stopped the Turks at the very gates of Vienna. However, the Austrians have declined in power since then, and Bourbon France has taken over as the most potent power in Europe. Austria is our ally, but an ailing ally, losing to the French in Italy and with the revolt in Hungary."

"Yes, Sergeant," Flockhart said, rubbing his throat. "When do we start to fight back?"

"Soon, Flockhart," Dunn said. "Very soon, and then you'll earn your generous pay as a soldier."

❄

The Cousland blacksmith shook his head. "No," he said. "I haven't had anybody ask me to remove a slave collar." He continued to shape his plough, running an expert eye along the ploughshare and tapping it with a hammer. "I don't remember ever seeing a slave collar, and I've lived here all my days."

"Did you hear of a blacksmith removing such a collar recently?" Redpath asked.

"Never," the smith replied. He held the ploughshare up to the light, examining it critically. "You'll have to try elsewhere."

Redpath nodded and walked away. "We've spoken to all the smiths in a ten-mile radius," he said. "It looks like Flockhart still wore his collar when he entered Edinburgh."

"Edinburgh will have blacksmiths, too," Duncan Grant growled.

"We'll find him," Redpath kicked his horse onward. "Wherever he may be. We'll find David Flockhart and take him back to his owner."

CHAPTER 8

DUTCH REPUBLIC, SPRING 1702

Flockhart looked up from cleaning his shoes. "There are the drums! We're not due a parade, are we?"

"That's the Assembly," Leishman said. "That means we've to gather around the Colours." He grinned. "Something's happening, Davie. Maybe the campaigning season has finally arrived. I hope you are in a mood to march."

"Why do we wait so long before we begin?" Flockhart asked, tying his shoes and grabbing his coat. "Could we not march in February or March when the ground is hard with frost?"

"We need to wait until there is grass for the horses," Leishman explained. "Not only for the cavalry but also the transport wagons, field bakeries, horses that drag the artillery and those that carry the wagons for the wives and other women."

"I see." Even after six months in uniform, Flockhart realised he still had much to learn.

"The cavalry can march faster than the infantry," Leishman said, "and the infantry will march twice as far in one day as the artillery."

Flockhart nodded as he fastened his coat. The drums still sounded the Assembly, and men were rushing past, some pulling on their coats or straightening their hats and others fully dressed. Flockhart grabbed his tricorne hat as they hurried from the tavern, running to the Colours.

During the seventeenth century, every regiment had a multiplicity of identifying flags; each company had its individual flag, or Colour, which an ensign held as a rallying sign. There were also individual Colours for the colonel, lieutenant colonel and the major. By the beginning of the eighteenth century, companies no longer displayed individual flags, with a regiment only carrying the colonel's, the regimental and royal Colours. Although this pageantry added to the attraction of the army for unsophisticated men, the Colours also acted as a rallying point if the regiment was scattered during a battle.

Flockhart glanced at the colonel's personal Colours. He flew a white flag with a gold thistle in the centre embellished with purple flowers and gold leaves and topped by a crown. A shield sat in the upper canton, quartered with the arms of Scotland, Ireland, England, and France. The regiment's other Colours carried a crowned thistle on a blue ground, showing the regiment was both royal and Scottish.

"We've had the crowned thistle since the days of Charles the Second," Leishman said. He pointed to the gold-lettered words. The inscription read *Nemo Me Impune Lacessit*.

"Can you read?" Leishman asked.

Flockhart shook his head. "I'm no scholar," he gave the customary answer of an illiterate soldier. Although many British soldiers were illiterate, such a state was more unusual in a Scottish regiment.

"That's Scotland's motto," Leishman said. "*Nemo me impune lacessit;* it means nobody assails me with impunity."

"What does that mean?" Flockhart asked.

"It means if anybody attacks us, we'll make them pay for it," Leishman paraphrased the words. "It means, who dares to meddle with me?"

Flockhart nodded. "That's a good motto," he said.

The regiment assembled in the centre of the town, with men

standing in their allocated places and a long train of wagons carrying supplies, tents, and wives, as they called the camp followers.

The drums rolled again, echoing from the surrounding buildings and causing the men to look at one another in anticipation. Flockhart felt the tension as the veterans stamped their feet, hitched up their trousers and exchanged meaningful glances.

"That's another beat I haven't heard before," Flockhart said.

"That's the General," Leishman replied. "It means get ready to march."

"March, where?"

Leishman grinned. "Ask the officers," he said. "For I am sure I don't know."

The colours flapped in a cool breeze as Flockhart looked around. Hundreds of men in scarlet coats, with the line companies wearing tricorn hats and the tall men of the grenadier company with impressively high mitre-shaped caps, impressed him. Leishman told Flockhart that the grenadiers wore their distinctive headgear to enable them to sling their muskets around their shoulder, freeing their hands to arm and throw their grenades.

Flockhart, always eager for knowledge, asked, "Why are these bombs called grenades?"

Leishman considered the question. "I believe the word comes from the Italian *granato*, a pomegranate, a type of fruit."

Flockhart stored the information away. After spending all his life ignorant of everything except the world inside the pit, he valued everything he could learn, whether useful or not. As he marched alongside the hundreds of men of the Royals, he felt that for the first time in his life, he was a small part of something important. Civilians left their homes to watch the regiment depart, with some shouting or waving to men they knew.

Officers rode tall horses, exchanging words with the NCOs. Flockhart knew some of the officers by name, with Captain Brisbane in charge of his company, and Lieutenant Murray, and

Ensign Forbes in his platoon. He noted that the officers were taller than most privates, with elegant clothes, long swords, and elaborate wigs.

Behind the fighting men, the wives on the carts and wagons waved and talked, exchanging banter with the civilians. Occasionally, a wife would clamber down from her wagon, run up to her husband in the ranks, exchange a few words and return.

Flockhart watched without emotion. Only one woman had shown any interest in him, and she had died two hundred feet underground. He did not expect to find another wife, for escaping from serfdom had been his ultimate objective. He marched mechanically, appreciating the air, the colour and the scenery of the Dutch Republic.

"You look quite relaxed, Davie," Leishman said. "Are you not worried we might be marching into a battle?"

Flockhart shook his head. He looked upward at the grey sky and took a deep breath. "No," he said. "Can you see the sky up there?"

"Yes," Leishman said.

"So can I," Flockhart said. "I seldom saw the daytime sky. I worked in the dark and only saw the night sky when I came home." He saw Leishman's expression of disbelief. "Can you breathe that air?"

"Yes," Leishman said.

"I worked in stale air filled with dust, air that could poison us and always fearful it could explode. Being out here, in daylight, walking without crouching, without fear the roof will collapse at any second, is better than you will ever understand."

Leishman shook his head. "Are you happy being a soldier?"

Flockhart pondered the question. He had never considered being happy. It was an alien concept. Happiness as a collier was drinking to excess as a temporary escape from the misery of existence. Life was short, brutal, uncomfortable, and dangerous; death could come with bad air, flooding, a cave-in or the black spit in old age, which would come around the age of forty for the fortunate.

"Yes," Flockhart replied. "I am happy being a soldier."

"Let's see if you still feel that way when we meet Johnny Frenchman," Leishman said.

"He can't be any worse than Lord Eskbank or Graham Cummings, the grieve," Flockhart replied.

"Johnny Frenchman will try to kill you," Leishman reminded.

Flockhart tapped his musket. "And I will try to kill him."

The drums beat the regimental march, *Dumbarton's Drums*, which dated back at least to 1675 when the colonel was Lord George Douglas, the Earl of Dumbarton.

"Dumbarton's drums beat bonny O," William Darvel murmured, and Flockhart listened to the words of the song.

"A soldier has honour and bravery-O,
Unacquainted with rogues and their knavery – O,
He minds no other thing,
But the ladies or the king;
For every other care is but slavery – O."

People no longer see me as a slave, Flockhart thought. *They see me as a free man, an honourable soldier in the Royal Scots, the Royal Regiment of Foot.* He lifted his head, held his musket firmly in his right hand and marched to war, prepared to meet whatever challenges the French threw at him.

❋

The Lord High Commissioner, James Douglas, Second Duke of Queensberry, stood at the window with a glass in his hand. He glanced outside, where the traffic on the Canongate was busier than usual that morning, with crowds gathering and a horse dragging a laden coal wagon uphill as a gang of street urchins jumped on the back. "Your money comes from your tenants and coal mines, doesn't it, Eskbank?"

"It does, my lord," Lord Eskbank agreed.

"I don't quite understand this colliery business, Eskbank. Tell me about it."

Lord Eskbank sipped at his claret to moisten his throat before he began. "We've had colliers and coal mines in Scotland from time immemorial," he said. "The monks at Newbattle had collier serfs in the thirteenth century, and maybe earlier."

Queensberry poured himself more claret. "Did they, indeed?"

Queensberry was an experienced politician, used to encouraging people to give him information. After Scotland failed to settle a colony in Darien in Central America, King William had employed Queensberry as a Royal Commissioner with instructions to calm any anti-English sentiment. Now he waited for Eskbank to continue, standing in silhouette at the window and calmly sipping his claret.

"Yes, My Lord," Lord Eskbank said. "At the beginning of the seventeenth century, King James VI had parliament pass laws that made colliers slaves. The colliers could only be free if the coal master, the landowner, gave him permission; we could reclaim our property if we had not given written permission for him to leave. If a collier left the pit without permission, he was a thief who had stolen his labouring body."

Queensberry nodded with his eyes fixed on Lord Eskbank. The driver of the coal wagon was furiously lashing behind him with his whip to drive the urchins off his vehicle. "Carry on, Eskbank."

"Yes, My Lord. Further Acts ordered colliers to work six days a week or pay a fine to their owners. Those who transgress can be whipped or made to go the rown, which means we tie them facing the horse at the gin – the horse-powered pump - so they run backwards until their owner decides they've had enough."

"Have you ever done that?" Queensberry asked. The coal wagon had trundled past, and a caddy was talking to a water carrier in front of the Canongate Tolbooth. Queensberry sipped at his claret.

"I do that to runaways and those who are insolent," Lord Eskbank said. "I have a persistent thief who I had flogged with forty lashes less one and made him go the rown for forty-eight hours at a stretch." He grinned. "If he fell, the horse would trample him underfoot."

"What did he steal?"

"Himself," Lord Eskbank said. "He tried to abscond." He finished his claret. "He's gone again, run away, much to my chagrin."

"I hope you catch him," Queensberry said without any interest. "How is the coal business these days?"

"Struggling," Lord Eskbank admitted. "We face competition from Tyneside pits and Liege in the Dutch Lowlands, together with new excise duties and tariffs. As you will remember, the terrible rains of 1695 and '96 caused flooding; I had to pump the pits dry around the clock to keep them working, which meant bringing in horses and men. Both need to be fed, and the bad weather meant poor harvests and higher prices."

Queensberry nodded, turned to look out of the window and continued. "You have saltworks, too, I believe."

"I have," Lord Eskbank agreed. "About 70% of my coal output goes to the salt pans. Without salt, my mines would have little reason to produce coal."

Queensberry poured them both more claret. "I know it is ungentlemanly to discuss money, Eskbank, but we've known each other for years."

"Ever since we studied at Glasgow University, My Lord."

"Ever since then," Queensberry agreed. "The Darien nonsense and King William's Ill Years must have taken quite a toll on your income, Eskbank."

"They did," Lord Eskbank agreed.

"You might be advised to seek alternative sources for your coal," Queensberry suggested.

"I would," Lord Eskbank seldom disagreed with his social superiors. "Where would you suggest, My Lord?"

"England," Queensberry said flatly.

Lord Eskbank nodded. "I was considering that possibility," he admitted.

"You know that I control the Court Party in parliament," Queensberry said, "you may not be aware that the Court Party is committed to a union with the English parliament."

"I believe I had heard something of that fact," Lord Eskbank said, wondering where Queensberry was leading.

"As well as me, we have the Earls of Mar and Seafield, a powerful clique of noblemen. If we unite with England, you will have free access to their markets for your coal and salt," Queensberry said. "We will also have the opportunity to trade with England's colonies in the Americas and English factories in the Indies. In our age of Protectionism, such trading possibilities are welcome."

"Yes, My Lord." Eskbank nodded, waiting. The Edward East longcase clock in the corner ticked softly, highlighting the silence in the room.

Queensberry continued, with his gaze fixed on Eskbank's face. "At present, you are in the Country Party, I believe, with the somewhat volatile Duke of Hamilton as leader."

"That is correct, My Lord."

"I presume you are opposed to any union," Queensberry said.

"I cannot see how it would benefit me," Lord Eskbank said. "Free market for my coal will also allow English coal into Scotland."

Queensberry smiled. "As the Commissioner, I have certain advantages, including the power to grant patronage," he said. "At present, London obtains its coal from Northeast England, yet London is a constantly growing city. In winter, it consumes coal like a greedy child consumes sweetmeats."

Eskbank swirled the claret around his glass, fencing with

words. "Are you saying you can grant me access to the London coal market, My Lord?"

"That would depend on how you voted when we debate a union with the English parliament, Eskbank," Queensberry said candidly.

"I would vote in whatever way you directed, My Lord," Eskbank said. "As long as it also favoured my interests."

"You're a grasping rogue, sir," Queensberry said. "But we understand each other. As long as our two desires run together, I am sure we can get along."

"I am sure we can, My Lord." Eskbank lifted his head challengingly. "However, I heard that some in parliament intend to loosen the bonds that tie us to England rather than tighten them."

"Are you of that persuasion, Eskbank?"

"Only if it favoured my interests, My Lord." Eskbank laid more of his cards on the table.

Queensberry smiled. "I'll ensure voting with the Court Party favours your interests, Eskbank."

"That would suit us both, My Lord," Eskbank said.

"You are Presbyterian, are you not?"

"I am, my Lord."

Queensberry finished his claret and refilled both their glasses. "Then it is unlikely you will support the Jacobite desire to return the Stuarts to the throne."

"I have no desire to return to a totalitarian Roman Catholic regime, My Lord."

Queensberry nodded. "A parliamentary union between Scotland and England would ease that worry," he said. "Don't you agree?"

"Perhaps so, My Lord. I have not given serious thought to the possibility."

Queensberry paced the length of the room and back, with his gaze never straying from Lord Eskbank's face. "It is a possibility which has dominated Scottish politics for some time," he said. "I presume you have attended parliament?"

"Not as often as I should," Eskbank admitted.

"That is an omission I am sure you intend to rectify," Queensberry said.

"I believe so, My Lord."

"Fletcher of Saltoun, Lord James Threipmuir and Sir Hugh Crichton are others I need to persuade," Queensberry said. "Fletcher is firmly against an incorporating union, and Threipmuir is deeply entrenched in the same belief."

"Yes, My Lord," Eskbank agreed.

"It would be better if Threipmuir were to change his mind," Queensberry said. "Or if he could not attend parliament."

"Yes, My Lord." Eskbank agreed again.

"You know Threipmuir well, I believe," Queensberry said. "You hunt together."

"We do, My Lord," Eskbank said.

Queensberry nodded. "And young Crichton has designs on your daughter."

"How the devil do you know that?" Eskbank asked, suddenly animated.

"It's my business to know such things," Queensberry said casually. "If Threipmuir and Crichton could abstain or vote according to my wishes, I would be grateful." He turned away to gaze out of the window again. "An English title would open the door for trade in England, don't you think, Eskbank?"

"I am sure it would, My Lord," Eskbank agreed.

"Then I think we understand each other," Queensberry said. "I am sure you have business to attend to, Eskbank."

※

Redpath and Grant entered the smithy in Haliburton Wynd, with Ruth Gordon following a moment later. The smith looked up from his forge and wiped the sweat from his forehead with a muscular forearm.

"What can I do for you, gentlemen?"

"We need information," Redpath said.

"What sort of information?" The blacksmith was a powerfully built man but immediately recognised the violence in his visitors. He held his hammer, ready to resist.

"We're looking for a runaway collier," Redpath said.

"Well, you won't find him here," the blacksmith replied. "There's only me in here."

"I see that," Redpath said as Ruth smiled at the blacksmith. "The runaway was wearing a brass collar. Have you seen a man wearing a brass collar?"

"There are some strange fashions this season," the blacksmith kept his eyes on Grant, who stood a yard behind Redpath, "but brass collars are a bit extreme."

"You haven't seen him, then?" Redpath asked.

"No," the blacksmith replied, gripping his hammer firmly. "Now, if you'll excuse me, I have work to do."

"Would this help?" Redpath slid a penny from his pocket and placed it on the anvil.

"No," the blacksmith replied.

"Maybe now?" Redpath added another penny.

"No," the blacksmith said.

"Here," when Redpath had been talking, Gordon had closed and barred the door before probing into the corners of the smithy. She held up a brass collar. "Flockhart was here."

"When was he here?" Redpath did not raise his voice.

"None of your damned business." The blacksmith was a brave man, confident in his strength. "Get out of my smithy."

"When was the runaway here?" Redpath asked again, still quietly. He glanced at Grant. "Ask him, Duncan."

"Get out!" The blacksmith swung his hammer in a clumsy blow that would have taken Redpath's head off if it had landed. Grant grabbed the haft, dragged it from the blacksmith's hands and threw it into the far corner of the smithy. As it landed with a clatter, Grant lifted the blacksmith from the ground as easily as if he was a child and slammed him face up over the anvil.

Redpath and Gordon watched dispassionately.

"Break his fingers," Redpath ordered quietly. "One at a time."

Gordon smiled as Grant snapped the little finger on the blacksmith's left hand. The blacksmith roared and struggled, but Grant held him down without difficulty.

"When was the runaway here?" Redpath asked. "You have ten fingers and ten toes," he reminded. "After that, my muscular colleague will sit you on your forge and roast you. Break another finger, Duncan."

"Six weeks ago," the blacksmith said as Grant grabbed his middle finger.

"Was he alone?" Redpath asked. "It will be easier for you if you tell us everything."

They left fifteen minutes later, leaving the blacksmith a bloodied mess on the floor.

"Flockhart's gone for a soldier," Redpath said. "Now we must find out which regiments were recruiting in Edinburgh six weeks ago, where they hold their recruits and where they are stationed." He tapped his cane on the ground. "We'll check the locally based regiments first and hope he's still in the area, and if not, we'll widen our field. We have a lot of work before us, and Lord Eskbank will have a large bill to regain his property, but we'll bring Flockhart back where he belongs."

CHAPTER 9

DUTCH REPUBLIC,
MARCH 1702

On March 10th 1702, the Royal Regiment left its quarters and marched to Rosendal to join the other British infantry regiments. With twelve battalions assembled, Flockhart had never seen so many soldiers or heard such a confusion of drums and shouted orders. He felt his back straighten as he marched, listened to the measured tread of thousands of feet, and wondered at the change in his circumstances since he left Stobhill Pit.

"Who's in charge of all these soldiers, Sergeant?"

Dunn balanced his halberd across his right shoulder. "Brigadier General Ingoldsby, Flockhart. Look for his carriage and four at the rear of the column."

A week later, the soldiers heard that King William had died on March 17th, 1702, and Queen Anne had acceded to the throne of Scotland, England, and Ireland. They gathered to renew their oath of allegiance to the sovereign.

"What does that mean?" Flockhart asked.

"It changes nothing as far as we are concerned, Davie," Leishman replied. "We march and fight for the sovereign, whoever that may be. Let the officers worry about the politics, and we'll take care of the French."

"Are we at war yet?" Peter Young asked.

"Not yet, Young," Leishman told him. "But we soon will be. Kings, queens, and princes can't abide peace when they can be grabbing somebody else's land."

On 15th May, the Grand Alliance of the Dutch Republic, Austria, and England declared war on France and her allies. As Scotland shared the same monarch as England, Scotland was also at war.

"That's us, lads," Leishman announced. "Now we have to earn our pennies."

While some of the recruits cheered, the older soldiers looked solemn, knowing what a bloody business war could be. Leishman looked at Flockhart and winked. "Take it one day at a time, Davie; one day at a time."

Two weeks later, the Royals were on the march again, feet crunching on the roads as the fertile land rolled past.

"Where are we going this time?" Young asked.

"One of our allies, either the Dutch or somebody else, is besieging the French in a place called Kaiserwerth," Leishman said. "That's a strong fortress on the Lower Rhine. We're marching to the Duchy of Cleves."

"I had never heard of any of these places," Flockhart said.

"Neither had anybody else until we started fighting King Louis," Leishman said with a grin, "and everybody will forget them again when the war ends. War is like that; we fight and die for places nobody gives a fig for."

The Royals' march ended at Kranenburg on the Lower Rhine, where the British regiments joined an allied force of Dutch and Germans. Baron Godard van Reede, the Dutch Lord of Ginkel, Earl of Athlone, assumed overall command.

"We're covering the siege of Kaiserwerth," Sergeant Dunn informed his platoon.

"What does that mean?" Flockhart looked over the sea of tents and listened to the babble of different languages from the allied camp.

"It means we're here to support the besiegers, but don't get too settled," Dunn advised. "Once the French realise we are here, they'll send an army to cut us up or at least drive us away from Kaiserwerth."

The sergeant's prophecy proved correct. As June wore on, Louis-François, Duke de Boufflers, and the Duke of Burgundy led a large French army through the forest of Cleves and onto the plains of Goch, hoping to separate the besiegers from their bases at Grave and Nijmegen.

"Strike the tents!" The allied drums beat the order as the sun eased to the west. "The French are heading across the plain!"

"We're on the march again," Leishman said, struggling with the heavy canvas.

"We've only just arrived," Flockhart said, hefting his musket. "Do we ever fight the French?"

"We'll fight them," Leishman said seriously. "You'd better pray it's not soon, Davie, and savour every hour you are alive."

"Marshal Boufflers is running Athlone into the ground," Sergeant Dunn said.

"Is that why we are retreating?" Flockhart asked.

"We're manoeuvring to find a better position," Dunn said with a sly grin. "Either that or Athlone is hoping that Boufflers eats himself to death. If the rumours are correct, Boufflers has over seventy cooks for his staff, and they drink fifty dozen bottles of wine daily."

Young laughed. "We're in the wrong army if the Frenchies have so much wine."

"That'll be the officers imbibing the wine," Leishman said. "Not the men who carry the muskets."

The allied army withdrew from Cleves, with heavy rain showers turning the road to mud and their tricorne hats clinging to their heads in a soggy mass.

Flockhart glanced over his shoulder at the long scarlet column that wound behind them, half-seen in the gloom of a spring night. "What's the point in an army that won't fight?"

"War is not only about fighting battles," Leishman said. "It's about manoeuvres and fortresses, getting the army in such an advantageous position that the enemy knows it can't win. The best victory is a bloodless one."

They slogged on, with the Colours furled above them and the drums tapping the pace. Flockhart fought his frustration. After the hard months of training, he wanted to prove himself a good soldier.

"You see," Leishman said. "Soldiers are hard to recruit and expensive to train and maintain. No general wants to see his men slaughtered by artillery or cavalry, so most avoid direct battles when they can."

Flockhart grunted and marched on, splashing through the muddy puddles. He watched squadrons of allied cavalry jingling out to scout ahead and heard the French cavalry was pursuing the allies, pushing on both flanks of the retreating column as they raced towards Nijmegen.

"How far have we marched?" Young asked.

"Nigh on two leagues," Sergeant Dunn replied.

"It feels a lot more than that," Young grumbled. "My feet are worn out."

"They'll harden," Dunn told him. "If you fall out, the French cavalry will kill you. Keep moving, Young!"

Flockhart looked to the right, beyond the screen of allied cavalry, and saw the enemy for the first time.

"I can see the French plainly," he said, "and nobody has fired a shot."

Dunn nodded. "We can see them, and they can see us. The French cavalry can charge us whenever they please." He shifted his halberd as if to repel an attack and grinned. "This is a strange affair."

"What are the French doing, Sergeant?" Flockhart asked as the drums beat more urgently, encouraging the infantry to move faster.

Dunn shifted his halberd from his right to his left shoulder.

"They're trying to get between us and Nijmegen, to hold us until their foot arrives so they can cut us up at their leisure."

"The French had better be careful," Leishman said. "If it's only their cavalry between us and Nijmegen, we have them between two fires."

Sixty squadrons of French cavalry and dragoons, with James FitzJames, Duke of Berwick in command, pressed on the retreating allies. They approached and withdrew, snapping up stragglers and harassing the rearguard and flank companies.

"The Duke of Berwick, eh?" Leishman shook his head. "That's the illegitimate son of King James VII and the Earl of Marlborough's nephew. His mother is Marlborough's sister, and Marlborough is our best general."

"Let's hope he hasn't inherited Marlborough's military skill."

Flockhart nodded. "God forbid, but why are some cavalry called dragoons?"

"Dragoons are mounted infantry rather than true cavalry, men who ride to battle but fight on foot like infantry," Leishman explained. "They ride inferior horses and get paid less than cavalry but still more than us."

"Everyone gets paid more than us," Young complained.

"Strange name, dragoon," Flockhart said.

"They used to be armed with a musket called a dragon," Leishman said, lifting his head. "Something's happening, boys!"

Lieutenant General Lord Cutts, in charge of Flockhart's brigade, ordered them to halt on top of a rise.

"We're making a stand here," Captain Brisbane shouted. "Ready the men!"

Cutts ordered three infantry companies to occupy a group of houses, and the rest waited, resting on their muskets, watching for events. Flockhart checked his flint was sharp, ensured his bayonet could slip easily from its sheath, and looked to his front. The French cavalry was ahead, a dense body of gloriously uniformed men armed with fusils and swords. Flockhart saw the horsemen waiting, with the horses pawing the ground and the men watching the allied infantry, ready to attack.

"They're moving," Leishman murmured. "Get ready, Davie."

Flockhart saw a tremor run through the Royals' ranks as men stamped their feet, tightened their grip on their muskets, and raised their chins defiantly.

"Here come the French!" Sergeant Dunn shouted. "Get ready, lads! Wait for orders!"

Captain Brisbane marched along the company. "Load!"

Flockhart bit open a cartridge and primed his musket, pouring a charge of powder down the barrel. Next, he spat down the ball, tamping it in place with his ramrod. He felt his heartbeat increase as he watched the French cavalry advance. He knew he would not feel like a real soldier until he had fought the enemy.

"Present!"

The British raised their muskets, a long line of weapons ready for the oncoming cavalry. Flockhart saw the French advance, holding their fusils and with their swords bouncing beside their saddles. They looked huge on their horses, and he wondered if the three slender lines of infantry could stand against such a horde of giants.

"Aim!" Brisbane shouted.

The muskets lifted, each one pointing towards the oncoming cavalry. Flockhart aimed at an officer riding in front, wondering how he would feel to see his ball plough into a human body. He closed his eyes for a second and remembered a rockfall down the pit, with two men crushed to death and another screaming as he was pinned under tons of rock and earth.

These colliers had no choice where they were. This French officer chose his station and intends to kill my colleagues in the regiment. Even at a distance, Flockhart saw the enemy's face; he was a young man with an immature moustache and wide eyes.

No, think of Lord Eskbank.

Flockhart imagined Eskbank on the horse, with his long nose and thin, sneering lips. He prepared to fire.

"They're going to turn," Dunn said.

The cavalry approached within three hundred yards, slowed, and turned away squadron by squadron, so within a few moments, the British were staring at the riders' backs and horses' tails.

Brisbane ordered his company to ground their arms, and Flockhart felt a mixture of relief and disappointment.

"Do we ever fight these rogues?" Flockhart asked.

"When we do," Leishman said soberly, "you won't want another battle. One is enough for any man."

"You've told me that before," Flockhart said.

The infantry marched on, following the drum.

❄

"I do like pearls," Elizabeth Ramsay lay on the bed, allowing the sunlight to warm her naked body. "I think every lady should have at least one string, don't you, John?"

Lord Eskbank lay at her side, listening to the sounds from Mylne's Court in the heart of Edinburgh outside. "I'm already out of pocket paying for this house for you, Elizabeth. The pearls will have to wait."

Elizabeth pouted. "I like pearls." She shifted on the bed, moving away from Eskbank. "Jamie Threipmuir gave his lady pearls. And a horse."

"Threipmuir doesn't have a wife as well," Eskbank said.

Elizabeth rose and walked to the window. "Maybe I should talk to Jamie Threipmuir; his mistress is nothing but a whore." She stood at the window, bending forward enticingly. "Or maybe you should not have both."

"I want to have both," Eskbank told her.

Elizabeth turned around. Lord Eskbank saw her in silhouette, with her body framed by the window. "Then you need more money, my lord." She remained still. "Or you have to reduce your expenses."

Eskbank stirred uneasily. He did not like to be lectured by his mistress or by anybody he considered his social inferior.

"The choice is yours, John," Elizabeth said. She yawned. "Many men would find pearls for a woman like me." Stepping away from the bed, she reached for her clothes. "Help me dress, John. I don't have my maid with me."

※

Flockhart stood with his platoon, chewing on excellent Dutch bread, and watched an anonymous Dutch general approach Lord Cutts. Although Flockhart was too far away to hear what was said, he could see Cutts gesturing to his men and expressing his willingness to fight. The Dutchman refused permission, pointing to the distant walls of Nijmegen.

"We're not fighting," Leishman said. "We're retiring to Nijmegen."

Flockhart sighed as the senior officers ordered the march to resume, except for a few grenadier companies that acted as rearguard. The Royals reformed into a column and marched through the incessant rain, with the French cavalry's vanguard halting four hundred yards before the grenadiers.

Both sides stared at the other, with the cavalrymen holding their reins, waiting for the order to attack and the grenadiers ready with loaded muskets. If any senior officers ordered the cavalry forward, there would be mayhem outside Nijmegen's walls.

"Get inside the town," the Royals shouted, waving their hats to encourage the men onward. The bulk of the Allies filed inside Nijmegen's gates, their shoes clattering on the cobblestones. The grenadiers remained outside the walls as cannon fire from Nijmegen landed among the French and occasionally dropped short. Flockhart saw the grenadiers lie down to save themselves from the Dutch artillery.

"Can't we fight?" Flockhart asked.

"We follow orders," Sergeant Dunn told him. "Move on, Flockhart!"

White powder smoke drifted across the walls, obscuring Flockhart's vision. When the cannon fire stopped and a breeze cleared the smoke, he saw the grenadiers had retired closer to the walls. The remainder of the Allied infantry had poured into Nijmegen, waiting for orders.

"Follow me, Royals!" Major Flockhart Hamilton, commanding the second battalion of the Royals, ordered. He led them beyond the walls to take over the covered way, the road between the defending ditch and the glacis, the smooth slope outside the walls. The Allied cavalry arranged themselves on the glacis, facing outwards.

"Now we'll see what happens," Leishman remarked as the officers rode around the men, giving sharp orders to adjust their positioning. "Will the French be fool enough to attack the walls?"

"Here come the Frenchies," Young said.

Flockhart saw the French cavalry arrange itself in order of battle, with shafts of weak dawn sunlight reflecting from steel and the horses tossing their manes. A quarter of a mile behind, the French infantry marched in a solid block, as precise as on a parade ground, and halted.

"You might get your wish for a battle, Flockhart," Leishman said. "The French look as if they're in earnest this time. See? They're bringing up the guns."

Flockhart nodded. He knew he should be afraid, but instead, he felt only tense excitement and a desire to prove himself a good soldier.

When the French artillery came up, the guns opened fire on the Allied cavalry, with the cannon in Nijmegen replying. The artillery was noisier than Flockhart expected, with the sound echoing and re-echoing from the walls. Smoke jetted out to settle on the Royals in the covered way and drift over the waiting cavalry. Flockhart saw ripples in the French ranks as the iron balls struck home and heard, high above the roar of the guns, the screams of wounded men and horses.

The French infantry and cavalry faced the Allied cavalry, only sixty paces apart, but with neither side firing or advancing. The Allies and French closed ranks as the opposing artillery caused casualties.

"I hate artillery," Leishman said.

Flockhart nodded, rubbing at his throat. "I know," he said.

"The French are retiring," Sergeant Dunn commented, standing three yards in front of his platoon with his halberd at a forty-five-degree angle.

Flockhart watched as the French cavalry turned away, squadron by squadron, to file between their white-coated infantry. The infantry followed, leaving their cannon isolated and firing at the town.

The Allied drums rattled next, ordering first the infantry and then the cavalry back inside Nijmegen's walls. Flockhart marched with the rest, unsure whether he was relieved or disappointed that there was no battle.

The artillery contest continued for a full day, batteries of French guns hammering the walls and Nijmegen's cannon replying. Unable to retaliate, the infantry remained on the walls, watching and hoping a French ball did not strike them.

Flockhart flinched when a cannonball screamed overhead, and another smashed into the wall twenty yards from where he stood, sending a shower of stone splinters in a wide arc around.

"Thank God we have walls to protect us," he said.

Leishman nodded. "It's worse when you're in the open," he agreed. "Being under artillery bombardment is the worst thing about being a soldier. You can't fight back but must stand in the ranks and take everything the enemy gives out." He touched the bayonet at his belt. "I always make it a point to kill artillerymen when I get the chance."

"Are they so bad?" Young flinched as a ball landed nearby, and a man screamed in pain.

"I think the French have a limited number of trained gunners," Leishman said, "so the more we kill, the less they'll have in the next battle."

Flockhart nodded. "That makes sense to me. Killing men from a safe distance is the mark of a poltroon."

Leishman glanced at him. "You're learning the language," he said. "You might make a soldier in a few years and a couple of campaigns."

"The guns are stopping," Young said.

The cannon fire eased away, then ended altogether, with the silence hard on Flockhart's ears. He peered over the battlements to see sections of French infantry guarding the artillery as the gunners prepared to depart.

"Should we not sally out and capture the guns?" Flockhart asked.

"You bloodthirsty rogue!" Leishman replied. "The French will expect that. War is like chess, with moves and counter moves. If we send out a few hundred cavalry, the French will send in a few thousand. They'll be waiting for us."

Flockhart nodded. He looked up as Private Darvel ran along the Royals' ranks. "The French!" he shouted. "The French! Those French poltroons have captured the supply wagons!"

CHAPTER 10

NIJMEGEN, DUTCH REPUBLIC, SUMMER 1702

"These French poltroons have captured our supply wagons," Darvel was tousle-haired with wild eyes.

Flockhart looked up. "They've what?"

"They've captured half the wagon train," the private repeated. "All the supplies and the women."

"The women?" Flockhart said. "God help the French. These women are devils incarnate. We won't need to fight at all; the women will tear the Frenchies apart!"

Leishman laughed. "Half will have French husbands before nightfall, and the rest will rob Boufflers blind. It's the supplies I am more concerned about. We need bread and beer."

A benevolent army provided a ration of a pound and a half of bread per man per day. The Navy's victualling board provided the flour, which the army's field bakeries made into six-pound loaves known to the soldiers as ammunition bread. As if to prove the soldiers should not take such benevolence for granted, the army charged them fivepence for each loaf. Fresh meat from the cattle accompanying the army was a welcome luxury, but the soldiers were expected to use their meagre pay to supplement the basic bread ration with vegetables. Every army in the field had developed the art of foraging to circumvent the constant drain on their wages, with the French the recognised experts but the British not far behind.

"What do we do about the women, Sergeant?" Flockhart asked. "Some of them are genuine wives."

"Including mine," Dunn said. "We leave it to the officers to negotiate something, Flockhart. The French will keep the supplies, but I doubt they'll want to be encumbered with a load of women. They'll either turn them loose or exchange them for some of our prisoners."

"Would they kill them?" Young asked.

"Unlikely," Dunn said. "The French are civilised Christians, not Turks." He stared towards the distant French camp. "We'll await developments."

The Royals remained ready in case the French attacked that night, and the next day, a sentinel gave the alarm.

"Something's happening out here, sir!"

"Beat to quarters," Captain Brisbane ordered, and the drummers rapped their ominous message. The infantry ran to the walls, muskets ready, with the gunners waiting with slow match and the cavalry ready beside their horses, waiting for the order to sally.

"The French are approaching the walls, sir!"

"Ready at the guns!" Brisbane ordered.

"Stand ready," Lieutenant Murray walked the length of his platoon.

A small group of French cavalry appeared, holding a flag of truce and escorting a company of women.

"What the devil are they doing?" Lieutenant Murray asked. "These women are all naked!" He raised his voice. "Somebody bring me a spyglass!"

"That's our wives, sir," Sergeant Dunn said. "Boufflers has had enough of them already."

The French cavalry halted at extreme cannon range and formed a line. Drawing their swords, they leaned forward in their saddles and used the flat of the blades to propel the women forward.

Lieutenant Murray stepped onto the parapet and extended the spyglass Ensign Forbes brought him. "Sergeant Dunn! Take a section and bring these women in! Watch out for French trickery!"

Dunn shouted for half a dozen men, including Leishman and Flockhart, as he ran outside the walls. "Keep your muskets ready, boys!" Dunn shouted.

Flockhart ran out with the rest, aware that every eye in the regiment was watching. He saw the French cavalry wait until the patrol was close before wheeling away.

"Leishman, Aitken, watch the French," Dunn barked. "The rest of you, get these women back into Nijmegen!"

Most of the women were brazen, ignoring their nakedness as they marched toward Nijmegen, with a few weeping and trying to cover themselves. One dark-haired, filthy-faced young woman was so upset that Flockhart removed his coat to shield her.

"It's all right," he murmured. "The quartermaster will find some clothes for you."

The woman could not have been above sixteen years old and hugged Flockhart's coat to her skinny body. "Thank you," she said, looking up at him through huge, red-rimmed eyes.

Unused to gratitude, Flockhart only grunted. He glanced at the array of naked women with little interest and no desire.

"What are you doing, Flockhart?" one of the veterans reeled up, grinning. "A recruity can't claim that one. I want her!"

The man was about forty, Flockhart judged, with a long, narrow face and basilisk eyes. He grabbed at the coat, ready to yank it off the weeping girl.

"Leave her," Flockhart said, feeling his temper rise.

"No recruit will give me orders. I'll do what I want, my God!" the soldier said. Half a head taller than Flockhart, he looked like a veteran of a lifetime in the ranks.

"No, you won't." Flockhart stepped in front of the woman.

The veteran glowered at Flockhart. "Get out of my way, boy."

"No," Flockhart did not move.

Seeing Dunn stride towards them, the veteran swore and stormed away. "I'll see you later, Flockhart." The young woman pulled Flockhart's coat closer to her.

"Why did you do that?" Dunn asked, glancing at the retreating veteran. "Do you know this girl?"

"No," Flockhart replied as he helped escort the women back to Nijmegen.

"Then why?" Dunn asked. "Hunnam is a bad-tempered bugger at the best of times."

"I don't know," Flockhart replied. "Maybe it's because that girl reminded me of my sister."

"You'll have to introduce us sometime," Dunn said.

"My sister's dead," Flockhart replied bluntly. He remembered Janet's scream as the ladders gave way under her, and she fell sixty feet down the shaft. He had scrambled to where she lay, still alive but broken, with both legs twisted under her, blood bubbling through her mouth, and her load of coal scattered around. She had lived for minutes, moaning through broken lips as Flockhart had tried to help.

"She's dying," Cummings the grieve had said and ordered another woman to pick up the coal. "Get back to work, Flockhart."

"I'm not leaving her to die alone," Flockhart replied.

The grieve backhanded Flockhart, knocking him to the ground. "Get back to work."

"I'm not leaving her to die alone," Flockhart said, spitting out blood. The dark pressed around them, stinking, thick, and ominous. Flockhart held his sister's hand, willing her to die quickly and end her agony. He never saw her again and never learned what happened to her body.

Flockhart looked up, realising that the wives were hurrying past with Sergeant Dunn watching him through musing eyes.

"Make sure you get your coat back, Flockhart, or you'll get into trouble."

"Yes, Sergeant," Flockhart said.

Leishman joined them, smiling.

"Some prize cattle here, Flockhart," Leishman said. "I see you've already chosen your heifer." He laughed. "I hope you've nothing valuable in your pockets."

"They're empty," Flockhart said. He had never owned anything in his life and never expected to. He felt the girl watching him and wished he had not made the gesture. Flockhart knew he would get into trouble for losing his coat, but he could not leave the girl to walk naked into a place full of sex-starved men. He had witnessed rape in the darkness of the pit and remembered the fear in the woman's face and the sordid lust of the man.

When Flockhart woke the following day, his coat hung on a pole beside his cot. Somebody had brushed it clean and stitched a loose button securely in place.

"Did anybody see who brought my coat back?" Flockhart asked.

Leishman shook his head. "No. That young woman must have sneaked in during the night."

"I thought I had lost it forever," Flockhart said, pulling on his coat. He put a hand in his pocket and found a plug of tobacco.

❇

"The French have surrendered the town of Kayserwerth," Sergeant Dunn announced with a smile. "And British reinforcements have arrived. We're on the march again, boys. More importantly, Corporal John has taken command. He leads the British, Dutch and various Allied troops."

"A corporal in command? Who is Corporal John? Is that good?" Flockhart asked.

"Corporal John is the best news possible if we want to win this war," Dunn said. "Corporal John is John Churchill or the Earl of Marlborough if you prefer. He is the general in charge of all our destinies."

"Is he any good?" Flockhart asked.

"Corporal John is probably our best general," Leishman replied.

When the drummers sounded the General, the Royals prepared to march, and then the stirring *Dumbarton's Drums* propelled them forward across the fertile Dutch countryside.

"Tell me about Marlborough," Flockhart asked.

Leishman grunted, splashing through a deep puddle. "Corporal John likes to fight, but the Dutchies will ensure he can't. They are too fearful of losing to chance a battle." He looked sideways at Flockhart. "Have you heard of the Marquis of Montrose?"

"No," Flockhart shook his head.

"He was a Scottish soldier about fifty years ago, and he put it well," Leishman said. "He wrote: 'He either fears his fate too much,

Or his deserts are small,

That puts it not unto the touch,

To win or lose it all.'"

Flockhart tried to analyse the words. "Do you mean the Dutch won't gamble on a battle?"

"That's what I mean," Leishman said. "As long as they're in overall charge, we'll be a very cautious army. Marlborough will have General Opdam whispering, 'Don't take risks,' in his ear."

"How can they tell us what to do?" Flockhart asked.

"Marlborough is in command of all the Scottish, English and Irish troops Queen Anne pays for, and he commands the Dutch when they're on campaign, in the field as we call it. However, Marlborough's commission only allows him to act when the Dutch Field Deputies agree, and they are mostly concerned with defending the Dutch Republic." Leishman grinned. "We are fighting for their country, after all."

The Allies marched and countermarched for the next few weeks as Marlborough attempted to bring the French to battle. Each time, his Dutch advisers, including General Opdam, advocated caution, and the French slipped away.

Flockhart did not know the reasons for the army's manoeuvres but marched with his battalion, followed orders, and gaped at the sights and villages of the new country he was traversing. He started the campaign with weaker legs than his colleagues, but after a few weeks of marching, he found he was as fit and able as any in the regiment.

"Where are we going now?" Flockhart asked as they erected their tents at the end of another march at the end of July.

"Only God knows, and then He'll have to check with Corporal John," Leishman said, gazing at the unfamiliar countryside.

"Marshall Boufflers has left one of his positions too far forward of his magazines," Sergeant Dunn explained. "That makes it vulnerable to our attack. I reckon Marlborough intends to disrupt the French supply lines to Brabant and Limburg. If we arrive there, Boufflers will have to fight or withdraw to protect his supplies."

Marlborough pushed his army on, with the supply wagons creaking in their wake. Flockhart marched with the rest, usually ignorant of their geographical position, content to be one of the mass, and out in the open. His mind drifted back to the pits as he remembered sitting in the darkness as a child, opening and closing doors to allow his elders access to the mine shafts. He recalled the chilling, stifling dark pressing on him, the constant fear and the hard, bright eyes of near-naked colliers as they approached him in the choking black.

"Davie! Are you with us?"

"What's happening?" Flockhart returned to the present.

"We're on the Heath of Peer," Leishman told him. "And those men over there are the French."

Flockhart realised he had been marching automatically without taking note of his surroundings. "They're close," he said.

The armies were only half a mile apart, as the drums ordered the Royals to draw up in battle formation. Flockhart stood in the first rank, with Leishman on one side and Young on the other, feeling the wind tug at his tricorn hat. The French were in plain sight, a long streak of white with flags fluttering above and cavalry on the flanks.

"Brace yourself," Leishman murmured. "Here come the guns."

Flockhart saw the gush of powder smoke and heard the terrifying roar of artillery. Two seconds later, cannonballs were bouncing and skipping among the men. One ball screamed over Flockhart's head to land in the supporting battalion. Two men began to scream, with one begging for death. Flockhart flinched until Sergeant Dunn stepped beside him.

"If a ball comes directly towards you, Flockhart, step aside if you can. Put your faith in the Lord."

"Yes, Sergeant," Flockhart replied.

"If it's meant for you, Davie, it will get you," Leishman said quietly. "But only one shot has your name on it, so the odds are on your side."

After fifteen tense minutes, the supporting French battalions marched away, with the others following. Their artillery was next, leaving a thin screen of cavalry as rearguard.

"They're not going to fight," Dunn said. "The Frenchies are withdrawing!"

As the French army began a rapid retreat, the Allies prepared to attack until the Dutch Field Deputies approached Marlborough. Flockhart saw the cluster of men around the commander, and then the drums beat the army to a halt. Flockhart felt the disappointment among the Royals as the French marched away, unmolested save for a few cannonballs.

"We would have beaten them hollow," Young opined.

"The French will retreat away from the Dutch border," Sergeant Dunn said, "and we'll gain a few towns, but we won't win the war until Marlborough defeats them in battle."

As a private soldier, Flockhart was only vaguely aware of the machinations of higher command. Apart from the information Dunn and Leishman fed him, his life revolved around the platoon and the company, with the daily grind of marching, standing sentinel, and eating. Despite his strengthening legs, he found the constant marching tiring, as did many of the men. Some recent recruits and a few older men staggered as the army pushed them onward.

"Keep moving," Dunn advised. "Don't think of the destination; only concentrate on the next step. One step at a time will get you there. Next to obedience, a soldier's prime duty is marching; fighting comes well down the list."

As the summer wore on, a trickle of men deserted, some hoping to return home, others vanishing into the local towns, and a few switching allegiances to join the French.

The Allies had no sympathy for any deserters they caught, and Flockhart saw the results, with those they caught immediately hanged. On one camp, he looked at an executed man swinging from a tree with his tongue protruding, his eyes bulging, and his head at an acute angle.

"A warning not to desert," Sergeant Dunn stood beneath the gallows, cleaning his pipe with a knife. He shrugged and put his knife away. "The French would not trust a deserter, and he'd spend the rest of his life looking over his shoulder."

Flockhart nodded.

When the Royals pitched their tents and the supply wagons rolled up, Flockhart sat outside, checking his musket for rust.

"That girl you helped is watching you again," Leishman nodded to his right.

Flockhart grunted, glanced up and returned his attention to his musket. "I see her," he said.

Leishman studied the woman, narrow-eyed. "She's a dirty-faced besom who wants a husband," he said.

"Aye, but I don't want a wife," Flockhart replied.

"Why not? She'll cook for you, keep your uniform clean and your bed warm."

"Women are trouble," Flockhart said.

Leishman grinned. "Are you running from one? Have you had too much wife before you donned the Queen's uniform?"

Flockhart shook his head. "Women are trouble," he repeated.

"You can be a close-mouthed bugger sometimes, Flockhart," Leishman said.

"Aye," Flockhart replied. "I can." He lifted his musket, ran a finger along the barrel and nodded, satisfied there was no rust.

When he closed his eyes, Flockhart could see Mary. She had not loved him, nor had he loved her, but they were a good partnership at the coal face as he hewed the coal, and she carried it away. A collier needed a wife, and Mary was suitable, being born and bred to servitude in the pits. Her death had shocked him more than he expected.

"I had a wife once," Flockhart explained, surprising Leishman. "She died on me."

"Ah," Leishman nodded. He knew Flockhart would only reveal more when it suited him.

March by march, Marlborough forced the French further away from the Dutch homeland, occupying the prosperous country of Limburg and Gelderland and ensuring much of the River Meuse was clear of the enemy. Flockhart and the Royals rarely saw the French, save for a few distant cavalry patrols. They were present when Marlborough's manoeuvring trapped the French, but the cautious Dutch forbade a battle, and the enemy retreated unscathed.

"Whose side are the Dutch on?" Flockhart asked after another abortive encounter.

"Their soldiers will fight like fury," Leishman replied. "Their leaders are not so keen." He smiled. "Look on each day you are alive as a gift from the Lord."

In September, the Royals set up their camp a few miles outside Maastricht, one regiment among many to cover the Allied siege of Venlo.

"Another siege," Flockhart said as he listened to the roar of the guns. Defenders and attackers fired their artillery, engineers dug trenches and tunnels, and the infantry drilled, stood guard, and died of disease and deprivation. Flockhart took the opportunity to learn about the British guns.

"Colonel Holcroft Blood is in charge of the artillery," Leishman continued with Flockhart's military education. "We have sakers, which are six-pounders, and minions, which are three-pounders, plus mortars and howitzers for besieging towns and fortresses."

"I didn't know there were so many types of cannon," Flockhart said, watching the gunners at work.

"The heaviest guns, the siege cannon, weigh a couple of tons and need eight horses to drag each one," Leishman said. "Think of that on a narrow, muddy road, and you'll realise why we make such slow progress."

The Royal Artillery wore red uniforms, with the officers sporting a large sash designed to act as a stretcher if a pole was inserted through the holes at each end.

"Sieges are what modern war is about," Dunn said, "capturing fortresses and denying them to the enemy; battles are secondary and unusual."

"Where are we anyway?" Flockhart asked.

"Limburg province," Dunn said. "The River Meuse is over there on the west."

Flockhart grunted. "I wish I had a picture of this country. I'd like to know where I am."

"Why?" Sergeant Dunn was instantly suspicious. "Are you planning to desert?"

Flockhart looked up. "Desert?" The idea had never entered

his head. He remembered the executed men, swinging from their trees as birds pecked at their sad corpses. "Where would I go?"

"Back to Scotland," Dunn suggested.

Flockhart looked around. The array of tents, the beating of drums, the sharp orders of officers and NCOs, the rough humour of the men and the colourful uniforms were all his home now. "If I returned to Scotland, Lord Eskbank would find me, and I'd be a slave again, bound to the pit."

"Is that worse than this?" Dunn asked quickly.

"Much worse," Flockhart said.

"Surely Lord Eskbank has given up on you by now." Dunn watched him through narrowed eyes.

"I hope so," Flockhart said, "but I doubt it."

Dunn nodded. "We'll see," he said. "You want a picture of the country. We call that a map; you must read to understand a map. Are you a scholar?"

"No." Flockhart had never considered reading. It was a skill for people far outside his social circle.

"Captain Brisbane gives reading lessons when we're in camp or winter quarters," Dunn said. "Maybe you could learn."

Flockhart nodded. "I'd like to learn."

"I'll tell him you're coming," Dunn said. "You'll need to learn to read if you hope to progress to a corporal."

Captain Brisbane was in his early thirties. He had a hard jaw, intelligent eyes, and used the Bible as a teaching aid. Brisbane was a martinet on the parade ground but gentle with his reading classes, encouraging his pupils with praise rather than driving them with the stick. He welcomed Flockhart to his class and began with the basics, imparting Christianity as well as literary skills.

Possessing a brain he had barely used, Flockhart listened to every word and learned quickly, thirsty for knowledge. His fingers were clumsy on the pen, and his letters crudely formed, but he persevered, labouring to learn the alphabet.

Captain Brisbane watched him, quick to guide and slow to criticise. Although half the class dropped out, the remainder proved apt pupils, probably because they wanted to learn, and Flockhart found himself soaking up knowledge.

"What were you before you joined the Royals, Flockhart?" Captain Brisbane asked kindly.

Flockhart had dreaded the question. He fingered the raw mark on his throat. "I worked underground, sir," he said, hoping Brisbane did not probe too deeply.

"Underground?" The captain had a livid white scar that ran from the side of his mouth to his ear. "Were you a collier?"

"Yes, sir," Flockhart replied quietly.

"Did your master release you from bondage?" Brisbane asked.

"No, sir," Flockhart admitted.

"You're a runaway, then," Captain Brisbane said.

"Yes, sir," Flockhart replied miserably. He straightened his back, wondering what Brisbane would say.

Captain Brisbane nodded thoughtfully. "Do you realise that if your master comes for you, we have no legal right to keep you here? The regiment will have to hand you over."

"Yes, sir," Flockhart said. He lifted his chin.

I'll run if that happens. I am not returning to the pit.

"Let's hope that never happens," Brisbane said. "The Royals won't want to lose a promising soldier."

The lessons continued most evenings, with Flockhart absorbing the new reading and writing skills while also increasing his Christian knowledge by learning chapters from the Bible.

The line companies of the Royals watched enviously as their grenadiers were involved when the Allies stormed Venlo.

"I haven't fired a single shot at the French yet," Flockhart said.

"Your time will come," Leishman reassured him.

When the Allies' assault captured Venlo's covered way, the town surrendered. In the Royals, drill and training continued.

Sergeant Lamb, one of the more aggressive grenadiers, gave lessons in swordplay, teaching the men the tricks and techniques he had learned in his twenty years in the regiment. To his surprise, Flockhart found he was a natural swordsman, with his muscular upper body and quick reactions.

"You interest me, Flockhart," Sergeant Lamb said as Flockhart polished his sword. "You're good with the blade, better than most men."

"Thank you," Flockhart replied. Ever since the woman had thanked him for his coat, Flockhart had realised that people liked to hear the term.

"We could make money, you and I," Lamb said. He was a thickset man with a broad face and small, cunning eyes.

"Could we?" Flockhart asked without interest. He had all he needed as a private soldier. He had companions, food, ale, fresh air, and a modicum of freedom, which was more than he had ever expected. He spent the pittance he earned on the necessities of life, with a fraction left for drinking money.

"We could," Lamb said. "Come and talk to me, Davie, boy."

"Yes, Sergeant." Flockhart had learned by example always to obey orders.

"Here's what we can do." Lamb ushered Flockhart outside the tented camp to the shelter of a group of trees. "I'll teach you some tricks with the blade, and then we'll find somebody who only sees you as a raw recruit and challenges you to a duel for money. We accept, fight him to the first blood, and pocket the winnings. What do you say, eh?"

Flockhart considered for only a moment. "No, Sergeant Lamb. I could not do that."

"Why not? Easy drink money, Davie, and you'll gain respect in the battalion."

"It doesn't seem right, Sergeant."

"What does that matter?" Lamb looked genuinely puzzled. "I could order you to fight."

Flockhart lifted his chin. "You could, but I might not win."

Lamb's smile vanished. He glowered at Flockhart and spat on the ground. "We'll talk about this later, Flockhart, when you've seen sense." Turning, he marched away.

"Flockhart," a female voice hissed from the side of a wagon. "David Flockhart!"

"What is it?" Flockhart kept his distance. He relaxed when he saw the speaker was the girl he had helped, looking as filthy as before.

"Be careful, David," the woman said. "Sergeant Lamb is a rogue, a rake and a pimp."

"I'll be careful," Flockhart said. He eyed the young woman. "Thank you. How do you know my name?"

"I asked," the girl said seriously. "I asked about the man who lent me his coat."

Flockhart frowned. "Why?" he asked, instantly suspicious. In his world, few people acted without an ulterior motive.

"I wanted to know," the girl replied. "Be careful of Sergeant Lamb; he knows every trick, runs a brothel, and gets drink for people. He'd be a bad enemy."

"I'll be careful," Flockhart assured her. He hesitated, unsure if he wanted to know this young woman. "I don't know your name."

"My name is Rachel," the girl replied, dropping her eyes shyly.

"Thank you," Flockhart said. "Thank you, Rachel." He walked away. When he glanced back, Rachel was gone.

CHAPTER 11

EDINBURGH, SCOTLAND, AUTUMN 1702

Lord Eskbank dropped his cards with a curse. "The devil must be on my shoulder today," he said.

"The run of cards has not been in your favour," Queensberry agreed. "How many hands have you lost tonight?"

"Too many, damn your eyes," Lord Eskbank said.

Queensberry chuckled and poured them both a glass of claret. "Console yourself with a drink, Eskbank. We both know that luck has a way of levelling out, and a man lucky on Monday can lose his fortune on Wednesday."

"I know that, damn it," Eskbank gulped at his claret, dragged the cards together and shuffled.

"Shall I deal another hand, My Lord?" Lord Threipmuir had been an amused spectator.

"Yes, deal another hand," Eskbank passed over the cards and drained his claret in a single swallow. "Bad luck can't last forever."

"That's the spirit, Eskbank," Queensberry said. "You have the money, don't you?"

"I have," Lord Eskbank forced a confident smile.

"I hope so, Eskbank," Queensberry said quietly, glancing at Threipmuir. "Your debts are beginning to pile up."

Eskbank looked at the cards that Threipmuir had dealt him and leaned back in his chair, knowing he would have to bluff to win anything at this table. He became aware of Queensberry watching him intently and lifted his glass for a refill.

"Have you spoken to young Hugh Crichton yet, Eskbank?" Queensberry asked casually as he passed the claret.

"I will," Eskbank said. He knew by his cards he would lose the next hand.

Queensberry smiled and raised the stakes again. "I hope the conversation goes well," he said.

※

"That girl is following you," Leishman said. "Don't look."

Flockhart grunted. "Which girl?" He had already guessed the answer.

"The dirty one you helped with your coat," Leishman confirmed.

"She's a bloody nuisance," Flockhart said, rubbing his throat. "I wish I had left her alone."

"Too late now, boy," Leishman told him. "Good deeds always land you in trouble. It's best to keep your head down and let life take its course."

Flockhart grunted. He knew about women. They were useful when one needed to pound the mattress, but other than that, they were unreliable at best and trouble at worst. The only exception to that rule had been his sister, and she was gone now; God rest her soul. Other colliers had called his wife dirty, bad-tempered and lazy and told him he was better off without her. Flockhart closed his eyes to avoid the memory, knowing he was lying to himself. Mary had done her best in the most terrible circumstances and had died carrying his child. He missed her.

"I don't know why you bothered with that one," Leishman said. "She must be the dirtiest woman I have ever seen."

Flockhart turned around. Rachel was twenty yards away, and

immediately she saw Flockhart looking at her, she began talking to somebody. Leishman was correct; Rachel had not washed her face for a month, and her hair was a tangled mess that formed a curtain across her eyes.

Why are you so dirty, Rachel, and why are you following me? You would be better with somebody else.

❋

After Venlo surrendered on September the 25th 1702, Marlborough turned his attention to besieging the two fortress towns of Stevensweert and Ruremonde. While most of the army remained outside Maastricht, a few battalions, including Flockhart's Royals, marched to besiege Stevensweert.

Stevensweert was situated on an island in the River Meuse, nineteen miles from Maastricht. The British settled down around the fort, dug siege trenches, and began a series of parallels that would eventually bring the besiegers sufficiently close to assault the town.

"You know how it works, lads," Dunn said. "We dig trenches parallel to the walls and set up the artillery. While the guns hammer the defences to make a practical breach, we dig closer and set up another parallel. By the time our guns have created a breach, we are close to the walls and threatening an assault."

Flockhart nodded. He eyed Stevensweert's walls, saw one of the Allies' cannonballs smash into the stonework with a cloud of dust, and wondered what life was like for the civilians inside.

Sergeant Dunn continued. "All the time we besiege them, the defenders are firing at our parallels and our guns, making sallies to disrupt our preparations, and hoping for a relieving army."

"Then we storm the place?" Young asked.

"Hopefully not," Dunn said. "If the defenders agree their cause is hopeless and resistance is pointless, they can surrender with honour and march out with flags flying and drums beating. However, if they decide to fight on, the attackers – us – will try to take it by storm. Storming a defended town is always bloody, and afterwards, the stormers have free rein to do as they like for a while."

Flockhart looked up. "What does that mean?"

"It means murder, plunder, drunkenness and rape," Dunn explained soberly. "It's not a sight for the faint-hearted or a place to hide an innocent young virgin like you, Peter."

"I'm not a virgin," Young protested vigorously. The section laughed cruelly.

Flockhart patted Young's shoulder. "We understand," he said. "We were all young once. Many years ago, in Adam Leishman's case."

At the beginning of October, two siege batteries opened fire on Stevensweert, hammering the defences with heavy cannon-balls and mortar shells. Dust and smoke rose from the town, and the defenders replied with artillery. Flockhart saw smoke jetting from the walls and flinched as cannonballs screamed overhead or plunged into the ground around him.

Sergeant Dunn lit his pipe, smiling. "Do you still prefer army life to working in the mines?"

"Yes," Flockhart replied. "Although I could do without the artillery."

Dunn nodded. "Everybody hates the enemy's artillery and loves our own," he said.

Stevensweert was a small fort, and Flockhart watched as the Allies made rapid progress, pushing their parallels close to the walls as the artillery hammered at the defences. On the morning of the third of October, as Flockhart checked his flint was sharp and his bayonet loose in his scabbard, the garrison beat a parley.

"Put your bayonet away, Flockhart," Dunn said. "The French have surrendered."

"I still haven't fired a single shot at a Frenchman," Flockhart said.

Dunn smiled. "You've been part of an army that has won a successful siege for the queen, Flockhart. That's more than most men in the country can claim." He shook his head. "I've never known a man keener to get into battle. Your time will come."

After the siege of Stevensweert ended and the Allies also captured Ruremonde, the Royals rejoined the main army. Marlborough marched to Liege, camping outside the French-held town that had joined the Sun King.

"What now?" Flockhart asked.

"Now we repeat the entire procedure," Dunn told him. "Marches and sieges are the life of the soldier." He lit his pipe and puffed foul-smelling smoke into the air. "Liege might be tough to capture." He grinned. "You might even get a chance to fight, Davie boy!"

"Maybe," Flockhart said. "Then I'd be a real soldier."

"God help you, Davie," Leishman replied quietly.

❇

"It's a fine day for hunting," said James Currie, Lord Threipmuir, Jamie Threipmuir to his closest friends.

"Indeed," Eskbank agreed, pulling on his reins to guide his mount around a particularly boggy stretch of ground.

They rode side by side through the Green Cleuch in the Pentland Hills, with a thin mist drifting across the surrounding hills and the sound of the Logan Burn pleasant in their ears.

"It's been months since I rode anywhere," Threipmuir said. "Except from home to Edinburgh and back."

Eskbank laughed. "It's time you got some fresh air in your lungs," he said. "I doubt we'll see any deer here today, but the Lord might bless us."

"He might," Threipmuir agreed. They followed the course of the Logan Burn with the hills rising on either side, dark with fading heather. A whaup circled overhead, calling plaintively as sheep bleated in the distance.

"What's that up there?" Eskbank pointed up the hillside,

where the thin white ribbon of the Loganlee Waterfall tumbled from a ledge.

"What?" Threipmuir asked. "I can't see anything."

"I saw movement." Eskbank scanned the steep slope. "It might have been a deer. What luck! There's something to tell your wife when you return."

Threipmuir eyed the slope. "We can't ride up there," he said. "It's far too steep."

"No, we can't," Eskbank agreed. "Come on, Currie. Dismount! There's fine grazing here for the horses, so they won't stray."

Both men carried long flintlocks at their saddles, and Eskbank led them up the grassy hill. Threipmuir, older, heavier, and out of condition, followed, puffing as he slipped on the greasy grass.

"Are you sure you saw a deer?" Threipmuir stopped for a rest, leaning on his flintlock.

"No," Eskbank replied. "I'm not sure. Let's get to the top of the ridge. We'll have a better view from there."

They climbed further, with the waterfall crashing down on their left and the serenity of the hills rising all around. When they reached the summit of the ridge, Eskbank stopped. "I can't see anything now," he said. "It might have been a hare. I only caught a glimpse of it. Maybe we should get back to the horses."

Threipmuir frowned. "After coming all this way?" He shook his head. "Not yet, Eskbank."

"If I was a hunted deer," Eskbank said, "I'd either run or hide, and I can't see anything running."

"It might be down there, then," Threipmuir faced the deep gorge the Logan Burn had carved in the hillside, where the water fell in a double plunge to the Green Cleuch. He stepped closer, balancing on the lip.

"There it is!" Eskbank said, pointing downward. As Threipmuir stretched over, Eskbank pushed him hard. Threipmuir overbalanced, yelled, and fell, landing fifty feet down the slope and tumbling head over heels. Eskbank waited until Threipmuir stopped rolling and followed him down, lifting a heavy rock.

※

The Royals were encamped outside the main siege works at Liège when they saw rising columns of smoke from the city's outskirts.

"What's happening?" Young asked.

"The French have burned the suburb of Walburge," Sergeant Dunn explained. "They'll be retiring to the citadel and the Chartreuse Fort. They'll have burned Walburge to ensure we can't shelter there."

"Will they fight?" Flockhart asked.

"I'd say so," Dunn replied. "You may have the chance to fire at a Frenchman yet, you bloodthirsty rogue."

"If I am to be a soldier," Flockhart said, "I want to be a real soldier, not just a man wearing a red coat."

"Your time will come," Dunn said. "Don't invite the devil, Davie. He'll visit when he wants to."

I've served my time in Hell, Sergeant, and I've met the devil. He wears soft clothes, rides a glossy horse, and his name is inherited wealth.

When the Allies surrounded Liège, Marlborough asked the Marquis de Violaine, commanding the citadel, to surrender and save bloodshed. Instead, de Violaine gave a defiant reply.

"It would be time enough to think of that six weeks after."

"He's going to fight," Dunn said. "This could be a bloody affair, lads. Keep alert in case the Frenchies try to sally."

The Royals provided cover and free labour while the Dutch engineer van Coehorn set up the Allies' cannons and mortars. They began the siege proper with an intense bombardment that hammered at the citadel's half-moon battery, sending dust and pieces of masonry flying into the air. Within three days, the Allied artillery had battered a breach in the outside wall of the half-moon battery.

"We'll see if Violaine is so cocksure of himself now," Leishman said.

"Look!" Sergeant Dunn nodded to the Allies' Grand Battery. "Here's Corporal John." The platoon watched as Marlborough rode to inspect the artillery with a small cavalry escort in case the French tried a sally.

Marlborough spoke to van Coehorn and a group of senior officers and issued crisp orders. Within half an hour, everybody knew what was happening.

"Corporal John wants twenty grenadiers of each regiment in the army as a forlorn hope, backed by ten battalions of front-line infantry." Dunn passed on the news. "They are to storm the fort, sword in hand."

Flockhart stamped his feet. "Will it be bloody?"

"Undoubtedly," Dunn said. "Marlborough has given orders to give no quarter to anybody in the fort. Violaine refused to surrender, remember, so Marlborough's only following the rules of war."

On the 23rd of October, Flockhart watched as the grenadiers prepared to attack, with each man carrying a satchel holding three grenades. The grenadiers were large men, the pick of the army, loud-voiced, and confident of success. When the drums beat the attack, the grenadiers gave a loud hurrah and surged forward like a scarlet flood.

"There goes the forlorn hope; enough brawn to sink a ship without a brain between the lot of them," Leishman murmured.

The grenadiers threw the first of their grenades through the breach and into the mass of the French defenders, with the explosions quickly followed by loud screams.

Sergeant Dunn watched and began to sing.

"Captain Hume is bound to sea,
And his brave company;
Hey, the brave Grenadiers,
Ho!"

Flockhart watched, wondering if the sergeant had been drinking, gathering Dutch courage for the carnage to come. When he decided Dunn was sober, he returned his attention to the storming party.

A moment later, the grenadiers threw their second grenades, resulting in more screams. One man's voice rose above the rest in a pitiful appeal for mercy or relief from terrible agony.

"War is a sordid, ugly business," Leishman murmured.

"People are sordid, ugly creations," Flockhart replied.

Once they had thrown their grenades, the grenadiers clambered over the palisades. Flockhart saw Sergeant Lamb in the leading group, with Adair from the Royal Regiment of Ireland, his only rival as a swordsman, a few yards away.

"What do we do?" Flockhart asked.

"We stand fast and wait for orders," Dunn replied. "There's enough trouble in this world, Davie. We don't need to go looking for it."

Flockhart heard the hoarse cheers as the British and French fought a vicious battle in the breach. The grenadiers thrust forward with swords and bayonets, killing and wounding as they captured the half-moon, roared over the palisades, and pushed through the retreating defenders.

"They call this place the *six-centpas*," Leishman said, packing a mixture of tobacco and dry grass into the bowl of his pipe. "It means the six hundred steps." He borrowed a light from a nearby artilleryman's slow match. "I thought you might be interested."

"Not even a little bit," Flockhart said.

"No?" Leishman raised his eyebrows. "You always seem eager to learn everything."

After the initial assault, the French collapsed. Flockhart saw them running out of the citadel, and despite Marlborough's orders to give no quarter, the British herded prisoners back to the Allied lines.

"We lost over a hundred and fifty killed and three hundred

and eighty wounded," Sergeant Dubb said that evening. "But we took the citadel. The Chartreuse fort will surrender soon."

"What will happen then?" Young asked.

"If they had surrendered immediately," Dunn said, "nothing would happen. But according to the rules of war, by holding out and refusing to surrender, the besiegers, us, can loot Liège to the bones."

Young grinned, stamping his feet. "Wine, beer, Geneva, and women," he said. "Women, women, and women."

Leishman shook his head. "That will be a new experience for you," he laughed at Young's expression. "I know, Peter; you've had hundreds of women."

When the French in the Chartreuse surrendered, men rushed into the town for loot.

Leishman elbowed Flockhart in the ribs. "Come on, Davie! See what we can pick up!"

Perhaps because they owned nothing and had no hope of bettering their lot, loot or booty was the soldier's chief obsession after drink and women. Flockhart had never seen so many men desperate to grab something, and as Liège had resisted, everything was fair game. Flockhart witnessed red-coated men breaking into houses, shops, and churches, stealing everything they could, however useless.

"The grenadiers have had the best pickings," Young said, with a woman's shift under his arm and a small brass crucifix. "See what you can find."

"I can't see anything I want," Flockhart watched a couple of dragoons carrying a heavy chair from a house while the owner wailed, hands covering her face. "I can't imagine lugging that on our next march!"

"You don't have to need it!" Leishman said. "Take away anything we can sell. Some of the officers will pay good silver for rubbish." He grinned. "Welcome to your next lesson on how to be a soldier, Davie. Our pay barely keeps us above starvation, but booty fills the gaps."

Flockhart nodded. "Captain Brisbane's lessons teach that theft is wrong," he said.

"It's only wrong if you are caught," Leishman said, smiling. "Seriously, though. Are kings not the greatest thieves in the world? In peacetime, we'd get hanged for stealing a sheep, a silk handkerchief or a pair of trousers, yet here is King Louis of France trying to steal half of Europe. It all depends on your status in society. Landowners steal the common lands and become earls or dukes, kings steal countries, and the world praises them as great rulers; larger countries steal smaller countries and become more important." He shrugged. "At the bottom of the pile, we scrabble to fill our bellies and clothe our backs and get hanged for stealing an egg."

"I see what you mean," Flockhart replied. "It puts our grabbing bottles of wine into perspective, doesn't it?"

Leishman nodded. "Only one thing though, Davie, when you are out for booty or even foraging for food for the pot, be very careful. Only a few weeks ago, a group of Boers – the farmers in the Low Countries – found a lone Hanoverian soldier out foraging. They hanged him from the nearest tree. Always be on your guard."

"I'll remember your words of wisdom," Flockhart said. His loot from Liège amounted to one half bottle of wine and a piece of cheese, while Leishman found considerably more, including a pocketful of coins.

With the fall of Liège, the campaigning season ended for the year, and the Royals marched back to the Dutch Republic. They halted in the neat little town of Breda in northern Brabant and settled down for the winter.

"Should we not be marching towards the French rather than away from them?" Flockhart asked, looking around his new quarters.

"Have you seen the weather?" Sergeant Dunn replied. "This rain will turn the roads to quagmires. We move with our supply wagons and wives. Could you imagine an army of ten, twenty or thirty thousand men, with all their transport, trying to move?"

Flockhart nodded. "Does that mean we sit tight all winter?"

Dunn smiled. "The campaigning season is over, Davie boy. Now we sit quiet over the winter, get fat, keep our flintlocks clean, and let our lords and masters plot their next years' moves."

Flockhart looked around Breda with its immaculate streets and comfortable houses. "Life could be a lot worse," he said.

CHAPTER 12

LONDON, ENGLAND, NOVEMBER 1702

※

Redpath leaned against a cartwheel and shook his head. "Another failure. That's four regiments we've visited and no David Flockhart."

They stood in the middle of London's Bishopsgate, with the ancient houses around them and a thin rain pushing smoke from a thousand chimneys to form a choking smog.

Gordon swept a hand across her coat. "There were some handsome officers, however."

"I don't doubt it, Ruth," Redpath said, "but we have a job to do, and Lord Eskbank is losing patience with us."

"Only three more regiments to visit," Grant said. "He'll be in one of them."

Redpath nodded. "So far, every regiment has been based in England. Now we'll have to travel to the Low Countries." He looked up as a group of soldiers swaggered past, some noisily drunk and looking for trouble. "That will be time-consuming and costly. Let's hope Lord Eskbank can foot the bill."

"He's paid up promptly until now," Gordon said, ignoring the leers of one of the soldiers.

"I heard he has gambling debts," Redpath said. He glanced at

Grant. "You may have to remind him of his obligations, Duncan."

Grant pressed his right fist into his left palm and smiled.

A swarthy, wiry soldier staggered close to Gordon. "Come with me," he slurred as his colleagues encouraged him with grins and lewd comments.

Gordon sighed and rammed a clenched fist into the leering soldier's groin. When the man retched and doubled up, Gordon crunched her knee into his face.

"Hey!" the other soldiers lurched forward until Grant lifted the injured man and threw him at them.

"Look after your friend," Grant growled, waiting until they supported the groaning soldier out of the street.

"We'll get to Harwich and find a packet to Holland," Redpath decided. "I'll write a letter to Graham Cummings, inform him of our progress, and ask for an advance to pay for transport and accommodation." He smiled. "We'll catch this runaway and bring him back in chains."

❄

Flockhart stumbled from Cornelia's Brothel arm-in-arm with Leishman on one side and Sergeant Dunn on the other. Dunn was singing, with the others joining in, making the streets of Breda echo to their voices.

"When we came to whores on shore,
Hey boys, ho boys,
When we came to whores on shore,
Ho!
When we came to whores on shore,
We made the guns to roar,
Hey, the brave Scottish boys,
Ho!"

"You did well at Liege, Adam," Dunn said. "If you hadn't found that money, we'd have had to use one of Lamb's women."

"And we'd all catch the pox," Leishman said. "These Breda women cost more but were clean and willing!"

They staggered through the quiet streets, lifted a hand to acknowledge the quarter guard's evening patrol, and pushed open the door of their house.

"Early parade tomorrow, boys," Dunn sobered up to remind them. "Make sure your uniforms are clean, your musket rust-free, and the bayonet is in its scabbard."

Leishman laughed. "My bayonet was busy tonight!"

None of them saw Rachel watching from the shadows of a recessed doorway. She waited until all three men were inside the house, then walked quickly to the brothel, drawing a handkerchief from inside her sleeve.

❄

"How much did you lose?" Lady Joanna asked as her husband walked into their front room. She stood beside the longcase clock, holding Charles in her arms.

"Did you think I lost?" Lord Eskbank asked.

"You always lose," Lady Eskbank said. "You are the worst card player I've ever known. How much did you lose?"

"A lot," Eskbank admitted, stepping across to the cabinet where he kept his drink.

"While you were squandering our money," Lady Joanna said grimly, "we had more trouble with our other possessions."

"What happened?" Eskbank poured himself a drink without offering the decanter to his wife. He held the glass to the window, admiring the colour of the claret. Ignoring the slight tremor of his hand, he sipped carefully, savouring the taste and effect.

"Another slave absconded from Stobhill Pit."

"Damn!" Lord Eskbank swore violently, drank the contents

of the glass in a single swallow, and poured another. "We'll have to find him, or we'll have no workers left. That's Flockhart's fault. We must find Flockhart and set an example. What the hell am I paying these Edinburgh rogues for?"

"Cummings traced the latest runaway," Lady Joanna said. "He hadn't gone far. I had him flogged, of course, and set him to running the rown." She smiled, remembering how she had watched the man suffer.

"Good," Lord Eskbank approved. He poured himself another claret with his hands noticeably steadier.

"I should take over the running of the pits," Lady Joanna said casually. "You are too soft with them. You'll have to trace the Flockhart creature, John."

"I have men working on it," Eskbank said. "They've found out he went for a soldier but don't know which regiment."

"Tell them to work harder. The longer Flockhart remains free, the more unsettled the colliers will get. I want him returned so we can make an example of him." She held the dog closer and whispered in its ear. "An example none of our possessions will ever forget."

Lord Eskbank finished his third glass. "Yes, Joanna," he said. "We'll string him up in chains at the pithead."

Lady Joanna smiled. "Now you're getting the idea."

❉

"Did you hear what happened to Cornelia's house?" Leishman asked.

"No, what happened?" Flockhart asked, rubbing furiously to remove a speck of rust from the lock of his musket.

"Soon after we left the other night, a woman put a stone through the window. When one of the whores came out, the woman cracked her in the face with a stone inside a handkerchief. Gave her a beautiful black eye and a bruised forehead."

Flockhart grunted. "Why?" He examined his musket, turning

his head sideways to ensure he had removed the rust. Sergeant Dunn was particular about rust.

"I am sure I don't know," Leishman said. He checked his uniform jacket for dust. "Whatever the reason, Madame Cornelia blamed us and has barred us from returning there. We will have to seek our pleasures elsewhere."

Flockhart grunted. "I've no money anyway, so sweet Sophie, or whatever her name is, will have to wait."

"We could always use Lamb's women," Leishman said. "They're cheap."

"We'd probably catch the pox," Flockhart reminded. "I'd rather turn into a monk."

Leishman grinned. "You're fighting for the wrong side, then, Davie. We're meant to be an all-Protestant army fighting the Roman Catholic French."

Flockhart turned his attention to the musket barrel. "So we are," he said. "I'll have to find another outlet then."

"The French nearly captured Marlborough, too," Leishman said.

"How did they manage that?"

"Corporal John was in a yacht on the river Meuse with some other high-ranking officers. They were journeying to the Hague, and a horde of Frenchies from Guelders ambushed them, chased away the escort, and captured the lot."

Flockhart listened, wondering what the Allies would do without their best General.

"As you'll know, officers can obtain passes of safe conduct, and most of the officers carried one. Marlborough did not, but his clerk, a man named Stephen Gell, had a pass for Marlborough's brother, Charles Churchill."

"Didn't the French recognise Corporal John?" Flockhart liked using Marlborough's nickname. It made him feel like a veteran soldier.

"Evidently, they didn't," Leishman said. "An Irishman called Captain Farewell commanded the French; he had deserted from the Dutch to fight for King Louis. Maybe he preferred French wine. Whatever his reason, he allowed Marlborough and the other officers to continue with their journey."[1]

"That was fortunate," Flockhart said.

"It was," Leishman agreed. "When Marlborough reached London, Queen Anne made him a Duke."

"Well done, Corporal John," Flockhart said. "Or rather, well done, Duke John."

None of the men were envious of Marlborough's elevation. The lives of the great and the good were so far above ordinary men that they inhabited different worlds. The rank and file knew they could never dream of achieving even the lowest commissioned rank, let alone rising to high command. Sergeant was their ceiling, and the very few who gained a battlefield commission were so rare that most privates viewed them as myths.

"Here's a health to the new duke!" Leishman unearthed a bottle of beer and poured half into Flockhart's eagerly proffered mug.

"The new duke!" Flockhart agreed.

They lifted their mugs as the rain battered at the window outside.

❄

Mungo Redpath looked over the rim of his tankard. "Are you still interested in finding this escapee?"

"I am," Cummings said. They sat in the inglenook at the White Hart Inn in Edinburgh, with a bright fire warming the room and the rotund landlord watching them from across the counter.

"All right, then," Redpath said. "Was this collar around his

---

1. Captain Farewell later deserted from the French and rejoined the Dutch with an enhanced position, so it is possible that some bribery was involved to allow Marlborough to proceed. In an age of shifting loyalties, men lost no honour when they fought for different sovereigns.

neck?" He dropped the brass collar on the table, where it landed with a clatter. Some of the tavern's clientele looked around, saw the size of Duncan Grant and immediately lost interest.

Cummings lifted the collar, read the inscription, and nodded. "Yes, that was his."

Redpath nodded. "He's gone for a soldier," he said. "Seven regiments recruited in Edinburgh the week the blacksmith removed the collar. We have visited those based in Scotland and England without success, which means Flockhart is overseas. If you want us to continue searching, it will cost."

"How much?" Cummings asked. "Lord Eskbank is not a patient man."

Redpath grunted. "We will have to sail to the Low Countries to trace him. That will not be cheap."

Cummings sighed. Lord Eskbank had ordered him to find Flockhart, whatever it cost. "Would five English guineas help?"

"Ten would help more," Redpath suggested.

"How long will it take to find Flockhart and bring him back?" Cummings produced a small leather bag, counted the contents, and slid it across to Redpath. "There are twelve English guineas in there."

Redpath recounted the coins and passed them to Gordon, who bit into each one to test its purity and placed them inside her coat. "My thanks, Cummings. I'll be in touch when I need more or when I have located Flockhart."

"Move quickly," Cummings said. "My master is pressing for results."

"Travelling is difficult in winter with bad weather and bad roads," Redpath said. "And in summer, the army is constantly marching or engaged in sieges. These things take time. Tell His Lordship to learn patience and assure him we'll find his property, however long it takes."

Cummings nodded. "I'll pass the message on," he said and watched as Redpath and his companions left. Gordon was last to leave the inn, allowing her hand to brush over Cummings' shoulder as she stood. He watched her step into the street and took a deep breath.

CHAPTER 13

BREDA, DUTCH REPUBLIC, SPRING 1703

"Have you thought of my proposition?" Sergeant Lamb asked as Flockhart sat in the tavern, nursing a pot of sour beer.

"I have," Flockhart replied. "I have no desire to make money by fighting people."

"No?" Lamb sat his considerable bulk beside him, smiling. "Then why are you a soldier?"

"Fighting for the Queen is different to fighting for personal profit," Flockhart replied. He saw Rachel hovering at the door and wondered what she wanted.

"You're turning me down?" Lamb sounded amazed.

"Yes," Flockhart replied.

"Then hell mend you, Flockhart!" Lamb threw himself up, shoving the chair over so it banged on the floor. He glared at Flockhart. "God help you if you're ever transferred to my platoon; I'd make your life such a hell you'll be glad to fight for me."

Flockhart grunted. "Yes, Sergeant." He watched Lamb march away, knowing he had made a bad enemy. He saw Rachel watching from the corner of a building, saw the bulge of a rock inside her handkerchief and wondered what she was doing. He shrugged and stared inside his nearly empty tankard. Rachel's life was no concern of his.

※

"What have these men done to deserve hanging?" Flockhart asked.

The gallows looked sinister in the dull rain, with the dead men swinging and the ropes creaking against the wood.

"They're probably petty thieves, rapists and deserters," Leishman said without interest. Every town and many villages had their gallows, with executed men and women decorating the skyline. They were as much part of the scenery as windmills or church spires.

Flockhart saw one man moaning as he hung in chains, with a penny loaf suspended just out of reach of his mouth. "What has that poor fellow done?"

"He is a French spy," Leishman said, glancing upward. "The Governor of Breda ordered him hanged in chains until he died of hunger or thirst, or the crows peck him to death."

Flockhart watched as the man strained to reach the loaf but only pushed it further away. He remembered the agony of hunger as a child, squatting in the crowding dark of the pit with water dripping all around.

The prisoner moaned something, looking at Flockhart through huge eyes.

"What's he saying?" Flockhart asked.

"He's asking for water," Leishman told him. "He's saying water, water for the love of God."

"I'll give him water," Flockhart said. He stepped closer, climbed up the body of one of the hanged men and emptied his water bottle in the prisoner's mouth. The man gulped gratefully, spilling much of the contents down his chest. Balancing on the swinging corpse, Flockhart took hold of the small loaf and pushed it into the man's mouth, patiently waiting as the man chewed desperately. Flockhart could not bear the look in the chained man's eyes.

"Congratulations," Leishman said when Flockhart returned. "You have succeeded in prolonging that poor fellow's suffering by a day. It would have been kinder to leave him to die."

"I don't like to see a hungry man," Flockhart said. "Or a hungry child."

"He was going to blow up the garrison's magazine, killing us all," Leishman said.

"Even so," Flockhart did not explain further.

He was a small boy again, three years old and crouching in the terrible blackness of the pit. He was alone, with nobody to heed his tears or alleviate his fear. His job was to open and close the gate when the putters passed, allowing them access with truckloads of coal. He waited in the blackness, hearing the creaking of the earth all around and hoping the roof did not collapse and bury him. He listened to the constant drip of moisture and felt the water underfoot, bitterly cold on his bare feet. Yet the hunger was worse, the constant ache of his shrunken belly. He did not know when he had last eaten. The day before, perhaps, or the day before that.

Death would have been welcome if he had understood the concept. Flockhart cried bitterly until the well of tears dried up. He had nothing left.

"Halloa, young fellow!" a girl shouted to him, her voice booming and echoing along the adit, the level passageway within the pit. Flockhart's sister was four years older than him, naked to the waist and chained to the truck she dragged over the uneven ground.

"Halloa, Agnes," Flockhart replied. He opened the gate to allow her passage.

"You look hungry," Agnes said. She was hollow-cheeked and red-eyed as she forced a smile.

Flockhart nodded.

"Here." Agnes tore off a chunk from the loaf she had tied

around her waist. It was filthy with coal dust and stinking with her sweat, but Flockhart ate it, gulping down the last morsel before Agnes changed her mind. He watched her drag the truck along the narrow passage, hearing her gasp with effort, and pushed shut the door. The darkness returned, pressing on him, but that small act of humanity had relieved some of his pain.

I miss you, Agnes. You were the best of sisters. Flockhart returned to the present. "I won't see anybody go hungry," he said.

Leishman shrugged. "If that's what you think," he said.

That night, as the garrison slept, Flockhart crept out of his quarters, carefully avoiding the Quarter Guard and the patrols. He carried a water bottle and a small loaf, with his bayonet at his waist. Flockhart knew he would either feed the suffering man or cut his throat and end his agony. By the time he arrived at the gallows, the man was dead, with blood pooling under his feet. Flockhart never knew who had given the prisoner peace as he sat below the gallows and ate the bread.

He did not notice Rachel watching from the shadow of the church, tucking her handkerchief up her sleeve.

❄

Lord Eskbank strolled inside Parliament House, looking around like he had never visited. The building was young by Edinburgh's standards, having been completed in 1639 for the meetings of the Estates, Scotland's parliament. Eskbank was aware of the sixty-foot-high roof resting on ornamental brackets; he ignored the hammer beams and cross braces and only glanced at the array of tapestries and royal portraits on the wall.

Portraits did not interest Lord Eskbank unless he was the subject. He had heard the legend that the famous Indigo Jones had designed Parliament House and knew that the Estates had voted funds for the First and Second Bishops' Wars inside this building. He did not care. Lord Eskbank discounted the history as he sought the modern incumbents rather than the great names of the past.

"My Lord!" Sir Hugh Crichton greeted him with a smile and an elaborate bow. "We are honoured by your presence!"

Lord Eskbank accepted the greeting as his due. "I thought it was time I did my duty to the country," he said.

Sir Hugh bowed again. "I am sure the country will appreciate your time, My Lord."

Lord Eskbank strode to his seat, dusted it with a flick of his sleeve, and realised that Sir Hugh was only a few steps behind.

"My Lord," Sir Hugh perched uncomfortably on a nearby seat. "Have you had time to consider my proposition?"

"Which one?" Lord Eskbank asked carelessly.

"Moira, My Lord. I requested your permission to ask for your daughter's hand in marriage."

"Ah, that one," Lord Eskbank remembered Joanna pestering him with Sir Hugh's name over the past few months. "Yes, Sir Hugh, I have given the matter a great deal of thought. Come, walk with me."

Sir Hugh stepped beside Eskbank as they walked up and down the echoing chamber.

He's young but well-favoured, I suppose, and he treats me with respect. Moira could do worse.

"You see, Hugh," Eskbank dropped the man's title. "My wife, Lady Joanna, believes you are a well-favoured and personable fellow, which is all to the good, but I have certain reservations."

"Oh," Sir Hugh's open, eager face fell. "What may they be, My Lord?"

"I am sure they are not insurmountable," Eskbank reassured him. "They relate to your political and religious persuasion."

The men turned at one end of the vast room and began the return walk, talking in low tones. "My religion, My Lord?" Sir Hugh looked confused. "I believe we are both Church of Scotland."

"Ah," Eskbank nodded sagely. "Yet I heard you supported the

Jacobite party in politics and opposed the proposed union with England."

"That is correct, My Lord," Sir Hugh said. They reached the top of the room and turned again, momentarily facing each other.

"The Jacobite party contains Roman Catholics and Episcopalians, Hugh. I am concerned you may mix too freely with them," Eskbank told him.

"I do not care for the Jacobites' religion, My Lord," Sir Hugh said. "I am with them because of their opposition to the proposed Union."

"If you were to marry my daughter," Eskbank said as they continued to pace up and down. "You would fall heir to my title with all its responsibilities. That includes my coal mines."

"Yes, My Lord," Sir Hugh agreed.

"My business interests include selling the coal I produce," Eskbank said. "And the union with England would increase my market and, therefore, your future market." He paused for a moment as they turned. "I would not allow my daughter to marry a man who threatened her with poverty."

Sir Hugh was quiet for a few steps. "Poverty, My Lord?"

"Poverty, Sir Hugh. My daughter should not live in poverty. A union with England will ensure my family continues to thrive."

"I understand, My Lord," Sir Hugh said. "I would not wish that on your daughter or, indeed, on any member of your family."

"I am happy to hear that, Sir Hugh."

They paced to another turn, with their footsteps echoing in the vast chamber.

"You will have to choose between your politics and your wife, Sir Hugh," Eskbank said sternly. "Let me know your decision before the end of the week." He strode out of the hall, leaving Sir Hugh Crichton standing alone under the high ceiling.

※

In March 1703, another eighty recruits joined the Royals, staring around them in confusion at the strange sounds and sights. Flockhart watched them arrive, feeling all the old soldier's amused contempt for the Johnny Raws.

"You'll soon be soldiers," Flockhart told them. "Then you can march with the Colours and face the French."

The recruits nodded, eager for acceptance. Flockhart watched Sergeant Dunn drill them, smiling at their clumsiness.

"You were like that last year," Rachel stood nearby.

"It seems like a long time ago," Flockhart replied.

Rachel was as dirty as ever, standing slump-shouldered as she watched the recruits. "A lot has changed in a year," she said. "Yet we seem to be in a wheel, marching, fighting, besieging. Everything changes for individuals, but the world stays the same."

Flockhart looked at her, surprised at the depth of her mind. Most people he had met only lived on the surface, lacking the ability or the desire to think beyond their most immediate necessities or sensual pleasures.

"You could be correct," Flockhart replied.

Rachel held his eyes for a moment, then walked away. Flockhart watched her, wondering what she did and how she survived. He realised he was watching the swing of her hips and looked away.

No. Never again.

Flockhart remained in the background as the recruits trained, content to be with his colleagues but still unsure if he was a soldier.

At the end of April, the drums rattled out, summoning the Royals to the Colours. The regiment hurried to organise themselves and began marching, with the long convoy of wagons bumping and lurching in the rear and the drums tapping the pace.

"We're on the move again," Flockhart said, stretching his legs on the road.

Leishman grinned. "Another year, another campaigning

season." He stamped his shoes. "I'm stiff after being in winter quarters so long, but we'll soon loosen up. I wonder where we'll besiege this year."

Flockhart looked up at the clouded sky and thanked the Lord he was not stuck in the dark misery of the pit.

While Flockhart marched with the Royals, other units of the Allied army besieged Bonn, a city beside the Rhine. The French Marshals Boufflers and Villeroy, learning that the Allies were dispersed, marched to catch them in their quarters.

"Here we go," Sergeant Dunn said. "We're the pawns in a chess game, lads, with Marlborough and the Frenchies deciding where we move."

After a few days, Flockhart was back in the routine of early morning marches, putting up tents and sleeping under stretched canvas. The Royals had spent three days hard marching and were preparing for another when Leishman ran to Flockhart's side.

"Can you hear that?" Leishman asked. "If that's not cannon fire, I am made of cheese."

"I always thought you were cheesy," Flockhart said. "Is it cannon fire? Or distant thunder? Nobody's said anything about the French being close."

"It's cannon fire," Dunn confirmed. "Our mounted patrols have clashed with the Frenchies."

"Pack up the tents!" The drums beat, officers barked orders, and the Royals ran to obey.

"What's happening?" Peter Young asked.

"The Frenchies are happening, that's what!" Sergeant Dunn replied. "While you've been lying at your ease, drinking beer and whoring like a prize bull, Boufflers has attacked Tongres. The Buffs and the Dutch Regiment of Elst are holding off the entire French army, damn it!"

The Allies struck their tents, packed the baggage wagons, and marched toward the distant sound of battle. Flockhart glanced at the long column of soldiers, with the wagons trailing behind and the artillery rumbling along on the clumsy wheels.

He shook his head, wondering how he could be a part of this mighty machine. For a second, he saw a passenger on the third wagon staring back and recognised Rachel balanced on top of a pile of tents, watching the long scarlet snake of the infantry march in front.

When they neared Maastricht, Marlborough summoned his senior officers, and within minutes, gallopers ran from regiment to regiment, junior officers carrying messages that saw drums rattle and battalions march. The army formed up in battle order, infantry in the centre, cavalry on the wings, and the artillery trundling toward.

"Now you might use your musket," Leishman said.

"I hope so," Flockhart replied. He was unsure if he was nervous or excited at the prospect of battle.

They watched Marshal Boufflers advance his army close to the Allies, with clouds of cavalry on the flanks and artillery formed up between battalions of infantry.

"Check your flints are sharp," Sergeant Dunn walked in front of his platoon, using his halberd to straighten the line. "You recruits follow the example of the old soldiers. Fire low and ignore the noise."

Captain Brisbane rode in front of the men, a glorious sight on his grey horse, with his wig descending to his shoulders. He turned his horse, briefly examined his company, nodded, and faced the French.

Flockhart heard somebody humming, realised it was Leishman and glanced along the line. Most men were staring ahead, two were silently praying, one recruit looked as if he was about to burst into tears, and Young was nearly leaning against Darvel for support.

Both armies watched the other, with colours flapping and snapping in the breeze, drums tapping orders and all the colour and spectacle of war. Flockhart heard a man retching behind him. He did not see which side fired the first shot, but within minutes, the Allied and French artillery were hammering at each other, with cannon balls screaming overhead and ploughing into the ground to bounce toward the waiting infantry.

"Stay in your ranks!" the NCOs shouted. "Whatever happens, stay in your ranks."

Flockhart heard a succession of screams to his right. "Close ranks!" a sergeant bellowed. "Close ranks! Face your front!"

The drums tapped out commands, officers rode in front of the men, and the cavalry trotted forward to reconnoitre the enemy as the guns continued to roar. Within a few moments, acrid white smoke covered the field, stinging Flockhart's eyes and obscuring his vision. He licked dry lips, tasting powder.

"Will they attack?" Flockhart asked. "I can hardly see."

"You never see much in a battle," Leishman said. "There is smoke and mud and confusion. We just follow orders and trust in God and our luck."

Flockhart flinched as a cannonball landed ten yards away, throwing up a fountain of dirt. It bounced once and rolled forward, seemingly innocuous.

"I've seen somebody try to stop a rolling cannonball with his foot," Leishman said. "The damned thing took his leg clean off at the knee. He bled to death before the surgeon reached him."

Flockhart watched the approaching iron ball as it tore up the grass. The soldiers in the ranks shifted aside to allow the missile passage and closed up again. Sergeant Dunn walked along the front of his platoon, using his halberd to pull the recruits into position.

"Stay with your colleagues," Dunn said. "Whatever happens, stay where you belong."

The Allied cannons roared in return, their orange muzzle flares bright through the smoke. Flockhart saw the gunners leap back as they applied the match, and the cannon recoiled with every shot.

"It's hard work being a gunner," Flockhart said.

"It's harder work standing to have gunners shoot at you," Leishman replied.

The officers rode in front of the Royals, seemingly impervious to the danger. With their tricorn hats, flowing wigs, and long cloaks, they looked like creatures from a different world as they appeared and disappeared in the smoke.

"They're firing less," Leishman said.

"Are they?"

"Yes, listen. There are fewer French cannon firing with each salvo."

Flockhart listened. "I can't hear any difference."

"It's just experience," Leishman said. "You'll learn in time."

The cannon roared again, with one shot passing so close that Flockhart ducked.

"It's well overhead," Leishman said calmly.

After another two salvos, Flockhart realised Leishman was correct, and the French artillery was diminishing.

"They're retiring, lads," Sergeant Dunn said. "We won't see a battle today."

Dunn was proved correct as the Allied artillery fire also slackened and stopped. The smoke clung for a few moments and then drifted away.

"Stay in formation," Dunn ordered. They watched cavalry patrols trot out, searching for the enemy. The cavalry returned within a quarter of an hour, and the news spread that the French were withdrawing.

"Don't they want to fight?" Flockhart asked, unsure whether to be relieved or disappointed.

"You'll get your fight," Leishman said. "Corporal John wants a fight. All he needs is a Frenchy to stand and face him and the Dutch not to interfere." He shook his head. "Once you've seen a real battle, Davie, you won't want to see another."

While Marshal Boufflers withdrew his army to Tongres, Marlborough settled his men around Maastricht. Marlborough split the Royals: he brigaded the first battalion with the Guards and four British line battalions, while the second battalion's brigade included the fearsomely Presbyterian Cameronians.

The Royals had barely set up their tents when the French in Bonn surrendered, and Marlborough had the army marching again, chasing the retreating French from Tongres.

Leishman winked at Flockhart. "No battles, Davie, but plenty of healthy exercise."

The summer passed in a wearying succession of marches and sieges, with the French always hovering just out of sight and Marlborough never managing to force them to battle. Flockhart got to know the countryside well, camping at Thys, investing Huy and listening to the tales of the capture of Limburg.

When they camped for more than a couple of days, Flockhart always saw Rachel watching him, and twice, he found gifts of tobacco or food in his pack.

"That dirty-faced woman likes you, Davie," Leishman said.

Young laughed. "Rather you than me, Flockhart. She's the filthiest woman I've ever seen."

"Maybe," Flockhart said, cutting a twist of tobacco in three, "but I doubt you'll reject a good pipeful from her."

Leishman smiled. "She has her uses," he agreed.

The two armies manoeuvred, each searching for an opening. Marlborough was desperate to fight, but Boufflers avoided battle until he was sure of numerical superiority to guarantee a victory.

By the end of September, the Allies had captured the fortified towns of Huy and Limburg, and Marlborough had chased the French out of Spanish Gelderland.

"What now?" Flockhart asked as they marched through the harvest month of October, with the rich countryside around them and a bite in the air. After nearly two years in the army, his life as a collier was already fading into a bad memory. The idea of being a serf, of being owned by a member of the landed gentry, wearing a slave collar, working underground and seldom seeing daylight only entered his mind during nightmares. He was Private David Flockhart of the Royal Regiment, an experienced soldier, and his life consisted of marching and outfacing the

Queen's enemies. He had comrades, even friends, lived in the outdoors and breathed fresh air and powder smoke.

"What now?" Flockhart repeated.

"Now?" Leishman replied. "We've pushed the French away from the Dutch border, so Boufflers can't invade; we've captured half Louis's border fortresses and put in our garrisons, and Corporal John has outfaced Boufflers whenever they try to stand. If only the Dutch weren't so cautious, we could have brought Boufflers to a general action and defeated him soundly, but that was not to be."

"It's been a quiet campaigning season," Flockhart said. "We only had one confrontation, and the French retreated."

"You're alive," Leishman said quietly. "That's the main thing, Davie."

At the end of October, after a summer of marching and manoeuvring, the Royal Regiment returned to the Dutch Republic for the winter.

"Drink and women," Leishman said with some satisfaction. "That's my aim for the winter season. Avoid patrols and sentinel duty, survive the drill and parades, and find a brothel beside a tavern with cheap beer and Hollands gin."

Flockhart grinned. "That sounds good to me, except for the brothel."

"Have you gone off women, Davie?"

They were in another neat little Dutch town, with a river flowing nearby and quiet Dutch people who watched them suspiciously and hustled their daughters out of the way of the British soldiers.

"I seem to be unlucky for prostitutes," Flockhart said. "Every woman I use gets hurt."

Leishman frowned. "You hurt them? Why?"

"Not me," Flockhart shook his head emphatically. "But three times now, I've been with a prostitute, and somebody's attacked them later."

Leishman grunted. "Did you not fall out with Sergeant Lamb?"

"I did," Flockhart agreed.

"He runs a brothel, remember. Maybe he's trying to force you to use his women, or maybe he's trying to give you a bad name so women avoid you."

"That's probably it," Flockhart agreed. He stamped his foot. "I'll either have to avoid women or have a wee word with Sergeant Lamb."

Leishman took a deep breath. "Be careful, Davie. Lamb's a dangerous man."

"I'll be careful," Flockhart said. *I'm not sure what I will do yet.* He rubbed the red mark on his throat.

CHAPTER 14

DUTCH REPUBLIC, WINTER 1703/04

"You're a very quiet man," Leishman said as they sat in a corner of the room. Sleet pattered on the multi-paned window, emphasising the comforting warmth of the house. "You've been with the regiment for years, and I know virtually nothing about you."

Flockhart cut a piece of tobacco for his pipe and passed the remainder to Leishman. "I am a soldier in the Royals," he said. "That's all I want to be."

"Were you always a collier before you joined the army?"

"Yes," Flockhart said. "I was always a collier."

Leishman leaned forward and touched the red mark around Flockhart's neck. "What caused that?"

Flockhart edged away. "That was a long time ago," he said.

"What are you afraid of?" Leishman asked. "Are you ashamed of something you have done?" He leaned back, setting a light to his pipe. "Believe me, Davie, whatever it is, I've done a hundred times worse."

"Have you?" Flockhart asked. "You've always been straight with me."

"And you with me, Davie," Leishman said.

Flockhart lifted his chin and fingered the mark the brass

collar had left. Whatever measures he had taken, the welt across his throat remained as a perpetual reminder of his servitude. "I was a slave, remember," he said, hearing the bitterness in his voice. "I was a collier, the property of another man."

"I know you were a slave," Leishman nodded. "How did that happen?"

"I was born into it," Flockhart said. "We are born into slavery, work as slaves, we're spurned by everybody else and die as slaves."

"Tell me about it," Leishman said.

Flockhart closed his eyes. He had tried to erase the memories, but they often returned at night when he lay in his tent or winter quarters. He could still feel the echoing darkness of the pit as he descended to the coal face. He remembered the pain as he had to twist himself onto his side and hack with a pick on an eighteen-inch seam, choking in the dust and fearing a rockfall at every moment. He remembered the fear of breathing poisonous air and the men and women coughing their lungs out with the black spit.

He remembered naked men eating and drinking at the pit foot and teenage and pre-teenage girls and boys, naked to the waist in the stifling heat, dragging trucks of coal along the ground. He remembered eight-months-pregnant women carrying weights of a hundredweight and over up flight after flight of rickety wooden ladders.

Leishman listened to him, silently puffing at his pipe. "How old were you when you started down the pit?"

Flockhart realised he had been thinking aloud as the memories flooded his mind. "I don't know," he replied. "I do remember sitting at a door, surrounded by darkness, and my father belting me for crying. I must have been three or four."

"Where is your father now?"

"Dead. He died of the black spit a few years later. The pit killed my sister and mother. My sister was fortunate; she died quickly. My mother lingered." Flockhart remembered his mother screaming as the roof collapsed and the tons of rock and earth landed on her, pinning her to the ground. Men had tried to free her, but the roof had been unstable, and the overseer ordered them to leave her. Two men had dragged Flockhart away, screaming for his mother, so his final memory had been of her outstretched hand and desperate, pleading eyes in the dark.

"My wife died down there as well." Flockhart sat with the tobacco in one hand and pipe in the other, staring into space. He had tried to block the memories of Mary, but now they returned, with her desperate smile and the hope of new life in her eyes as she told him she carried his child. *There was no hope; there is never any hope in a collier's life. There is only the drink to grant a few hours of oblivion from the hell of existence.*

"Davie?"

Leishman's voice propelled Flockhart to the present, and the noises of his quarters around him prompted him to rise and open the window, allowing the winter chill to flood the cosy room. He thrust his head outside, gulping in the cold, fresh air.

"Shut the bloody window," Peter Young roared.

Flockhart shut the window, nearly ran outside, closed the door behind him, and leaned against the wall. He needed air and space. He looked up at the stars, partly seen through a clouded sky, and thanked God he was no longer in the pit. Flockhart took a deep, shuddering breath to control his memories.

"Davie?" Rachel came close, as dirty as ever, and her ugly, elvish face puckered in concern. "Are you all right?"

"I need to walk." Flockhart could not talk. He lurched away, avoiding the night patrols as he stalked the streets. The memories were always worse at night. He heard revelry from a tavern, a child's laughter from a house, and a couple disagreeing outside a building. The sounds helped erase the ghosts of sound from the past, the chipping of picks on the coal face, the sobbing of children carrying huge loads of coal, and the groaning of the roof above. Cool rain washed his face, calming him down. Flockhart did not mind the rain; it had often been damp down the pit, but the rain was cleansing, not laden with dust and dirt.

Flockhart stopped beside a tree.

"Davie? Are you all right?" Rachel asked again.

"Are you still here?" Flockhart asked, struggling free of his thoughts.

"Yes."

Flockhart touched the cold bark of the tree. "Trees are wonderful things," he said. "They survive everything that nature throws at them: wind, rain, sunshine, even thunder and lightning. They shelter cattle and give homes to insects."

"Yes," Rachel looked at him curiously. "They are just trees." She stood bareheaded under the slanting sleet, with water dripping from her tangled hair.

"They survive until man cuts them down." Flockhart spoke without realising Rachel had interrupted. "If we didn't interfere, trees might survive forever."

"Maybe they would." Ignoring the sleet, Rachel looked at him oddly. "But trees help us build houses and carts and barns and ships. We need trees; that's why God put them in the world."

Flockhart took a deep breath as he considered her words. "You're right, Rachel," he conceded. God put them in the world for a purpose. "I wonder what his purpose was with us."

"You're a strange man, Davie Flockhart," Rachel said. "I've never met a man like you before."

"Maybe you were fortunate," Flockhart said.

"I don't think so," Rachel said when Flockhart walked away. She remained at the tree for some time, touching the bark where Flockhart's hand had been.

❄

As the days lengthened, the officers intensified their training, drilling the men by platoon, company, and battalion, reminding them of the realities of army life and instilling some fitness after the lazy days of winter.

The Royals returned from another hectic drill session and were recovering in their quarters.

"Well, boys," Sergeant Dunn said, "last campaigning season was a disaster. We hunted the French across the Netherlands, but they avoided battle. In other theatres, Marshal Villars defeated our Imperial Allies at Hochstadt, and Marshal Tallard's Frenchies recaptured the fortress of Landau on the Rhine."

"Is that bad?" Young asked.

"It is," Dunn informed him. "Landau is fifty miles north of Strasbourg, and by capturing the fortress, Tallard ensured France has direct communications with Bavaria. The French already hold Kehl and Old Breisach, fortress towns that dominate the Rhine crossings." He waited for his men to absorb the information. "In war, communications are vital. The easier it is for France and Bavaria to communicate with each other, the more they can combine against us."

Flockhart nodded, fingering his empty pipe.

"Don't forget the fighting in Italy, where Marshal Vendome is keeping the Austrians occupied and menacing their south." Dunn shook his head. "We are holding our own in the Low Countries, but the French are kicking the Imperials from Monday to Hell's back door. If France boots the Austrian Empire out of the war, Louis XIV can concentrate all his forces against us."

"What does that mean, Sergeant?" Young asked.

"It would mean the enemy would heavily outnumber us," Dunn said. "If I can see that, so will Corporal John. I'd expect him to do something about it." He grinned. "Prepare for some long marches this season, boys, because I think we'll be fighting to help Austria, not the Dutch Republic."

Flockhart looked out of the window at the frost-rimmed Dutch town. "I'm looking forward to spring," he said. "Getting outside again with the fresh air and sunlight."

"It could be a hard year," Dunn told him. "After the French gains on the Rhine, Maximilian Emmanuel Wittelsbach, the Elector of Bavaria, made a treaty with Louis XIV. As a German ruler, he should owe allegiance to the Austrian emperor, not to the French, which makes him a traitor in my eyes."

"Loyalties seem to be very fragile," Flockhart said.

"There's division in the Allied camp," Dunn said. "I can smell the tension in the air." He stretched his legs and grinned. "It's all above ordinary musket men like us, lads. We just obey orders and follow Corporal John."

"What sort of division among the Allies, Sergeant?" Flockhart refused to allow Dunn to sidetrack him.

Dunn glanced at him. "The Dutchies want another cautious campaign along their border, but our Duke of Marlborough wants something more ambitious. According to his secretary, a bottle companion of mine, he's fed up marching us into a favourable position for battle only for the Dutch to back off or the French to run away."

"Do you think we'll fight without the Dutch? Leave them to fight alone?" Leishman asked.

Dunn shook his head. "We need each other to defeat Louis. Individually, neither of our armies is large enough to face the French. I think this could be an interesting campaigning year, though, boys."

"You might get your battle yet, Flockhart," Leishman said.

Dunn nodded. "That is a strong possibility. According to Corporal John's secretary, the Dutch want us to remain on the line of the Moselle River, but we're going to High Germany."

"Where's that?" Flockhart asked.

"Deeper into Europe," Dunn replied.

As the campaigning season opened, the British army was abuzz with speculation and anticipation. In March, with snow remaining in sheltered spots and a bitter wind howling over the flat countryside, the Royals sent six hundred men to join Brigadier-General Ferguson. They augmented the four-thousand-strong British force near Maastricht, joined General Overkirk's Dutch army, made their encampment, drilled incessantly, and waited for orders.

At the end of April, with the roads sufficiently dry to be usable and the fields planted, Marlborough gave his orders for the forthcoming campaigning season.

"Here we go, boys," Leishman said as he saw the gallopers passing orders from unit to unit and the officers packing their baggage. "Back to war."

Except for the garrison at Maastricht, the British assembled at Hertogenbosch, where Marlborough inspected them on the 27th of April. It was the first time Flockhart had seen the commander-in-chief up close, and his impressions were of an agile, intelligent man in his fifties. For a second, Marlborough stared into Flockhart's eyes and then moved on. It was a fraction of time Flockhart knew he would never forget, an instant that cemented him to the army with a personal connection.

Shortly after, Marlborough led the army away, with thousands of hard shoes crunching on the Dutch roads, and the men facing an always uncertain future.

"It's marching season again," Flockhart said. He glanced back at the supply wagons, saw Rachel perched on the leading wagon with a chattering group of women and looked away.

"Let's see if the French actually fight this year," Leishman said. He winked at Young. "Cheer up, Peter, there will be more women wherever we go next."

Young grunted, hawked, spat on the ground and said nothing.

Major-General Churchill, Marlborough's brother, led the British across the Meuse at Ruremonde and to Bedburg, where Ferguson's Maastricht detachment joined them. The two forces merged seamlessly, the scarlet British uniforms flowing like blood along the arteries of Europe.

"We're going to Bavaria," Dunn informed his platoon. "It's about two hundred and sixty miles away, so we have some marching ahead of us."

Flockhart did not hear who started the song, but at the beginning of each day's march, somebody would start to sing, and others joined in.

"So, dearest Polly, the war it has begun,
And I must march along by the beating of the drum.
Come dress yourself all in your best and sail away with me;
I'll take you to the wars, my love, in Higher Germany."

The men sang for a while, until the routine of the march took over, and the crunch of shoes on the ground, the tapping of the drums, and the flapping of the Colours were the only sounds.

Flockhart found that marching could be a thirsty business, and his throat was too dry to sing as the column of men kicked up dust. Cavalry rode on the flanks and ahead, scouting for the enemy as the wagons followed in the rear, rumbling and jolting over the rutted roads.

Each day, the British paid for supplies, and the men ate well. They camped overnight or billeted in towns and left when the drums ordered them out.

"The sky's getting darker," Leishman said. "There's going to be a storm."

Flockhart raised his head, mouth open to catch any raindrops. He did not mind marching in the rain.

On the 19th of May, the weather broke, with hailstones as large as musket balls pelting down. The men bowed their heads, carters tried to protect their horses, and women searched for cover. The army marched on, the miles slowly passing as they penetrated the heartland of Europe.

"I'll buy Polly a pony, and on it, she shall ride,
I'll buy Polly a pony to ride all by my side.
We'll stop at every alehouse and drink when we
    get dry,
We'll be true to one each other and marry by
    and by."

"Where are the French?" Flockhart asked as the hail passed over. They marched on, their uniforms steaming and their feet splashing through muddy puddles.

"I doubt they even know we're coming," Leishman replied.

They halted at Cassel beside the River Rhine, where the local elector inspected them in the suburbs of Mainz, with half a dozen Allied generals looking anxiously for His Highness's approval.

"It's strange that these veteran soldiers wait for some lordling's words," Leishman said. "I doubt the elector has ever marched a mile in a soldier's shoes or seen an angry Frenchman."

Flockhart remembered the fear with which the colliers watched Lord Eskbank and the obsequious manner with which all his servants and underlings treated him. "Aye," he said. "We bow and scrape to rubbish that doesn't deserve our attention."

After a day's halt, they marched on, leaving hundreds of sick men behind. Marlborough's men always followed the same routine. They started at three o'clock in the morning and marched for six hours, covering between twelve and fifteen miles. When they arrived at the area Marlborough had chosen to camp, the commissariat already had supplies ready.

"This is soldiering as it should be," Sergeant Dunn said. "All we have to do is pitch the tent, boil the kettle and relax." He grinned. "If you men had seen the shambles when King William was in charge during the War of the League of Augsburg, as they call it now, you'd appreciate how lucky you are under Corporal John."

Flockhart lay on his back with his arms behind his head,

staring at the sky. "I would not be anywhere else for the world," he said and looked up as Rachel appeared.

Rachel joined him, lying at his side with a faint smile on her face. "You are a strange man, Davie. Most men dream of escaping the army." She ran a stubby finger down his tunic. "Your button is coming loose. Give me your coat, and I'll fix it."

"I'll do it later," Flockhart said.

"I'm neater than you, and I'll do it now," Rachel poked him. "Come on, off with your coat."

Flockhart sighed and obeyed.

"Don't you want to leave the army?" Rachel took a small packet from inside her travelling cloak and began to work on Flockhart's coat.

"To do what?" Flockhart asked. "I'd rather die than return to what I used to do, and I've no skills for anything else. I could be a beggar, I suppose."

Rachel nudged him with her hip. "Have you no higher ambition? You could open an inn in London or Edinburgh or become a carter, travelling from place to place."

"I'd need money for both these," Flockhart pointed out. "I know nothing about running a tavern, and I've never driven a cart in my life, let alone bought one."

Rachel sighed. "Do you have any plans for the future?" she asked.

"I'll follow the drum for as long as I am able," Flockhart said. "I might make sergeant one day."

Rachel shook her head. "You are not a man of vision, Davie, are you?"

"No," Flockhart said. "I am only a man." He grinned at her, wishing she would wash some dirt from her face.

"Do you have hopes for the future?" Flockhart asked, knowing a female camp follower could only dream of attaching herself to a corporal or a sergeant. Rachel would have no higher ambition in life. *What else could she possibly do?*

"Yes," Rachel replied unexpectedly. "I have."

"What's that?" Flockhart watched as Rachel deftly sewed on his button. Her eyes were serious inside a dirty face.

She looked up and flicked away a loose strand of hair from her eyes. *She has fine eyes.* "I may tell you sometime," she said, and handed back his coat.

CHAPTER 15
HIGH GERMANY, MAY 1704

The weather broke at the end of May, pouring down rain and turning the roads into quagmires so bad the teams of horses could hardly drag the artillery. Mud clogged the wheels, infantry slithered and fell, and the gunners had to push their charges to make any progress.

"Keep moving!" the officers ordered. "Forward!"

The men obeyed, trudging through the sucking mud, reversing their muskets to prevent the rain from entering the muzzles, cursing, swearing, feeling the sodden uniforms chafe their rain-softened flesh and pushing on. Left leg, right leg, left leg, right leg, on and on relentlessly.

The march continued from Liège to Bedburg, Kerpen, and Bonn, deeper into Germany than any British army had ever penetrated. Twenty-one thousand men, including fourteen thousand British, followed Marlborough, a scarlet snake sliding into Europe with muskets, artillery, and drums.

"I hear that Marshal Villeroy's Frenchies are following us," Sergeant Dunn said. "He's got forty-two battalions and sixty cavalry squadrons."

"That's more than we have," Leishman quickly calculated.

"He has about thirty thousand men," Dunn agreed.

"With that advantage in numbers, Villeroy might want to fight," Leishman said.

"Maybe," Dunn agreed. "Until he does, we'll march."

Marlborough led them through the flat lands of the Landgraviate of Hesse and crossed the River Neckar on the 15th of June 1704. Marching for three successive days, then resting for twenty-four hours, Marlborough preserved his army's strength so the men would be fit to fight when they met the French.

Despite the weather, the army was in good spirits, for they knew Corporal John looked after them. They ate better than most had known in civilian life, and Marlborough ensured that a field hospital travelled with the men to care for the sick and wounded. Flockhart heard that Thomas Gardiner, once King William's surgeon, oversaw the hospital.

"We're marching to meet one of the best generals the Austrian Empire has got," Sergeant Dunn said. "General Eugene. You might know the name."

Flockhart shook his head. "I have never heard of him."

"Eugene is a strange character," Sergeant Dunn was always willing to share his knowledge. "He was born in Paris and is part French, but loyalties are flexible, as you know."

"Yes, Sergeant," Flockhart replied.

"Prince François Eugene of Savoy is related to Cardinal Mazarin, who was once Louis XIV's First Minister. I've never seen him, but he's said to be extremely ugly and was intended for the church." Dunn cut off a quarter inch of tobacco and packed it into the bowl of his pipe, pressing it down with his thumb. "He lay with male lovers among the pages at court while his mother was a witch, or so people say."

"A witch?" Flockhart repeated.

"That's what some people believe," Dunn said.

Flockhart looked away. He remembered some of the colliers discussing witchcraft and their fear of witches.

"Do you believe in witches?" Dunn asked.

"I don't know, Sergeant," Flockhart replied.

"Nor do I," Dunn admitted. "Witch mother or not, General Eugene is now Louis's implacable enemy. In a previous war, he defeated the Ottoman Turks, and in 1690, when the French ravaged Piedmont, he emasculated some of his French prisoners."

Flockhart grunted. "That's barbaric," he said. "I thought we had rules for war."

"We have," Dunn said. "Not everybody follows them."

When Eugene and Marlborough discussed strategy and tactics at Mindelheim on the 10th of June, the British soldiers raised a glass to their famous ally.

"Come on, Davie, boy," Leishman said. "We requisitioned a bottle or two of beer."

Flockhart joined them in singing a song to honour the Austrian General.

"Drink, drink, drink we then

A flowing glass to Prince Eugene."

Officers, sergeants and men repeated the toast across the British army as they wondered where they would march next.

"Marshal Ferdinand de Marsin and the Elector of Bavaria are advancing on Vienna," Dunn explained. "If they take Vienna, the Austrian Empire will fall. However, Marshal Tallard is in Alsace, threatening the German states."

"What will Marlborough have us do?" Young asked.

Sergeant Dunn pursed his lips. "Corporal John has not told me," he said. "He has a choice to either move back to hold the Lines of Stollhofen to keep Tallard in Alsace or stop Marshal Marsin and the Elector of Bavaria's march on Vienna," Dunn said. "I think the latter is more likely. Or they might split their forces and send the Elector of Baden to Stollhofen."

As Flockhart and the other soldiers marched, waited, and wondered, Eugene and Marlborough had a second meeting at Grossheppach. As a result, Eugene and twenty-eight thousand men marched to Stollhofen.

Flockhart looked around as the army marched, aware he had

never expected to see such places as the neat towns he visited. He seemed a long way from the hopeless despair and constant toil of the colliery pit. Flockhart relished the fresh air, ate the fresh bread, and drank the beer and wine with his comrades. He also heard that Marlborough had allowed some infantrymen to ride in his coach when they dropped from exhaustion.

"That's Corporal John," Leishman did not sound surprised. "He looks after his men, and we fight for him."

They marched on, muskets ready, red coats swinging, deeper and ever deeper into Germany.

> "So, dearest Polly, the war it has begun,
> And I must march along by the beating of the
>   drum.
> Come dress yourself all in your best and sail away
>   with me;
> I'll take you to the wars, my love, in High
>   Germany."

When they stopped at towns, the British found the local women handsome and friendly. They brought wine for the thirsty soldiers, ogled these fit new men, and flirted outrageously until their fathers grabbed their arms and dragged them indoors.

"Rachel's watching you," Leishman said. "She didn't like you talking to that German wench."

"We weren't talking much," Flockhart said, smiling. "I can't speak German, and her English was worse."

"Listen!" Leishman lifted his head. "We're on our way again."

The drums rapped, sergeants shouted, and the Royals formed up to march again.

"Where are we heading?" Young asked.

"Towards the River Danube," Sergeant Dunn was the fountain of all wisdom as far as the private soldiers were concerned. The officers might know more, but few would deign to talk directly to an ordinary man in the ranks.

The army marched until marching was everything they knew, and perpetual movement was their life. Town after town, camp after camp, they plodded on, now heading towards Donauwörth, a settlement on the banks of the Danube.

The name Donauwörth was on everybody's lips, although few had heard of it even a few days previously, and even fewer knew where it was. They marched forward, desperate to reach this new destination.

"We're very vulnerable, extended in this manner," Dunn said. "Our columns stretch for miles, so if the French take us with a flank attack, they'll rip right through us."

Flockhart looked over his shoulder, where the long scarlet column wound over the German countryside, with the interminable lines of supply wagons behind. "Where are the French, Sergeant? How can they miss seeing us?"

"Maybe they're marching twenty miles away, saying the same thing about us," Dunn said. "Keep moving, Davie boy! We're close to Donauwörth."

"What happens then?" Flockhart asked.

Dunn shook his head. "Ask the Duke of Marlborough," he said. "He knows more than I do."

On the second of July, at three in the morning, Marlborough sent six thousand Allied troops towards Donauworth. Two hours later, the remainder of the army followed, marching at their usual measured pace.

"Here we go," Dunn said. "Make sure your flints are sharp, boys, and keep your cartridges dry. We might see some fighting today."

Flockhart killed his flicker of anticipation, for he had heard similar stories through the last two campaigning seasons. After two years of marching with the Royals, he still wanted to prove himself a soldier. He wanted to fire his musket at a Frenchman, even at the cost of his life.

"What's happening, Sergeant?" Leishman asked.

"According to my bottle companion, a rogue named Count

D'Arco has an entrenched camp on the heights of Schellenberg," Dunn said. "That's on the north bank of the Danube, overlooking Donauwörth. D'Arco has a mixed force of French and Bavarians, and he's dug himself well in. We aim to shove him out." He glanced at Flockhart. "You're going to get your battle, Davie."

"Do we want Donauwörth?" Leishman asked.

"We do," Dunn replied. He explained the situation to his platoon. "It's only a small town, but it's in a good location where the Wörnitz River joins the Danube. It will be a fine place for Marlborough to cross the Danube and establish a secure base for supplies and to fall back on. But to ensure it's safe, we'll have to clear the enemy from the Heights of Schellenberg."

"We'll be attacking uphill," Young said.

"We will," Sergeant Dunn agreed. "If the enemy holds the Schellenberg, they will control the Danube crossing and hamper our movements."

The army marched slowly across a difficult tract of mountainous country, with cavalry guarding the flanks.

"The French must be nearby," Flockhart nodded to the cavalry.

"Keep your flints sharp," Dunn ordered. "Cavalrymen look pretty, but when it comes to fighting, we're the soldiers with the muskets." He looked up at the teeming rain. "I thought Scotland was bad for rain until we came here. We're marching through a torrent."

The rain hammered down like punishment from an angry god, lashing the toiling men as they bowed their heads and splashed ankle-deep through mud and puddles.

"Today makes it thirty-two days in a row," Young said. "Thirty-two days of rain."

The road narrowed into a steep-sided valley called the Gieslingen Defile, where the column marched through calf-deep, surging water.

"At least the Frenchies can't ambush us here," Flockhart said, indicating the steep slopes. "Their flints won't raise a spark in this weather, and their cavalry can't ride down a cliff."

They marched two abreast on the narrow road, heads down, rainwater dripping from hats that gave no protection but sat on their heads like cold, shapeless lumps, adding to their misery. They held their muskets barrel-down, hoped for a break in the weather, and wondered if the French would fight so they could end this war.

"I hear the Elector of Baden will add his army to ours," Sergeant Dunn growled, cursing as he slogged through a deeper-than-normal puddle. "That will increase our full force to eighty-five thousand men, compared to the French seventy thousand."

Leishman looked up briefly. "If we outnumber the French, they won't fight."

"They're well dug in," Dunn reminded. "That will give them an advantage."

The Allied army emerged from the streaming defile to find the Elector of Bavaria had damaged the bridge across the Wörnitz River. Grumbling but defiant, the Allies spent a long, damp morning marching to Ebermorgen, crossed there, and halted in front of D'Arco's position. Tired after days of constant marching, the men heard the drums call them into battle formation.

"No rest for the wicked," Leishman said, "or the Royals."

Flockhart gazed up at the steep green slopes, where the enemy positions were clearly visible, with the snouts of cannon poking through embrasures and palisades augmenting the dark soil of trenches. "It will be a hard fight to gain that place."

They watched Marlborough ride forward to inspect the enemy's positions, escorted by a cavalry detachment.

"Corporal John will find the weakest place to attack," Sergeant Dunn said. He grinned without humour. "At least the Frenchies won't run away this time. They need the Schellenberg Heights and know they have all the advantages remaining in position."

As he dried his musket and checked his flints and cartridges, Flockhart saw French and Bavarian soldiers toiling to improve the trenches and palisades on the Heights. A strong unit of Bavarians torched the small village of Berg at the base of the steep slopes, with smoke coiling from the damp buildings to form a dark cloud against the bright grass.

"D'Arco's trying to prevent us using Berg as a defensive base," Sergeant Dunn explained.

Flockhart watched the villagers flee in a disconsolate mass, husbands shielding their wives, mothers carrying young children and the elderly hobbling as best they could. *War is hardest on the innocent,* he thought.

"D'Arco's got good quality, veteran French and Bavarian infantry," Dunn said, watching the civilians without visible emotion. "Plus dismounted dragoons and a couple of artillery batteries. He also has a garrison of French regulars and Bavarian militia in Donauworth. They will fight."

"How many are there holding the Heights?"

"Marlborough's secretary told me there were thirteen thousand on the Heights," Dunn said.

Flockhart rechecked his flint and his ammunition, ensured he had spare flints and that his bayonet and sword were loose in their scabbards, and looked ahead. He could taste the tension in the air as the Royals prepared for battle. He heard somebody singing, although he did not recognise the voice.

> "Oh, cursed are the cruel wars that ever they should rise,
> And out of Bonnie Scotland press many a lad likewise.
> They took my husband from me and all my brothers three,
> And they sent them to the cruel wars in High Germany."

"When we go forward, lads," Dunn reminded. "Obey orders and fire low."

Flockhart nodded. He saw the veterans preparing themselves and the young soldiers trying to copy their elders.

By tonight, I'll be a real soldier.

Using the smoke from the burning village of Berg as cover, Marlborough ordered up a battery of artillery. The enemy retaliated immediately, and when the Dutch and Allied German artillery joined in, the battle began in jetting smoke, flaring muzzles, and plunging cannonballs.

"Ignore the guns and listen for the drums, boys, listen for the drums," Sergeant Dunn walked the length of Captain Brisbane's company, adjusting a coat here, setting a tricorn hat properly there, encouraging the nervous and calming down the excited. He tapped his halberd on the ground; a sun-browned, medium-height man with troubled eyes and a loud voice. "Follow the drum, obey orders, look to your front and fire low. If anybody is hit, close ranks and continue, as I've trained you."

The men nodded, with the veterans looking thoughtful and the unblooded either keen or scared.

"Keep your head up, Davie," Leishman murmured. "If the Good Lord has decided that it's your time, there's nothing you can do to save yourself."

Flockhart nodded, swallowing hard. At five to six, Colonel Holcroft Blood's artillery began a heavy bombardment of D'Arco's position, with the cannonballs arcing and screaming through the air. Five minutes later, Marlborough ordered the leading division forward.

"That's us, boys!" Sergeant Dunn said. "Keep your positions, fire low and keep your flints sharp."

The Royals' officers dressed the line, riding calmly in front despite the enemy's fire. Captain Brisbane adjusted his wig, drew his sword, and turned to face the enemy. Flockhart glanced along the Royals' line. The colonel's company was in the centre, with the second in command immediately to the right. The remaining companies deployed in order of seniority, with a half company of grenadiers on either flank. When the drums rapped out commands, the men reduced from six to three ranks, their fighting formation, with each man the correct half distance of a pace and a half from his neighbour.

Here we go. In an hour, I will be a real soldier, Flockhart thought. *Or I'll be dead.*

The drums beat steadily as the senior officers, wigs tossing in the breeze, divided the line companies into divisions and platoons. Each group of six platoons was called a firing.

Come on! Flockhart urged silently. *This preparation is taking an age.*

An Imperial battery rolled up behind the Royals and joined Colonel Blood's, with the noise deafening as the Allied guns hammered at the enemy. Firing uphill, the Allies' guns were at a disadvantage, but the gunners knew their duty. Flockhart saw the iron balls skip over the front-line earthworks where the Bavarians waited and landed among the supporting French. Each ball caused a swirl in the white-coated ranks, but the French stood still, accepting casualties like the brave veterans they were. Flockhart saw a haze hover over the defending soldiers and realised with a start it was blood from the stricken men.

The orders rang out, and Flockhart checked his priming, ran a thumb to test the sharpness of his flint, and the platoon moved into close order, each man one foot apart. The company officers stepped in front of their men as the colonel and his drummer strode seven measured paces in front of the ensign with the regimental Colour. The lieutenant colonel waited ten paces behind the fighting line, ready to take command if the colonel fell.

"It's like a ceremony of death," Leishman murmured. "But it's worked out to be efficient when we join battle."

With the ritual complete, the colonel spoke to his drummer, who tapped the advance; the other drummers repeated the order, and the Royals moved forward slowly, impersonally, each man with his musket held against his shoulder and his feet shuffling through the long damp grass.

Flockhart glanced along the line of steadily advancing British infantry. In addition to both battalions of the Royals, there were the First Guards and the heavily Welsh 23rd Foot, with Brigadier-General James Ferguson of the Cameronians in command. There was also some Dutch infantry in their iron-grey uniforms and some German regiments Flockhart did not know. He knew General John Wigand van Goor commanded the division but could not see him in the thick smoke.

"God save the Queen!" somebody shouted, and others joined in so all the British infantry chanted the same refrain.

"God save the Queen! God save the Queen!"

The four-word request to the almighty deity sounded ominous when shouted by thousands of deep male voices.

"Fix bayonets!" the officers ordered, and Flockhart reached for his bayonet so the eighteen inches of polished steel thrust from the muzzle of his musket.

The enemy was behind a deep ditch, with an entrenchment beyond. Flockhart saw the evening sun glinting on musket barrels and the flash of artillery through the murk of white powder smoke.

The Allies advanced in six roughly parallel lines, with eighty English Guardsmen as the forlorn hope and the leading four lines of infantry ahead of a double line of horsemen. As the infantry advanced, more Allied horsemen carried fascines from a wood on the left, dropping them on the ground for the infantry to collect.

"The forlorn hope will throw fascines into the entrenchment," Sergeant Dunn explained. "We will walk over the fascines and assault the enemy."

"After today, Davie boy," Leishman said, "you'll be able to say you've been in a battle. These Frenchies and Bavarians are going to stand."

Flockhart nodded, licked his lips, tasted gunpowder, and faced the enemy.

CHAPTER 16

SCHELLENBERG HEIGHTS, RIVER DANUBE, SUMMER 1704

No sooner had Leishman spoken than the French and Bavarian artillery opened up on the advancing infantry. After a salvo of cannon balls, the guns fired grape, which sliced into the Allied ranks, killing, maiming, and wounding. Flockhart heard dreadful screams from the wounded and saw a film of blood rising in the air.

"Don't look, Davie," Leishman advised. "Just look to your front and trust to your luck."

"Better killed outright than wounded and left on the ground," Flockhart said. He saw a human head rise above the Royals, trailing a red streak of blood. For a moment, Flockhart saw the face of the man, Private Milne, with his eyes and mouth open, and then the head fell back down.

With Brigadier Ferguson leading the first line, the Allies advanced steadily, moving uphill towards the nearly invisible enemy. When a cannonball howled overhead, with the wind of its passage knocking Flockhart's hat askew, he was glad he was no taller.

"Keep in formation," Sergeant Dunn shouted. "Face your front!"

Flockhart saw a discharge of grape scythe into a group of

mounted officers, wounding one man and disembowelling a screaming horse. He saw General Goor fall, shot in the eye, and Lieutenant-Colonel White, in command of the Royals, falling mortally wounded.

"The French are targeting the officers," Leishman said.

"Colonel White was a good man. We'll miss him," Dunn said as the Royals marched on, leaving their dead and wounded on the grass. Flockhart saw White's wig lie beside him, partially red with blood.

"Close up!" the NCOs shouted. A drummer sprawled on the grass with his drum at his side. Bavarian musket balls hammered at the drum, puncturing it with holes. The drummer, a boy of fourteen, began to scream. The Royals marched past, leaving him behind.

The Allies advanced, with their artillery firing over their heads and the French and Bavarian guns slicing them with grape that killed or wounded a dozen men with each discharge.

Flockhart realised the powder smoke was already restricting his vision. He could see twenty yards in either direction, with the enemy lines lost behind grey-white smoke.

"Keep in step!" Sergeant Dunn roared. "Follow the drum!"

Flockhart glanced to his left, where Leishman was marching like an automaton, his face set and eyes glaring forward. On Flockhart's right, Young's mouth was open as he sucked oxygen into his lungs. He held his musket in white-knuckled hands.

A French cannon roared ahead, with grape whirling and howling around them. A man three files down from Flockhart screamed and fell, with blood spurting from the stump of his missing left arm. Another man marched for four steps with the top half of his skull sheared clean off. When he crumpled, the man behind him stepped over his still-twitching body and marched on, dyed with blood and spattered with his colleague's brains.

Flockhart took a deep breath. He now understood the countless hours of drill when men marched, manoeuvred, and countermarched until their movements were mechanical. Without such enforced discipline, Flockhart doubted that mortal men could continue to march into the horror of cannons firing canister.

The forlorn hope dashed forward with the fascines, threw them in a ditch, and retired, duty done, before the French guns. The survivors formed up on the flanks, ready to advance again.

"That was quick," Leishman commented. "And the Frenchies hardly fired at them."

The Allies marched on, then stopped in cursing confusion. Rather than throw the fascines into the defending trench, the forlorn hope had tossed them into a natural hollow, leaving the deep defences intact two hundred yards uphill.

"That's a bugger," Leishman said as Captain Brisbane and Major Hamilton discussed their next move with Brigadier Ferguson.

When the advance halted before the entrenchments and palisades, the French and Bavarians added musketry to the cannonade, with Allied soldiers falling. Flockhart saw the Bavarian infantry with their light blue uniforms and red stockings leaning over or climbing on the parapets to get a better shot at the British. Further over were the French in their bourbon white coats, while he also saw a flash of red and blue, vague through the smoke.

"Are those British deserters fighting for the French?"

"No; they are either Irish or Swiss guards," Leishman said. "They both wear red uniforms with blue facings."

The smoke thickened, hiding everything except what was immediately in front.

"What now?" Flockhart asked as they approached the entrenchments with musketry and canister felling men with every discharge.

"We earn our pay, die like soldiers and wait for orders," Leishman replied.

Captain Brisbane appeared before the company. "Fire back, men," he ordered casually. "Volley fire on my word."

Glad to have something to occupy his mind and body, Flockhart followed the manoeuvres hours of practice had drilled into him. He remembered his initial training when Sergeant Dunn told the recruits that a well-trained infantryman could fire two rounds a minute, but each minute dragged when the enemy was firing at him.

"Load!"

Flockhart bit off the end of the cartridge, held the one-ounce-weight lead ball in his mouth, and poured the powder into the musket's muzzle. He felt surprisingly calm, as if the enemy were not intent on killing him. Spitting the ball down the barrel, he folded the paper and rammed it home to prevent the ball from rolling out. He glanced left, where Leishman was ready, waiting for orders.

"First Firing, take care!" Brisbane shouted as the drummers beat a ruffle to emphasise the order.

The six platoons of the first firing readied to fire, checking their flints and holding their muskets steady. The first rank knelt on the damp grass while the other two ranks of the first firing moved into close order behind them.

Each man shifted so his left shoulder faced the French, with his left foot extended and nearly touching the right foot of the man in front. Flockhart ensured his position was correct so the man in front did not obstruct his musket barrel.

"Present!" the drums hammered out a flan.

Flockhart aimed, with the heavy weapon easy in his hands. He saw the enemy as a vague shape, the men's heads and upper bodies bobbing above the entrenchments. On both sides of him, the Royals had lifted their muskets, a long row of steel and wood.

Sergeant Dunn walked along his platoon, using his halberd to shift the angle of a muzzle here and there. He had trained his men to aim at the enemy's stomachs, but the battlements would be the target here.

"Steady boys," Dunn said. "Remember your training."

"Fire!" Captain Brisbane shouted, and Flockhart pulled the trigger.

The bark and recoil of the musket were reassuring. Whatever happened now, Flockhart knew he had fired at the enemy; he was a soldier who had fought for the queen.

That's one shot. I have nine more before I must change the flint. Look for a medium size; the large flints snap, and the short don't always spark. Remember the sergeant's training.

"Reload!"

The officers followed the same procedure for the second and third firings, with the grenadier companies joining in the third. Powder smoke hung around the Royals, stinging their eyes, tasting acrid on dry tongues, and irritating nostrils and ears.

The enemy's positions did not look damaged, but Flockhart could hardly see through the blanket of smoke.

With the enemy muskets and cannons tearing holes in their ranks, some of the infantry began to waver, looking over their shoulders as if preparing to retire.

"Bayonets! Bayonets!" the order sounded along the ranks. "Charge!"

With their bayonets already in place, the Royals' first line charged forward, with the defenders firing constantly, so the dead and wounded men began to fill the trench. Flockhart leapt into the entrenchment and scrabbled up to face the enemy. Bayonets clashed with bayonets, men thrust upwards at the Bavarians, snarling, shouting obscenities and falling as the defenders fired down at them.

"Push on!" Sergeant Dunn stood on a dead body in the ditch, thrusting upwards with his halberd. With a more extended reach than a musket and bayonet, he jabbed into the chest of a defender, roaring as the Bavarian screamed and fell back. Flockhart leapt onto the earthwork, scrabbling for purchase as he slithered on the wet soil. He saw faces above him: a Bavarian soldier aiming a musket at him and an officer shouting orders. When the Bavarian fired, the ball passed close to Flockhart without hitting him, and he felt his handhold give way. Shouting, he tumbled back down into the ditch, landing on a screaming, wounded man.

Sergeant Dunn was halfway up the parapet, using his halberd for balance as he slashed at a defender with his sword. The Bavarian swung back, another lunged at Dunn with a bayonet, and Flockhart tried to climb up to the parapet again.

The Bavarians roared in triumph as the British attackers recoiled, and Bavarian grenadiers leapt over the parapet and surged forward on the assaulters' front and flanks. Flockhart saw the sun glitter from the enemy bayonets as they ran down the slope, shouting. One man slipped and fell to roll downhill towards the British. Sergeant Lamb stepped forward and plunged his halberd into the man's stomach.

Lamb stopped, faced the oncoming Bavarians, and roared a challenge.

"Come and fight a man, you Bavarian bastards!"

"Hold!" the officers shouted. "About face! If you are loaded, fire!"

A scattering of shots barked out, knocking down a few of the Bavarian grenadiers, and the officers gave the order to reload.

Flockhart realised he was swearing as he worked, glanced around, and saw Leishman kneeling at his side.

"Where's Peter?"

"I don't know," Leishman replied.

With the tall grenadiers running downhill towards them, the British infantry loaded in frantic haste. Flockhart bit open a cartridge, poured the powder down the musket barrel and nearly dropped the ball from his mouth until he saw Captain Brisbane calmly waiting. He steadied his nerves, spat in the ball, and rammed home the wad.

"Present!" Brisbane shouted as the drums sounded again.

Flockhart aimed and wondered how the Bavarians felt as hundreds of British muskets levelled at them while they floundered down a slippery grass slope.

"Fire!"

The volley was precise, with nearly every musket firing together. Only eight misfired, and one nervous man had neglected to remove his ramrod, which hissed through the air to land, quivering, in the ground.

The Royals, backed by the Guards, reloaded, no longer rushed as the volley had settled their nerves and slowed the Bavarians. They fired a second volley, felling a score of men and in a minute, the Allies were engaged in a deadly battle with the Bavarians and French. It was unusual for infantry to resist a bayonet charge as the defenders normally gave way and retreated. This time the British and Dutch refused to retire and met the enemy with bayonets, musket butts and swords.

A tall Frenchman with a curled moustache charged at Flockhart with his bayonet extended. Flockhart parried as Sergeant Dunn had taught him and swung the butt of his musket. It connected with the Frenchman's arm with a solid thud, knocking the man sideways. As the Frenchman staggered, another came roaring from Flockhart's right. Lacking the time to finish the first man, Flockhart thrust with his bayonet, only for the second man to parry. Flockhart ducked the return thrust, then lunged forward with the top of his head, catching the second Frenchman under the chin. The man staggered, spitting teeth and blood, and Flockhart plunged his bayonet into his stomach.

Before Flockhart recovered his blade, the first Frenchman was on him, slashing sideways. Flockhart ducked again, felt a stinging nick on his shoulder, pulled out his bayonet and stabbed, swearing.

Flockhart saw the Frenchman's mouth working as he shouted something, and then warm blood gushed onto him. Leishman was down, wrestling with a bald giant. Flockhart grabbed the giant's head and hauled backwards with his left hand while stabbing one-handed with his musket and bayonet. He felt the blade sink in again and again; the giant reared back, yelling. Leishman rolled free, kicked the giant full force in the face, lifted his musket and thrust the bayonet into the man's mouth.

Young was shouting, backing away from a wiry Bavarian, until Sergeant Dunn casually bayonetted the enemy. "Fight them, lad!"

Flockhart realised the French and Bavarians were retreating, leaving a scatter of dead and wounded, Allied and enemy, on the ground.

The drums tapped to reform, and Flockhart stepped back into his place, gasping for breath, with his hat missing and his shoulder stinging. He lifted a discarded hat from the ground, ignored the still-wet blood and jammed it on his head.

"Adam?"

"I'm all right," Leishman said. He checked his bayonet and automatically reloaded his musket, looking towards the French lines. "That was hot while it lasted."

Flockhart nodded. The Royals were reforming, checking to see who was dead, listening to the moans and screams of the wounded as Captain Brisbane paced the length of the regiment and gun smoke drifted across the bloodied slopes.

The Bavarian infantry began to fire again, and the French artillery roared out, spattering the Allies with grapeshot.

"We'll be going in again," Leishman said. "We can't stand here and let the Frenchies shoot us to bits, and Corporal John is not a man to retire."

Flockhart looked forward where the French and Bavarian earthworks reared up before them, with the defensive ditch a formidable obstacle in front, now scattered with dead and wounded men. "Aye," he agreed. "I reckon we will."

The drums tapped again, ordering the advance, and the Allies moved forward in disciplined lines, with cannonballs and canister hammering at them.

"Push on!" the NCOs shouted. "Keep in formation!"

Flockhart stepped over the writhing body of a desperately wounded Frenchman and launched himself up the slope. The

Bavarians fired another volley, killing or injuring more men, and then the Royals slithered or leapt into the defensive ditch and scrambled up the slope to the defences. The French and Bavarians met them with bayonets and close-range musketry, so they clashed again on the earthworks.

Flockhart pushed up the slope, saw a Frenchman waiting for him and lunged with his bayonet. He had a vision of the defender, a long-faced, dark-haired man with a broken nose, and then they were fighting desperately, clashing bayonets as each sought an opening to kill the other.

To Flockhart's left, Leishman was tearing at a defender's musket, trying to grapple it from the Frenchman's hand. On his right, a Royal was doubled up, screaming as a defender plunged a bayonet into his belly and ripped sideways, with the entrails pouring out. He saw Leishman ram a thumb into his opponent's eye, gouging, and then he had to concentrate on the enemy immediately in front.

The broken-nosed man was wily, leaving an opening and then closing Flockhart's attack down, trapping his bayonet and attacking again. With the advantage of height and a secure position, the defender gradually pushed Flockhart back. Flockhart fought desperately, blocking the Frenchman's lunges, nearly unbalancing as he pulled back to avoid a sideways slash.

The noise was terrific, a cacophony of screams, curses, yells, the rattle of drums and the clash of metal on metal.

"They're coming again!"

Flockhart did not know who shouted the warning but saw French and Bavarian soldiers again erupting from the earthworks to attack the Allies in the flanks. The Allies recoiled, with Flockhart pleased to step back from his dangerous French opponent. The Allies withdrew back down the slope, leaving a litter of bodies as the French and Bavarians taunted them with insults and began to fire into the now disorganised soldiers.

"Form up!" Dunn ordered. His hat was missing, and blood wept from a gash on his head. "Form up!"

The platoon came together. Flockhart noted the gaps in the ranks where men lay dead or wounded. He could not see Young. The drummers frantically plied their drumsticks, each company with its individual signal as officers rallied their men. Captain Brisbane was shouting something, his words lost in the general bedlam.

Ensigns lifted the colours high to act as rallying points as the flanking attacks pushed back the supporting regiments and the defenders fired volley after volley into the Dutch and British lines.

"Stand!" Dunn snarled, grabbing a man who turned to run. "Stand in line!"

The Royals rallied around the Colours, with musket balls whipping the air around them. Flockhart glanced at Leishman, who stood erect, facing his front.

"You're a soldier, Davie!" Leishman said. His smile seemed genuine.

Sergeant Dunn lifted his head. "Cavalry!" he shouted.

"French or British?" Leishman asked.

Cavalry was the queen of the battlefield, for unsupported infantry was not expected to stand against a cavalry attack. A few men glanced over their shoulders as if preparing to run.

"Ours!" Dunn replied after an anxious look to the flanks.

Lieutenant-General Henry Lumley led the Allied cavalry to support the beleaguered infantry, with the horsemen rolling up the enemy flanking attack and pushing them back to their defences. Peering through the rolling smoke, Flockhart had only fleeting glimpses of the cavalry action, with a confused picture of gleaming swords, flailing hooves, and running men as the enemy retreated.

With part of the pressure relaxed and their flanks secure, the Allied infantry reformed and reloaded. Behind them, Prince Lewis of Baden had marched up with the remainder of the Allied army.

"Prince Lewis is attacking the French left!" Sergeant Dunn informed his platoon. "Now we'll be going forward again!"

The Royals' drums beat the advance. Men looked at each other. Flockhart drew a deep breath, tried to ease the niggling pain in his wounded shoulder and hefted his musket.

"Here we go again," Dunn said, raising his halberd. "May God go with us all, lads!"

As the Allies, French and Bavarians slaughtered each other in the centre, the French sent units to hold back the Allied attack. Seeing the enemy line weakened, Prince Eugene ordered in his Imperial Grenadiers. Flockhart was too busy to see the Imperial Grenadiers capture a now thinly held line of gabions and swung left to take the defenders in the flank.

"The Bavarians are weakening!" Leishman shouted. "They're wavering!"

"Face your front, Leishman!" Dunn snarled.

Flockhart saw two more Royals' officers carried wounded from the field as he slogged uphill into the cannonade and musketry. He saw the broken-nosed Frenchman standing on the parapet, taunting the British, making gestures with his hands and lifting his bayonetted musket in defiance.

"I want him!" Sergeant Lamb shouted. "Leave that bastard for me!"

Flockhart nodded; after meeting the broken-nosed man once, he had no desire to cross bayonets with him again.

The Allies surged forward, and Flockhart pushed up the slope to the entrenchments. He felt the wind as a musket ball zipped past his ear, and then he was fighting again, thrusting his bayonet towards a flinching defender. The man countered but slipped. Flockhart plunged his bayonet into the Frenchman's neck, somebody pushed him from behind, and he fell over the wall inside the entrenchment.

Confusion. Flockhart saw men, living, dead and dying, all around him. The French and Bavarians were holding with difficulty as the Allies pushed harder. Flockhart struggled to his feet and saw a surge of dismounted British dragoons rushing at the defences.

"Here, Frenchy!" Lamb mounted the earthworks with his musket in his left hand and his sword in his right. He killed a defender with almost casual skill and looked around him, pointing at the broken-nosed Frenchman. "Me and you, Frenchy!"

The broken-nosed man moved towards him, holding his musket two-handed, with blood dripping from the point of the bayonet. He shouted something Flockhart did not catch and stood, waiting for Lamb to approach him.

Recognising that two champions were about to clash, half a dozen soldiers stopped to watch. Flockhart saw the Frenchman advance and feint to the left, wait for Lamb's response and prepare to slash at his stomach. But Lamb was a cunning veteran. He pretended to fall into the Frenchman's trap, hesitated, and thrust upwards with his sword. Poised for the slash, the Frenchman moved a fraction too late, and Lamb's sword blade caught him under the chin. He collapsed, gargling in blood, and Lamb finished him with a swift thrust to the heart.

That Frenchman would have killed me easily, and Lamb mastered him in seconds. Lamb is a very dangerous man.

"They're breaking!" Sergeant Dunn shouted as he cracked the butt of his musket against a French head. "Chase them, boys!"

Flockhart ducked under a wild swing, stabbed forward, heard his man squeal, and saw him limp away, holding a bleeding thigh. He heard trumpets and saw Lumley's cavalry sweeping around the flanks as the Allies fired volley after volley at the retreating enemy.

"Cease fire!" Captain Brisbane ordered. "Cease fire! You'll hit the cavalry."

The Royals obeyed, grounding their muskets and watching the Allied cavalry complete the rout. French, British, Bavarian, Austrian and Dutch casualties lay in mutual suffering on the ground while gun smoke drifted across the field, only partially concealing the horror.

British and Prussian cavalry charged the retreating French and Bavarians. "Kill! Kill and destroy!" they roared.

Flockhart glanced at the wounded Royals writhing on the ground and quashed any sympathy for the fleeing enemy. He watched, aware he had taken another step toward becoming a soldier.

The broken remnants of D'Arco's stubborn army ran down the opposite slope, heading for pontoon bridges across the River Danube. The Allied cavalry rode among the fugitives, sabring those who ran or resisted and taking prisoner those who surrendered. Not all cavalry accepted prisoners; Flockhart saw some slashing at men who begged for quarter with upraised hands.

When scores of panicking wagon drivers rushed onto the single pontoon bridge across the Danube, the bridge collapsed, tipping many into the river. Others voluntarily leapt into the water, desperate to escape the scything sabres. After the recent rains, the river was swollen and fast flowing, so even strong swimmers struggled, and the current swept hundreds away. Others struggled in the river, with heavy boots dragging them down. The Danube washed their drowned bodies ashore miles downstream.

Flockhart sighed, sat on a dead man's chest, fished some poor-quality tobacco from his pocket and lit his pipe.

CHAPTER 17

SCHELLENBERG HEIGHTS, RIVER DANUBE, SUMMER 1704

"Well, Davie," Leishman said. "You've been in a battle now. How did you like it?"

"Not at all," Flockhart crouched, utterly exhausted. He seemed to have been fighting for hours. "Not at all." He puffed smoke into the air and looked over the field with its prone or writhing casualties. "I hope the kings, queens and electors are happy with their victory," he said.

Leishman nodded, produced a twist of tobacco, and handed half to Flockhart. "I doubt they'll care," he said. "I don't know what kind of tobacco you use, but it stinks. Have a smoke and be thankful you're alive."

Flockhart nodded and accepted the tobacco. When he closed his eyes, he could see a hundred images from the battle for the Heights.

Leishman patted his arm. "Rachel's watching you," he said.

Flockhart opened his eyes and saw Rachel a hundred yards away. He lifted a hand, Rachel acknowledged, smiled, and turned away.

"She's ensuring you are still alive," Leishman said softly.

"I'm still alive," Flockhart confirmed. "I haven't seen Peter Young, though."

"I didn't see him fall," Leishman said. "We'll look for him later."

Flockhart slumped to the ground as waves of exhaustion joined the reaction. "Later." He looked up. "What the devil are the Bavarians doing in Donauworth? They're torching the place!"

After Marlborough captured the Heights, the Elector of Bavaria ordered the Donauworth garrison to burn and evacuate the town.

"Look! They're destroying everything." The Royals watched as the French and Bavarians began to break down the bridges and torch the buildings.

Captain Brisbane rode to the front of his company. "Don't get too comfortable, men. We have more work to do. We have a town to capture and a fire to extinguish!"

"You heard the captain!" Sergeant Dunn shouted. "On your feet! Come on, you lazy scoundrels! Earn your pay!"

Flockhart pushed himself upright and joined the other Allies in pushing into Donauworth. The engineers were busy working on pontoon bridges across the Danube and barely looked up when the Royals marched across and began fighting their way into the suburbs.

"Street fighting is different from anything else," Leishman warned Flockhart. "Don't get separated and watch for Frenchies firing from windows. Don't go into a house on your own."

Flockhart nodded, trying to assimilate the new knowledge that Leishman threw at him.

Captain Brisbane addressed his company. "We'll take the town one street at a time. Ten men to each building, men. Shout out before you enter in case there are civilians inside. If in doubt, shoot."

The battalion marched in at the double to face a stubborn French rearguard. Scots and French exchanged musketry through a fog of blue-grey smoke, with Flockhart too busy concentrating on loading and firing to think about the bullets that whizzed around him.

"Advance!" Brisbane ordered, marching in front of his company. The Royals pushed on through the burning town, coughing in the smoke and hoping the buildings did not collapse on top of them. Threatened by encirclement and capture, the French and Bavarians withdrew in the dark hours before dawn, leaving devastation behind them.

Smoke blackened and exhausted, the Allies watched them go. Flockhart rested on his musket, feeling the heat from the surrounding burning buildings.

"Heads up, lads," Sergeant Dunn ordered. "We're not finished yet!"

"Put the fires out!" Captain Brisbane commanded. "Help the locals!" He organised chains from the river, with men carrying wooden buckets of water to throw on the flames. The retreating French and Bavarians had crammed straw into the houses and set torches to the thatch, making a roaring hell of what the previous day had been a beautiful town.

"Sergeant!" Flockhart pulled smouldering thatch from a house as Leishman threw buckets of water over it. "Over here!"

Dunn hurried over and used his long-handled halberd to haul down a section of blazing thatch and trample it underfoot. "What have you found, Flockhart?"

"The house is full of sacks, Sergeant," Flockhart said. "They may be gunpowder."

"Stand back, lads!" Dunn thrust his halberd into the nearest sack. "This one's full of flour," he said and tried the next. "This one is oats." He grinned. "The army will eat well tonight."

The Allies found three thousand sacks of oats and flour in Donauworth and twenty thousand pounds of gunpowder. They also captured an array of Colours, tents, camp gear, and nineteen pieces of artillery. The more fortunate of the Allied soldiers found valuables, with D'Arco losing his silver dinner service, among other possessions. Flockhart, busy with firefighting, gained nothing.

As the night eased on, a thin drizzle helped quell the flames, and Flockhart looked over the battlefield, where camp followers and locals had arrived. They robbed and stripped the dead and wounded, leaving the slopes a horror of naked men and pieces of men with pools of blood in the hollows. Wives of the missing searched frantically for their husbands, sometimes arguing with the ghouls for possession of a shirt, a handful of coins or a pair of boots.

"You'd better get that wound seen to," Dunn noticed the blood on Flockhart's shoulder.

"It's only a scratch," Flockhart objected, rubbing his throat.

"If it festers and goes bad, you might die," Dunn said. "I've spent months training you to be a soldier, and I don't want that time wasted. Get to the surgeon!"

Ten paces away, Rachel nodded her agreement. "I'll take him," she volunteered.

"I know the way," Flockhart said sourly.

The surgeon glanced at Flockhart's wound, grunted and slapped a handful of some foul-smelling ointment on top. "It's only a scratch," he said. "Get back to duty."

Flockhart thanked him and left, pulling on his shirt. He was thankful to leave the hospital tent with its row of desperately suffering men and the pile of amputated limbs outside.

"What are you doing?" Rachel waited for him outside the tent.

"Putting my shirt on," Flockhart replied.

"It's torn and covered in blood," Rachel said.

"I'll wash it when I can," Flockhart told her, desperate to get some sleep.

"Give it to me," Rachel said, holding out her hand. "I'll wash it now and stitch the tear. Come on!"

"Thank you." Flockhart gave in and handed over the shirt.

"Who flogged you?" Rachel ran a hard finger over the welts on Flockhart's shoulders and back.

Flockhart lifted his head. "It was a long time ago."

"In the army?" Rachel asked. She looked closer. "No, these scars were not caused by the claws of the cat."

"Not in the army." Flockhart realised that Rachel was genuinely interested, and her brown eyes were sympathetic. "I was caught running away from my owner."

"Your owner?" Rachel sat beside him, looking at his face.

Flockhart explained some of his previous life, too tired to protest.

"I didn't know there was slavery in Scotland," Rachel said.

"Colliers and salt workers are enslaved," Flockhart said.

Rachel looked at him thoughtfully, touched his arm and walked away to wash his shirt. "I'll see your wound tomorrow," she promised over her shoulder. Flockhart watched her for a moment, feeling that something had changed between them. He sighed and lurched to his tent, too exhausted to care.

※

After Rachel had bandaged his wound and washed and repaired his shirt, Flockhart sat outside his tent. He smoked his pipe and listened as his colleagues swapped lies and exaggerated stories about the victory of Schellenberg.

"I must have killed five of them," Young boasted. "Maybe even six, including two Bavarian Grenadiers."

"I never saw you kill anybody," Darvel said as Lamb watched with a sneer on his face. Alone among the company, Lamb had not washed the battlefield blood from his face and uniform.

"I need a woman," Darvel said, stretching. He stared at Rachel, who sat nearby. "You'll do. Come with me once you've learned how to wash."

Flockhart glanced up. "Leave her," he said quietly.

Darvel stood up, glaring. "Who are you to tell me what to do? You've still got crib marks on your arse!"

Flockhart unsheathed his sword and placed it across his thighs. "Leave her," he repeated quietly.

Darvel opened his mouth to say something, met Flockhart's gaze, and walked away. Lamb watched, nodded, glanced at Rachel, and strolled off, smiling.

Rachel touched Flockhart's arm, wordless.

"According to Marlborough's secretary, the British lost twenty-nine officers and four hundred and seven men killed," Leishman said, "with another eighty-six officers and over a thousand wounded. Many of them will also die, so it was an expensive victory. Overall, our army had 5,400 casualties." He swept the stem of his pipe over the Royals' camp. "Our regiment was in the forefront of the action, so we lost more than most. The first battalion lost Captain Murray, Ensigns McDougal and McIlroy killed, with one sergeant and thirty-eight men, plus ten officers and a hundred and three men wounded. The second battalion lost two officers and seventy-three men killed and fifteen officers and a hundred and ninety-six wounded, including twelve sergeants."

Flockhart knew that Leishman had a macabre fascination for casualty lists. He listened, already aware of the gaps in the ranks and thankful he had survived. He felt like a veteran soldier now after his first major battle.

"Corporal John ordered that our wounded should be taken to the hospital immediately," Leishman continued, "and all the now widowed women and their children are to be sent home. Widows are to help nurse the wounded, and then Marlborough will give them passes and passage money for the journey home."

"He has a lot of humanity in him," Rachel joined in easily. "I like the duke."

"We all do," Leishman said. "Except the enemy!"

Everybody laughed at the simple joke.

"There will be vacancies for sergeants in the second battalion," Leishman said, "and we can expect new officers and a host of replacement recruits in the next draft."

"Campbell's Scots Dragoons did well," Flockhart said. "They began the battles mounted as dragoons, dismounted to join the assault as infantry, and ended as cavalry during the pursuit." He smiled. "The army pays them more than it pays us, so we should all transfer to the dragoons." He realised Rachel was looking at him.

"I thought you were not interested in money," Rachel said.

"It might be useful," Flockhart replied, wondering why Rachel was smiling.

"They'll look up to you as an old soldier now," Rachel said. She ran her hand across his shoulders. "How's the injury?"

"It's not worth mentioning," Flockhart said.

Rachel smiled, her teeth white in a dirty face. "My ministrations are better than the surgeon's." She inched closer to Flockhart.

※

After their defeat at Schellenberg, the French retreated further into Bavaria, with the Royals included in the Allied army that followed. Marlborough left a garrison in Donauwörth to ensure a secure passage over the Danube for reinforcements or withdrawal. His victory allowed him to march his army between the French and Vienna, relieving the immediate threat to the Imperial heartland and ensuring the Austrian Empire remained in the war.

"Corporal John has buggered up the Frenchies' plans," Leishman said bluntly, "and now we're chasing them all over Bavaria."

The French and Bavarians withdrew to Augsburg, behind the barrier of the Lech River, where they reorganised and prepared to fight again.

Once again, Flockhart found himself marching, with the Allies capturing and occupying towns in supposedly hostile Bavaria.

A short siege saw the town of Rain fall into Allied hands, and they pushed on to Augsburg, where the French and Bavarians had settled. The Allies halted within sight of the French and Bavarians' camp, set out strong pickets, and waited.

"Here we are again," Leishman said cheerfully as they erected their tents, lit their pipes and sat in the sun. "Us on one side, and the French and Bavarians on the other, with cannon and fortifications in between."

"I'll wager they retreat without a fight," Young said.

"I'll take your money," Darvel told him.

Sergeant Lamb arrived in his platoon with a broad grin. "Orders, boys! The officers want us to burn, loot and plunder!"

Flockhart listened without understanding. "Why? Marlborough flogs men who plunder."

"Not here," Lamb said with satisfaction. "The Bavarians are our enemy, and they're supplying the French army in Augsburg with supplies, so the more we plunder, the less the farmers can send to the garrison." He stamped his boots on the ground. "If we plunder Bavaria, the Elector will have to send detachments of his army to defend it, meaning his army will be weaker if we fight him again."

Flockhart nodded. "That's a new strategy," he said.

Peter Young grinned, and men licked their lips, smiling. "Let's get going, then!"

Each regiment sent out strong parties to burn, loot and destroy, with the result that the land around Augsburg became a smoking waste, with the soldiers returning laden with farm produce, drink and anything portable they could find.

When Flockhart joined the patrols, he marched through a devastated countryside, with smoke rising from once prosperous farms and villages. A few peasants watched the Allies' passage with hate in their eyes. Local villagers caught one party of raiders and killed them without mercy, while Bavarian and French patrols skirmished with the looters with mixed results.

As usual in eighteenth-century warfare, prisoners were exchanged, man for man and rank for rank. When not marching or looting, the army continued to train, with parades and senior officers inspecting reviews and ensuring tight discipline.

"The penalties for drunken behaviour have not altered," Captain Brisbane warned his company. "Hand the food to the commissariat and return to your quarters when you return from your patrols."

As the British Army recruited many of its men from the bottom level of society, the hopeless, shiftless and criminal, many men avoided the orders. Flockhart saw drunken men reeling around the camp, with some normally steady soldiers causing problems for the NCOs.

"We'll have to keep an eye on Sergeant Dunn," Flockhart said. "He gets a little boisterous when he's taken too much to drink."

"Aye," Leishman agreed. "Especially since Lamb is the provost sergeant. He doesn't like Dunny, and he'll delight in having him disrated at the very least." He sighed and nodded to his right. "Talk of the devil; Dunny only sings that Tangier song in battle or when the drink controls him."

Flockhart heard Dunn singing.

"Captain Hume is bound to sea,
Hey, boys, ho boys,
Captain Hume is bound to sea,
Ho!
Captain Hume is bound to sea,
And his brave companie;
Hey, the brave Grenadiers,
Ho!"

Dunn staggered up with a bottle in his right hand and his hat missing.

"We'd best rescue him before Lamb puts him under arrest," Flockhart said.

"Why?" Young asked. "Sergeant Dunn's always shouting at us."

"He could do much worse than shout," Flockhart reminded him. "How many men has he had flogged in the past year? Only one, and that was for assaulting a woman. We're lucky to have him."

Dunn saw them coming and waved his bottle at them. "Join me, lads, for the honour of the regiment!"

"Come on, Sergeant," Flockhart put an arm around his shoulder. "Lamb is on the prowl, and he'd love to break you to the ranks."

"I'll kill him!" Dunn bawled drunkenly. "Bring me to him!"

"I rather think he'd kill you," Flockhart said. "Come on, Sergeant."

Leishman took hold of Dunn's other arm and helped guide him to his tent.

"Careful," Rachel had a knack of appearing when needed. "Sergeant Lamb is around."

They ushered Dunn inside his tent, removed his bottle and remained with him until he fell asleep.

"He'll have a sore head tomorrow," Rachel said primly.

Flockhart agreed. "You're a strange woman, Rachel," he said. "You're not like the other wives."

"I'm nobody's wife," Rachel replied quickly. "I never have been."

Flockhart nodded, watching her. "I know," he said.

CHAPTER 18

ESKHALL, SCOTLAND
SUMMER 1704

"Have you seen my pearl necklace?" Lady Joanna asked.
"No," Lord Eskbank replied. He stood at the open door of his wife's dressing room.

"I am sure I placed it on my dressing table," Lady Joanna said. "Either I have lost it, or one of the servants stole it. I never did trust that Polly Darkin girl. She only came here because she was in trouble in England. I'll have a word with her."

"Best do that," Lord Eskbank said. "Although it's more likely you mislaid it somewhere."

Lady Joanna glared at him. "Those are my mother's pearls," she reminded him acidly. "That little rogue will have taken them or sold them. I'll whip the skin off her doup until she confesses, and I'll see her dangling with a necklace of hemp rather than pearls."

Lord Eskbank looked away. "Whatever you think best," he said. "The female servants are your concern."

Lady Joanna opened the drawers in her dressing table, scrabbling through the contents. "I don't like to have a thief in the house. God knows we are poor enough without the maids stealing the bread from our mouths." She emptied the drawers on the floor. "Damn the girl. Polly!" She raised her voice to a shriek. "Polly! Come here!"

Polly Darkin hurried into the room, standing with her head bowed and her hands in front of her.

"Did you steal my pearl necklace?" Lady Joanna asked.

"No, my lady." Polly was a twenty-year-old girl with a pale face and a pronounced English accent.

"Liar!" Lady Joanna slapped her. "Liar! Liar! Liar!" She punctuated each word with a hard slap, back and forth across Polly's face.

Lord Eskbank watched for a few moments, then walked away. He could hear his wife screaming abuse and the maid crying and protesting even as he left the house to stroll in the garden.

The gardener lifted his hat in acknowledgment as Lord Eskbank whistled softly to himself, listening to the birds in the trees. He wished he had brought his gun to shoot them, decided he could not be bothered returning to the house, and continued his stroll. Far away, he heard Lady Joanna continue her tirade above the maid's denials and tears.

❄

When Elector Maximilian of Bavaria saw Marlborough's army ravaging his land, he tried to form a truce with the Allies. The negotiations were far advanced until the Elector learned that Camille d'Hostun de la Baume, Duc de Tallard, Marshal Tallard, had brought a sizeable French reinforcement to his aid. Tallard had marched thirteen thousand men through the Black Forest. As Tallard's men included hundreds of veteran Irish mercenaries, thirteen hundred French veterans, and over two thousand cavalry, the Elector quickly weighed the odds, decided the French had more chance of success, and switched allegiance again.

"There's no such thing as loyalty nowadays," Leishman sighed. "The world's going to the dogs."

When Marlborough learned of the Elector's betrayal, he did not hide his anger.

"Burn and destroy," Marlborough's generals gave the orders. "The Elector of Bavaria has broken his treaty with us. Burn and destroy!"

The raiding parties marched and rode out again, turning the comfortable Bavarian countryside into a desert as far as the walls of Munich and darkening the skies with acrid smoke. Flockhart grew tired of listening to the despairing cries of countryfolk as soldiers destroyed their crops, burned their homes, and stole their livestock.

"Is this war?" he asked.

Leishman nodded. "This is war," he said. "The part without glory, but which many of the soldiers enjoy—looting, drinking, and the occasional rape. God save the Queen."

"God save the Queen," Flockhart intoned dutifully.

While the troops pillaged the helpless countryside, mounted patrols inspected the French and Bavarian camp at Augsburg, with an occasional skirmish when the French retaliated.

"The French have their camp well-fortified," Sergeant Dunn reported. "They'd slaughter us if we tried to attack."

"We can't just sit here and do nothing," Flockhart said. "We're turning the country against us by looting and ravaging."

Marlborough pulled back his army and turned his attention to the fortress town of Ingolstadt. He sent his unreliable ally, the Margrave of Baden, with fifteen thousand Imperial troops to besiege the city, with the Royals joining the covering army.

"Do we want Ingolstadt?" Flockhart asked.

"It could be useful," Leishman replied, "although I think Marlborough is here to try and lure the French away from Augsburg to fight him in the open."

The Royals settled in, posted pickets, and sent out patrols to find supplies and forage. When Flockhart returned from an extended patrol, Sergeant Dunn greeted him with a smile.

"We might be called on soon," Dunn said.

"Why is that, Sergeant?" Flockhart asked.

"The Elector of Bavaria has left his camp at Augsburg and merged his army with Tallard's reinforcements," Sergeant Dunn explained.

Flockhart nodded. "Will we fight them?" He remembered the slaughter of the Schellenberg and the aftermath of guilt and elation.

Dunn stuffed tobacco in the bowl of his pipe. "Maybe," he said. "I reckon we've annoyed the Elector by burning half his country. He might want revenge." He applied a flame to his tobacco, puffing blue smoke. "On our side, Prince Eugene of Savoy has joined Corporal John. As Eugene is one of the Empire's best generals, the Elector is facing two good men."

Flockhart tested the edge of his bayonet on his thumb. "Let's fight them, then."

"You're a bloodthirsty rogue, Davie," Dunn said, shaking his head.

Dunn's prophecy proved correct, as the French and Bavarians left their camp, and the Allies followed. Flockhart lost count of the marches in Bavaria as the French, Allies, Bavarians, and Imperialists manoeuvred to find a position where they could defeat their enemy.

At midnight on the 11th of August, Marlborough's army was back near the Schellenberg Heights, camping between the Danube and the Kessel rivers. The men were tired and confused, wondering where they were heading.

"We know Bavaria now," Flockhart said as they crouched over a campfire and ate boiled Bavarian beef and Bavarian eggs. "And Bavaria knows us. Surely, the Elector wants to boot us out of his country."

"He must face us soon," Young said, "or he won't have a country to rule."

Sergeant Dunn lifted his voice. "The scouts tell me that the Frenchies are only three miles away," he said.

Flockhart clamped a requisitioned long-stemmed clay pipe between his teeth. "That's no distance," he said. "I wonder if they'll stay to fight or bid us a fond farewell and march away."

Leishman shrugged. "If we fight, we'll beat them. If we don't, we know we'll live another day." He peeled the shell from an egg. "I don't know about you, lads, but I'd rather live a bit longer, so if the Bavarians choose not to fight, it's grand with me."

"I'll pass your suggestion to Prince Eugene," Dunn said. "In the meantime, make sure your muskets are rust-free and your flints are sharp."

On the 12th of August, Marlborough and Eugene clambered to the top of the church in Tapfheim, within a stone's throw of the Danube. When they extended their spyglasses, they could clearly see the French and Bavarians' camp in the Danube valley, in the Plain of Hochstadt. Marlborough saw the enemy in a strong but not impossible position, situated on a hill, with the three-hundred-foot-wide River Danube on their right and the River Nebel guarding the front. Villages dotted the enemy's front, each a possible strongpoint. Dense woodland protected the left flank.

"I think the Frenchies are making a stand," Sergeant Dunn said. "It could be a bloody day if they do."

Flockhart nodded. He sensed somebody to his right and saw Rachel sitting on a wagon wheel, watching him. She mouthed, "Take care," and stepped away, turning again after fifteen yards. When her gaze met Flockhart's, he saw her concern and raised a hand in acknowledgment.

Marlborough began the battle by sending a stream of brave men to the French camp, each man claiming to be a deserter. The pseudo-deserters fed Marshal Tallard the idea that the Elector of Baden had joined Marlborough, hoping to dissuade the French from attacking a supposedly stronger force. At that time, the joint French and Bavarian army had around sixty thousand men and a hundred cannon, giving them eight thousand men and forty guns more than the Allies.

"Eat well tonight, boys," Sergeant Dunn advised. "We might need all our strength tomorrow. And grab all the sleep you can tonight."

"I never mind the fighting and killing part of soldiering," Darvel said slowly. "The worst thing is being so tired all the time." He shook his grey head. "I've been a soldier for longer than I care to remember; I've fought at Sedgemoor and the Low Countries, and I've never got enough sleep yet." He checked his flints. "Sleep when you can, piss whenever you get a chance, and drink whatever you find." He closed his eyes and was asleep in seconds.

"Good advice, boys," Sergeant Dunn said.

When Marlborough ordered his pioneers to hack down trees to improve the roads for their artillery and supply wagons, French cavalry patrols rode to investigate. Flockhart heard the fighting, with the crack of fusils and the more resounding roar of muskets.

"We're not involved," Dunn said. "Don't look so hopeful, you blood-hungry scoundrel."

"Have you any news about the French dispositions, Sergeant?"

Dunn smoothed a hand down the shaft of his halberd. "They have a strange formation, Davie; rather than having the cavalry on the wings, with a strong reserve ready to exploit any weakness, they have infantry and cavalry in alternate blocks. Now, try and grab some sleep. We'll need all our energy when the fighting starts."

Flockhart nodded. "Marlborough will see us through," he said.

Leishman sat splay-legged on the ground, puffing smoke. "Maybe so," he said quietly. "Maybe so." He looked at the bustling camp. "I wonder how many of these lads will die when he does."

"I can't sleep." Flockhart slid his bayonet into its scabbard and began to clean his musket. "It will be another bloody day," he said. He felt the rising anticipation around him as the Royals prepared themselves, mentally and physically, for battle.

Rachel watched from a distance, her hands twisting together.

※

Lord Eskbank sat in Queensberry's house at the foot of the Canongate. The windows were open to the sound of the traffic rumbling over the cobbles outside, while inside, soft-footed servants attended to the men's desires. Queensberry lifted his glass in salute, with the flame from the tall candle in the centre of the table reflecting in the glass. "I believe you are considering joining our party, Eskbank."

"Indeed, I am, Queensberry," Lord Eskbank agreed. "After due consideration and taking your advice, the Court Party seems my natural home."

"A wise choice, Eskbank, a wise choice indeed. Welcome aboard." Queensberry sipped at his claret, eyed Eskbank over the rim and listened as a cart clattered past. "Let's consider the present economic and political state of the nation."

Lord Eskbank nodded. He sat back in the comfortable armchair and nodded to the single manservant who remained in the room. "Is he safe?"

"That's Campbell," Queensberry said. "He won't say anything. I can guarantee his silence."

Eskbank relaxed a little.

"We'll go back a century," Queensberry said. "We both know that King James VI tried to bring Scotland and England closer after he added the English throne to that of Scotland."

Eskbank nodded. "Yes, My Lord."

"And we both know further attempts to unite the two kingdoms were made at various times in the latter part of the seventeenth century."

"None succeeded," Eskbank said.

"None succeeded," Queensberry agreed. "Discussions began again last year, as you know. There are a couple of major stumbling blocks. The Scottish Kirk does not trust the Anglicans, and the English parliament vehemently opposes the Scots having free trade with English colonies in the Americas."

"Protectionism rules supreme," Eskbank said. "It's a shame our Darien colony failed."

"It is," Queensberry agreed. "I'll come to that in a minute. In 1700, Sir Edward Seymour, the Tory leader in the English House of Commons, said Scotland was a beggar and whoever married a beggar could only expect a louse for her portion." He leaned back in his chair. "And that's the Tory opinion of Scotland."

Before Eskbank finished the claret in his glass, Campbell added more, then stepped back, expressionless.

"Away back in 1688, the so-called Glorious Revolution placed William of Orange and his wife, Mary, on the Scottish throne." Queensberry lifted a be-ringed finger to prevent the servant from refilling his glass. "Dutch William arrived after we rid ourselves of the Catholic King James VII and at the invitation of the Scottish Convention of Estates."

"Queen Mary was entitled to rule through her Stuart blood," Eskbank said.

"Precisely so," Queensberry agreed, "and she was a good Protestant, like William. Our parliament got rid of the Estate of Bishops and became a much stronger body. You'll be aware that King William tried to control Scotland by appointing ministers, like myself, Argyll and Atholl. Aristocrats such as us have followings and the power to appoint clients."

"I am aware of that," Eskbank said. "I am not so aware why King William accepted the crown."

"William of Orange was involved in a long war with the French," Queensberry replied. "He welcomed our manpower to defend his territories, and the fact that Scotland and England are both Protestant helped."

Eskbank nodded. "William was the guardian of Protestantism."

"Don't make too much of that," Queensberry said. "In the last war, Roman Catholic Spain was his main ally. He used his religion when it suited him." He sipped at his claret. "Maybe he was sincere, although I believe defending the Dutch Republic was his prime objective."

Lord Eskbank glanced at Campbell, who refilled his glass.

"As one would expect, the Scottish nobles fell out about William's accession to the throne," Queensberry said. "Augmenting the situation were disagreements between Scotland and England. William's war with France was expensive in Scottish lives; he was a poor general, and our soldiers were often at the forefront of his bloody defeats. The wars compromised our Continental trade, while the English Royal Navy, the navy of our ally against the French, used their Navigation Laws to prevent us trading with North America." Queensberry watched carefully as Lord Eskbank shifted in his seat. "In short, Eskbank, Scotland had the worst of all worlds, fighting a war with no benefit to us. Then came King William's Ill Years, when bad weather ruined our harvests and produced famine."

"I remember," Eskbank said. "I had a lot of trouble with flooded mines after the heavy rain."

"We tried to revive our fortunes with a trading company known now as the Darien Company. I believed you invested rather heavily in it?"

Lord Eskbank nodded. "I did, damn it all," he said. "A great deal of my money sunk into the swamps of Central America."

"Our English allies refused to support the scheme; William valued his Spanish allies more than his Scottish subjects, and the planning was poor," Queensberry said. "Many people began to clamour for an end to the Regal Union, so we no longer share a king with England, and we can gang our ain gait."

"I have heard that mentioned," Lord Eskbank agreed.

"With no shared monarch, we would not be involved in the

Continental wars, would not lose so many men in battle or disease and could trade with whoever we liked in Europe," Queensberry said.

"What do you think?" Lord Eskbank asked.

"I believe the opposite," Queensberry said. "And for many reasons. I believe we should have a parliamentary as well as a regal union with England. Firstly, our soldiers, the Queen's soldiers, are engaged in a war in Europe against a very dangerous man. If Louis XIV of France wins, he will dominate Europe in a manner no monarch has for centuries. Secondly, an English union will allow us to trade with their American colonies, and thirdly," he dropped his voice, "if we arrange it well, the commissioners who approve the union could have financial and maybe other rewards."

"Financial rewards?" Lord Eskbank looked up as Queensberry had hoped he would.

"We should be rewarded for helping the fight for Europe's freedom from tyranny, don't you think?" Queensberry asked smoothly while signalling Campbell to refill Eskbank's glass.

"Indeed I do," Eskbank agreed.

"The English will benefit from a union as we will, Eskbank," Queensberry said. "Queen Anne has asked me to steer the Treaty of Parliamentary Union through the Estates for the benefit of both our nations."

"Will we both benefit?" Eskbank asked, looking sideways at the man people called the Union Duke.

Queensberry nursed his glass. "Scotland is stifling because of European and English protectionism. We need trade to thrive, England needs our men to fight against King Louis, and they need to ensure the French influence does not spread over here. If the exiled House of Stuart returned to power in Scotland, the nation's ruler would lean towards Catholic France rather than Protestant England."

Lord Eskbank nodded. "That would never do," he said. "There would be civil war."

"Quite possibly, and French armies tramping all over the country. We'll have to overturn this Act of Security our parliament has passed," Queensberry said. "That Act says that Scotland and England can't share a monarch unless the English parliament grants Scotland free trade with the plantations, and guarantees the Scottish parliament, religion, liberty and trade are free from English or any other foreign influence."

Lord Eskbank nodded. "We should certainly overturn that Act," he said.

Queensberry nodded. "Then there is the Wine Act that allows trade with France even if our shared monarch is at war with that nation, and the Peace and War Act that allows Scotland to make peace even if England is at war. These acts are surely hostile to the Regal Union."

"I agree," Lord Eskbank said, nodding to emphasise his understanding.

"I presume you will support me in opposing these measures and pushing for a full Parliamentary Union with England?" Queensberry asked. "Of course, you must be worrying about your gambling debts, the money you owe me. Think no more of them, Eskbank. Your support will be more than sufficient payment."

"You have my promissory notes," Eskbank reminded.

"I have them here." Queensberry produced them, smiled, and burned them, one at a time, at the tall candle. The papers curled, smoked and burst into flames. Queensberry held the burning paper until the flames licked his fingers, then dropped the charred remnants into the fireplace. "And now I have none. Do you I have your word?"

"You have my word," Eskbank said as the ashes of one of his burdens blew away in a blast from the flue.

"That's sufficient for me," Queensberry smiled. "I believe you have also agreed on the marriage between Sir Hugh Crichton and your daughter."

"I have, My Lord," Eskbank said.

"A good choice of husband," Queensberry approved. "Sir Hugh has also joined the Court Party. On your recommendation, he tells me."

"Indeed, My Lord."

"And My Lord Threipmuir met with an accident, I hear," Queensberry said.

"Yes, My Lord," Eskbank agreed. "He was hunting in the Pentland Hills and fell into a waterfall."

"How unfortunate for him," Queensberry said. "Still, it's an ill wind that blows no good, and his demise favours our cause, eh?"

"Indeed, My Lord," Eskbank agreed.

"Excellent," Queensberry said. "I have kept copies of the promissory notes, of course, which I will retain until I have proof of your dedication to the Union."

"Of course," Eskbank said, and they toasted each other in mutual suspicion and dislike.

CHAPTER 19

EDINBURGH, SUMMER 1704

Elizabeth Ramsay posed in front of the looking glass before she turned around. Wearing nothing but her new string of pearls, she smiled at Lord Eskbank.

"They suit me, I think."

"They do," Lord Eskbank agreed.

"Where did you get them?" Elizabeth asked, running the pearls through her fingers.

"From a reputable person," Lord Eskbank said. "They are Scottish freshwater pearls fished from the River Tay. I believe they have an interesting history with royal connections."

"Let's add to it, John," Elizabeth said, stepping towards him.

Eskbank smiled. "Keep them on," he said.

"I intend to," Elizabeth said, shifting her upper body so the pearls swung to and fro. "Don't they make a lovely sound? Come on, my lord, let's make pearl music together."

Lord Eskbank began to remove his clothes.

※

Marlborough's army woke at two in the morning, with half-asleep men breaking up the camp and packing the tents onto wagons to be driven to Reutlingen. NCOs and officers supervised, snarling superfluous orders to hide their anxiety. Camp followers and children bustled around, getting underfoot, and Rachel came to say a brief goodbye to Flockhart.

"Don't do anything foolish," Rachel said. "Stay alive and keep out of harm and cannonball's way."

"I'll do my best," Flockhart promised.

Rachel touched his arm and walked away. Flockhart watched her climb onto a wagon until the drums summoned him back to duty.

The Allied army marched towards the French positions, men aware they would be fighting in a few hours, knowing the enemy might kill or hideously maim them, and hiding their fear behind black humour.

"Think of the booty when we beat the Frenchies again," Leishman said. "Cheer up, Peter; you look like you lost a guinea and found a farthing."

Young forced a smile. "If I lost a guinea, I wouldn't be here," he said. "I'd be on my hands and knees, scouring the ground until I found it!"

Marlborough commanded ninety squadrons of cavalry and fifty-one battalions of infantry. Along with the fourteen Scots, English, Irish, and Welsh infantry battalions, there were Hanoverians, Danish, Hessians, and Dutch. The British also contributed nineteen mounted squadrons, with seven cavalry regiments, including two of dragoons.

"Who commands our cavalry?" Young asked.

"Lieutenant-General Henry Lumley commands the horse, and Major-General Charles Ross commands the dragoons," Leishman told him. "They're both good men."

Flockhart watched the cavalry jingle past, thousands of mounted men with ornate uniforms and sharpened swords, a picture of martial glory determined to close with the enemy, maim and kill.

Cavalry are the prettiest of soldiers and as brutal as any.

The British infantry marched in three brigades. Brigadier-General Archibald Rowe commanded one brigade, his fellow Scot, Brigadier-General James Ferguson, the second, and Brigadier Frederick Hamilton, the third. Flockhart did not see the generals, only the back of the man immediately in front, and Leishman at his side as they marched forward through early morning mist. The drums kept them in step, beating them to battle and throbbing through their heads.

The army advanced in columns through the early hours of the morning, with the rising sun burning away the faint mist and glistening from the dew. Fields of grain waved in the morning light as the forward Allied squadrons pushed back parties of French and Bavarian foragers.

"It's a beautiful morning," Flockhart observed, looking at the sun easing through the pearl-grey mist. As always, he appreciated the morning light. After years of campaigning, he was weather-beaten and hard, with his chest and arms as powerful as ever and his legs as strong as any other British infantryman.

"It is indeed," Leishman agreed. "A good day for a battle."

Flockhart looked over his shoulder, where smoke from cooking fires rose over the now distant Allied camp as the wagons trundled away. It was strange to think that somebody on one of the wagons cared whether he lived or died.

"Face your front, Flockhart!" Sergeant Dunn growled. "Yesterday is behind us, and we'll need all our concentration to win today."

Flockhart jerked his head to face forward. All around him, the Allied army marched forward with determined, grim faces. Their shoes rose and fell on the damp ground, with the jingle of cavalry a background to the constant beat of the kettle drums.

Nobody sang.

Marlborough followed the army, riding in his campaign carriage and giving orders to his senior officers. At seven in the morning, the Allied drums signalled for the army to halt, and the senior officers rode to some rising ground, extended their spyglasses, and studied the plain of Hochstadt spreading before them.

"Look ahead," Dunn said.

Flockhart nodded. "I see them," he said.

The enemy encampment was spread over the plain, with the Bavarians and French seemingly content to remain within their tents.

"Have they not seen us?" Leishman asked. "Have their scouts and foragers not reported that we're coming?" He grinned. "Did they not hear the drums?"

As Leishman spoke, the thunder of French and Bavarian drums reached the Allies.

"They're beating to quarters at last," Young said.

As the officers ordered the Allies into battle formation, Flockhart watched the enemy wake up. Messengers galloped from unit to unit across the plain, infantry battalions and cavalry squadrons formed up, and artillerymen ran to their guns. The sun warmed away the last of the mist, so the coming battleground was bright.

Flockhart peered forward. He knew the enemy might kill him today or, worse, leave him mutilated and crippled for life, but at that moment, he did not want to be anywhere else. He could understand the appeal of military life when he saw both armies formed up in their bright uniforms and with the Colours arrayed, limp but evocative, above each regiment.

"Armies are very colourful things," Flockhart mused.

"The glory attracts fools like us," Leishman replied.

The British and Hanoverians wore various shades of scarlet, with the Dutch and Austrians wearing grey. Flockhart saw the dark blues of the Hessians and the formidable Prussians in the same colour.

"Men dress in such pretty clothes to slaughter each other," Leishman continued. "How simple we are to fall for the blandishments of our leaders."

Flockhart grunted, concentrating on watching the enemy in

front as the Allied drums signalled the advance. Flockhart stepped on again, with the French and Bavarian artillery opening fire when the columns came into range. A round shot slammed into the Royal Irish Regiment, killing a private, the first casualty of what would prove to be a bloody day.

"That's heavy metal," Sergeant Dunn said. "The Frenchies are firing twenty-four pounders by the sound."

"I'll duck if a ball comes this way," Flockhart said.

Flockhart ignored the French and Bavarian foragers running back to their lines as the Allies advanced. He saw smoke and flames curling upwards as the enemy put torches to the small villages in front of their lines that the Allies might have used for cover.

"Some people have already lost their homes because of this battle," Leishman murmured.

"They outnumber us in infantry and artillery," Young said. "Does Marlborough not see that?"

"Corporal John knows what he's doing," Dunn replied. "Obey orders and trust your luck."

"You won't be harmed unless it's your time," Leishman said. "And if it's your time, nothing can save you."

When the battle was imminent, Marlborough left his campaign carriage and mounted his horse. Flockhart glimpsed him, wearing a scarlet uniform with his knight of the garter ribbon bright on his chest, and then the commander-in-chief was gone, and other matters occupied Flockhart's mind.

With the Allied columns facing the French, the regimental chaplains began their usual Christian service, with psalms ringing across the land.

"We're singing about God's love as we prepare to slaughter other Christians," Flockhart said. "Is that not strange?"

"It's always been that way," Leishman murmured. "Our Christian duty is to obey our leaders and fight for the queen."

"Ah," Flockhart nodded. "I thought it was to love one another."

"That's after we've slaughtered half of them," Leishman said.

The drums hammered their orders, splitting the Allied army as Marlborough and Eugene rode to inspect the enemy positions. Forty cavalry squadrons rode beside them in case the French tried to capture the Allied leaders.

Marlborough pushed his cavalry across the Nebel River, with Eugene's Imperialists on the right wing of the Allied army, struggling through dense woodland as Marlborough's force halted, watching.

"The Austrians are a bit tardy," Young said. "I hope they fight better than they march."

"They had difficult territory to traverse," Sergeant Dunn replied. "Eugene has the harder journey here, moving through a forest against superior numbers." He smoothed a hand along the staff of his halberd. "Eugene's men are not all Austrian; he also has Danish and Prussian infantry."

"They're all bloody Austrian to me," Young said.

As the Imperialists formed up, the enemy artillery hammered their infantry, blasting bloody lanes in their ranks. Eugene's reply was late and less effective due to the ground being uneven and riven with ditches. Adding to the carnage, Marlborough's guns on the Allied left wing tore bloody holes in the enemy's ranks.

The combined French and Bavarian army waited for the Allied advance, rank upon serried rank of the most successful infantry in the world, backed by massed squadrons of cavalry and parks of artillery. Colours hung above the regiments, and the martial tapping of drums reached across to the Allied army.

"I'll wager you wish you were back underground now, Davie," Leishman said.

"You'd lose your money," Flockhart told him. "I'd rather die in the open than live as a slave down the pit." He inspected his musket, checked the flint was sharp, and looked to his front. He was among his friends, with the regimental Colours to his left and the drums rattling their incessant tune.

The Imperialists continued to take their formation as the sun rose, birds sang, and Flockhart wondered why men should kill each other on such a beautiful morning. The artillery hammered on, blasting men who could neither defend themselves nor retaliate. The infantry stood in dense, colourful blocks, each man praying and hoping the enemy gunners did not target their battalion.

"Stand your ground," Sergeant Dunn said as he walked along his platoon, pushing men into position with his halberd. "Our turn will come in time. Fill the gaps and stand your ground."

Flockhart held his musket close, watched the powder smoke drift slowly across the rival armies and hoped he could get at least one of the French gunners at the end of his bayonet. He watched Marlborough ride along the front of his army, not even flinching as a French cannonball landed close by.

"Marlborough's a brave man," Leishman commented.

"I wonder what he plans to do?" Flockhart asked.

Dunn leaned on his halberd. "By the look of our positions," he said, "he'll send the bulk of the infantry to attack the villages on the enemy's flanks, launch our cavalry against the Frenchies and have the Imperialists keep their left wing occupied." He looked up as a cannonball screamed overhead. "He never asks my advice, though."

Young gave a nervous smile. "Maybe he should."

"Maybe he should," Dunn agreed.

Gallopers hurried from Marlborough's small group of staff officers, taking orders to the subordinate commanders. Flockhart watched one gorgeously dressed young officer approach Lieutenant General Lord John Cutts and Major General Wilks, commanding the twenty-strong column on the Allied left.

"That young gallant is the Prince of Hesse," Dunn said as a man approached the Royals. "He's bringing a message for us. Check your flints, boys; we could be fighting soon."

"Things are happening," Leishman murmured.

The Royals' drums began to tap, ordering the regiment

forward, and Lord Cutts' column moved towards the village of Blindheim, known to the British as Blenheim, at the right of the French line. They marched slowly, keeping in step with the officers in front and the Colours held in the centre of each battalion.

"This could get bloody," Leishman said. "Look at the numbers the Frenchies have."

The French had twenty-seven battalions of infantry in and around Blenheim, including some of their best men, and waited behind entrenchments and palisades. Flockhart saw the French had barricaded every street with trees, heavy wooden chests, and wagons, behind which the defenders waited, muskets at the ready.

"We'll need the surgeons after this day," Leishman displayed his love of statistics. "Corporal John has seventeen surgeons ready for the wounded."

"Plus the regimental surgeons," Flockhart added, not to be outdone.

Cutts' column consisted of four brigades, including two British, with Brigadier-General Rowe, colonel of the Royal Scots Fusiliers, commanding one and Brigadier-General Ferguson the other. A brigade of Hessians and another of Hanoverians completed the column. Marlborough formed the Allies with a line of infantry in the front and a double line of cavalry behind. A further line of infantry, commanded by the Earl of Orkney, remained in support.

"Look to your front," Sergeant Dunn shouted. "Keep your flints sharp, fire when ordered and keep in formation."

French artillery fire ploughed through the Allied ranks, causing incredible pain as the iron balls tore off arms and legs, eviscerated men and left screaming remnants strewn on the already bloody ground.

Flockhart saw the French technique as they aimed the balls to bounce along the ground. Each landing spread stones, dirt, and fear into the Allied ranks before they crashed into an unfortunate file of defenceless soldiers.

The drums continued to tap as Lord Cutts' column pushed forward. Twenty battalions and fifteen squadrons strong, Cutts' men advanced, suffering under the French cannonade yet keeping perfect discipline.

"Close up!" Captain Brisbane ordered. "Close the gaps!"

Flockhart heard the swish of feet through the grass, the harsh breathing of nervous men, and the flapping of regimental and company Colours. Always in the background, dominating their thoughts and ordering their movement, the tapping of the drums. He cursed as something warm spattered over his face, wiped away Private Simpson's brains and blood, and marched on.

The column advanced to the banks of the river Nebel, with French outposts withdrawing before them amidst an inconsequential spatter of musketry.

"I'd say the French have two battalions facing us," Sergeant Dunn shouted above the sound of the guns. "They might fire a volley before they retract."

Flockhart grunted. He felt the heat of the sun through his hat and heard a terrible scream as a French cannonball crashed into a file of men. The Allied infantry closed the gap and marched on, a line of British in the van, then the Hessians, then British, and finally the Hanoverians.

"We'll take these water mills," Dunn said as the French garrison withdrew from a pair of mills beside the Nebel River. As the Allies approached, the French set fire to the mills, which blazed furiously.

"Maybe we won't," Flockhart commented quietly. He lifted his chin as the enemy twenty-four-pounder fired, and cannon balls crashed into the Allied column, knocking down men and throwing hats, muskets, heads, and pieces of human bodies into the air. A film of blood ascended to fall on the surrounding troops. Flockhart grunted, looked down momentarily, then lifted his chin, blinking away the red mist.

The Allies leading line forded the Nebel, splashing knee and thigh deep to cross to the marshy ground on the far side.

The drummers struggled over the bogland, with their beats irregular until the NCOs snarled at them to concentrate. When the leading British troops were only thirty paces from their earthworks, the French and Bavarian garrison of Blenheim fired. Volleys of musketry crashed out, and musket balls screamed and whistled among the advancing British.

Out in front, Archibald Rowe's brigade took most of the initial casualties as they approached the enemy palisades.

"We'll only get one shot at them," Rowe shouted. "We can't afford to stop and reload, so don't fire until I strike the palisade with my sword."

The leading line understood. The infantry marched, grim-faced, into the storm of musket balls and case shot. The defenders' cannon fired continually, with the smoke soon forming a screen through which the British advanced. When Rowe's brigade was fifteen yards from Blenheim, the French infantry fired another ferocious volley, backed by the fusils of dragoons outside the village. The orange flashes of massed muskets flared through the smoke like petals of death.

Dismounted and striding ahead, Rowe kept his men in hand, refusing to give the order to fire until he thrust his sword into the enemy's palisade. Men and officers fell, dead and wounded, screaming or writhing in silent agony all around him. He reached the palisade, halted, and rammed his sword into the timber.

"Fire!" he said, and the troops finally fired at the defenders.

The two forces clashed with muskets and bayonets, British soldiers trying to clamber over the palisades and the French equally determined to throw them back. Fresh infantry surged forward to reinforce the defence, firing volley after volley at the British.

After a prolonged struggle, the defenders pushed the Allies back and slowly, reluctantly, the British withdrew, still firing. Rowe fell, shot in the thigh, along with the commanding officer and second-in-command of the Royal Scots Fusiliers. The French released their cavalry, hoping to catch the Allies while they were disorganised, but the Hessians, led by Brigadier Wilkes, formed up and repelled them with musketry and a steel hedge of presented bayonets.

As the French and Bavarians repulsed Rowe's brigade with thirty per cent casualties, Ferguson's brigade and the Hanoverians crossed the Nebel River beside the lower of the two burning mills and advanced to the front.

"What is Ferguson's brigade trying?" Flockhart asked.

Leishman shouted above the noise. "They'll attempt to get between Blenheim and the Danube to take the village in flank."

The French commander had dismounted his dragoons and stationed them in an orchard. He waited until Ferguson's brigade came close and met them with blasts of grapeshot and concentrated musketry that pushed them back, cursing, frustrated, and still fighting. With Colonel Dormer of the First Foot Guards killed, the brigade reformed, filled the gaps in its ranks, and advanced again with the same result.

As the British recoiled in bloody chaos, a French cavalry attack hit the right flank of Rowe's brigade, scattering some men and capturing the Scots Fusiliers' Colours. The situation looked bad until the second line of red-coated Hessian infantry attacked the French cavalry with volleys and bayonets and recovered the Colours.

"They're slaughtering us," Young yelled.

"We're keeping them occupied," Sergeant Dunn said calmly. "Check your bayonets." Like all the others, he was speckled with the blood of dead and wounded men, and his face was black with powder smoke. "We're going in again."

Flockhart took a deep breath of the acrid air and glanced at Blenheim village. The palisades were scored with British cannon and musket balls but stood as tall and defiant as ever. Bavarian and French heads bobbed above the timber and earthworks.

"Ready, lads!" Dunn shouted as the drums rolled again, and

the officers marched to the front, swords drawn. Captain Brisbane did not look back, trusting his company to follow. The Colours floated above the regiment, smoke-stained, one ripped by enemy shot but undeniably rallying spots.

"Keep in formation, men," Dunn said and stepped ahead, holding his halberd.

The Royals marched on to the beat of the drum straight into the French musketry. Once again, Flockhart saw the orange spurts from the smoke-wreathed palisades and heard the whistle of lead balls and screams of wounded men. The Royals halted to fire a volley, fixed bayonets, and charged, but the French behind the palisade held firm and repelled the third attack as they had the previous two.

"These Frenchies know how to fight," Leishman gasped. His hat was missing and his tunic torn, but he was unhurt.

The French cavalry threatened Cutts' flank again until Lumley sent five Allied squadrons against the enemy's eight. The French cavalry drew their fusils and immediately fired.

"Look at that!" Leishman said as the British cavalry ignored the fusil fire and charged, sword in hand. They pressed the French back until more French cavalry arrived, and the infantry in Blenheim added volleys of musketry. Outnumbered and taking casualties from the village and French swords, the British cavalry withdrew, losing officers and men.

"The French won that one," Young said.

"Maybe they did, but the cavalry took the pressure from us," Flockhart said, "so they did their job."

"Those Frenchies were the *Gens d'Armes*," Sergeant Dunn said. "One of their best regiments."

The British cavalry withdrew in disorder until the Hessian infantry advanced again and fired a few volleys that stopped the French cavalry. Horses and men tumbled to the ground, kicking and screaming.

"Thank God for the Hessians," Flockhart said.

"We're not doing well so far," Sergeant Dunn commented.

"The French have repulsed us from Blenheim and pushed us away from Lutzingen." He stretched his neck, staring across the smoke-wreathed field towards Eugene's flank. "The Prussians and Danes are having no better luck, lads. The Frenchies are winning this battle unless Corporal John has something in his locker."

CHAPTER 20

BLENHEIM, BAVARIA, SUMMER 1704

※

After the double repulse, Lieutenant General Lord Cutts led his men against Blenheim again, with the defender, the Marquis de Clerambault, pulling in further infantry. De Clerambault made every house a strongpoint, and the streets and alleys were densely packed with men.

"Where are the Frenchies coming from?" Leishman asked as he saw the reinforcements marching into Blenheim. "We're attracting them like bluebottles to a pile of dung."

"They're coming from the right wing," Dunn said. "I hope Marlborough can see what's happening."

"We're not making much impression on their defences," Flockhart said.

The Royals watched as the Prince of Holstein-Beck led two Dutch brigades in an attack on the village of Oberglau. The defenders, French and Irish, held their fire until the Dutch were close, then blasted them with volleys that broke the attack. The Dutch retired hastily, a mishmash of confused and frightened men. Marlborough had to send in three more infantry battalions plus artillery to restore the situation, but the honours had gone to France.

"Now we can see why the French are reputed to be the best soldiers in the world," Leishman said. "If the French had counterattacked after Oberglau, they'd have split our army in two."

"Keep pushing!" Dunn ordered, his face powder-blackened and his hat torn by a musket ball. "We are the Royal Regiment! Leave the decisions to the senior officers and concentrate on your duty! Check your flints; we're going forward again!"

The Royals advanced into Bavarian and French volleys, losing men as they slid across grass greasy with Scottish and Allied blood. They fired in return and closed to fight at the palisades with bayonets and musket butts until the Allied drums beat the retire.

With the French and Bavarians pouring in men to defend their village strongpoints, other sections of their line were weakening.

"The villages are where it matters," Leishman said. "We're draining the French strength here, and Marlborough will know it."

Flockhart nodded. The Royals had withdrawn temporarily, and he cleaned his fouled musket barrel. "They're draining our strength, too. We can't keep advancing against an impregnable defence."

At around five in the evening, as Flockhart and the Royals battled with the French in Blenheim, Marlborough ordered the bulk of his army across the Nebel and attacked the main French body.

"What's happening?" Young asked.

"Corporal John knows the French have weakened their centre to defend Blenheim," Dunn explained. "He's hitting them with all his force."

Flockhart thumbed a new flint and glanced over to his right, where rolling volleys and thick smoke showed the fighting was intense. He could not see anything through the smoke and concentrated on loading his musket. The Royals were back at their starting point, counting their casualties and preparing for a fourth assault.

"Can you feel that?" Leishman asked. "I felt a breeze."

Flockhart looked up as a slanting wind temporarily shifted the smoke. He watched the fighting to his right as Marlborough's main force thrust through the French centre. When the French infantry scattered, Marlborough ordered his cavalry forward. Flockhart heard the thin trill of a trumpet and saw the Allied cavalry charge at their French counterparts.

The French cavalry, thinned of infantry support by the relentless assaults on the villages, stood for a few moments. They halted, fired their fusils at the great mass of Allied horsemen with their drawn swords, then turned away, withdrew and reformed.

"The cavalry is doing well," Leishman was watching the centre.

Flockhart nodded, waiting for the drums to order the Royals to advance once more.

The Allied cavalry charged forward, slashing with their swords as the French fire emptied a dozen saddles. When the supporting Allied infantry fired volleys from extreme range, further weakening the French, smoke blanketed the scene. Flockhart saw some horsemen emerging with the lower half of their mounts hidden in the smoke, tendrils trailing from their heads.

The Allied cavalry charged, withdrew, reformed and charged again, with horses screaming and men, Allied, French and Bavarian, falling to be trampled by the heavy hooves in the next attack. In the intervals when the Allied cavalry reformed, infantry fired at the densely packed French, moving closer each time so their shots were more effective.

"The French are breaking!" The shouts came from the Allied centre. "The French cavalry are running!"

"The French in front of us are not running!" Sergeant Dunn

grunted as Blenheim's defenders fired another volley, refusing to give way despite the developments in the centre.

As the French cavalry broke, the Allies followed, cutting them down or forcing them into the River Danube. As the cavalry fought, Marlborough ordered his artillery and Hanoverian infantry to deal with the stubborn French infantry. Abandoned by their cavalry, the white-coated French infantry refused to run, closing ranks as Hanoverian volleys and blasts of case shot massacred them. Ultimately, the Allied cavalry charged, destroying the survivors who died, still lined in disciplined ranks.

"Brave men," Leishman murmured. "What a waste of brave men."

The left of the French and Bavarian army retired hurriedly, while the garrison in Blenheim realised their position was becoming untenable. As Ferguson's brigade watched the front, the garrison attempted to slip out of the rear, only to meet waiting Allied infantry.

"They're trapped," Flockhart said. "They can surrender or fight to the finish."

"Let's hope they surrender," Leishman replied. "Although I can't see the French giving up easily."

The Scots Dragoons foiled the garrison's second attempt to break out, and they withdrew behind their palisades, now isolated from the main French army but still dangerous and very numerous.

"We'll have to attack them again," Flockhart said, looking around the depleted ranks of the Royals.

"They're a stubborn bunch," Leishman said.

"Check your flints are sharp, boys," Dunn said. "Fill up with ammunition and keep your bayonets loose in their scabbards. Marlborough will have to send us in again."

Now a veteran, Flockhart had automatically prepared for the next assault. "How many French are there, I wonder?"

"Thousands," Dunn replied dryly, "but Corporal John is going to sort them out."

The Allies brought in reinforcements and surrounded Blenheim village to ensure the garrison could not escape. Flockhart watched the horses drag in the artillery and watched as the bombardment began.

"Poor buggers under that," Leishman said as the cannon fired solid shot to break down the walls and grape to thin out the defenders.

"It would be better if they parleyed," Flockhart agreed.

With the Allied guns still pounding the French and Bavarian positions, Marlborough sent reinforcements ready for a final attack.

"Ready, lads," Dunn said for the third time. He looked forward at Blenheim, stamped his feet and smoothed a hand over the haft of his halberd.

The drums hammered out their messages as the Allies readied themselves, and then the generals launched their men forward. The Earl of Orkney sent eight battalions against the French defending Blenheim's churchyard, and Lieutenant General Richard Ingoldsby led four battalions against the right of the village. A regiment of Irish Dragoons waited to support Ingoldsby, ready to exploit a breakthrough.

"Come on, boys!" Dunn said, striding forward. Flockhart took a deep breath and followed, marching in line with his musket loaded and his hat pulled low over his face.

The artillery fired over the advancing Allies and then stopped as the infantry blocked their line of fire. The Allies marched forward, losing more men to the defenders' fire. Once again, Flockhart heard the whine and whistle of passing musket balls as he walked into the wall of smoke that surrounded the village.

He saw the orange-white muzzle flares, automatically obeyed the order to aim and fire, and then the drums beat the charge.

Weakened and dazed after the day's fighting and intense

bombardment, the French still tried to fight, but the Allies swept on with bayonets and muskets. This time, the attackers had the advantage.

Flockhart advanced with Leishman on one side and Sergeant Dunn in front. He saw Lamb stop beneath the palisade, order a private to bend over and used his back to help mount the timber stakes. Lamb was laughing as he landed among the defenders, slashing to the right and left with his sword and bayonetted musket.

"Come on, Davie!" Leishman shouted. He clambered up the rough timber with Flockhart, half a head shorter, a few feet behind.

The cannonade had taken effect on the defenders, and Flockhart jumped down to a scene of carnage, with dying men and pieces of men strewn among the desperate living. He saw Leishman struggling with a slender Frenchman, feint right, and plunge his bayonet into his opponent's belly, rip sideways and withdraw. More French appeared, shouting as they attempted to push the Allies out.

"Come on, lads!" Lamb shouted, bounding forward with his platoon at his back.

Flockhart sparred with a wounded Frenchman, allowed him to escape and followed Leishman into the waiting French. Leishman charged, shouting, and a Frenchman parried his lunge and disarmed him in seconds.

Leishman stood still with his eyes wide and his hands at his side, momentarily helpless.

"Adam!" Flockhart shouted, running forward. He saw the Frenchman poised above Leishman with his bayonet ready to plunge down and leapt the final few feet. The Frenchman saw him coming a fraction too late.

"Adam!" Flockhart yelled again. His bayonet clashed against the French musket, diverting the bayonet a vital eighteen inches so it rammed into the ground instead of through Leishman. Flockhart felt the thrill of contact. Unable to halt his leap, he crashed into the Frenchman, so they fell in a tangled heap.

Flockhart reached for the man's throat, hearing somebody snarling in animal-like fury. He saw the Frenchman's eyes glaring wide, saw his mouth contorting and tightened his grip. Since he worked down the pits, Flockhart had powerful hands and arms. He felt the Frenchman's throat constrict under his fingers and squeezed, ignoring everything else except his desire to kill.

Flockhart felt the man's life end. He knew he had killed him, watched something fade from his enemy's eyes and released his grip. Despite the battle raging around him, Flockhart stared at the Frenchman, feeling a sense of comradeship with the dead man he could not explain.

That's the first man I've killed with my bare hands. I am sorry, my friend, but I had no choice.

"Davie," Leishman had rolled clear and stood at Flockhart's side with his bayonetted musket in hand. The French had withdrawn behind the smoke of the burning buildings. The only Frenchmen Flockhart could see were the dead and wounded.

"You saved my life, Davie," Leishman sounded shaken. "You are more than just a bottle companion or a colleague, Davie; you are a friend."

Unsure what to say, Flockhart said nothing. He stood still, leaving the Frenchman's broken body on the ground. He lifted his musket and stared forward. Across the village, the fighting had stopped as French drums beat for a parley. When a chance gust of wind momentarily blew away the smoke, the two enemy forces stared at each other in mutual respect. As the fighting ended, all hatred faded away, and two groups of men met, panting, exhausted and glad to be alive amidst the crazed monstrosity of war.

"What's all this about?" Flockhart asked. "Why are we killing each other?"

"Because it's our duty, lad," Sergeant Dunn replied. "It's our duty to the Queen."

Flockhart looked at the man he had strangled. The Frenchman lay twisted and pathetic in death, with a face no different to many in the Royals. Flockhart wondered if he had a sweetheart, if his mother hoped for his return home, and if he was a veteran or a pressed recruit.

"Thank you," Leishman patted Flockhart's shoulder. "I'll never forget."

Flockhart could not control his tears, although he had not cried since his first day in the pit when he was four years old.

CHAPTER 21

BLENHEIM, BAVARIA, JUNE 1704

As the French in Blenheim surrendered, Flockhart learned the extent of the Allied victory. The French army had dominated Europe for decades, with Louis the Fourteenth, the Sun King, threatening to become the most powerful man on the continent. Europe had quailed when French armies conquered wherever they marched, creating a reputation for invincibility.

Marlborough and Eugene's victory at the Battle of Blenheim brought that idea to a shuddering crash. Twenty-four battalions of French infantry and twelve squadrons of cavalry surrendered to the Allies, which was an unprecedented event.

"We've defeated them," Sergeant Dunn said in a tone of wonder. "According to Corporal John's secretary, we killed, wounded or captured forty thousand enemy soldiers, with a hundred and twenty-four cannons, all their tents and ammunition, over a hundred and seventy standards, nearly a hundred and thirty Colours and God knows how many kettledrums." He sat on a French corpse, stuffing tobacco into his pipe. "If you lads had been through the last war when King Billy tried to be a general, you'd know what that meant."

"King William was a brave man," Leishman said.

"Oh, aye, there's no doubt about his courage," Dunn agreed. "He was a brave man but a mediocre general at best."

"What happens now?" Flockhart asked. "Have we won the war?" He thought about the uncertainty of peace. If Queen Anne decided to disband the Royals, he would be a footloose beggar with no home or reason for existence.

What about Rachel? The question surprised Flockhart. *Rachel can look after herself, probably better than I can.*

"What happens now?" Dunn repeated. "That's out of our hands, Davie boy." He grinned. "I'll tell you one thing, though. There will be a bounty for this day's work."

"A bounty?" Peter Young looked interested. Flockhart had hardly seen him during the battle, but now he appeared, looking strangely clean.

"Aye. We'll all get a little extra pay for winning this battle," Sergeant Dunn said.[1] He grinned, puffing a coil of smoke from his pipe. "Did you lads hear about the meeting between Marshal Tallard and Corporal John?"

"No," Leishman said. "We don't mix in that sort of company."

"A bit beneath you, are they?" Dunn drew on his pipe. "Well, according to Marlborough's secretary, Tallard bowed and said, 'I congratulate you on defeating the best soldiers in the world.'"

Corporal John politely returned the bow and replied, "Your lordship, I assume, excepts those troops who have had the honour to beat them."

Flockhart and Leishman smiled, with Young looking confused until Leishman explained what Marlborough had meant.

Dunn blew out more smoke. "Marlborough allowed Tallard

---

1. The bounty for those who fought at Blenheim was one pound for a private soldier, two pounds for a sergeant and fourteen pounds for a lieutenant; a full colonel pocketed seventy-two pounds. A generous government doubled the bounty for wounded officers.

to shelter in his carriage after the battle, for the French marshal had private grief, as his son had died in the battle."

Flockhart looked away, remembering the soldier he had strangled. "Losing a battle and a son on the same day would be hard."

"That's a soldier's lot," Young said callously. "Tallard probably wanted his son to have riches and glory, not an ounce of lead in the guts."

Leishman began to clean his musket. "Marshal Tallard isn't the only man mourning today," he said. "There were six hundred and seventy British killed and more than fifteen hundred wounded. Our regiment was in the worst of the fighting, and we lost twelve officers, added to the thirty killed and wounded at Schellenberg a few weeks back."

"Too many," Flockhart said. "We'll be hard-pressed to find replacements."

Dunn eyed Flockhart, puffed his pipe, and said nothing.

Flockhart never learned how many of the Royals' rank and file died, but, judging by the gaps in the ranks, they paid a grievous price for Marlborough's victory.

"Does anybody have any spirits?" Dunn asked. "I always need a drink after a battle."

"Good idea, Sergeant," Young said.

Flockhart slumped down as reaction set in after the sights and sounds of terribly wounded men and the stench of raw blood. Already, the human ghouls were busy stripping and robbing the dead and slitting the occasional throat if an injured man objected to their ministrations. War always brought out the worst in people.

The drums sounded again, calling the Royals back to duty. Flockhart stood, thankful that somebody else made the decisions.

"Come on, lads," Sergeant Dunn said, removing his hat, dusting it by banging it against his thigh and replacing it on his head. "The drums are calling us to erect the tents."

Rachel was waiting when the officers organised the Royals. She peered at every face, trying to recognise people behind layers of powder smoke, blood, sweat and filth. She half-smiled when she saw Flockhart.

"I'm glad you are alive," Rachel said. "It saves me the trouble of finding a replacement soldier."

"I'm glad too," Flockhart looked at her, shaking his head. "You're a strange little thing, Rachel," he said. "You're not like the other wives and camp followers."

"I am what I am," Rachel said. "As you are what you are."

"How did you come to follow the drum?" Flockhart asked.

Rachel accompanied him to one of the few quiet areas of the camp and plumped down under a tree. Flockhart joined her, his mind still full of the horrors of battle.

"I was born to the drum," Rachel said. She pressed close to Flockhart, pleased to have his undivided attention. "My father was a soldier, although I never met him and don't know who he was." She leaned against the tree. "I am unsure if my mother met him more than once, either."

Flockhart nodded. "Is your mother still around?"

"She may be, I don't know. She vanished years ago. Mother was a camp follower," Rachel spoke without bitterness. "She was a temporary wife when she was lucky and a prostitute when things were bad. I grew up in one of the regimental brothels, or running free when my mother had a soldier to herself."

"That's a tough upbringing," Flockhart said.

Rachel looked away. "Maybe. It's all I've known." She was quiet for a while. "Few people wanted to know the little bastard girl I was or the woman I have become."

Flockhart sensed the hurt behind the words. "You've become a fine woman," he said.

Rachel shook her head and tossed her tangled hair from her face. "Do you know the first time a man was ever kind to me without expecting a reward?"

"No," Flockhart saw two men carrying a writhing casualty to the hospital tent. He was glad he had escaped serious injury.

"When you lent me your coat," Rachel said. She looked up at him, her face dirty and streaked with sweat through powder stains and her eyes pleading, although Flockhart was unsure what she wanted.

"You needed it," Flockhart said. "You looked scared," he paused. "And vulnerable."

Rachel nodded. "I was scared. You didn't have to do that."

"You reminded me of my sister," Flockhart explained.

"Tell me about her," Rachel demanded, lifting her chin.

More men walked past, some boasting of their supposed deeds, others quiet, and many looking shocked with experience of battle. One youngster was openly weeping, while the veterans looked nonchalant.

"She was a bit like you but younger," Flockhart said.

"Where is she now?" Rachel asked.

"She's dead," Flockhart replied.

"Oh," Rachel accepted the answer without further comment. Death was normal to her. She had seen men die of wounds or disease all her life. Men had marched proudly to battle in the morning and never returned or came back maimed or broken in body and mind.

"Will you stay in the army?" Rachel asked.

"I think so," Flockhart said. "It's a better life than I used to have."

"Somebody told me your old master could demand your return," Rachel said. She produced a short clay pipe and stuffed rich tobacco into the bowl.

"That's correct," Flockhart said guardedly.

"I hope he doesn't do that."

"So do I," Flockhart said. He hesitated for a moment. "Why? Why do you hope he doesn't do that?"

"You must know by now," Rachel said simply. "I like you, and you were kind to me."

Flockhart felt her stirring against him, pushing closer. He nodded. "You're different from the other women."

"I am not," Rachel denied immediately, then asked. "Which other women?"

"The other wives and the women in the brothels," Flockhart said.

"I am not a prostitute," Rachel told him, "and I don't want to be a temporary wife."

"Aren't all wives temporary?" Flockhart asked. "Down the pits, men and women could die any time, and few soldiers live long lives."

"When I choose my man," Rachel said. "I expect him to stay loyal to me, even when we're apart. I don't want him running to a prostitute or another woman as soon as I am not here."

Flockhart pulled his pipe from his pocket, swore when he saw the stem had snapped in half during the battle, tamped a mixture of tobacco and grass into the bowl and borrowed a light from a passing grenadier.

"Here," Rachel reached inside her top and handed him a twist of tobacco. "I can get you better tobacco than that rubbish you smoke," she said.

"Would you do that for the man you choose?" Flockhart asked.

"Yes," Rachel said. "I'd do that for you."

"Me?" Flockhart already knew the answer but sought confirmation. He wondered why any woman would wish an ex-slave as her man.

"You are the man I have chosen," Rachel said.

Flockhart puffed on the stub of his clay pipe. "That's good," he said. "That's good." He looked at her sideways, trying to smile. "I won't go running to any prostitutes; they are usually unlucky with me anyway."

Rachel smiled. "They would be even more unlucky if we were together." She exhaled a long ribbon of smoke. "When we're together," she amended.

"When we're together," Flockhart agreed.

CHAPTER 22

BLENHEIM, BAVARIA, SUMMER 1704

"Do you notice the difference in that woman today?" Leishman nodded to Rachel, who was busy washing clothes in a wooden tub.

"There's a little difference," Flockhart agreed, checking his musket for signs of rust. He had not told Leishman about his conversation with Rachel.

"She's cleaner," Leishman said. "She was always a midden, with a filthy face and tangled hair."

"So she was," Flockhart agreed. "She looks quite presentable now."

"She looks tasty," Leishman said. "She's certainly not the prettiest girl in the camp, but she has something."

Flockhart watched as Rachel worked, bending and rising over the wooden tub, with water splashing over the sides and her hips swaying with her effort. He saw her hands, red with cold, and wanted to do something to alleviate her discomfort. "She does have something, doesn't she?"

"She also lacks something," Leishman said.

"What's that?" Flockhart asked.

"A man," Leishman smiled. "Every one of these women has a

man among the battalion, even the oldest and ugliest, but not Rachel."

Flockhart nodded.

"She still likes you, Davie," Leishman said. "And looking at her now, you could do far worse."

"Aye, maybe I could," Flockhart said. "And she could do far better than me."

Leishman laughed. "She's a whore's bastard," he said. "She should be thankful to have any sort of man."

"I'm still legally a slave," Flockhart reminded. "Owned by Lord Eskbank. He could still drag me back to the pit, and if Rachel was my wife, he could grab her and condemn her to a lifetime of unpaid work underground."

Leishman counted his flints, arranging them in size order before carefully packing them away. "He could only do that if you had been married in a church by a Kirk minister. He'd have no legal authority over a mistress, or a temporary wife, or whatever you choose to call her."

Flockhart lifted his head. "I never thought of that," he said. He watched Rachel bending over the washing tub and smiled.

❇

"This is the last regiment he could be in," Mungo Redpath said. "The Royal Regiment, Pontius Pilate's Bodyguard."

"We've travelled halfway across Europe for this man," Ruth Gordon remarked. "And visited every blasted regiment Queen Anne has. Lord Eskbank must be desperate to locate one little serf."

"It's a matter of pride now," Redpath said. "For His Lordship and us. We'll lose our credibility if we can't bring him back."

Ruth nodded. "It's been a lucrative contract, but I've had enough travelling."

"There's been a battle here," Grant observed. "Look at all the dead bodies."

"Let's hope our man Flockhart is still alive," Gordon said. "Or we'll have to pick through all the dead to find proof."

"That's a tedious task," Redpath agreed, "especially after the ghouls have stripped them of their clothes."

"We'll cut off somebody's ears and say they were his," Gordon said casually.

They walked into the Allied camp with the usual collection of camp followers, pimps, prostitutes, merchants, sutlers and pickpockets watching them.

Redpath approached a wiry private with a bandaged hand.

"Is this the Royal Regiment? Orkney's Foot?" Redpath asked.

The private nodded. "Aye. Are you going to join?" he nodded to Grant. "That fellow would be a fine grenadier if they can find a uniform big enough."

Redpath laughed as Grant glowered at the soldier. "No, we're looking for a man named Flockhart."

"I don't know him," the private said. "There were over fifteen hundred men in the regiment. Less now, though. Whose company is he in?"

"We don't know," Redpath spun a small coin in the air.

The private ignored the implied bribe. "If this fellow's a big lad, like your silent friend there, he'll likely be a grenadier. Otherwise, he'll only be in one of the marching companies, like me."

"He's not big," Redpath said. "He's a touch under average height and probably with a scar on his throat."

"Ask one of the NCOs, then," the private soldier said helpfully. "Sergeant Dunn or maybe Sergeant Lamb, they know everything that is happening."

"Where will I find them?" Medium asked.

"Sergeant Dunn is on guard duty, but Sergeant Lamb is over there. He's the loud-mouthed fellow giving sword fighting lessons."

Redpath replaced the coin in his pocket and walked on with Gordon and Grant at his back. Redpath waited until

Lamb dismissed his dozen pupils before calling out. "Sergeant Lamb!"

"That's me," Lamb agreed. He recognised the potential violence inside Grant and kept his sword handy. "Who are you, and what do you want?"

"My name is Mungo Redpath, and my companions are Ruth Gordon and Duncan Grant. We are looking for a man named Flockhart."

Lamb grunted, still holding his sword. "I know of three men of that name in the regiment. Why do you want him?"

"That's our affair."

"Keep looking, then," Lamb turned away.

Redpath nodded to Grant, who moved to block Lamb's escape. "We might be able to help each other," Redpath said.

"In what way?" Lamb put his sword on the on-guard position as he faced Grant, confident of his ability to kill this silent civilian. He smiled.

"I have silver," Redpath said. "You have information. We could exchange."

"Call off this fellow before I spit him," Lamb said.

"Step away, Duncan," Redpath ordered quietly.

When Grant obeyed, Lamb slid his sword into its scabbard. "How much silver, and what do you want to know?"

"A lot of silver for the correct information," Redpath said. "Does one of your Flockharts bear the Christian name of David?"

"Two of them are called David," Lamb replied. "It's a common name."

Redpath nodded. "When did they join the regiment?"

"How much silver, did you say?" Lamb countered.

Redpath produced a silver Spanish dollar. "A silver Piece of Eight. That's for a start."

Lamb accepted the coin, checked it for authenticity and squirrelled it into his pocket. "Big David Flockhart has been with us for fifteen years. Silent Davie Flockhart since late 1701. He's a torn-faced bugger."

Redpath glanced at Gordon. "Silent Davie Flockhart sounds like a man I am interested in. Where might he be?"

"He might be anywhere," Lamb said. "But I could take you to where he is." He smiled ingratiatingly at Redpath, who handed over another silver dollar.

"Take us to him," Redpath said. "There's more silver if we see him, and he doesn't see us."

Lamb smiled. "We could form a decent partnership," he said. "What do you want Flockhart for?"

"That's still our affair," Redpath said.

"Are you a Messenger-at-Arms?" Lamb asked. "You look official."

"Something of the sort," Redpath said.

"Is Silent Davie running from something?" Lamb gave a greasy smile. "Did he join the army because he murdered somebody? We've had murderers in the ranks before."

"I am sure you have," Redpath said.

Lamb led them through the camp, heading for Flockhart's company. He stopped beside a stunted tree and indicated two men cleaning their muskets.

"That's him," Lamb said.

"Which one is him?" Gordon asked.

"The smaller of the two," Lamb said. "The ugly one."

Gordon glanced at Redpath. "He should be easy," she said. "Ugly men always succumb to flattery. Let me try first."

Redpath nodded. "You bring him to us, and we'll do the rest."

"Where?" Gordon watched as Flockhart stooped inside his tent.

"We know where he is," Redpath said. "Take him to the village."

"Blenheim?" Gordon asked, smoothing a hand down her skirt and patting her hair in place.

"Yes. Duncan and I will wait beside the church. There's a yew tree in the churchyard; that's our marker."

Gordon smiled. "Ugly men are always grateful when women pay attention to them. I'll deliver him to you soon after dark."

Grant stamped his feet on the ground as Redpath nodded slowly. "We'll be waiting," he said. "Find your way around the camp first."

Grant and Redpath strolled back through the Royals' camp, with Redpath ignoring the glances of the wives and Grant smiling at them, aware of his masculinity. Gordon waited until they had left and then walked away, learning the camp's geography, emphasising the swing of her hips, and enjoying the soldiers' reactions. She halted at the Grenadiers' section and settled beside a wagon, ogling the tallest and broadest men the Royals had to offer.

※

Rachel waited until the strangers had left before entering Flockhart's tent. Flockhart glanced over as she entered.

Ignoring the other eleven men who shared the tent, Rachel eased to Flockhart's side. "Davie! I must talk to you!"

"Why?" Flockhart was checking his flints were sharp.

Rachel looked at the other men, some of whom were mildly interested in her appearance. "Come outside!"

Flockhart glanced at Leishman, who shrugged and nodded to the still-open flap. Flockhart sighed and followed Rachel outside the tent. "What's the matter?"

Rachel nearly dragged Flockhart to a corner beside a wagon. "Some men are looking for you. Lamb showed them who you are."

Flockhart felt his always-present tension increase. "What sort of men?"

Rachel hesitated. "I don't know. Sergeant Lamb thinks they are Messengers-at-Arms. There are two men and a woman."

Flockhart felt his world collapse. "Lord Eskbank's sent them," he said. "They've found me after all this time."

"Let me help," Rachel said.

What can I do? Flockhart wondered. *If I stay, they can drag me back to Lord Eskbank and the pit. If I run, the army will shoot me for desertion.*

"Trouble?" Leishman had followed them from the tent.

Flockhart nodded. "Trouble for me," he said. "You'd best keep out of it, Adam."

Rachel took Flockhart's hand. "Come away, Davie."

"What's happening?" Leishman asked, raising his eyebrows.

"Sergeant Lamb has led three civilians to Davie," Rachel explained. "One is a woman, but the others might be Messengers-at-Arms."

"Did you murder somebody?" Leishman asked, half smiling.

Flockhart realised that Rachel was anxiously waiting for him to run. "Lord Eskbank will have sent them to take me back," he said.

"After three years?" Leishman dropped his smile.

"It must be Eskbank," Flockhart said. "Nobody else outside the Royals knows anything about me." He looked around as Sergeant Dunn emerged from the side of the wagon.

"Are the civilians still there?" Dunn asked.

"I'll look," Rachel slid away. She returned fifteen minutes later. "No. The men have left the camp, but the woman is at the Grenadiers' company."

"I must run," Flockhart said. "I'm not going back to the pit."

"You've seen what happens to deserters," Dunn reminded him. "You can't desert." He gripped Flockhart's shoulder. "You're not alone, Davie; you're a Royal. You're one of us."

"I can't remain here, either," Flockhart said, rubbing his throat. "Lord Eskbank has the law on his side."

Leishman looked around. "Maybe the officers could help. Captain Brisbane and Major Hamilton are decent men."

"No officers," Flockhart shook his head. "They'd follow the law, which gives Lord Eskbank the authority to own me."

"Maybe the Messengers-at-Arms will go directly to the officers and take Davie away," Rachel suggested. "We'll have to get him out of the camp."

"If they were genuine Messengers-at-Arms, they'd have approached the colonel rather than sneaking around the camp," Dunn reasoned. "If they had any legal authority, they'd have used their power. I don't think any sheriff or any court sent them."

"Who are they then?" Flockhart asked.

"I think they are private individuals working for Lord Eskbank," Sergeant Dunn said. "With no legal authority whatsoever."

"What will we do to protect Davie?" Rachel cut to the heart of the matter.

"Nothing," Dunn told her. "If they have no legal authority, they can't do anything. They might report his whereabouts to Lord Eskbank, but that's all."

"So, I am safe?" Flockhart asked.

"Safe from legal action at present," Sergeant Dunn said. "When Lord Eskbank contacts the colonel, we'll have to reconsider, and that may never happen."

❄

Flockhart heard the slight rustle as the tent flap opened. He remained motionless and opened his right eye slightly. He saw the figure enter the tent and pause, looking about her. Despite the darkness, Flockhart knew immediately that the incomer was a woman by the way she moved. For a second, he thought it was Rachel, but he realised the incomer was taller, with more generous curves.

Trouble, he told himself. *That's the woman His Lordship sent for me.*

The woman glanced at the faces of the sleeping men. Some

were twitching, dreaming of the horrors they had witnessed during the recent battles; others were snoring as if nothing had happened, and one lay awake, quietly sobbing. Flockhart was used to men crying at night, either young recruits wondering why they had agreed to follow the drum or men emotionally and physically exhausted after a battle. The incomer ignored the crying man and looked at Flockhart.

She crawled across the tent, carefully avoiding the recumbent bodies.

"You're awake," Ruth Gordon said.

Flockhart nodded.

"Can I join you?" Gordon whispered.

"Why?" Flockhart knew that most soldiers would respond enthusiastically to a woman's nighttime visit. He wondered how best to keep this woman off guard.

"Why do you think?" the woman crouched at the bottom of Flockhart's bed, wearing a low-cut top and an appealing smile. Even in the dim light, Flockhart could see she was attractive.

"There's hardly room in here," Flockhart said. Even with the days' casualties, sleeping soldiers crammed the tent.

"We can go somewhere better," Gordon whispered.

Flockhart put a hand over her mouth. "Sshh. You'll wake the men." He rolled from his cot and guided her from the tent, keeping alert for the routine night patrols.

"I know a place we can be alone for an hour or so," Gordon said. "Or longer." She allowed her hand to drift across Flockhart's groin.

"Why pick me?" Flockhart asked. "Marlborough has tens of thousands of men in his army."

Gordon looked at him, allowing him to see her eyes roam from the top of his head to his feet and back. "Some are brutes; many are lushy drunkards, a few are just boys. You are a handsome young man, fit and active."

They halted at the camp's periphery, with the tents softly

white and a low murmur from the wounded who remained on the battlefield.

"Come on," Gordon said, with a hand on Flockhart's arm. "The surgeons have ordered the churchyard cleared first. It's quiet there."

Flockhart nodded. "Is it not sacrilege to do such things on holy ground?"

"Genesis chapter one, verse twenty-eight, orders us to be fruitful and multiply," Gordon said, emphasising her smile. "If it's God's word, where better to obey than in God's holy acre?"

"Where indeed?" Flockhart agreed.

They moved cautiously away from the encampment and into the churchyard. As Gordon had said, the medical orderlies had taken away the casualties, although cannon and musket balls had pitted the walls of the church. Powder smoke clung to the ground, acrid and cold, and a scimitar moon shone uncaring light on the serried ranks of gravestones.

"Is the church open?" Flockhart asked.

Gordon screwed up her face. "I don't know," she admitted.

When a deceptive wind shifted clouds across the sky, the moonlight flitted across the gravestones, casting shadows that added to the surreal atmosphere. Flockhart strode to the church door, ignored the hoot of a watching owl, and tried the handle.

"It's locked," he said.

Flockhart heard the heavy tread behind him and shifted sideways, reaching for the bayonet inside his shirt.

"David Flockhart!" the voice was deep and as hard as the hand that clamped on his shoulder. "You are a runaway collier, the property of Lord Eskbank."

Flockhart turned, keeping one hand on the hilt of his bayonet. The man who held him was huge, taller and wider than anybody Flockhart had seen before, with a broad face and arms as muscular as most men's legs.

"I am David Flockhart, a private soldier in the Royal Regiment of Foot," Flockhart kept his voice level. "I am nobody's property." He had to crane his neck to glare into the giant's eyes.

"You're coming with us," a second man loomed from the gloom. He was of medium height and build, with no distinguishing features, yet Flockhart knew he would stand out in any crowd. This second man had a presence that nobody could ignore.

"Who are you?" Flockhart asked, fighting to remain calm despite the hammer of his heart.

"Who we are doesn't matter," Redpath replied. "Who you are, does."

Gordon sidled up on Flockhart's left side. "It's best if you don't struggle, Davie," she said, smiling. "Duncan Grant can break you with one hand."

"He's a big fellow," Flockhart agreed without slackening his hold on the bayonet.

"Come on, Flockhart," Redpath said as Grant tightened his grip.

"I'll take the bayonet," Gordon put a small hand on Flockhart's arm. "In case you are tempted to try anything silly."

Flockhart saw the movement from the corner of his eye.

"That's my man, Mistress!" Rachel appeared behind Gordon with something in her hand. She grabbed Gordon's hair and pulled her violently backwards. "Get away!"

Gordon staggered, recovered and laughed. "Do you think you can intimidate me, little girl? I've been dealing with your type for years."

"What is my type?" Rachel asked, stepping back. She was nearly a head shorter and much lighter than Gordon but thrust forward aggressively. She pushed at Gordon. "Who are you?"

Gordon rode the attack, laughing.

With Rachel distracting Gordon, Flockhart grabbed Grant's thumb and twisted backwards, using all his strength. Although Grant was huge, Flockhart's powerful grip bent his thumb back.

Grant gasped, trying to break Flockhart's hold. He swore, unused to such resistance.

"Enough," Redpath said wearily. He pulled a pistol from beneath his jacket and pressed it against Flockhart's head. "Release him and come with us."

Flockhart saw Redpath suddenly stiffen as Leishman pressed the muzzle of his musket against his skull. "Drop the pistol. Drop the pistol, or I'll spread your brains across the kirk wall."

"You're making a mistake," Redpath said calmly. "I have the law on my side."

"Do you think I care a tinker's cuss for your bloody law?" Leishman spoke in a harsh whisper. "I'll count to three and then blow a hole in your skull."

Redpath glanced at Grant, who still struggled in Flockhart's grip.

"You won't fire," Redpath told Leishman. "You'd swing for it."

"One," Leishman said. "Drop the pistol, fellow."

"I'll kill your friend," Redpath warned. "And the law will let me walk away."

"Two," Leishman's grip on the musket was steady. "Drop the pistol."

"Hanging is not a nice way to die," Redpath sounded as calm as if he were discussing the weather on Edinburgh's High Street.

"Three," Leishman said and pressed the trigger. Flockhart saw Redpath's expression alter to terror as the hammer fell. The musket roared, with the ball smashing through Redpath's skull and spreading brains, blood and fragments of bone across the church wall.

"I warned you," Leishman said with no emotion at all.

As Leishman dealt with Redpath, Sergeant Dunn came behind Grant and crashed the butt of a musket against his head. Grant staggered but remained on his feet. Flockhart twisted Grant's thumb, hoping to disable him, but Grant ignored the pain and tried to grab Dunn's musket.

"You're next, big man," Leishman said, drawing his bayonet.

Grant swung his arm, dragging Flockhart across the ground, and aimed a clumsy kick that missed Flockhart's groin by a handsbreadth. Flockhart released Grant's thumb and rolled away, leaving Dunn to face the giant alone.

Grant charged forward, fists swinging, but Dunn ducked away and thrust his musket barrel hard into Grant's groin, following with an upward swing of the butt. Grant yelled once and collapsed as Dunn crashed the musket butt onto his head.

Flockhart stood up in time to see Gordon dropping a knife from her sleeve into her hand and slashing at Rachel, who dodged with the ease of long practice. Rachel swung her weapon, a fist-sized stone in a handkerchief, catching Gordon squarely on the hand. Flockhart heard the crack of breaking bones as Gordon gasped and dropped her knife, which Rachel kicked to one side and swung her stone again. Gordon crumpled without a sound.

"Thank you," Flockhart said. He looked at Redpath's body. "What do we do now?"

Sergeant Dunn prodded Grant with the toe of his boot. "We have a choice," he said. "We can walk away and hope these two don't run to the authorities, and we all swing, or we ensure they can't run anywhere."

"How do we do that?" Flockhart asked.

"Like this," Dunn said and ran his bayonet through Grant's throat.

"What about her?" Rachel nodded to Gordon. "We can't leave her," Rachel said. "She'd be bound to talk."

"I can't kill a woman," Leishman said.

"Nor can I," Dunn said and glanced at Flockhart, who shook his head.

"Not me," he said.

Rachel lifted her stone, hesitated and shook her head. "Not like this," she said.

"We'll leave her here," Sergeant Dunn decided. "Take any

money and valuables from her and let her take her chance. She can stay or leave as she wishes."

"She might tell the colonel," Leishman said.

"Who would believe a woman was involved in such an affair?" Dunn asked. He watched as Rachel removed another knife, a gold ring, and a small purse from Gordon. She handed the knife and ring to Dunn.

Flockhart nodded. "What about the others, Sergeant?"

"Leave them where they are," Leishman suggested.

"Strip them stark," Rachel said. "If somebody finds two civilians, they'll be suspicious. If they find two naked men, they'll think they're battle casualties the locals have stripped."

"You're right," Dunn agreed. "Good thinking."

Rachel bent over Redpath's bloodied remains. As she ripped off his clothes, she found a heavy leather purse. Shielding her actions with her body, Rachel opened the drawstring, saw that the purse contained gold and silver coins, smiled, and tucked it away inside her jacket.

With the bodies stripped, Rachel took the clothes and threw them over the churchyard wall.

"Somebody will take them," she said casually. "Where's that woman?"

"She must have recovered and run," Sergeant Dunn said. "Good luck to her. She'll struggle in a strange country with no money and nothing to sell."

Flockhart nodded. "There's been sufficient killing." He indicated the battlefield, where dead and wounded still lay in their thousands, Allied, Bavarian and French side by side. Men and women moved among them, stripping them of clothes, possessions and dignity in a final display of man's inhumanity to man.

CHAPTER 23

BAVARIA, AUTUMN 1704

"Rachel," Flockhart asked. "You used to be a dirty little creature. You never washed your face or brushed your hair."

"Yes," Rachel agreed.

"Now you are the cleanest woman in camp," Flockhart said. "What happened?"

"You did," Rachel said simply.

"I don't understand," Flockhart replied.

"You should," Rachel told him, unsmiling. "Why do you think I rarely washed?"

"I can't imagine," Flockhart replied.

"Would you want to bed a filthy woman?" Rachel asked.

"No," Flockhart replied immediately, then closed his eyes as her meaning became clear. "No, I would not," he said more slowly. "And I don't know many men who would."

"That's why I rarely washed," Rachel said quietly. "If men did not find me attractive, I would be safe."

Flockhart nodded. "You're a clever little rogue, aren't you?"

"It's not easy for a bastard girl to grow up in the army," Rachel said with a touch of bitterness. "Especially when my mother was a whore, and I hardly saw her."

"I can only imagine," Flockhart said. "You did a good job of raising yourself."

Rachel raised her chin. "I don't want my children to follow the drum," she said. "I want a better life for them."

"Children?" Flockhart said. "Do you want children?"

"Want them or not," Rachel said, "if you bed me, they'll come along by and by."

Flockhart shivered. He had never considered having children. The thought scared him: the responsibility of having to care for people apart from himself. "The army is not a place for children," he said.

"I agree," Rachel said with feeling. She looked up. "The drums are calling for you."

Flockhart stood. "You look better when you've washed," he said. "Much better." He looked at her for a moment, unsure what to say. "You are very attractive."

Rachel smiled. "Thank you," she said. Leaning forward, she touched a button on his uniform. "Your button is loose. You need that stitched on, or you'll lose it."

"I'll do that tonight," Flockhart said.

"No, I'll do it tonight," Rachel told him. She gave him a rare smile. "I'm better with a needle than you are."

※

After the victory of Blenheim, Marlborough split his army. He sent Brigadier Ferguson with six infantry battalions to escort the prisoners to Holland. The remainder of the army, including Flockhart's battalion of the Royals, marched deeper into Germany.

Flockhart shouldered his musket, ensured Rachel was safe with the wives, and slogged on. They headed across Swabia and crossed the Rhine at Philipsburg on 7 September 1704.

"We are marching forever," Leishman said.

Flockhart nodded, enjoying the crisp autumn air. "I could do that," he said. "As long as Corporal John feeds us, I could march until Judgement Day. Every morning brings new sights and new places." He glanced back at the baggage train, where Rachel sat on the leading wagon with other wives. "I can't think of a better life than soldiering."

"It's hard on the women," Leishman said.

Flockhart remembered the semi-naked women in the pit, shackled to laden trucks or carrying hundredweights of coal up narrow wooden ladders in the stinking dark. "There are worse things," he said. He remembered women giving birth deep underground and returning to work the next day, girls of seven and eight sobbing with exhaustion as they laboured under weights grown men could hardly lift.

Leishman looked at him curiously. "Are you all right, Davie?"

"I am all right," Flockhart tried to shake away the memories. He felt his throat itch where the slave collar had been and rubbed at the welts.

The Royals' next task was to join the army that covered the siege of Landau, a Bavarian town by the Rhine. Flockhart admired the beautiful valley of the River Queich, kept his musket clean, his flints sharp and joined in Chaplain Samuel Noyes's psalms and prayers. He felt the Lord had blessed him by releasing him from the pit, although the fear of Lord Eskbank dragging him back was always present. Flockhart thanked the Lord for sending him good friends who helped him dispose of the two men at Blenheim church and sang with a clear conscience.

The Royals camped in autumn-damp fields with the reassuring drums establishing order and the daily drill so routine that Flockhart knew he would feel something was missing if the officers did not call them to parade. Sometimes, Flockhart would wake up in a panic, staring around the tent to assure himself he was safe with the regiment. After the incident with Redpath and Grant, he watched any smartly dressed civilians in case they had come to claim him. With every new campsite or town, Flockhart worked out routes to run, although he knew the chances of escape in a foreign land were slim. He learned a few words of German to increase his chances, warned Rachel of his intentions and knew she would accompany him.

"How about Adam and Sergeant Dunn?" Rachel asked.

"I can't ask them to desert," Flockhart replied. "It's best to tell them nothing and leave them safe with the regiment."

Rachel considered for a moment. "We're better on our own," she agreed.

When the chill winds and blasting rains of October ended the campaigning season, the Royals joined other regiments in marching to the neat riverside town of Germersheim. They boarded river boats that transported them down the Rhine to their winter quarters in Holland.

Rachel softly sang her favourite song as the boat cruised down the Rhine.

> "My friends I do not value nor my foes I do not
>   fear,
> Now, my love has left me, and I wander far and
>   near.
> And when my baby it is born and a-smiling on
>   my knee
> I'll think of lovely Davie in High Germany."

Flockhart felt Leishman's eyes on him as Rachel sang. "That song is not about me," he growled.

Leishman grinned. "Yes, it is, Davie, boy. That song is entirely about you." He laughed. "You are lucky to have a wife like Rachel. Do you know how many men she's rebuffed to keep faithful to you?"

Flockhart shook his head, rubbing at his throat.

"Nor do I," Leishman admitted. "She's too good for the likes of you and me, Davie boy."

Flockhart shifted his stance to view Rachel. She was small

and slight, with large eyes and a snub nose. Flockhart realised Rachel would never be anything but small and slender, yet she had matured in the last couple of years. Rachel no longer looked like a scared youngster but a full-grown woman.

"Maybe you are right," Flockhart said. "She is too good for the likes of me."

Why would any decent woman want a runaway collier serf? Rachel would be better with Adam Leishman, Sergeant Dunn, or nearly anybody else in the Royals. I am not suitable for a husband and certainly not suitable for a father. All I want is to follow the drum, drink with my friends and breathe fresh air until some French ball ends it all. After that, it will be a soldier's grave under the sod and eternal peace.

How about Rachel?

Flockhart found he was watching everything she did, listening to the intonations of her voice, and thinking about her when he should have been attending to his duty.

Damn the woman. She's getting under my skin, Flockhart thought, smiling. And Rachel caught the smile and understood better than he ever could.

※

"I haven't got Flockhart back yet," Lord Eskbank said.

"No, My Lord," Cummings stood before Lord Eskbank with two tall candles sending flickering shadows across the room and a bright fire in the grate.

"What's happening with the scoundrels you sent after him?" Eskbank asked.

"I don't know, My Lord," Cummings admitted.

"What do you know?" Lord Eskbank asked, pouring himself a glass of claret.

"Redpath informed me he had traced Flockhart to the Royals, My Lord, in High Germany. He was travelling there to bring him back."

"When was that?"

"Some months ago, My Lord."

"You paid him with my money," Lord Eskbank finished half the glass in one swallow. "I think your friend has taken my gold and run."

"I don't believe he would do that, My Lord," Cummings said. "Mungo Redpath is an honourable man. Perhaps some accident has befallen him."

Lord Eskbank drained the glass, thumped it on his desk, stood up and pointed a quavering finger at Cummings. "I gave you a task to do, Cummings, and provided more than sufficient funds. Nothing happened; the money has vanished, Flockhart remains free, and half my property is laughing and planning to abscond."

Cummings stood still, unable to reply.

"You are a married man, are you not?" Lord Eskbank said with a sudden smile.

"Yes, My Lord."

"With a family?"

"Yes, My Lord. I have two sons and a daughter." Cummings realised that Lady Joanna had entered the room and was standing beside the window, listening to the conversation. He was sure she was smiling.

Lord Eskbank poured himself a glass of claret, glanced at his wife and poured another. "I'll tell you what I want, Cummings. I want you to go to High Germany, find Flockhart and bring him back here. I don't care how you do it or what measures you take. If he is dead, I want you to bring me back proof of his demise."

"How can I do that, My Lord?"

"By thinking of your wife and family," Lord Eskbank said, passing the second glass to his wife. "If you fail your allotted task, I will find another grieve."

Lady Joanna stepped forward, still smiling. "If you lose your position, Cummings, what will happen to your wife and family?"

"They'll be beggars, vagrants forced to roam the country," Lord Eskbank replied to his wife's question.

"You can't do that to them, John," Lady Joanna said. "I am sure you'll make provision for them."

"I will," Lord Eskbank said. "As vagabonds and beggars, Cummings' wife and children are liable to be taken into my care. They are strong, fit, well-fed and will be useful down my mines."

"I am sure your grieve understands his position," Lady Joanna smiled at Cummings. "Don't you, my man?"

"Yes, My Lady," Cummings replied.

"Bring Flockhart back alive," Lord Eskbank said. "Or bring back proof of his death." He finished his claret as Lady Joanna watched Cummings, smiling.

CHAPTER 24

DUTCH REPUBLIC, SPRING 1705

F lockhart watched Sergeant Dunn drill the latest recruits, wondering if he had ever been as clumsy and unresponsive as these newcomers. As an old soldier and veteran of battles, marches, and sieges, he knew the recruits looked up to him with respect.

"They'll learn," Leishman said, puffing at a long-stemmed pipe.

"They'll have to," Flockhart replied. "If they hope to take their place in the Royals."

Leishman glanced at the clear sky. "It will be campaigning season soon," he said. "I wonder where Corporal John will take us this year."

"Wherever it is, we'll have to go," Flockhart said. He shook his head as one particularly clumsy recruit tripped and nearly brought the next man down. Sergeant Dunn prodded the culprit with the butt end of his halberd. "I hope these lads improve before we meet the French."

When the winter eased away, and a weak sun gradually dried the ground, supplies creaked in for the coming campaigning season, some by river and canal and others along the roads. The French sent mounted patrols to disrupt the Allied supply convoys, with a few encounters between the rival armies. In one such affair, Colonel Jemmy Campbell's Scots Dragoons almost annihilated a French raiding party, much to the Royals' delight.

In April, the Royals left their winter quarters, marched past Maastricht, and wound through wooded hills to the Moselle valley. At the end of May, both battalions camped outside the city of Treves. Flockhart found the march both pleasurable and routine, enjoying the movement. Leishman was less happy.

"This is a bleak country," Leishman said.

Peter Young screwed up his face and looked up at the incessant cold rain. "The weather makes it worse," he complained.

Leishman nodded. "The weather and the shortage of supplies. We've little forage for the horses and less for us. Marshal Villars and his Frenchies have swept the place clean."

"They're doing to us what we did to Bavaria last season," Flockhart said.

Leishman grunted. "If it weren't for your Rachel, we'd be worse."

Flockhart nodded contentedly. "Rachel is the best forager in the army," he said. "But even she is finding it hard to bring home food. The Frenchies have done a good job."

Joined by the Dutch and a collection of forces from various German states, Marlborough led his combined army past the Moselle and the Saar and marched towards Sierck-les-Bains.

"What's at Sierck?" Young asked, splashing through a deep puddle.

"The French," Sergeant Dunn replied laconically. "Marshal Villars has a large French army camped near Sierck."

"Larger than ours?" Young asked.

"Larger than ours," Dunn confirmed.

"Is Villars a good general?" Young asked.

"He's one of the best Louis has," Dunn replied.

Flockhart adjusted his musket, spat on the ground, and marched on. "Let's have a look at him, then," he said. He glanced over his shoulder at the long scarlet column behind them to where the baggage wagons rolled and creaked over the road. Although he could not see her, Flockhart knew that Rachel was there, sitting inside the leading wagon, sheltering under the canopy and staring out as they rumbled through the countryside. Flockhart smiled; it was good to be an infantryman, surrounded by his colleagues and with a woman who cared for him. The poor weather did not matter, nor the shortage of rations. Flockhart was content with his lot and had no desire to change.

The poor weather encouraged desertions, with men slipping away from the Allied army almost daily. Flockhart listened to the Royals grumble without joining in. The weather was cold, the soil poor compared to the Low Countries or Lothian, and the villages bleak and uninviting. Even Rachel returned from her foraging trips with little good news.

"The villagers have all fled," she said, "taking everything with them. I found one scraggy hen that will have to do us and a couple of handfuls of meal."

"That's better than nothing," Flockhart said, "and far better than anybody else has found this campaign." He smiled at her. "We couldn't do without you, Rachel."

Marlborough halted his army a few miles from Sierck, sent out patrols that occasionally skirmished with the French, and stood still.

"What are we waiting for?" Flockhart asked. "We can advance and smash them."

"We're waiting for Prince Lewis of Baden," Sergeant Dunn explained. "Once he brings his army to join us, we'll have equal numbers to Marshal Villars."

Flockhart grunted, cut a section of mixed tobacco and dried grass in three, and handed Dunn and Leishman each a piece. "I dislike depending on allies," he said. "They can be good, like the Hanoverians, or hesitant, like the Dutch higher command."

"The Dutch soldiers are stubborn fighters," Leishman said.

"Aye, they are," Flockhart agreed. "It's their leaders I dislike."

Dunn chewed the tobacco. "You have a talent for finding

decent tobacco," he said. "Foraging is your one redeeming quality."

"I don't find it," Flockhart said. "Rachel finds it."

"In that case, you have no redeeming qualities," Dunn said. "Yet you're a lucky man. All the wives I've had left me."

"That's because you're a mean-spirited poltroon without a Christian bone in your body," Leishman told him.

Dunn laughed and bit off more of Rachel's tobacco. "I thought that might be the reason."

The Allies and the French remained within a day's march of each other, with Villars remaining static behind his prepared positions and Marlborough not risking an attack against superior numbers.

After waiting for a frustratingly long time without Prince Lewis showing, on the 17th of June, Marlborough ordered his men to march north from the Moselle to the Meuse.

Marlborough had to disengage from Marshal Villars' army without exposing his vulnerable flanks to a French attack. To confuse the enemy, he divided his army into different columns.

"We've not done anything except camp and march," Young said.

"You've lived another month," Leishman said. "Be grateful for that."

"What's happening now?" Young asked.

"We're returning to the Low Countries," Sergeant Dunn replied. "The French are causing trouble there again. They've captured Huy, besieged Liège and are ravaging the land."

"Can we not fight them here?" Young asked. "Without all this marching."

"We have to defend our Allies' lands," Dunn explained.

"The campaigning season is wearing away," Young, an expert in complaining – the favourite habit of British soldiers after drinking, "and we haven't fired a single ball."

Flockhart grunted. "No, but we're alive, and as Adam says,

that's always a bonus." He looked to the dark sky. "It's a beautiful night, Peter."

Young trudged on. "You're a strange man, Davie."

"I know," Flockhart agreed.

On the 20th of June, Marlborough ordered the Earl of Orkney to take all the grenadiers, plus a hundred men from each battalion, towards Marshal Villeroy's army at Liège. François de Neufville, Marshal Villeroy, was a Lyon-born nobleman and a close friend of King Louis XIV. He was a personally brave man but was never accepted as a top-quality general. The British soldiers were confident that Marlborough would defeat him.

"I'm sure I'm wearing out my feet, marching all across Europe," Young said.

Flockhart nodded. Detached from the main force, he looked in vain for Rachel. For the past few months, he had felt uneasy when he did not know where she was.

Orkney's detachment marched and counter-marched for the remainder of June, shadow boxing with the French without ever coming within firing range. When the French retired, Orkney led his men back to the main Allied army.

"The experts sitting around the drawing room fires call these operations a war of manoeuvre," Leishman explained. "I say it's a way of tiring us out."

"It's healthier than being in camp," Dunn told him. "The longer we're in camp, the more diseases spread. We've always got fewer sick men when we're on the march."

With Marlborough's army back from the Moselle valley, the French withdrew from their siege of Liège. Marlborough split his force again, with the first battalion of the Royals among the troops he sent to recapture Huy. General Schultz and the Earl of Orkney commanded this section of the Allied army.

"Captain Brisbane," Orkney said, "the first Royals are short-handed. Take your company and reinforce them."

"Yes, My Lord," Captain Brisbane said and gave immediate orders for his company.

"On the march again," Young said.

"Still alive and breathing," Flockhart added, wishing he knew where Rachel was.

The siege was short and sharp, with the Royals not playing a significant part. Huy had one castle and two forts named Picard and Rouge to defend the town. On the 6th of July, the Allies brought a battery of twelve cannon and six mortars to bear on Fort Picard. As the bombardment began, the Royals formed part of the infantry force that attacked the outer defences.

"Here we are again," Leishman said. "You guard my back, Davie, and I'll guard yours."

Flockhart nodded. "As always," he agreed, rubbing a hand over his throat.

The French put up a brief resistance at the outer defences, but when the Allies forced the covered way and slammed their ladders against Fort Picard's walls, the defenders fled to the castle.

"That was short and sweet," Flockhart said. "I never fired a single ball."

"The French have also abandoned Fort Joseph," Sergeant Dunn told him. "Orkney has done well here."

Huy surrendered the following day, and the Allies took possession.

"Another victory for Corporal John," Leishman said. "The Frenchies may as well pack up and go home when he arrives."

As always, the capture of a town unleashed a horde of looters, with soldiers and camp followers picking what they could find. Rachel was one of the first into Huy and returned from her foray with a smile on her face and French bread and wine under her arm.

"You're a lifesaver," Flockhart told her. He felt he was becoming dependent on Rachel and suddenly realised he did not care.

Damn it. I like that woman.

CHAPTER 25

DUTCH REPUBLIC AND SPANISH NETHERLANDS, SUMMER 1705

YORLING Marlborough's return to the Low Countries altered the tactical position as the French army, with Marshal Villeroy and the Elector of Bavaria in command, retreated behind their heavily fortified Lines of Brabant.

"We'll have to winkle them out," Leishman said.

"That won't be easy," Dunn replied. "The French are famous engineers, and their defences run from Antwerp to Namur." He shook his head. "That's a seventy-mile line of fortifications!"

"That's a long line to defend," Flockhart said. "The French can't be strong everywhere."

"They must be scared of us," Young said. "We don't build fortifications."

"Corporal John will think of something to get past them," Dunn said. "He always does."

Flockhart nodded. He wished Rachel was with them.

※

"We're marching again," Sergeant Dunn said. "Full load of

ammunition, men, check your flints are sharp, and I'll inspect your muskets for rust later."

"It's nearly dark," Young said.

"I know. Get ready."

Flockhart glanced at the sky. It was July, the height of summer, with warm, pleasant nights to march through.

The men knew what Corporal John required of them. They moved on, following the drum, marching in step as the fertile countryside eased past. With their muskets pressed against their shoulders and tricorn hats shading them from the sun or dripping with rainwater, they marched hour after hour and day after day.

Marlborough had used deception to fool the French. Pushing a detachment to the extreme south of the French lines as if to threaten Namur, he waited until Villeroy moved the bulk of his men to reinforce that section. To bolster the supposed threat, Marlborough sent his pioneers to build bridges across the Mehaigne River in full view of French patrols.

"With Corporal John, half the battle is won before the first shot is fired," Sergeant Dunn said.

"What does that mean?" Young asked.

"It means he's pulling the French all over the place," Dunn said. "Villeroy doesn't know which way to turn."

On the 17th of July, with the French concentrated on the south, Marlborough marched the remainder of his army to the opposite flank. Flockhart eased into the routine of the march, enjoyed the cooling mist and occasional light rain showers, and wondered what the morning would bring. He tried to learn some German words, for in addition to Scots and English, Marlborough led Danish and German soldiers.

At four in the morning of the 18th of July, the advanced units of the Allied army marched in three columns towards the French at Elixheim and Hespen. The Royals were one of only three British units involved, moving through a now-dense fog.

"Where are we?" Flockhart asked.

Sergeant Dunn shook his head. "Even Marlborough's secretary did not know," he said. "I only know Marlborough's ordered us to clear whatever is in our path."

Flockhart shrugged. "Then that's what we will do."

The Royals pushed onwards, seeing a body of white-coated soldiers before them. The surprised French shouted a challenge, fired a quick volley and withdrew, with tendrils of mist clinging to them as they hurried back.

Dunn gave quick orders, and his platoon fired at the retreating Frenchmen, with no visible casualties on either side.

"Move on!" Captain Brisbane ordered. "Keep moving!"

With the French pickets retreating before them, the Royals pushed on, keeping in formation as they hoped to capture the village of Elixheim with its bridge.

"Move on!" Brisbane commanded as the light strengthened and the morning sun began to dissipate the mist. Isolated trees showed ghostly through the silver-grey, with the sound of running water distorted as the Royals moved forward.

Flockhart heard musketry on either side, smelled acrid powder smoke and followed Brisbane.

"Double!" Brisbane ordered.

The Royals ran through enclosed fields, with the occasional French musket ball whistling among them, and entered an area of marshland. Flockhart swore as mud sucked at his shoes and splashed his legs. He struggled on, slower now as the marsh slowed their advance.

"Push on!" Captain Brisbane ordered. He stopped, turned around and gestured them on, waving his sword to prove the urgency. A few musket balls pattered into the mud, but Dunn ordered his platoon to hold their fire.

"It takes too long to reload, boys. Only fire to save your life."

Flockhart nodded, stepping carefully, cautious in case the next step saw him plunge into deep mud that sucked him under. The marshland stretched to the banks of the Little Gete River, which flowed sullenly between soft banks. Flockhart hesitated a little, for he had never learned to swim, but Dunn plunged in after Brisbane.

"Come on lads! Ford the river!"

Flockhart took a deep breath and stepped into the Little Gete. He felt the pull of the current against his legs and waded slowly on, with Leishman and Young overtaking him. He held his musket high, swore when he stumbled, and pushed on, desperate to reach the relative security of the opposite bank.

The French defences rose on the far side of the river, a combination of earthworks and palisades, with formidable artillery redoubts. White-coated soldiers flitted to and fro, shouting at each other.

"Come on, Royals!" Brisbane ran to the closest earthwork, slashed at the gaping defender and vaulted over the low wall. Sergeant Dunn followed, shouting as he scaled the wall with Leishman and Young at his heels. Flockhart struggled from the river, thankful it was shallow, and ran forward, roaring.

Captain Brisbane was well in front with the sun flashing on his sword. That single unexpected charge had smashed through the outer French defences.

"Onward!" Brisbane shouted.

The company followed, chasing the surprised defenders without causing many casualties on either side. Flockhart saw French soldiers surrendering as others fled, with some dropping their muskets. He saw an entire regiment of French dragoons galloping in the opposite direction.

"We've broken through the French lines!" Sergeant Dunn shouted, more in surprise than jubilation.

"Take formation in case they try a counterattack," Brisbane ordered.

With the Allies still disorganised from the assault, the French mounted a vigorous attack. French and Bavarian cavalry and infantry launched themselves, shouting and hammering encouragement with their drums.

"Form a line!" Brisbane shouted, pointing to one of the tree-lined sunken lanes. "Prepare to receive cavalry!"

The remnants of the mist clung to the ground as the counter-attack gathered momentum. The Royals fired a volley, and then a unit of Bavarians were on them with bayonets and rifle butts. Flockhart heard somebody laughing and saw Lamb jumping into a group of Bavarians, slashing and thrusting with his bayonet. Other grenadiers joined him, pushing back the assault on the flanks as the rest of the Royals held the line.

"Reload!" Brisbane shouted as the first Bavarian assault recoiled. The Royals reloaded quickly, gasping with effort. Flockhart thrust with his ramrod, replaced it in his rest and looked up. The Bavarians and French were coming again.

"Make ready! Present! Fire!"

The volley rang out, halting the attackers.

"Reload!" Captain Brisbane ordered.

As the infantry struggled for superiority, Marlborough ordered the pioneers to flatten the defences, creating a passage of level ground to enable the Allied cavalry to enter and reinforce the advance force.

"Here comes the French cavalry," Leishman said as the Royals heard the thunder of hooves ahead. Flockhart glanced over the broken ground with its sunken lanes, entrenchments and clumps of trees. He tightened his grip on his musket.

"I've never faced cavalry before," he said.

"You might not have to. Here come our Horse!" Sergeant Dunn shouted.

Flockhart checked his musket, realised the flint was dull, and quickly fitted another. He was surprised that his hands were steady.

"Relax, lads," Dunn said. "Their cavalry can't charge in case our Horse take them in flank."

When the Allies repulsed the initial French and Bavarian attacks, Marlborough reorganised his men so they were better prepared for the next onslaught. The broken ground did not favour horsemen, and the Allies soon gained the upper hand.

After a couple of hours, a British cavalry patrol probed forward.

"The French cavalry are retreating," Leishman read the signs. "Leaving the Bavarian infantry unsupported."

Flockhart watched as the Bavarian infantry formed a hollow square and withdrew without breaking formation. The Allied cavalry and dragoons surrounded them, looking for an opening, but the Bavarians kept them at bay with musket volleys whenever they came too close.

"Our cavalry should charge immediately after the Bavarians have fired and when they are still reloading," Leishman said.

"They should," Dunn said. "But look at head height. See the grenadier caps? The Bavarians have a company of grenadiers inside the square, ready to reinforce whichever side has fired. Our horse can't break in."

"Stubborn lads, the Bavarians," Flockhart said. "I wish they were fighting on our side."

"Maybe they will in the next war," Dunn said, grinning. "Give it one year of peace, and it will be all change and swap partners."

With the enemy withdrawing, Marlborough consolidated his army, waiting for reinforcements.

"Why don't we push on and smash the Bavarians?" Young asked. "They're too dangerous to allow them to recover."

"We don't know where Villeroy or the Elector is," Sergeant Dunn reminded him. "It's best to wait for the Dutch to join us first, or the enemy will merge, so they outnumber us and pound us into the dust."

With the Allies penetrating his defence line, Villeroy withdrew towards the River Dyle, losing many men to desertion.

"That's another victory for Corporal John," Sergeant Dunn said as he watched hundreds of French prisoners marching to the rear. "We captured about twenty of their Colours and eighteen guns."

Flockhart nodded. "So much for their invincible lines," he said, stuffing some of Rachel's tobacco into the bowl of his pipe.

As the French retreated, the Allies followed, picking up another 1,500 prisoners as they advanced.

"We're moving again!" Sergeant Dunn shouted as the drums summoned the battalion. The Royals joined the pursuit, marching towards the River Dyle, watching the disconsolate French prisoners slouching in the opposite direction and enduring days of torrential rain.

Marlborough sent the first battalion of the Royals in hot pursuit of Villeroy's men. Flockhart heard the crackle of distant musketry and heard later the first battalion had skirmished, with three companies pushing too far forward and taking casualties from a smart French rearguard.

"We're still chasing them," Sergeant Dunn said. "March on, my fellow sufferers."

Marlborough's advanced cavalry screen crossed the Dyle River on the 29th of July.

"We're pushing them back to France," Leishman exulted.

Flockhart stared into the distance, wondering if the French would stand and fight. He had not seen Rachel for days and hoped she was all right.

Rachel's a survivor. She'll be with the baggage train, foraging like a queen. The Queen of Foragers, that's my Rachel.

"Halt!" the order came from above, passed back by a relay of gallopers. The drums tapped a confirmation, and the army stopped, with Colours drooping in the rain and the men wondering what was happening.

"What's the to-do, Sergeant?" Flockhart asked. It was usual for the rank and file to march in complete ignorance of what they were doing the next day or even where they were. Flockhart's platoon was fortunate that Sergeant Dunn had a source of information.

"Corporal John wants the army to cross the Dyle, but the Dutch won't let him," Dunn said.

"Why not?" Flockhart asked.

"They're scared to risk anything," the sergeant explained. "They seem to think we can defeat the Sun King by remaining on the defensive."

After another abortive attempt to cross the Dyle, which the Dutch frustrated, Marlborough ordered his army to destroy the French fortified lines. With the months dragging on, the Allies marched back to Holland for the winter.

"That's another campaigning season completed, and we're all still alive," Leishman said.

Flockhart nodded. "And a long winter before us," he added.

"Maybe we'll get peace soon. One more victory might settle the issue," Leishman said.

"What will happen then?" Flockhart asked his habitual question.

"Only the good Lord knows," Leishman replied. "We might remain here to ensure King Louis keeps the peace, we might be sent back to Scotland or England, or the Queen may disband one of our battalions, and we'd all be civilians again."

Flockhart nodded. He did not want the army to post him back to Scotland, and he did not want to be a civilian again. He thought of his previous life, touched the red mark on his throat and hoped the war would last forever.

CHAPTER 26

SCOTLAND AND THE DUTCH REPUBLIC, WINTER 1705/06

"Who's that?" Abigail Cummings looked up in sudden alarm.

"It's me. Get the children," Cummings whispered from the dark. "Hurry!"

"What's happening?" Abigail struggled from her bed, adjusting her nightdress and blinking the sleep from her eyes.

"We're leaving," Cummings told her. "Keep your voice down! Gather your things."

"What? Why?" Abigail scratched a spark from the tinderbox and applied it to a candle. Wavering light illuminated the bedroom.

"I've got another position away from Lord Eskbank. Hurry, Abigail. There's no time to explain!"

They stumbled from the tied cottage with the children bundled up against the chill. Cummings ushered them onto the cart he had outside. He whipped up the horse and steered for the gates of the estate, feeling the jolt of the cart on the unmade road. An owl hooted through the night, answered by its mate.

"What's happening, Father?" a small, tired voice asked from the back of the wagon.

"We're going somewhere safe," Cummings said, dismounting to open the gate.

"Hoi!" the gatekeeper shouted. "Who's that?" He emerged from the lodge, blunderbuss in hand. "Where do you think you're going?"

Cummings did not reply but whipped the horse and ran at the side of the cart with the gatekeeper following. He heard the blast of the blunderbuss, and something hot seared the side of his head.

❄

Winter sleet rattled at the tavern windows, roaring around the eaves and threatening to lift the roof from the building.

"God help sailors on a night like this," Rachel said as she hugged her tankard.

"We're fortunate that we're snug in winter quarters," Flockhart replied.

Rachel looked at him sideways as they sat at the battered table. Although the room was crowded, they sat alone in a corner, with the smoke-stained plastered wall behind them and the fire at Rachel's side.

"Have you ever wondered what you'll do when you leave the army?" Rachel asked.

"Leave the army?" Flockhart repeated. He stared into the fire for a few moments. "I try not to," he said. "I don't think I can leave."

"You can't stay a soldier forever," Rachel said. "The constant marching in bad weather and sleeping in tents in the rain will wear you out. Oh, it's fine now when you are young, fit and healthy, but how about in ten years or twenty when you are an old, done man?"

Flockhart lifted his tankard without drinking. "I suppose I'll soldier until I die," he said. "Or, if I'm lucky, I'll end up a Chelsea

Pensioner."[1]

"What would happen if the war ended, and the Queen disbanded the Royals?" Rachel mentioned the scenario that Flockhart most dreaded.

Flockhart sipped from his tankard, looked up as two men in the far corner of the room began to argue, and returned his attention to Rachel. "The Queen won't do that," he said. "We're the Royal Scots, the Royal Regiment, the oldest Foot regiment in the army. She might disband the newer regiments but not the Royals."

The two men were civilians, and one was English. Flockhart slid further into the corner, apprehensive in case Lord Eskbank had sent somebody else to hunt him down. He touched his throat and slid a hand to the bayonet at his waist.

"There are two Royals battalions," Rachel reminded. "If peace came, the Queen might disband one of them. You could be begging in the streets in a couple of years."

"Let's hope for a long war, then," Flockhart said.

Rachel understood her man. "How about me?" she forced Flockhart to consider the future. "Would you abandon me to pauperism?"

Flockhart stared at her. "You could find another soldier in the regiment," he said.

"I don't want another soldier," Rachel told him. "I only want you."

Flockhart looked away, trying to understand that Rachel's affection was more profound than the day-to-day necessities of life. Most soldiers' women, he knew, were faithful when their men were alive, but necessity had bred a pragmatic breed. If a soldier's wife lost her man to battle or disease, she would soon find a replacement in the ranks. Some women could lose their man in the morning and be sharing a comrade's bed that same

---

1. The Royal Hospital at Chelsea was completed in 1692, with its complement of long-serving ordinary soldiers.

night. There was little place for romantic love in the ranks of Queen Anne's army.

"You can do better than me," Flockhart said at length. He smiled without humour. "You're an intelligent woman, Rachel. You can think things out. You know I have no schooling; I can barely read and write. I have no trade, no skills and no future. If I left the army, the best I could hope for would be casual labouring."

"I know," Rachel said candidly. "But I also know you helped me when I needed it most; you have a decent heart somewhere." She watched as one of the barmaids added coal to the fire. "I can't see coal without thinking of you slaving down the mines," Rachel changed the subject slightly. "You never know; you might have hacked out that coal yourself."

"Maybe," Flockhart was never happy discussing his past.

"You don't want to return to that life," Rachel tried a new tack.

"I don't," Flockhart agreed.

"I've mentioned this before," Rachel said. "Would you not prefer to run an inn or a tavern?"

Flockhart sighed. "I've no skills in counting," he said, "no money to buy or rent an inn, and if I return to Scotland or England, the authorities will grab me and hand me over to Lord Eskbank."

"Even after all this time?" Rachel asked.

"His Lordship is a vindictive man," Flockhart said.

"You don't have to return to Scotland," Rachel said quietly. "We can stay in the Netherlands."

"We?" Flockhart repeated.

"We," Rachel said firmly. "You and I, together."

Flockhart stared into the fire, wrestling with the idea that Rachel wanted more from him than the transient relationship of a military camp follower.

"Why?"

"Why not?" Rachel asked.

Flockhart nodded. "You'd be a good innkeeper," he said cautiously.

"So would you," Rachel told him. "Most soldiers would drink away the takings. Look at them, ten thousand lushes armed with muskets, hunting for whores and alcohol. You don't act like that."

"No," Flockhart said quietly. "I can't afford to get drunk in case Lord Eskbank sends somebody else after me, and I don't need a whore."

Rachel nodded. "Think about it, Davie. Don't push my idea aside. We could make it work."

"I'll think about it," Flockhart promised. "We'd need money, though, far more than a soldier earns. Eightpence a day less stoppages won't buy or rent us a tavern."

"There are ways around that," Rachel said without adding details.

Flockhart was on sentry duty that night, and as he stood at his lonely post, holding his musket to him and watching through the echoing dark, he thought of Rachel's words.

He would have Rachel with him forever, acting as man and wife. But he'd have to leave the regiment, leave Leishman and Sergeant Dunn. He'd miss their company, the friendship forged over long marches and bitter battles. He'd also miss the open air, the sky above as they marched, the camaraderie of the Royals and the rough humour that lightened the days.

Flockhart sighed, peered into the dark countryside outside the town as he thought he saw movement and relaxed when he heard a fox bark.

What should I do? Rachel has put me in a quandary now. He shrugged. *Maybe not. I don't have a brass penny to my name, let alone enough to rent a tavern. Rachel is dreaming.*

Flockhart heard somebody moving and cocked his musket. "Who goes there? Advance and be recognised!"

"Remember me?" Ruth Gordon stepped from the shadow of a building in front of Flockhart.

"I remember you," Flockhart said warily, keeping his musket aimed at her body. He had hoped never to see her again.

Gordon remained two yards away. "You murdered my colleagues."

"I murdered nobody," Flockhart replied.

"That's not what I heard," Sergeant Lamb joined them, sliding from an alleyway. "I heard you are a runaway collier who murdered two men who came to arrest you."

Flockhart fingered his throat. "Is that what you heard?"

"I could have you arrested here and now," Lamb said, standing beside Gordon. "We'd send you back in chains and let your owner decide what to do with you."

Flockhart looked around, but the area was deserted. Neither Sergeant Dunn nor Leishman was in sight. When he lifted his musket, he realised that Gordon had a pistol pointed at his groin.

"That won't avail you," Gordon said. "You left me stranded and alone in Bavaria."

"Did I?" Flockhart played for time, hoping that somebody, an officer or NCO, would happen along. The street remained frustratingly quiet.

"We've decided not to arrest you," Lamb said. "Not this time. This poor lady needs money to pay for her passage home, and you're going to provide it."

"Me?" Flockhart's laugh was genuine. "I don't have a farthing to scratch myself with."

Gordon jabbed the muzzle of her pistol painfully into Flockhart's groin.

"You will do," Lamb told him. "You may remember that I gave you a proposal once. I said you could fight for money, and we'd split the proceeds. You turned me down. Now, you'll fight, and Ruth and I will pocket the money."

"I'm damned if I will," Flockhart said.

Gordon jabbed him with her pistol again. "How's your woman? She hit me with a stone last time we met."

"She didn't hit you hard enough," Flockhart said.

"If you refuse my proposal," Sergeant Lamb said. "We'll have you arrested, and Ruth here will cut Rachel up."

"I won't kill her," Gordon said pleasantly. "I'll just leave her so mutilated she won't want to live."

Flockhart felt something lurch inside him. He knew Gordon was not exaggerating.

"You've gone very quiet," Lamb said.

Gordon smiled. "Shall I give you details, David? I'll start by cutting off her nose. Slowly."

"When do you want me to fight?" Flockhart asked. He saw Lamb smile and touch a hand to the sword at his waist.

"Tomorrow evening," Lamb said. "I have an opponent marked out for you."

Flockhart closed his eyes. In the last ten minutes, his world had turned upside down.

※

"So, you're my husband's mistress, are you?" Lady Joanna asked, leaning against the door jamb. "I wondered what you'd be like."

"I am," Elizabeth Ramsay replied.

Lady Joanna allowed her gaze to slide over Elizabeth from head to foot and back. "At least he has good taste."

Elizabeth rose from her chair and gave a mock curtsey. "Why, thank you, My Lady."

"He gave you my pearls, I see," Lady Joanna said.

Elizabeth fingered the pearls. "I wondered where they came from."

"From my dressing table," Lady Joanna said. "We blamed Polly Darkin, one of the maids." She slid onto a chair and glanced around the room. "He keeps you in some style, I see. For a common whore."

"I am not a whore," Elizabeth said evenly. "And if you were a good wife, His Lordship would not need another woman."

Lady Joanna laughed. "How little you know my husband."

Elizabeth strolled to the sideboard, poured herself a glass of claret, and sipped delicately, smiling at Lady Joanna. "Perhaps I know him better than you. I know I can satisfy his desires."

Lady Joanna smiled and took the glass from Elizabeth's hand. "We have things to discuss, my Lady Whore."

CHAPTER 27

DUTCH REPUBLIC, WINTER 1706

Flockhart stood at one side of the circle of spectators with his opponent opposite.

"You men know what you have to do."

Flockhart nodded while his opponent, Harkins, a flint-eyed veteran of Howe's Regiment, eyed him coldly. "I hear this is your first contest, Jock."[1]

"It is." Flockhart had nothing against the veteran.

Harkins nodded, drew his sword and examined the blade. "Did you learn fencing before you joined the army?"

"No," Flockhart replied.

"To the first blood, then," Harkins said, saluting with his sword.

"First blood." Flockhart saw the crowd as a blur of faces, some interested, some only hoping to win a wager. He knew most would bet on the veteran, who had previously won duels, while he was an unknown quantity. Flockhart saw Leishman at the front of the crowd with a stubby clay pipe between his teeth. Leishman nodded when he caught Flockhart's gaze. A few feet

---

1. Oliver Cromwell's soldiers seemed to be the first to call Scotsmen "Jock", so I have kept the term for a veteran soldier fifty-odd years later.

away, Rachel looked anxious, giving an obviously false smile to encourage him.

Behind Rachel and huddled in a camouflaging shawl, Gordon pulled back her sleeve to reveal a long knife, nodded towards Rachel, and lowered her arm.

Flockhart grunted, understanding the implied threat.

Lamb acted as referee, smiling as he stood at the side of the ring. "Are you men ready?"

"Ready," Harkins said.

"Ready," Flockhart replied.

Lamb held a silk handkerchief in the air. "When I drop this handkerchief, you will fight to the first blood."

Lamb opened his fingers, and the square of blue silk fluttered free. Less than a second later, Harkins ran at Flockhart, slashing at his left leg. Flockhart parried quickly, surprised at the ferocity of the attack. The crowd were shouting, most of them cheering for Harkins.

They've put money on me to lose, Flockhart told himself. He jumped back as Harkins slashed again, a backhanded swipe aimed at his right thigh.

"Fight him, Flockhart!" Lamb roared. "I've got money on you!"

Flockhart parried the next slash, wondering if he should allow Harkins to inflict a flesh wound to end the bout. He saw Gordon stepping closer to Rachel and knew he had to continue. He cursed, ducked and swung his sword upwards, catching Harkins' blade with his. Harkins tried to pull back, but Flockhart had anticipated the move and followed, pushing his sword against the older man's weapon.

Flockhart knew he was stronger and held Harkins' blade captive, driving the older man back step by step. He saw beads of sweat appear on Harkins' face, saw the veteran's confidence slowly fade, and knew he had the upper hand. As Harkins weakened, Flockhart continued to press, slid his left foot, tripped his opponent, freed his blade, and inflicted a nick on the man's shoulder.

Flockhart stepped back. "First blood," he said and helped Harkins to his feet. He heard Lamb's roar of triumph and looked at Rachel. Gordon had merged with the crowd.

"The first victory of many," Lamb said as he collected his winnings. "And your ugly little woman will live another day."

※

Recruits came to the Royals in small parties throughout February and March, sailing directly from Leith in the royal warships *Weymouth, Nightingale* and *Bonadventure*.

Flockhart and the other old soldiers were always interested in watching new blood arrive, partly to assess their quality and partly to glean information about life back home.

"Here come more recruits!" The veterans gathered around, wiry men with stern, weather-beaten faces and basilisk eyes who surrounded the nervous newcomers.

"What's the news then?" Flockhart asked. "What have you got to tell us?"

"The politicians are discussing a union between Scotland and England," a fresh-faced recruit replied, recoiling slightly from Flockhart's iron visage.

Flockhart glanced at Leishman, who looked disinterested. "Anything else? Have you any news about Lord Eskbank of Eskhall?"

The recruit nodded, eager to be accepted. "Yes. Lord Eskbank is one of the Scottish representatives for the Union negotiations."

"Does that mean he'll be moving down to London?" Flockhart asked hopefully.

"I don't know," the recruit replied.

Along with the recruits, a munificent government supplied the Royals with a full supply of new clothing to replace the threadbare and sadly battered uniforms they had worn for years. Flockhart lifted his bright scarlet coat.

"Rachel will be pleased," he said. "She says she is always darning and sewing my old coat together, while my stockings have more holes in them than the lines of Brabant."

Leishman puffed smoke into the air. "Don't be too joyous," he said. "The colonel will deduct the price from your pay."

Flockhart nodded. "I'd have to pay for new clothes anyway, and I'll never miss what I've never had."

"You're a philosophical fellow, Davie; I'll say that for you," Leishman added more tobacco to his pipe. He eyed Flockhart through a cloud of blue smoke. "You'll never amount to anything with that attitude, but you'll be content."

Flockhart nodded. "I have few worries," he said.

"Sergeant Lamb being one," Leishman replied. "There are ways of getting rid of him."

"I know," Flockhart said softly. He did not mention Gordon's threat to Rachel, not even to Leishman.

When the winter eased and the 1706 campaigning season began, Sergeant Dunn explained what he knew about the French positions.

"According to my bottle companion in Marlborough's quarters," Dunn began, "The French have three armies in northern Europe. Marshal Villeroy commands around sixty thousand men in Brabant, ready to do battle with us. There are another 25,000 French on the Upper Moselle, including the French Household Cavalry, the famous Maison du Roi. Lastly, Marshal Villars has 40,000 men facing the Margrave of Baden."

Dunn's platoon listened and nodded. "We'll be fighting Villeroy, then," Flockhart said.

"I'd say so," Dunn agreed. "He's one of Louis's favourites and a veteran, but I'd say Marlborough will have his measure."

"Let's hope so," Flockhart replied.

Rachel joined them, accepted as an equal as she slid beside Flockhart and sat cross-legged on the ground. "I don't know how true my information is," she said, "but the women in town tell me that King Louis is pressing Villeroy to face Marlborough in battle."

"How would they know?" Young asked.

"Women stick together," Rachel informed him. "They pick up information from the wives of French deserters, and, unlike you, Peter, they can work things out. The Frenchies say that Villeroy thinks our victory at Blenheim was a fluke, and he contained Marlborough easily last year."

"That's not what happened!" Young protested.

"We know that," Rachel told him, smiling, "but according to the deserters' wives, some French are disparaging Villeroy's courage and encouraging him to face Corporal John in open battle."

Leishman blew more smoke into the air. "I'll wager the men who do that have never smelled powder smoke in their lives."

"Their courage comes out of a bottle," Rachel agreed.

On the 18th of May 1706, Villeroy marched his army from Louvain, hoping to outflank the Allies in Brabant.

"The French have started this year's season!" Sergeant Dunn was first with the news. "Get ready, boys; we'll be on the march soon. Flockhart! I saw a speck of rust on your musket; get rid of it! Young, check your flints are sharp, Leishman, you're on picket duty, McLeish, get that uniform cleaned before some farmer ploughs it up." Dunn moved away to spread encouragement to another section as the drums rolled and officers adjusted their wigs before taking another parade.

Flockhart grinned to Leishman as he examined his musket for non-existent rust. "We're back to war again," he said.

In May, the Royals were on the move, marching to Bilsen, ten miles from Maastricht, to rendezvous with the rest of the Allied army.

"The Dutch are already here," Leishman said, "but the Danes are still about thirty miles and two days' march away." He sucked at an empty pipe. "The Hanoverians and Prussians are still in their winter quarters."

"Lazy buggers," Flockhart commented without heat. "I hope they join us soon."

"If we count the Danes," Leishman said, "we'll have 130 cavalry squadrons, 90 guns, and 75 infantry battalions. Fifteen battalions are British, including four Scottish, while four more Scottish battalions, the Scots Brigade, are marching with the Dutch."

"I heard we had 74 battalions and 122 squadrons," Dunn corrected. "That's what Marlborough's secretary told me."

"Either way," Flockhart said. "We have sufficient to spread the fear of God into the French."

"I wish the Prussians were with us," Young said. "These lads know how to fight."

From Bilsen, they marched towards Mont St Andre as rumours swept over the army. Men exchanged news they had heard or what the sutlers, wives, or washerwomen thought.

"Did you hear what the French plan next?" Young asked as they marched over the rain-lashed roads.

"Not a word. The Sun King hasn't spoken to me for days."

"Marshal Marsin and the French Household Cavalry will combine with Villeroy and ambush Marlborough."

"Who told you that?" Flockhart asked.

"Corporal Muirhead's wife."

"It must be correct then. Agnes Brown knows more than any general," Flockhart replied seriously. "You'd better tell Captain Brisbane to pass it along to Corporal John."

"Do you think I should?" Young asked.

"Only if you want to be on latrine duty from now until Judgement Day," Flockhart told him.

As the Allies marched, tension mounted. Villeroy besieged a minor fortress on the Little Gete River, and his cavalry patrols ravaged the surrounding land.

The Allies marched from campsite to campsite, grousing,

grumbling, perplexed by the seemingly pointless movement yet obedient to the insistent demands of the drums. Following the drum was their life, the only life many of them could understand. They were soldiers, the poor, bloody infantry, underpaid, despised by the countries they protected, unwanted, underappreciated, yet proud of their regiments and loyal to their companions.

March, march, follow the drum, eat poor rations, camp in the rain, the sharp end of Queen Anne's diplomacy, march, march, march, and eventually fight an enemy who was the mirror image of themselves. Unless fatigue, exposure, or disease claimed them before the battle.

The next few days, as messages came to Marlborough informing him of Villeroy's movements, he pushed his army across the smiling countryside. Initially intending to threaten Namur, Marlborough heard the French were gathering in the Louvain area and headed in that direction. The following day, 19th of May 1706, spies told him Villeroy was marching towards Tirlemont, still in the Spanish Netherlands.

"I feel dizzy with all this marching and counter-marching," Young said.

"There are worse things in life than marching," Flockhart told him. They watched the cavalry trot forward, the sun glinting from their accoutrements. Flockhart took a deep breath, glanced at his companions, and then over his shoulder to the camp followers. He could not see Rachel but knew she was there.

The rumours spread, with each telling adding more to the story. Flockhart listened, smiled and marched on.

"Ignore the nonsense," Sergeant Dunn said. "Marlborough has ordered the Duke of Württemberg, the Danish commander, to march to us and send the cavalry in advance. All the rest is speculation or lies."

On the 20th of May, rain fell in a deluge that turned the roads into quagmires and halted the passage of wheeled vehicles. The army halted, with the men grumbling at the weather and the higher command anxious to press on.

"Where are we now?" Young asked as rainwater wept from the brim of his hat.

"We're here," Flockhart replied. "And tomorrow, we might be somewhere else." He lifted a hand to acknowledge Rachel's wave, held his musket upside down to prevent rain from entering the muzzle and sucked his empty pipe.

As the Allies waited in frustration, Villeroy and the Elector of Bavaria combined their armies and began to march south.

"The Frenchies are looking for a battle," Leishman said.

"So are we," Flockhart replied.

Marlborough marched the army across the now sodden countryside, with the wagons struggling on the rutted, part-flooded roads and men wading through ankle-deep puddles. They slogged around the swollen Little Gete and to the rising ground at the head of the river. Every step splashed in mud, with the land beside the river like a bog and bruised grey clouds overhead, threatening more rain.

At the head of the river, ridges of higher ground rose from marshland, with the rivers Mehaigne and Little Gete separated by a single ridge that descended to a broad plain.

"This area is grand cavalry country," Leishman commented. "Villeroy will throw the Household Cavalry at us, and they're said to be the finest cavalry in Europe."

Flockhart swore as his feet sank calf-deep in a muddy puddle. "Aye? Well, the Royals are the finest infantry, so let the bastards come."

"You're a bloodthirsty bastard, Davie," Leishman said.

Flockhart grunted. "I'll do my duty," he replied.

A little after midnight on the 22nd of May, Marlborough ordered a substantial body of 700 dragoons to escort the Earl of Cadogan, the quartermaster general, on a reconnaissance. Two hours later, in the chilling grey of the pre-dawn, the drums woke the Allied camp, and they were on the march by three.

"Why send Cadogan in front?" Young asked.

"The Earl of Cadogan is an important man," Leishman said. "Marlborough thinks a lot of him."

"He does," Sergeant Dunn agreed. "Cadogan is Marlborough's eyes and ears; he deals with the Army's intelligence. I hear he has a whole raft of agents in the Low Countries and even in France, feeding him information about French military movements."

Flockhart grunted. "He doesn't need them. Sergeant Muirhead's wife knows all there is to know. Just ask her, eh, Peter?"

Young swore in reply.

"There will be a battle today," Flockhart said. "I can feel it." He peered forward through a rising mist. "Villeroy wants a fight, and Marlborough won't disappoint him."

Leishman nodded, stumbling in the half-dark. "You could be right," he said. "God preserve us; you could be right."

Marlborough pushed his men forward in eight columns along a four-mile front. Most British infantry were on the right under the Earl of Orkney, with Lumley's British cavalry in support. The Dutch infantry took the centre, supported by Danish cavalry, with the Dutch cavalry riding on the left wing.

As the army marched, Marlborough sent a galloper to the Royals, and news spread down the ranks that Marshal Villeroy and the Elector of Bavaria had formed their army ready for battle.

"They're waiting for us," Sergeant Dunn said. "Villeroy wants revenge for Blenheim."

"Where?" Leishman asked.

"The French right is mainly cavalry, based at the village of Taviers," Dunn said. "Their centre is at Ramillies, a mile and a half to the north." He ran a hand over the blade of his halberd. "I hear Villeroy has his men very strongly posted, with his left between the villages of Offuz and Autreglise."

The names meant little to Flockhart, but the positioning of Villeroy's army did. "We should be on the right of the army," he said, "the post of honour, so we will face the men in Offuz and Autre-Eglise."

"That's true, Davie, if Corporal John decides on a head-on attack," Leishman said. "There are the drums." He stamped his feet. "God be with us, Davie. If I die, take my things before the ghouls do, and if I'm badly wounded, end it quick for me."

Flockhart nodded. "I will, Adam, and you do the same for me."

They shook hands, both aware of the horrors the day would unleash.

The drums beat for the Royals, with each company following the drums to march into position. The men concentrated to hear their company's signals and moved as ordered, precise and slow, with Marlborough the brain behind the movement of tens of thousands of men.

Flockhart stared in front, aware of the men on either side of him, the colours drooping in the damp air, and the mounted officers riding to and fro. He wondered where Rachel was and what was happening back in Scotland, and then he halted as the drums stopped.

The army stood still, save for the busy messengers. Horses snorted, men shuffled their feet on the wet ground, and a whiff of smoke came from a distant chimney.

Early summer crops rippled across the fields, while the natural ridges of the landscape concealed much of the Allied army, giving the scene a surreal effect. Somewhere, a man coughed, the sound unnaturally loud in the tense hush.

Marlborough formed up his army in a long line facing the enemy and slowly advanced across the open plain. The Royals were on the right, forming on the Heights of Foulz, from which they had a fine view of the low ground and the French in the distance. The Earl of Cadogan commanded the advance guard, riding well in front of the Allied army.

"Why's Cadogan so far in front?" Flockhart asked.

"Marlborough relies on him," Dunn replied. "Cadogan will

tell Corporal John how the French are positioned and give sound advice. Once we start fighting, he'll carry Marlborough's instructions to the generals."

"He's an important man, then," Flockhart said.

"Perhaps second only to Marlborough himself," Dunn replied. "Look ahead! Is that not a sight to thrill the blood?"

The plain of Ramillies stretched ahead, with the French infantry advancing in two columns, with each front a battalion strong. The artillery lumbered forward between the infantry, with teams of horses pulling the sinister guns.

"I hate the artillery," Leishman growled, as he always did before battle. "They stand out of danger and murder us from afar. I never give an artilleryman quarter."

Flockhart nodded. He remembered the effects of roundshot and grape at Blenheim, with maimed men screaming for relief or death. Musket shot was bad enough but seemed kind compared to the damage cannons inflicted, while soldiers with bayonets at least faced their enemy man to man.

In their white uniforms and black tricorn hats, the French infantry looked impeccable and formidable as they advanced in perfect formation beneath their flags. Behind them, the eighty-two squadrons of cavalry, including the famous *Maison du Roi*, assembled on a ridge that stretched southward from Ramillies to the Mehaigne. Between Ramillies and Offuz, two more lines of infantry waited, with a further twenty battalions waiting behind entrenchments at Ramillies.

"There's plenty of them," Young said.

"There are," Leishman agreed. He nodded to the ground between Offuz and Autreglise. "And more over there."

Flockhart saw the lines of soldiers in Bourbon white, backed by squadrons of eager cavalry.

"They have a strong position," Leishman said, "but Villeroy has placed his cavalry to counter ours rather than exploiting the plain on his right." He laughed. "He's already dancing to Marlborough's tune."

Flockhart rested on the muzzle of his musket, listened to the drums, Allied and French, and saw both armies set out like colourful pieces on a gigantic chessboard. He knew the analogy was well-used but very apt before a formal battle.

"We're moving again," Leishman said. "The drums are summoning us. Good luck, lads."

At one in the afternoon, the Allies came into range of the French artillery.

CHAPTER 28

RAMILLIES, MAY 1706

"Here we go," Leishman said as the sharp bark of artillery sounded, with flashes of orange flame and jets of dirty grey-white smoke. "God, how I hate standing still for these bastards to murder us."

"The French have the same number of men as we do," Flockhart said. "According to Aggie Brown." His smile convinced nobody. "And the defence is always favoured against the offence. This day will be bloody."

"Every battle is bloody," Leishman spoke through gritted teeth when the French artillery fired again.

As the British advanced against the French left at Offuz and Autreglise, Villeroy shifted some of his men to counter the attack. Flockhart watched the white-clad battalions march away, solid blocks of soldiers, inheritors of a tradition of victory that stretched back for decades. Only Marlborough's success at Blenheim spoiled the French record, and Villeroy's battle-hardened infantrymen were determined to rectify that blemish.

"The French will expect the swampy ground to act as a barrier to Offuz," Leishman said. "Nobody can advance rapidly and in order through a bog."

"Villeroy has positioned his men well, damn him," Flockhart said.

When the British line descended into a fold in the ground, invisible to the French, Marlborough sent the rear line rapidly to their left.

"What's happening?" Young asked.

"Corporal John has fooled the French again," Flockhart explained. "He's put his best regiments, us, against the French left. Villeroy responded by weakening the rest of his position. Now, Marlborough will launch an attack on the French centre and right while we hold their left." He nodded forward. "See that little village there?"

"Taviers," Leishman explained, relieved to be temporarily sheltered from the French artillery.

"What about the village?" Young asked.

Taviers looked suddenly vulnerable, a place of peace about to be shattered by men of war. Fate had placed Taviers in the cockpit of Europe, ripe for predatory kings and professional soldiers to exploit.

"Taviers is in front of the French right," Leishman said, "and beyond the marsh that acts as a moat. If we take it, we could enfilade the French cavalry with volley fire. That's why Marlborough has sent fourteen battalions of Dutch and Scots Dutch to capture it."

The Allies' left and centre advanced, drums beating, men in step, tricorn hats on heads, and muskets held in front of them. Flockhart thought it very pretty, very martial, and very dangerous. Once again, he understood the attraction of military life, except for the strict discipline and the horror fields of battle.

The French artillery continued to pound the Allies as the Royals emerged from the dip. The roundshot ploughed bloody lanes in the ranks, cutting men in two, smashing bodies, taking off arms, legs and heads and leaving shattered, screaming remnants on the ground. A film of blood rose in the air to descend on the subsequent lines of steadily marching men.

"Dear Lord, save me from artillery," Leishman prayed. "Let me live long enough to get close and grant me the strength to shove my bayonet in the gunners' guts."

As Marlborough launched the second line of Dutch and Danes at the French centre and right, the Allied right stood still, containing the French left without firing a shot. The battle to the Royals' left raged on, with both sides firing volleys, drums hammering orders, and the screams of the wounded and the dying.

Villeroy sent five regiments of dismounted dragoons, three battalions of Swiss infantry and a brigade of Bavarians to hold Taviers.

"The Frenchies are disorganised," Leishman sounded calm despite the artillery fire. "Their counterattack is advancing in dribs and drabs."

As Villeroy's men moved forward, the British artillery targeted them, knocking men down without slowing the advance. A colonel rode at the head of the Bavarian brigade and pushed forward to inspect the marsh, searching for the best passage for his men. He sank deeply into the mud and floundered within a few moments. A group of Allied horsemen splashed in, rescued the colonel and took him prisoner.

While the Bavarians were still negotiating the marsh, the dragoons and Swiss met the Dutch and Scots Dutch in Taviers. The fourteen Allied battalions blasted the Swiss and dragoons, causing many casualties and sending them back in a disorganised mob. Their panic affected the Bavarians, and their officers only restored order with difficulty.

"We're making progress," Flockhart said.

"Let's capture these blasted guns," Leishman said. His eyes were wild, jerking from side to side as they entered a bank of acrid powder smoke.

As the Dutch, Scots, Swiss and French contested Taviers, a galloper approached the Allied right with orders from Marlborough.

"We'll be moving soon," Leishman said. He nodded when the drums tapped the advance.

"Here we go, Davie boy. Remember, if the French kill me, you take my possessions."

Flockhart nodded, marching forward in step as the colours fluttered above them. "You do the same for me, Adam."

"There's a bog and a river ahead," Sergeant Dunn said. "Keep in formation, boys, and help anybody who sinks!"

Flockhart found the soft ground sucking at his feet, with men around him swearing. One recruit panicked as the bog pulled him under until Sergeant Muirhead pulled him bodily out, although at the expense of one of his shoes.

"Never mind your shoe," Muirhead said. "You'll get another from the casualties later. March on!"

The bog stretched to the Little Gete River, which Flockhart thought looked broad and deep as the Royals reached its banks.

I'll have to learn to swim.

The officers rode in front, splashing through the river, the morning sun reflecting on the water droplets. Captain Brisbane stopped mid-channel and waved his company across. "On you come, men! It's not too deep." The river surged to his horse's hocks, breaking around the animal in creamy brown water.

The Royals waded in. Flockhart gasped at the force of the current, felt his feet sinking on the muddy riverbed, and pushed on. He focused on the far bank, fixed a point in his mind, and tried to ignore the prospect of drowning.

"You hate artillery, Adam," Flockhart said. "I hate fording rivers. I can't swim."

Leishman put a steadying hand on his arm. "I've got you, Davie!"

Flockhart stepped onto the far bank, breathed a deep sigh of relief and marched on. One by one, Orkney's British regiments crossed the Little Gete and approached the village of Autreglise. Flockhart saw some squadrons of British cavalry on their right flank and felt more secure, knowing the French could not attack from that side.

"We can't be far away now," Young said.

"Save your breath for fighting," Sergeant Dunn snarled.

The enemy left consisted of a mixture of French, Bavarians and Spanish. They held for a while, exchanging volleys as the Allies pushed forward, then began to withdraw.

Musketry crackled ahead of the Royals, with the enemy firing volleys with long gaps between. Men fell, wounded or dead, and the British ranks closed, leaving the casualties behind.

"Close up!" the officers and NCOs ordered. "Close ranks and move on!" The colours fluttered above, bright against the morning sky, as clouds of powder smoke wafted across the battlefield. The British halted, fired a volley, reloaded, and advanced, with the drums beating, officers marching in front, and the NCOs using their halberds to keep the men in line.

"Push them back," Captain Brisbane shouted.

The Royals responded, increasing their pace as they advanced into now dense clouds of smoke.

When the Allies appeared before them, the French broke and fled, with the Allies following, killing, wounding and taking prisoners.

"Don't break ranks!" Major Hamilton roared. "There may be French cavalry around!"

Flockhart saw a galloper approach Orkney, and a few moments later, the drums ordered the Royals to halt. The men stopped, panting, glad they were unhurt and wondering if they had won the battle. When Flockhart looked around, he saw that the Allies' entire right flank had halted, with men and officers looking at each other in confusion.

"What are we stopping for?" Young asked. "We've got them on the run!"

"God knows," Leishman replied. "Count your blessings that we're still alive."

Flockhart checked his flint, found it dull and quickly replaced it.

"Halt!" an officer shouted to one company who were reluctant to stop. "Halt!" The men slowed with some shouting obscenities that the officer wisely chose to ignore.

The drums beat the retiral, and the British began to withdraw, grumbling and unhappy to break off an engagement when they were successful.

Encouraged by the British retiral, the enemy flooded back, firing ragged volleys as a battery of artillery hammered at the redcoats. Orkney took direct command, ordering the Guards and the Royals to form a rearguard.

"We had them on the bloody run!" Young said. "We had them beat."

When the French followed, the Royals and Guards faced about and replied with volley fire that stopped the pursuit.

Captain Brisbane ran through the orders.

"Make ready!"

Flockhart obeyed mechanically, hardly listening as he presented his musket.

"Fire!"

The sheet of aimed one-ounce bullets halted the pursuit. As the enemy hesitated, the British reached Little Gete, and the French followed without coming close.

Fording the river under fire was unpleasant, but Orkney had the Guards cover the Royals, and then the Royals covered the Guards until both regiments were safely across.

Brisbane's company acted as rearguard, lining up to repel a French assault that did not occur. The French did not cross the river, knowing they would be vulnerable in the marsh, but contented themselves with firing at the withdrawing British.

"Give them a volley," Captain Brisbane ordered, "and then retire by platoons!"

"How far are we retiring?" Flockhart asked as the British returned to their original positions.

"As far as the officers tell us," Sergeant Dunn replied.

The drums rattled their orders, turning the first British line to face the French. The second line marched below the ridge crest, then altered direction and marched to reinforce the Allied centre.

All the months of training have been worth it, Flockhart thought as he marched with the rest. He wondered what Marlborough's strategy was, shrugged and trusted to the officers' judgement.

While the Royals were engaged, Marlborough had sent twelve battalions against Ramillies, with the artillery hammering the village. Henry de Nassau, General Lord Overkirk, led a Dutch cavalry attack up the French-held ridge south of the village, scattering the Bavarian and French cavalry. However, the supporting infantry presented a line of bayonets and controlled volleys that halted the Dutch cavalry. Seeing the Dutch in disarray, the French *Maison du Roi* charged and pushed them to their original starting point.

"Look!" Leishman nodded with his head. "There's Corporal John!"

General Marlborough galloped into the melee, wig flying as he shouted to rally the Dutch cavalry. Three squadrons formed behind him, and he charged into the enemy, sword in hand. Some of the retreating cavalry crashed into Marlborough, knocking him off his horse, and the battle swirled around him, men roaring, swords clashing, and horses pounding and whinnying. Captain Richard Molesworth, once a Royal Scot, galloped forward, lifted the duke, and returned with him to the Allied lines.

"We nearly lost Corporal John!" Dunn shouted. "Thank God for Rickie Molesworth!"

As the Dutch struggled with the French, thirty-nine squadrons of Allied cavalry arrived from the right wing. The Danish cavalry swung wide, outflanking the French. The Allies advanced in four lines, cavalry supported by infantry, slowly at first, then with greater speed. They smashed into the French cavalry, surged through the gaps in the enemy squadrons, circled and attacked them in the rear and flanks.

The French right-wing broke, with riderless horses galloping past the infantry as the victorious Allied cavalry reformed. Marlborough lined them facing north, with Villeroy dragging his remaining cavalry from the left wing to counter them. In the village of Ramillies, pockets of stubborn French infantry clung on, refusing to flee or surrender.

Still waiting for orders, Flockhart and the Royals watched what they could see of the battle through the powder smoke.

"Doesn't Marlborough want our help?" Flockhart asked.

"Stay out of it and keep alive," Leishman said calmly. "Don't hunt for death, Davie; he'll find you soon enough."

The Allies and French reformed, with the cannon firing at the opposing infantry and the constant orders to close the ranks.

"Bloody artillery," Leishman's hands gripped his musket so tightly his knuckles gleamed white. "I hate gunners!"

"We know," Flockhart replied. "You've mentioned it before."

The Colours flapped above them, marking each battalion and daring the enemy to advance. At six in the evening, trumpets and bugles sounded their shrill notes, and the Allied cavalry advanced.

"This is the crisis," Leishman said. "Either the French will break now, or they'll hold on, and we'll have to rethink our tactics."

Flockhart rested on his musket, watching the course of the battle. Rather than face the superior numbers of the Allies, the French cavalry hesitated. Flockhart saw a ripple run through the French ranks, with some men turning and others remaining still. The officers took control, and they withdrew in good order.

"What's happening?" Young asked.

"They're beat," Leishman said with more relief than triumph. "Without their supporting cavalry, the French infantry can't stand."

When Marlborough's drums rattled advance, the Allied

centre moved forward, marching against the unsupported French infantry and artillery between Ramillies and Autre-Eglise. Simultaneously, the Dutch and Saxons overcame the final French resistance in Ramillies and mounted a flank attack on Offuz.

"When will we be involved?" Flockhart asked.

"We're holding down the French opposite us," Leishman explained. "If we stay put, these lads can't get involved."

Villeroy was not finished yet. He had no French cavalry but ordered the Elector of Bavaria's Bavarian and Spanish Horse Guards to attack. Marlborough countered by sending forward two British cavalry regiments, which routed the enemy. With no cavalry and the British centre advancing, the French began a full retreat.

"There goes the cavalry," Leishman said as Lumley's horse trotted across the French line of retreat. The Greys charged the *Regiment du Roi*, scattering them, and the French retreat became a rout. The Greys captured the *Regiment du Roi's* Colours, equipment, and scores of men.

"That's another victory for Corporal John," Leishman said when the Allied infantry finally halted, although the British cavalry continued to harass the fleeing enemy.

Villeroy retreated hastily. He set torches to many of his stores to prevent the Allies from profiting from them, threw the remainder in the Dyle, and fled to the rivers Senne and Dender.

"The French are running hard," Sergeant Dunn said. "We've broken their spirit as well as their army."

The cavalry pursued the French as far as Louvain, then halted. The French continued to retreat, abandoning town after town to Marlborough's men.

"We lost around five thousand men in that battle," Sergeant Dunn said the following day, puffing on his pipe, "mainly the Dutch and Danes for once."

"How about the enemy?" Leishman asked.

"According to Marlborough's secretary, they lost three times that number, with fifty guns, eighty Colours and standards and much of their baggage." Dunn looked pleased. "It was a decent victory."

Rachel smiled. "I know about their baggage," she said, feeling the money belt she had fashioned to carry her pickings.

After the battle, Rachel joined the scavengers robbing the dead. Some had been wives looking for their husbands; others were ghouls who slit the throats of the men they stripped of their clothes. Rachel was more practical, only taking what she could easily carry or sell to an officer.

CHAPTER 29

SPANISH NETHERLANDS, SUMMER 1706

As the French and Bavarians withdrew to Brussels, they felled trees and dug ditches to block the roads and slow down the Allied advance.

The Allies pressed on into the Spanish Netherlands. They took Louvain, brushing aside French resistance without trouble. Marlborough captured Brussels on the 28th of May, and the Allies cheered when they learned Brussels and the Duchy of Brabant switched their allegiance to the Emperor of Austria.

Marlborough's army marched, capturing town after town, village after village. When Marlborough captured Alost and marched his men over the Dender, Villeroy retreated again, marching hurriedly to the river Lys. Marlborough split his army and laid siege to fortresses and towns.

Flockhart and the Royals formed part of the army that protected the sieges of Menin, Ostend and Dendermonde. Life reverted to its summer routine of marches and sieges, putting up tents, digging entrenchments and taking down tents, following the beat of the drums.

"The French must be sick of walking backwards," Leishman joked.

Flockhart flinched at Leishman's choice of words. He remembered being shackled to the horse in the darkness of the pit, facing the nose of the horse as the blood flowed down his back, and Cummings and Lord Eskbank watched.

"Now you'll walk backwards," Lord Eskbank said. "Until I decide otherwise."

The horse moved in a circle, driving the pump that thrust water from the pit by lifting a chain of thirty-six buckets. Stumbling in front, Flockhart shuffled backwards, knowing the horse would trample him if he stopped or fell. After only a few circuits, he felt dizzy; after half an hour, he was sick, vomiting the contents of his stomach onto the ground as the horse moved inexorably towards him.

Flockhart lost count of the hours, feeling only the pain in his legs and the sickness inside him as he moved backwards with the horse's nose inches from his face. He could hear the constant clump of its hooves on the floor of the pit and the grind and creak of the pump. Time lost all meaning, while Flockhart's life was only pain and discomfort. He knew nothing else yet refused to give in and allow the horse to trample him underfoot.

The lantern shone from above, an alien intrusion into Flockhart's suffering.

"He's still alive," Cummings' voice broke into his introspective thoughts.

"And upright," Lord Eskbank sounded surprised. "Release him and put him to work."

Flockhart looked up, dazzled by the light. When Cummings unfastened him, he could not balance to walk forward but staggered and fell. Lord Eskbank kicked him in the ribs.

"Get up! You've got work to do! I'll teach you to steal yourself away! You're my property, body and soul!"

"Davie!" Leishman was staring at him. "Are you all right?"

Flockhart saw the ranks of weatherbeaten tents, heard the beating of drums and remembered where he was. "I'm grand," he said, forcing a smile.

Once again, Flockhart pushed the memories of the pit to the back of his mind, although he continued to watch any civilians suspiciously. He held his musket and reached for the bottle of Geneva that Leishman offered him.

Brussels, Ghent, Bruges: Marlborough's army captured town after town, pushing the French out of the Spanish Netherlands with a speed unprecedented in modern European warfare. The succession of successes was apparent to the toiling privates of the Royals as they marched and camped through the long summer of 1706.

When the French surrendered Ostend to the Allies, Marlborough split the Royals, sending one battalion with General Overkirk and Lieutenant-General Ingoldsby's force to besiege the town and fortress of Ath.

"Another week, another siege," Young said as the Royals took up their positions. "Why doesn't French Louis accept his sun has set before we take all the Spanish Netherlands and move into France?"

"He's a king," Leishman said. "They think differently from other people. They have the divine right to rule, or so they say."

Flockhart kept quiet, wondering what peace would mean to him. He did his duty, spent time with Rachel, and dreaded the war ending.

The pioneers dug the first parallel of the siege trenches on Monday the 18th of September, with the artillery batteries wheeled into place the following morning. Flockhart was in the supporting company as the grenadiers pushed forward towards the walls of Ath. He watched Lamb advance, throwing his grenades as the defenders retaliated with volleys of musketry and showers of grapeshot.

More blood, deaths and agony, so one king can say he owns a town where the inhabitants only want peace.

"Stand steady, men," Captain Brisbane ordered his company. "We'll sit tight unless the French try a sally."

Sergeant Dunn checked his men, smoothed a hand over the shaft of his halberd and watched.

"Keep your flints sharp, lads, and watch your front."

Waiting in the forward trenches, Flockhart came to expect Rachel to arrive periodically with sustaining broth and news of what was happening elsewhere in the siege.

"Sergeant Lamb's making quite a name for himself," Rachel said as she eased into the trench beside Dunn's platoon. "I heard talk of him being promoted."

"To what?" Flockhart asked.

"I heard Captain Brisbane talk of Lamb getting a battlefield commission," Rachel said. "He's been prominent in each storming and always shows leadership."

"God forbid!" Leishman said, supping at Rachel's broth. "Lamb would make Jean Martinet look like a kindly patriarch!"

"His only rival is Corporal Adair of the Royal Regiment of Ireland," Rachel continued.

"Adair the swordsman?" Flockhart asked.

"That's the fellow," Rachel said, "Well, we'll see what happens." She squatted in the shelter of the sandbags, spooning more broth into the eager bowls of Flockhart's section. "I heard that Prince Eugene's had another victory in Italy. He smashed the French at Turin and saved Savoy for the Grand Alliance."

"Eugene and Marlborough are winning this war," Leishman said. "We'll have peace soon, and all get back home." He grinned. "I can hardly remember what Scotland is like."

Flockhart exchanged glances with Rachel, who touched his arm with her forefinger. "It will be all right," she mouthed. "Everything will be all right."

"Careful!" Sergeant Dunn shouted. "Watch your front!"

"Get back out of danger," Flockhart moved to shelter Rachel. "Go on!"

Despite their defeats in battle and precipitous retreats, the garrison of Ath, French and Spanish, did not tamely surrender. They met the besiegers bomb for bomb and exchanged insults in various languages.

"Davie!" Rachel looked up as Dunn's platoon lifted their muskets.

Flockhart pushed Rachel to the bottom of the trench as the defenders sallied from Ath in a flood of white uniforms and determined, fiercely-moustached men. "Stay down!" Flockhart ordered as he aimed and fired.

"Make ready!" Dunn shouted as his platoon hastily reloaded.

The sally had nearly caught the Allies by surprise, overwhelming the forward pickets without a sound and charging into the Royals' trenches.

Flockhart glanced at Rachel lying in the bottom of the trench, straddled her with his legs and waited for the French.

"Here they come!" Dunn shouted. His platoon met the sally with a spatter of musketry, knocking down a few men without slowing the hundreds that came behind.

"Stand your ground!" Captain Brisbane ran up, sword in hand and wig askew. "Don't give them an inch!"

Flockhart reloaded, spitting the ball into the muzzle of his musket and ramming home the wad. He glanced at Rachel, crouched in the bottom of the trench and guarding the remains of her pot of broth. "You stay under cover!"

"I can fight!" Rachel said.

"We need you alive!" Leishman told her.

The French pushed on, intending to break down the besiegers' entrenchments, capture and spike some of the artillery and delay the Allies as long as possible in the hope that a relieving army could lift the siege. They ran along the forward trench line, throwing grenades before them.

Waiting in the second parallel, the Royals fired into the mass, repelled a half-hearted assault on their trench and waited for the French to gather their strength.

"Fix bayonets!" Brisbane shouted.

Flockhart slid his bayonet into place, watching the oncoming white flood.

"Make ready!" Brisbane stood on the lip of the trench to make himself visible to his men. He ignored the French balls that whistled around him, balanced the blade of his sword on his right shoulder and watched the enemy approach.

"Present!"

Brisbane's company slammed the muskets to their shoulders and aimed. Flockhart saw some of the French hesitate as they faced the wall of muzzles.

"Fire!"

Flockhart fired and immediately began to reload. He heard a roar from his right and saw a man fall, holding a hand to his face.

"They're still coming!" Young shouted.

Brisbane nodded, glancing behind him to see if any support was coming. "They're heading for the gun battery," he said. Make ready! Present!"

The French were shouting, encouraging each other with loud cries. Flockhart felt movement beside him and saw Rachel pick up the wounded man's musket.

"Get back down!" Flockhart snarled. "Or get out and run before the French get here."

"I'm staying," Rachel said calmly. She checked the musket's priming, lifted a cartridge from the wounded man's pack, loaded and held the weapon to her shoulder.

"Fire!"

Flockhart was too concerned with watching Rachel to see the effects of their volley. Rachel fired like a veteran, hardly flinching at the recoil of the heavy musket. She looked up as Flockhart nodded approval, and then the French were only a few yards away.

"Meet them!" Brisbane ordered.

Flockhart climbed to the lip of the trench and swore as Rachel joined him. "Get back!" he snarled.

"I'll be damned if I will!" Rachel replied, slotting a bayonet in place.

"You're a bloody fool!" Flockhart shouted.

Rachel laughed and tossed back her hair. "We're all fools,

fighting for a monarch who doesn't know we exist and doesn't care if we live or die."

A platoon of French advanced towards them, bayonets extended. Flockhart did not see the British counterattack until Corporal Adair appeared on the flank, threw two grenades and followed with a disciplined charge that saw a phalanx of tall Irishmen smash into the French.

"Forward!" Captain Brisbane shouted.

Flockhart ran to support the Royal Irish. He glanced at his side and saw Rachel was still there. She was slower than the men as her skirt hampered her but she was determined to prove her worth.

Faced with an attack on two sides, the French faltered. Flockhart saw them turn to run, heard Rachel shout, and saw her stumble.

"Rachel!" he held out a hand.

"I'm all right!" Rachel looked up, with sweat and dirt smeared over her face. "Watch out!"

A stray Frenchman had halted and lunged at Flockhart with his bayonet. Flockhart parried, swung his musket and smashed the butt into the Frenchman's face. The man roared and staggered, so Flockhart finished him with a thrust to the stomach, ripping the blade sideways.

"Thank you, Rachel," Flockhart gasped.

The Royal Irish had completed the counterattack, sending the enemy running. Rachel came to Flockhart's side as Adair looked at Flockhart, panting and cleaning the blood from his sword.

"You're Flockhart."

"I am," Flockhart admitted.

"I've heard of you," Adair slid his sword into its sheath.

"And I've heard of you," Flockhart told him.

They sized each other up momentarily; then the drums summoned them back to their lines.

The Royals did not participate in the assaults that captured Ath and watched as the garrison surrendered at the beginning of October.

As if God had seen sufficient bloodshed for one year, heavy rain hammered down, turning roads into muddy rivers and hampering any movement or further fighting. Marlborough ordered a review of his army, which meant days of cleaning and polishing, with fighting men becoming gloriously uniformed automatons. Rachel kept busy, ensuring Flockhart's uniform was pristine before helping Leishman and Young.

"How about you, Sergeant Dunn?" Rachel ran an experienced eye over him. "You look smart even without my help."

"I've found myself another wife," Dunn replied. "Esther is a good woman, a sergeant's widow."

"How many wives have you had?" Rachel asked.

"Three," Dunn replied. "Four if you count my first. I was a seaman then."

"Why would you not count her?" Rachel asked.

Dunn grinned. "It was only for a few days when I was in port."

"I don't want that sort of marriage," Rachel said solemnly. "I want one that lasts many years."

Leishman glanced from Rachel to Flockhart, smiled and said nothing.

Dunn hefted his halberd. "In this life, Rachel, we don't know if we'll have a tomorrow, let alone a next year. Take each day as a gift, and don't think of a future that might never happen."

"Wise advice for a soldier's wife," Leishman said.

"Perhaps," Rachel replied calmly. "But I won't take it. I don't want my children to grow up as I did. I want something better for them."

"You don't have any children," Leishman said, again glancing at Flockhart.

"Not yet," Rachel said. "But I intend to."

Flockhart remained silent, ensuring there was no rust on his musket.

The Royals took their place in the grand parade, with Marlborough and his senior Generals inspecting them unit by unit. Flockhart stood with the rest, once again feeling as if he was part of something important. Marlborough merely glanced at him as he passed, yet Flockhart sensed something charismatic. He stiffened more, and then Marlborough rode away, and Flockhart was only one man amongst thousands, less than a pawn in an army of tens of thousands.

Flockhart allowed his gaze to wander and saw Rachel standing among the spectators. Despite all the soldiers on parade, she only watched him, and Flockhart felt something swell inside him. He was unsure what it meant or even what it was, but he knew Rachel was becoming even more important than the regiment.

When Marlborough and the senior officers rode away, the drums sounded to dismiss the parade, and the Royals returned to their camp.

"That will be the end of the campaigning season," Leishman said. "Now for a comfortable winter back in Holland."

Flockhart nodded. There was no talk of peace, and he could relax for a few months. He closed his eyes, yearning for the war to last forever.

CHAPTER 30

LOW COUNTRIES AND SCOTLAND, WINTER 1706/07

F lockhart nodded as Rachel counted a handful of small coins on the ground and noted her tally in a small book. He looked up as Lamb appeared at the front door of the house.

"Another winter, Davie," Lamb smirked. "Are you ready to make me some money?"

"You're a bastard, Lamb," Flockhart said.

"So I've been told," Lamb replied. "I have a meaty bout waiting for you. Newly promoted Sergeant Adair, the champion swordsman of the Royal Irish. How about that?"

"How about it," Flockhart replied.

Lamb laughed, pointed to Rachel, ran a meaty finger across his throat and sauntered away.

Rachel swept her coins into a leather purse and closed the drawstring. "What was that about, Davie? What hold does Lamb have over you?"

"Nothing," Flockhart said.

"Don't lie to me, David Flockhart," Rachel warned.

Flockhart shook his head. "It's best you don't interfere," he said.

Rachel saw the steel in Flockhart's expression. "I'll find out," she told him. "And I'll sort it out." She left the room, worried and determined.

※

Queensberry smiled at Lord Eskbank over the rim of his claret. "That's the end of the old song," he said. "The Treaty of Union is signed, and we are all one country now. Great Britain." He rolled the syllables around his mouth. "Great Britain. It has a ring to it, doesn't it?"

"The people might protest," Eskbank warned. "They don't want to lose their nationality. Petitions are coming into the Estates from all four corners of Scotland."

"North Britain," Queensberry corrected with a small smile. "Scotland no longer exists. We're ready for any riots. We have English regiments placed on the Border and in the north of Ireland, ready to march into North Britain to put down any insurgency."

"Won't the Queen's Scottish regiments defend the country?" Eskbank asked.

Queensberry sipped at his claret. "We've made sure they can't. They're on the continent, following the drum with Corporal John, well out of the way. We'll change their names from the Scots Dragoons to the North British Dragoons and the Scots Fusiliers to the North British Fusiliers. Within a generation, the old name of Scotland will only be a memory."

"I see," Eskbank nodded.

"Here's to our success and new titles," Queensberry raised his glass. "A toast to Great Britain and mutual prosperity for you and I!"

"Great Britain and mutual prosperity!" Eskbank echoed. He thought of his gambling debts and Elizabeth Ramsay. "Prosperity!"

※

"Sergeant Adair!" Rachel lifted her skirt above her ankles and stepped towards him.

"That's me," Adair said and frowned. "You're Flockhart's wife, aren't you?"

"I am," Rachel agreed. "I believe you two are due to duel soon."

"We are," Adair said. Tall and broad, he spoke with a musical Ulster accent.

"I'd like a word with you," Rachel said.

Adair glanced around the street. "My quarters are over here." He hesitated for a second. "You've no need to be scared of me."

"I'm not," Rachel assured him. "I have something I want to discuss."

❄

Lord Eskbank adjusted his wig, ensuring it was at the correct angle, lifted his gold-topped cane and tapped it on the floor. "Are you ready?"

"Yes," Lady Joanna stepped away from the mirror. She glared at the two maidservants who had helped her dress. "Get out!" she said.

The maids curtseyed and fled.

Lord Eskbank held the door open for his wife, and they swept down the stairs together. A man-servant opened the front door, and the coach was waiting outside, with the coachman on his seat and the twin matched grey horses groomed and perfect. When a footman opened the coach door and let down the steps, Lady Joanna entered. Lord Eskbank followed.

"Queensberry House," he ordered and sat back to enjoy the ride.

"Is that all our money troubles behind us now?" Lady Joanna asked.

"It is," Eskbank confirmed. "Between the money London paid us for voting according to plan and our share of the Equivalent, we will have no debts and a little to spare. The new title will help as well." He smiled across to her in the padded interior of the carriage.

A group of farm servants watched as they passed through the tall gates of the estate, with one man spitting on the ground to show his dislike.

"Who is that insolent fellow?" Lady Joanna asked.

"A tenant," Eskbank said. "I don't know his name."

"Evict him," Lady Joanna said. "And his family. We can't allow that sort of attitude."

Eskbank nodded. "I'll do that when we return," he replied.

"Traitor!" somebody shouted, with the accusation hanging in the air as the carriage rumbled past.

"What did he say?" Lady Joanna asked.

"Traitor," Eskbank repeated. "Perhaps alluding to my voting for an Incorporating Union."

Lady Joanna smiled. "How amusing. A tenant who thinks his opinion matters. What do the lower orders understand about politics?"

Lord Eskbank laughed. "What do they understand about anything? They are barely better than the brute beasts."

The carriage rolled on, passing through the fertile Midlothian countryside with the small, thatched cottages of the tenant cottars and larger houses of the tenant farmers who paid their rents to Lord Eskbank and his fellow landowners. The serrated ridge of the Pentland Hills rose in the west, with the Moorfoots to the south.

"I think I'll improve some of the estate," Lord Eskbank mused. "I'll clear some tenants away and enclose the land. Enclosure is in fashion now, and it will increase our rents."

"Good idea, John," Lady Joanna agreed. "These cottars' huts are so unsightly."

When they rolled past the first pit village, the population was quiet, with the workers below, but Lady Joanna tutted. "This is a horrible place," she said. "Do we need such ugliness near the house?"

"It brings in revenue," Eskbank said. "I intend to increase coal production in the future." He leaned back in the padded seat. "I'll have my people find where the coal deposits are under the commonalities, take the land, and create more pits to increase our wealth. I have plans now that we are out of debt."

"Good," Lady Joanna leaned back in her chair. "We are even more out of debt than you imagine, John." She felt inside her skirt and produced her mother's pearls. "You no longer have a mistress."

Eskbank stared at her, wordless.

"She is spending somebody else's money now, John." Lady Joanna allowed the pearls to run through her fingers, smiling. "We had words."

"Whose money is she spending?" Eskbank asked.

"Hugh Crichton's," Lady Joanna said. "She keeps an eye on him for me, and I keep an eye on her. That way, we still control Moira through her husband's mistress."

Eskbank nodded. "You're a clever puss, aren't you?"

Lady Joanna smiled again and returned the pearls to her pocket.

❋

"Why?" Rachel bound the long cut in Flockhart's forearm. "Why are you fighting these foolish duels? I know it's not for money."

Flockhart watched Rachel tie up the makeshift bandage with a neat knot. "No, it's not for money," he agreed.

"That's five you've fought now," Rachel said.

"Is it?"

"And you've won them all," Rachel sat beside him. "What's happened to you, Davie? Have you begun to enjoy fighting?"

"No," Flockhart said.

"God forgive you; do you want an excuse to kill?"

"No," Flockhart said again.

"Then why?"

"I have a reason," Flockhart said.

"Then tell me it," Rachel asked. "I tried Sergeant Adair, but he didn't know, and you face him next. Why?"

"I have a reason," Flockhart repeated. He heard the drums tapping. "That's the assembly, Rachel. I have to go."

"We have new Colours for the Royals," Lieutenant-Colonel Hamilton addressed the assembled battalion. "Scotland and England have now joined in a parliamentary union, so as well as sharing a monarch, we now share a parliament."

If the colonel had expected cheers and jubilation, he would have been disappointed in the lack of enthusiasm from the Royals' ranks.

"We are now known as Great Britain, and our Colours will display the interlocked crosses of St Andrew and St George."

The men said nothing, standing in disciplined silence under the chilling rain.

"We also have a new regimental badge, the Royal Cypher, within the circle of St Andrew, surmounted by a crown."

Nobody cheered. Flockhart had no interest in any parliamentary union. He watched as the colonel desperately tried to create enthusiasm among his men. Politics did not interest Flockhart; he had no vote or hope of ever getting such a thing. Flockhart had a vague knowledge of Scottish history, picked up in a dozen conversations over the past few years, but Scotland to him meant slavery under the rule of Lord Eskbank and his like.

Leishman had more interest and shared his knowledge.

"It was all corruption," Leishman said. "Did you notice that the Duke of Argyll, Red John of the Battles as people call him, left the army before the vote for union?"

"I noticed Argyll left," Flockhart said. "I didn't know about the voting."

Leishman nodded. "Argyll will be promoted for voting for the union,[1] and others will also pocket their thirty pieces of silver."

Flockhart glanced over to Rachel, who was busy washing clothes. "What do you think about it, Rachel?"

"I think they are all corrupt," Rachel said. "Argyll, Queensberry, Eskbank, and the whole stinking pile of them. A set of corrupt thieving poltroons, the lot of them." She took out her anger on the shirt she was washing, banging it on the side of the tub. "Well, hell mends them, and it will when they end up there."

"It was a crooked deck of cards to begin with," Leishman said. "The English government had regiments waiting on the Border and in Ireland, ready to invade if the voting went the other way, and warships to intercept our merchantmen."

Rachel looked up from slaughtering the shirt. "Scotland would fight back," she said. "Could Queen Anne afford another war?"

"Fight back with what?" Leishman asked. "Nearly every Scottish regiment of the Queen is over here with Marlborough. There is only a small force of about 1,500 men in the country, and Queensberry controls that, ready to put down any disturbance among the people."

"We should still fight," Rachel said. "We've been Scotland for hundreds of years."

"Who would we fight for?" Leishman asked. "The Duke of Hamilton, who doesn't know what day it is? King James the Eighth, who is in Louis the Fourteenth's pocket? The Earl of Mar, perhaps, who decided that Queen Anne should nominate the Scottish commissioners and who bribed any opposition to change sides? Or the Church of Scotland, which only cares for the Presbyterian cause. The people are fine, Rachel. It's the lead-

---

1. The Duke of Argyll was promoted to Major-General and accepted payment of £20,000 and an English peerage for his vote. Other Scots who switched from the opposition to pro-union for personal gain included Sir Kenneth Mackenzie, William Seton of Pitmedden, and the Earl of Glencairn. Queensberry gained a substantial financial reward and the dukedom of Dover.

ers, the landowners and that type who have betrayed us, and until there is a real leader, there is nobody to fight for."

Flockhart touched Rachel's arm. "Our time will come," he said quietly. "Maybe our children will see it, or our grandchildren, or their great-grandchildren, but this is not the end."

"We don't have any children," Rachel said.

"Not yet," Flockhart replied softly.

Rachel took a deep breath and nodded, understanding his meaning.

❄

Flockhart stood in the centre of the ring with his sword in his hand, facing Sergeant Adair. He saw Lamb walking around the crowd, taking bets, collecting money and laughing like a good-natured showman.

"You and me, Flockhart," Adair balanced his sword by its point, tossed it in the air, caught it by the handle and gave a few practice strokes with a speed that Flockhart knew he could never match.

"You and me, Sergeant Adair," Flockhart agreed. He flexed his muscles, preparing for the hardest bout he had ever fought.

"We both knew it would come to this," Adair said.

"It was inevitable," Flockhart said. "You're the best swordsman in the Royal Irish, and people say I am fairly good."

"People say you are the best swordsman in the Royal Scots," Adair corrected.

"People say many things that are not true," Flockhart said. He swished his sword. "How much money have you put on yourself to defeat me?"

"One guinea," Adair said.

"You could have wagered more," Flockhart said. "You are better than I am."

"If I win," Adair told him, "I'll be thankful to be alive. If I lose, I won't care about wealth."

"Then why fight?" Flockhart asked.

Adair looked at him, his eyes sad. "Why do any of us fight? For the thrill of the thing, I suppose. Even men who gamble enjoy the thrill rather than the money." He sighed. "You must have money on the outcome."

"Not a penny," Flockhart told him.

Adair frowned. "Your wife told me that. She came to see me a few weeks ago."

"She's a good woman," Flockhart said. "Too good for me."

"She said Lamb makes you fight," Adair said.

The crowd were becoming restless, demanding the two duellists stop talking and start fighting.

"We'd better give them a show," Adair said.

They fought, moving quickly yet without fire, neither giving the other an opening.

"Your Rachel is watching," Adair said as they stopped after a furious five minutes.

"She always does," Flockhart told him.

They fought again, with their swords clashing together without either man gaining an advantage. Flockhart saw the crowd as a blur in the background.

"Who is that woman behind Rachel?" Adair asked. "She's watching your wife, not us."

Flockhart nodded. "If I don't fight, she'll kill Rachel."

"Ah, is that the way of it? I understand," Adair replied. "Fight!"

They fought again, gasping with effort as the crowd cheered, groaned and shouted bad advice.

"You're good," Adair said in their next exhaustion-forced break. "Nearly as good as me."

Flockhart nodded. "You're better," he said.

Adair grunted, looked sideways at Rachel and grinned. "Let's end this," he said. Standing up, he suddenly lunged into the crowd, scattering them before him. Flockhart joined him, unsure what was happening until Adair wrapped a hand around Ruth Gordon's neck.

"I saw you!"

Gordon dropped a knife down her sleeve and slashed at Adair, who blocked the swipe with ease, twisted Gordon's wrist until she dropped the weapon and dragged her into the centre of the open space.

"What's happened?" Captain Brisbane bustled up. "What are you doing with that woman, Sergeant Adair?"

"She's a pickpocket, sir," Adair replied. "I happened to see her dip inside a woman's cloak."

"Which woman?" Brisbane asked. "Come on! Out with it!"

"That woman there, sir," Adair pointed to Rachel.

"Come down here!" Brisbane ordered, and Rachel obediently left the crowd. "Have you lost anything?"

Rachel felt inside her coat. "Why, yes, sir. My purse is missing! There's not much inside, but it's my purse!"

"Search her!" Brisbane ordered.

Adair was quick to step forward. "She put it in her right pocket, sir," he said and dived a hand inside. "Here. Is this your purse?" he asked Rachel, who nodded quickly.

"I stitched my name on it, sir. Rachel."

Brisbane took the purse from Adair and turned it over. "Yes, there's the name. Rachel, bold as brass."

"I didn't take it!" Gordon denied hotly.

"Who are you?" Captain Brisbane demanded, raising his voice. "Does anybody know this woman?"

"He does!" Gordon pointed to Sergeant Lamb. "He'll vouch for me!"

Lamb shook his head. "I will not, madam. I have never seen you in my life before this very minute."

Brisbane nodded grimly. "I'll have you flogged and drummed out of camp, whoever you are," he said. "And it's the gallows noose if you ever return." He raised his voice again. "The duel is over, and all bets are cancelled. Go about your business!"

Flockhart met Lamb's eye, saw the raw anger and lifted a derisory hand. *If Lamb does anything against Rachel, I'll put a musket ball in his head and hang happy.*

Flockhart watched as Gordon was paraded through the camp with a hempen noose around her neck, as a drummer played the Rogue's March, and the female camp followers jeered and threw horse manure at her. When she reached the entrance, Rachel, as the only known victim, landed a hefty kick on Gordon's backside to help her on her way.

The women crowded around, adding more kicks and blows.

"We know your face now, Ruth Gordon," Rachel warned. "If you come back, we'll see you dangling."

Gordon turned around for a rush of women to attack her, kicking, slapping and punching until she fled, pursued by a howling mob.

"How did you do it?" Flockhart asked.

"Do what?" Rachel tried to look innocent.

"How did you do that?" Flockhart nodded to the rapidly retreating Gordon.

Rachel smiled as they walked back to their quarters. "I knew Lamb had a hold on you, and it wasn't because you're scared of him. That meant it must be something to do with Adam or me. I guessed it was me."

Flockhart grunted.

"Do you think I care that much for you?"

"Yes, you do," Rachel told him. "During one of your bouts, I saw you looking behind me, and I saw Ruth Gordon there, so I guessed she was involved. I told Sergeant Adair, and he and I worked out the plan. I gave him my purse days ago so he could find it in Gordon's pocket."

Flockhart grunted again. "You were right."

"Why didn't you tell me?" Rachel asked.

"I didn't want to worry you," Flockhart said.

Rachel nodded. "I'd prefer you to tell me and let me worry about worrying." She linked her arm with his.

CHAPTER 31

EDINBURGH, SCOTLAND AND THE LOW COUNTRIES, SUMMER 1707

Edinburgh was busy, with crowds on the High Street, men and women shouting, and angry people waving their fists.

"There seems to be some agitation," Lady Joanna said. "Listen to what they are saying."

The crowd surged forward when they saw Lord Eskbank's coach.

"No Union!" they roared. "No Union!"

"More of the lower orders with ideas above their station," Lady Joanna said. "Why doesn't the army clear them away so people who matter can go about their business in peace?"

"There's Lord Eskbank!" somebody roared. "Another of the traitors."

When someone threw a stone that crashed against the body of the coach, Lady Joanna quickly withdrew from the window. "The cheek of it!"

"Drive on!" Lord Eskbank shouted as more stones came towards them. Two rattled off the carriage's bodywork, and one bounced between the horses. "Drive on, for God's sake!"

"Traitors!" the crowd followed, roaring their hatred as they released a barrage of stones, dead cats, and other missiles. "No Union! Get the traitors!"

"The rabble is annoyed," Lady Joanna commented. "Whip behind, driver! Give them a taste of the lash!"

The driver obeyed, flicking his whip behind the carriage to try to catch some of the crowd. They retaliated by including him in their targets, and a stone the size of a human fist crashed beside him.

"Overturn the coach!" someone roared. "Drag the traitors out!"

"Get out of this, driver!" Lord Eskbank said. "Get out of the city!"

With the crowd howling in frustrated anger and missiles hammering against the carriage, the driver turned down the steep slope of the West Bow into the Grassmarket. More people waited there, also chanting, "No Union!" They greeted the carriage with more stones and tried to block its passage. Lord Eskbank took a brace of pistols from inside his coat.

"We'll have to fight our way clear," he said. His hands were steady as he loaded his pistols.

The driver lashed out with his whip, driving back the most forward of the crowd and opening a narrow lane. He moved the horses forward, swearing as lustily as any cavalry trooper. The coach rocked as a surge of people crashed against the side, shouting "Traitor!" and "No Union!"

Lord Eskbank checked the priming of his pistol. "I'll shoot the first one to enter the carriage," he promised.

"Give me a pistol," Lady Joanna held out her hand. "I'll shoot the second."

"I knew I married a game one," Eskbank said, reversing a pistol and pressing it into her hand.

"We're through!" the driver shouted as the coach burst through a thin line of protesters into a clear road.

Lord Eskbank looked behind him. Hundreds of people glared at the coach, with dozens gesticulating. He had expected the protesters to be from the lowest order of society but saw a great many respectable people involved. Everybody was chanting their dislike of the Union and their opinion of the commissioners who had signed Scotland's independence away.

"Traitors! No Union!" the crowd followed for a couple of hundred yards but returned to the city when Lord Eskbank's coach picked up speed.

"Back to Eskhall," Eskbank said. He uncocked his pistol and removed the flint in case of accidents. "I think we should retire to our new property in England until the rabble calms down. Our English tenants will welcome their new master."

Lady Joanna nodded. "I agree," she said. "I'd like to see what we own down south." She smiled at him. "You did rather well back there."

"So did you, Joanna," Eskbank told her.

※

Flockhart disliked parades in which a collection of noblemen, princes, and senior officers watched the soldiers perform. The grand parade as the army awaited the campaigning season to start was no different. The Duke of Marlborough and the Earl of Orkney watched as the British infantry marched, manoeuvred, and fired volleys by platoon.

The foreign dignitaries clapped politely, but for the first time since joining the Royals, Flockhart felt out of place. Without moving his head, Flockhart slid his eyes sideways to view his neighbours. Leishman was stony-faced, staring ahead as the regulations demanded, while Young looked even more apprehensive performing in front of the senior officers than he did facing the French.

We're performing for the useless. That's how this parade feels. We are not training for war; we are performing to entertain the foreign observers. I don't feel like a soldier today.

As the parade ended, the weather broke, and torrential rain

hammered down. Within half an hour, hail and heavy rain had flattened scores of tents in the camp, flooding the interiors and sending the contents into the streets between the lines.

"It's going to be a wet season for campaigning," Leishman said, sucking on an empty pipe. "I can't see much fighting this summer."

It was August before the rain eased sufficiently for Marlborough to allow them to march.

"At last," Flockhart said as he checked his equipment. "We might feel like soldiers again rather than ducks."

Sergeant Dunn smiled. "You're alive, Davie boy. Thank your God for another summer of life and accept what comes."

The Allies splashed along deeply puddled roads in search of the French, who were anxious to avoid a battle after the disasters of the previous year. After a few days, the rain began again, and Marlborough halted his frustrated army at Soignes.

"March, halt, and shelter," Young said. "Is that all we do?"

"It's a soldier's life," Dunn said.

Rachel eased closer to Flockhart. "You've been different these past few weeks," she said. "What's on your mind?"

Flockhart examined his musket for rust, scraping off a minuscule speck on the hammer. "You are," he said.

"Me?"

Flockhart nodded. "You."

"Why?" Rachel asked.

"I don't like to see you living like this."

"I've always lived like this," Rachel reminded. "It's not a hardship to me."

Flockhart nodded. "Maybe it's all right, then," he said, but Rachel knew he was unhappy.

A break in the weather saw Marlborough again pushing the army after the French.

"Maybe this time we'll finish the war," Leishman said.

"Maybe so," Flockhart agreed. For once, the prospect did not dismay him. He glanced over his shoulder at the transport wagons, did not see Rachel, and looked forward again, vaguely disappointed.

As the Allies approached Ath, intending to cross the Dender River, they saw the orange reflection of flames on the low clouds.

"The Frenchies have burned their camp," the news spread from man to man. "Vendome has run away rather than face us."

"It's not been a great summer," Flockhart said.

"You're alive, I'm alive, and your Rachel is alive," Leishman growled. "Reaching winter still breathing is always good for a soldier."

When the army reached the stone bridge across the Dender, it found the French had blocked it with ditches, flanking breastworks, and a heavy barricade of recently felled logs. The Allied cavalry reconnoitred cautiously, expecting a blast of grapeshot and musketry. They returned smiling to report that the French had retired without firing a shot.

"Somebody's gone to a lot of trouble to make this palisade," Leishman said as they examined the barricade. "And then they ran away without even trying to defend it."

"That saves us the trouble of pushing them away." Flockhart rested on his musket. He watched Rachel jump from a wagon and head purposefully for the burning remains of the French camp.

"Where's she going?" Young asked.

"Foraging," Flockhart replied. "She'll find something tasty to eat, mark my words." He watched until Rachel was out of sight, then checked his musket for rust. There was always something for a soldier to do.

The French had left in a hurry, as the supplies of beef, tobacco, and wine they abandoned proved. Rachel returned with a full bag and a broad smile.

"We'll eat well tonight, boys," she said. Not even Flockhart saw her count the contents of her second leather purse that evening.

The campaigning season of 1707 eased to a close, with Marlborough continuing to press the French and Vendome conducting a masterly retreat without the two armies ever coming to battle. For Flockhart and the Royals, life consisted of marching, camping, and keeping their equipment clean.

"We're pushing them back every day," Leishman said. "The Frenchies have run to the river Marque with the fortifications of Lille to protect him. We're inside France."

"On to Paris, then," Young said.

"No," Dunn shook his head. "We don't have the numbers to attack Paris, and we can hardly overwinter in a hostile country. Vendome is playing for time and wearing the days away until the season ends."

"Maybe we should overwinter in France," Flockhart said. "We would be using their resources and food, impoverishing the enemy."

Dunn grunted. "Every supply convoy would be in danger, and the population would be hostile. Best be in a friendly country with secure supply lines, Davie."

As the year dragged on, the weather returned to rain, and the Allied army struggled to progress. The men marched through glutinous mud, sinking knee-deep as they tried to move, with frequent halts until the draught animals could drag the artillery and supply wagons forward.

"Did you hear the army is raising more Scottish regiments?" Leishman asked as they huddled in a leaking tent with the wind threatening to lift the canvas with every gust.

"No," Flockhart rarely listened to gossip. He worked on his musket. "I must have the most unfortunate musket in the army. Whatever care I take, it seems to attract rust."

"Since the Union earlier this year, the Duke of Atholl has raised another regiment."

"Has he? I wonder if the men had any choice. You know the

Highland way; the young men must do what the chief says, or he'll evict their family." Rachel looked out the flap at the teeming rain. "I'm getting too old to live in a tent, lying in a puddle of water surrounded by hairy men lying in their shirts."

"What do you want?" Flockhart asked.

"You know what I want," Rachel said. "I want a place to call my own. I want a home with a patch of land to grow what I eat rather than foraging for food. I want a view at my front door and a way of making money that does not involve stealing from the dead."

Flockhart smiled. "That's a dream," he said. "The likes of us shouldn't have false hopes. Just take each day as a gift and enjoy the daylight."

Rachel shook her head. "No, Davie. We've had nothing all our lives. Surely, we can gain something better after all our effort and struggle."

Flockhart touched her arm. He understood, yet he knew dreaming of the impossible only led to disappointment. He made a final check of his musket, covered the lock and muzzle with a dry cloth, lay back, and looked at Rachel, content for the moment. The patter of rain on the outside of the tent was strangely comforting.

"We're going back to Flanders, boys," Dunn poked his head inside the tent. "Say goodbye to sunny France."

Rachel inched closer to Flockhart and put an arm over his lean, hard body.

❄

Lord Eskbank looked out of the coach window at the English countryside, glorious in the autumn tints of russet, red, and gold. "This is a rich country," he said. "Fertile fields, snug little villages, comfortable inns and pleasant weather. I think we will like it here."

"I am sure we will," Lady Joanna said. "The people seem

delighted to have the Union with us, so unlike the ungrateful rabble in Edinburgh. I do find travelling tedious, though. How far to our new house?"

"Not far now," Eskbank said. "About ten miles. I am glad we changed horses at the last inn. These beasts should last for the remainder of the journey without any more halts." He stared out of the mud-spattered window. "Two hours, and we'll be there."

The carriage jolted on, occasionally crashing into a deeper-than-usual rut as they pushed further south. The land was flatter than Lord Eskbank was accustomed to, with extensive views over broad fields and a mixture of enclosed and unenclosed land. He examined the farms, hoping to collect some farming techniques he could use at home.

"There's a horseman behind us," Lady Joanna said. "A man on a brown mare."

"He's been there for a while," Eskbank told her. "A fellow traveller. He was in the last inn as well."

Lady Joanna settled back in her seat and closed her eyes. "Wake me when we reach our new house, John." She ran a hand over her pearls and settled down to sleep.

The road rose on an incline, slowing the carriage as the horses strained to pull the weight. The driver resorted to the whip, and they crested the rise and dipped to a copse, with trees crowding close to the road. Birdsongs sweetened the air, with a flock of pigeons exploding from the trees.

The cool shade was a contrast to the brightness of the open road. Lord Eskbank pulled the curtains wide to allow more light to enter the carriage and frowned as a rider stepped into the middle of the road ahead.

"Tell that poltroon to get out of our way!" he shouted.

"Yes, My Lord," the driver said and waved the rider aside. "Move away, fellow! Let us pass!"

The man remained immobile, blocking the road.

"Tell him who I am, damnit!" Lord Eskbank ordered.

"This is Lord Eskbank's coach," the driver shouted. "Step aside, fellow."

In reply, the man produced a brace of pistols. "Step down from your seat, driver, or I'll let daylight into your skull."

"Good God! It's a highwayman! And he is trying to rob me! Me!" Lord Eskbank said. He pulled his pistols from inside his coat and began to fit the flints.

"Put the weapons down, My Lord." The rider on the brown horse yanked the door open and pointed a wide-barrelled blunderbuss inside the coach. "Get out."

"I'm damned if I will," Lord Eskbank replied, struggling with a powder horn.

The highwayman reached in, grabbed Lord Eskbank by the sleeve and dragged him outside, where a third man landed a hefty kick, grabbed his pistols and dragged him to his feet.

"Up you get, Scotchman!"

"That is Lord Eskbank," Lady Joanna protested as the highwayman hauled her outside. "I'll see you dancing on the gallows, you rogue."

"You! Driver! Get down!" The first highwayman pointed two pistols at the driver and shoved him beside Lord Eskbank. He covered them while the blunderbuss man frisked all three and removed all their valuables. He examined Lady Joanna's pearls for a few moments, glowering at her.

"Who did you say you were?" the first highwayman asked.

"I am Lord Eskbank, and you will hang for this day's work," Eskbank said.

"Maybe, My Lord Scotchman, but you won't see it." The highwayman levelled his pistol and fired, with the ball crashing into Eskbank's chest.

"You rogue!" the driver sprang forward, only for the second highwayman to fire his blunderbuss, the discharge throwing him backwards and killing him instantly.

"I suppose you'll kill me, too?" Lady Joanna asked calmly,

spattered with the blood of her husband and servant. She looked the killers in the eye.

"Not yet," the first highwayman said. "We have other plans for you."

"As you wish," Lady Joanna said, curling her lip as she looked over the trio. "Who's first?"

"Me," the taller of the three said, throwing off his cloak. "Do you remember Polly Darkin, your maid?"

Lady Joanna frowned. "What the deuce has that little minx got to do with anything?"

"You had her hanged for theft," the highwayman said. "She was my sister, and we'll make you pay for her death."

"What?" Lady Joanna asked in sudden alarm. She began to scream as the highwayman grabbed her.

CHAPTER 32
DUTCH REPUBLIC, MARCH 1708

"The Jacobites are making trouble in Scotland again," Dunn said so casually that Flockhart knew he was leading up to something.

"Are they, Sergeant?" Flockhart concentrated on his musket, intent on removing anything Dunn could construe as rust. *I can play your game, Sergeant Dunn.*

"So I have heard," Dunn sat in the corner of the room, with his long-stemmed pipe between his teeth, enjoying his morning smoke. Flockhart and Leishman waited for further news while Rachel sat at the back of the room, darning a tear in Flockhart's shirt. "I don't know the details yet. Are either of you men waiting to welcome the Pretender?"

Flockhart glanced at Leishman and shrugged. "Jamie Stuart's never done anything for me," he said. "Nor against me."

"Nor me," Leishman said.

"I hear the French are sending a fleet to Scotland to aid the Jacobites," Sergeant Dunn continued, "and the army is sending men to support Queen Anne's garrison."

Flockhart nodded. "Are we going?"

Dunn nodded. "Yes, but some officers are concerned about our loyalty."

Flockhart felt Rachel's eyes on him. "I've already said I don't care a farthing about the Pretender."

"The Pretender is a Stuart," Rachel said quietly.

"That's right," Dunn agreed.

"It was his Stuart ancestor that enslaved the colliers and salt workers," Rachel said with a meaningful glance at Flockhart.

"Was it?" Flockhart asked.

"It was," Rachel said. "King James VI enslaved them about a hundred years ago. Before that, they were free, and now another Stuart wants to bring back the Roman Catholic church, like the Frenchies we've been fighting for years."

"I didn't know the Stuarts made my ancestors slaves," Flockhart said.

"They did," Rachel said flatly.

"How do you know all these things, Rachel?" Flockhart asked.

"I read books," Rachel said, smiling. "It's a whole new world you should try."

"I swore an oath to serve Queen Anne," Flockhart said. "I'll keep my word."

With Flockhart's loyalty to Queen Anne confirmed, Sergeant Dunn dripped in more information. "Corporal John's secretary, my old companion of the bottle, told me that the Earl of Cadogan had garnered more intelligence about the Jacobites."

"What's happening, Sergeant?" Rachel asked.

"Cadogan found out that a fleet of French privateers under the Comte de Forbin is preparing to embark James Stuart and fifteen infantry battalions for a descent on Scotland. They'll land somewhere, maybe in the Forth, and join a Jacobite rising to put the Stuarts back on the throne. It will be a return to Roman Catholic absolutism, and Louis XIV will have taken us out of the war."

"Does that mean we'll be fighting for Louis against the Dutch and Imperialists?" Flockhart asked.

Dunn shrugged. "Maybe. Who knows the minds of kings and

politicians? I think it's more likely to create a civil war in Britain, armies of French and British marching and counter-marching against each other, plundering towns and farms."

"All the horrors of war in our homeland," Leishman said.

"Yes," Dunn agreed.

"What do you think of that, Davie?" Leishman asked.

Flockhart was silent for a few moments before he replied. "I don't have many fond memories of my homeland," he said. "Scotland, or at least Lord Eskbank and his ilk, treated me abominably, but I'd find it hard to fight for Louis, whose men have been trying to kill me for years."

"What will you do?" Rachel asked.

Before Flockhart replied, somebody rapped sharply on the door.

"Flockhart!" Captain Brisbane's voice sounded from the street outside.

Flockhart hurried to the front room. "Sir?" Flockhart opened the door, hastily fastening his shirt buttons.

"This man wants to see you, Flockhart," Brisbane stepped aside, allowing Flockhart to see Cummings standing behind him.

As Flockhart felt nausea rising inside him, Captain Brisbane walked away, leaving Cummings standing outside the door with rainwater weeping from the brim of his hat. Flockhart stared at him, with all his old fears returning.

"Who is it?" Rachel asked, fastening her skirt as she bustled to the door.

"This is Mr Cummings," Flockhart explained. "Lord Eskbank's grieve."

Rachel took in the situation at once. "Well, bring the poor man in then, Davie. We can't leave him standing out there in the rain."

Flockhart stood reluctantly aside, and Cummings entered, removing his hat to Rachel. The scar on the side of his head looked raw, but Flockhart did not ask any questions. Cummings stood in the front room, dripping water onto the floor as Rachel stirred the stove to life, and Flockhart eyed the bayonet that hung in its scabbard behind the door.

"Yes, Mr Cummings?" Flockhart said. He heard footsteps behind him and knew Leishman and Sergeant Dunn had entered the front room. "Have you come to try to take me back to Lord Eskbank?" He fingered the mark around his throat.

Cummings remained standing. "Lord and Lady Eskbank are dead," he said brutally. "They were travelling to their new lands in England, and a highwayman killed them both."

Flockhart nodded. After participating in major battles, the deaths of two people who had only done him harm did not upset him. "What happens now?" He saw Leishman move to the front door, blocking Cummings' exit. Rachel had a fire glowing in the stove and lifted the poker as if to encourage the flames.

Cummings squared his shoulders. "His Lord's property, including the mines and the colliers, has gone to Lord Eskbank's son-in-law, Sir Hugh Crichton, now the new Lord Eskbank. He has never seen you but wants you returned alive or proof of your death."

"I am not going back alive," Flockhart said, edging towards his bayonet, "and you cannot prove a live man dead."

"Yes, I can," Cummings said. "I have spoken to your company commander, Captain Brisbane. There were three men named David Flockhart in the Royals. Only two remain; the French killed one David Flockhart during the Battle of Ramillies."

Flockhart frowned. "That was not me."

"His Lordship does not know that it's not you," Cummings said. "I will obtain a copy of the casualty returns for His Lordship and show him your name. As far as he will know, you are dead."

"Thank you," Flockhart said. He felt as if somebody had lifted a massive weight from his shoulders. He noticed Rachel replacing the poker beside the stove. "The Messengers at Arms could still come for me."

"No," Cummings shook his head, visibly relaxing as he felt the tension ease. "He couldn't."

"By escaping from Lord Eskbank, I am guilty of theft in stealing my own body," Flockhart reminded.

"No," Cummings replied. "By law, your owner," he emphasised the word, "had a year and a day to retrieve his property. It is much longer than that since you left."

"A year and a day?" Flockhart repeated.

Cummings smiled for the first time. "That's correct," he said. "Legally, you have been a free man since October 1702."

Flockhart shook his head. "Oh, dear God. I am free?"

Instinctively, Flockhart fingered the marks across his throat. He had often felt as if the brass collar was still attached, confining his throat. Now, he felt only rough skin and the rasp of coarse hairs where he needed to shave.

"What will you do now?" Cummings asked.

Flockhart thought of his last few years, the winters in Dutch towns and summers campaigning. He thought of the camps, with their ordered ranks of tents, confusion of camp followers, pimps, prostitutes, merchants, wives, and soldiers. "We have a war to win," he said. "The Royals gave me a home. I belong here now."

Cummings held out his hand. "I wish you the best of luck, Flockhart."

"Thank you." Flockhart ignored Cummings' hand. There were too many bitter memories. "Are you going back to be the new Lord Eskbank's grieve?"

"No," Cummings said. "I left that situation two years back. I only came here to tidy up loose ends."

Flockhart watched as Cummings left the house for the long journey back home. He felt Rachel slip her arm inside his.

"We'd better prepare for parade, lads," Dunn said. "The war is not over yet."

Flockhart nodded. "Yes, Sergeant." He felt numb, unable to comprehend what had just happened.

Dunn glowered at him. "Make sure you've no rust on your musket!"

Flockhart nodded. "Yes, Sergeant."

"We march in three days," Dunn said quietly. "We might be fighting on Scottish soil in a couple of weeks."

❄

On the 8th of March 1708, the Royals marched from their quarters at Ghent, along with other line regiments and the Foot Guards. They arrived at Ostend on the 15th of the month, where the Royal Navy and transport vessels waited to carry them across the German Ocean to Scotland.

Martha's Pride was familiar. The last time Flockhart had boarded her, he had been a nervous recruit. Now, he was an experienced soldier who had seen bravery, horror and death in all its guises. He was also a free man. Flockhart tried to absorb the idea that he was equal to everybody else. Nobody owned him or could drag him back to slavery.

"Flockhart!" Sergeant Dunn pushed him forward. "Get up the blasted gangplank!"

"Yes, Sergeant."

He strode on board with the other Royals, confident of his fighting ability and his standing among his peers.

"We're bound for Tynemouth," Dunn told his men. "If the French expedition lands, we'll be chasing them through Britain. It will be the Royals' first campaign in our own country since we defeated Monmouth at Sedgemoor. No looting, boys, and be nice to the civilians. They are on our side. Mainly, anyway."

The storm hit the convoy a day after they departed from Ostend. Flockhart saw the sky darken from the south, and then the shipmaster ordered the crew to take in sail. The seamen leapt aloft, scrambling up the rigging with an agility Flockhart could only admire.

"Get the redcoats below," the shipmaster bellowed through a speaking trumpet. "I don't want them littering my deck!"

"Come on, lobsters!" the seamen ushered the Royals below deck. "You're in the road up here." Petty officers reinforced their orders with stinging cuts from their ropes' ends.

As the men filed below, Flockhart remembered the stifling, crowded conditions and dodged away. Crowded between decks in a ship was too similar to working underground in Stobhill Pit. *I'll die in the open air.*

Flockhart found a relatively sheltered spot between the mainmast and the foremast, away from the officers in the stern. He lodged himself beside the bulwark, ignored the screaming wind and lashing spindrift and wondered what the future held.

"Flockhart," the voice made Flockhart turn.

Sergeant Lamb stared at him across the breadth of the foredeck. "What the devil are you doing here?"

"I'm going to fight the Jacobites," Flockhart said.

"You wouldn't know a Jacobite if one bit you in the arse," Lamb told him.

Flockhart did not reply. He held onto the rigging as the ship pitched and rolled in the short, choppy seas. A capful of spindrift spattered him, making him blink.

"I think you're planning to desert," Lamb said.

"I am not," Flockhart replied.

"You were going to jump over the side and swim to land," Lamb accused him.

"I can't swim," Flockhart said, immediately realising he had made a mistake as Lamb grinned.

"I always knew you were a fool, Flockhart, but now I know you are also a knave." Lamb drew his sword. "You cost me a great deal of money, Flockhart. I had all my gold wagered on your last bout with Adair."

Flockhart checked the deck. It was empty save for the

helmsman at the stern a hundred feet away and hardly seen for the spray that exploded across the ship whenever she ducked her head into the sea.

"I'm going to kill you, Flockhart," Lamb said. "Either by steel or by water."

Flockhart drew his sword, feeling the weapon familiar in his hand. "One of us will die, Sergeant Lamb." He knew Lamb was the better swordsman.

At least I'll die free, and Rachel will find another husband. Adam Leishman will look after her.

"Come on then!" Flockhart stood in the On Guard position, allowing Lamb to attack. *He might exhaust himself or fall overboard. Wear him down.*

Lamb held Flockhart's gaze as he advanced, probing with a series of attacks, left, right and low to the left thigh. Flockhart defended, clashing his blade from Lamb's, feeling the man's strength equalled his own.

When Lamb pulled back, Flockhart pushed forward. He saw slight hesitation in Lamb when he thrust to his left, feinted right and swore as the sergeant held his blade, turned it and attacked. Flockhart found himself on the defensive, moving backwards as Lamb's blade flicked at his face, then his groin, and sideways to his ribs.

"You can die slowly or quickly, Davie boy!" Lamb's point stabbed into Flockhart's side, scoring his ribs. "Which do you want?"

Flockhart attacked again, desperately searching for an opening against a man who was immeasurably his superior at swordplay. Lamb parried, struck and pulled back, leaving Flockhart with another wound and his blood seeping onto the deck.

"Try again, Davie boy, try again!" Lamb laughed, daring Flockhart to come at him.

Flockhart held onto the rigging with his left hand, feeling his strength draining. The deck underfoot was slippery, and the swaying ship threw him from side to side.

Lamb pushed forward, thrusting like a fencing master, then using all the subtlety of a master swordsman to trap Flockhart's blade with his own.

Flockhart parried and thrust, stretching forward. At that second, the bow dipped into a trough of the waves, dipping Flockhart underwater. The ship rolled, throwing him from his precarious stance and into the sea. He heard Lamb's loud laughter, and then the sea closed over his head.

I can't swim!

Flockhart heard a terrible roaring in his ears, gulped down water and flailed his arms and legs as he sunk deeper beneath the waves. The pain in his chest was terrible; he knew he was drowning.

Sorry, Rachel, I let you down.

※

Flockhart felt rough hands on his body. He tried to talk, felt his chest heave and spewed out seawater that seemed red hot in his throat.

"He's still alive," a man said casually.

"Cut his throat then," a woman's voice advised.

"Dinnae bother. He'll be deid soon. Just take what we can."

"He's a redcoat, a soldier," the woman said.

"He won't have much of value then."

Flockhart tried to move. He felt somebody ripping off his coat and somebody else hauling down his breeches. His shoes had gone, taken by the sea. He tried to protest but only managed to make a slight croaking sound.

"Shut him up, Meg," the man said. "Cut his throat."

Flockhart felt somebody grab his hair and haul back his head. He looked into the bitter eyes of a young woman with dirty blonde hair and saw the flash of a knife.

Rachel crept from under the canvas cover of the ship's boat. She held onto the bulwark as *Martha's Pride* rocked in the heavy sea, steadied herself and held tight to a rope. She knew the Royals were below and wondered how to join them.

The sound of steel clashing on steel came to her. Rachel looked forward and saw two men fighting desperately across the foredeck.

"Davie!" Rachel saw Lamb press Flockhart back, flick his sword forward and withdraw, laughing. She saw Flockhart stagger and attack again, slashing with his sword.

Lamb parried easily and lunged forward.

Martha's Pride dipped to a wave, and when Rachel raised her head, Flockhart was gone.

"Davie!" Rachel rushed forward and jumped after him. She saw him sinking under the water and dived, kicking hard to reach him. A current caught them both, pushing them towards the Fife coast.

"Come on, Davie!" Rachel shoved him to the surface. She felt the current drag her away, stronger than she had expected. "Don't leave me, Davie."

The fickle current pushed them apart, and then Rachel was amongst the surf on a shingly beach, gasping as she forced herself to stand.

A brace of seagulls watched her, with the wind flicking up feathers on the back of its neck. Rachel looked along the beach and saw a man and a woman looking down on Flockhart's body.

She staggered towards them in time to see the woman drag back Flockhart's head and press a knife to his throat.

"No!" Rachel lifted a stone from the beach and smashed it against the woman's head. When she fell, her companion ran.

Flockhart heard a yell of fear and saw a youth running away, with his feet slipping and sliding over the shifting shingle. Dazed, he looked around and spewed some more seawater.

"Now, here's a pretty picture."

The voice was familiar as Rachel knelt at Flockhart's side.

"I don't know, Davie. I leave you alone for five minutes, and look at the mess you get yourself into. What are we going to do with you?"

L'ENVOI

For many years after the Peace of Utrecht, travellers wondered at the name of the inn that stood beside the road at Soutra. Any traveller who called in could stand at the front door and admire the sweeping vista over the Lothian plain towards the Firth of Forth. The Collier's Arms had a musket on brackets above the bar, quietly rusting as the years smoothed past, and a drum inside the door, with the artwork fading with every season.

There was always a warm welcome from the serious-eyed, stocky man who ran the Arms along with his smiling, immaculate wife, while their growing brood of children would help or get underfoot, depending on their mood. Any passing ex-soldier, up or down on his luck, would be assured of a warm seat beside the inglenook fire, a good meal and a bed for the night.

In the cool light of the morning, the landlord could often be seen sitting outside the inn, gazing into the distance as his wife prepared for the day ahead. The landlord sometimes rubbed a hand across the still-visible red marks around his throat. At other times, he would hum a tune, and one or two of the regular clients in the inn would join in.

L'ENVOI

"So, dearest woman, the war it has begun,
And I must march along by the beating of the drum.
Come dress yourself all in your best and sail away with me;
I'll take you to the wars, my love, in Higher Germany."

Regular customers always remarked that the landlord never closed the shutters on his bedroom window and kept the interior of the inn bright, with cruise lamps, candles, and a fire always burning.

On an autumn evening, when his old friend Adam nursed a pint of home-brewed ale and the wild geese winged overhead, the landlord and his wife would sit outside, happy in each other's company. If they were in the mood and the ale flowed freely, they would talk about the old days when they followed the drum with Corporal John.

ABOUT THE AUTHOR

Born in Edinburgh, Scotland and educated at the University of Dundee, Malcolm Archibald has written in a variety of genres, from academic history to folklore, historical novels to fantasy. He won the Dundee International Book Prize with *Whales for the Wizard* in 2005 and the Society of Army Historical Research prize for Historical Military Fiction with *Blood Oath* in 2021.

Happily married for over 42 years, Malcolm has three grown children and lives outside Dundee in Scotland.

※

To learn more about Malcolm Archibald and discover more Next Chapter authors, visit our website at www.nextchapter.pub.

Printed in Great Britain
by Amazon